The Imposter

MARK DAWSON

A BLACK DOG PUBLISHING ebook.
First published in Great Britain in 2013 by Black Dog
Ebook first published in 2013 by Black Dog
This ebook published in 2013 by Black Dog
Copyright © Mark Dawson 2013
Formatting by Polgarus Studio

The moral right of Mark Dawson to be identified as the author of this work has been asserted by him in accordance with the Copyright, Designs and Patents Act 1988.

All the characters in this book are fictitious, and any resemblance to actual persons living or dead is purely coincidental.

All rights reserved. No part of this publication may be reproduced, stored in a retrieval system or transmitted in any form or by any means, without the prior permission in writing of the publisher, nor to be otherwise circulated in any form of binding or cover other than that in which it is published without a similar condition, including this condition, being imposed on the subsequent purchaser.

ALSO BY MARK DAWSON

The Art of Falling Apart
Subpoena Colada

In the Soho Noir Series
The Black Mile
The Imposter

In the John Milton Series
One Thousand Yards
The Cleaner
Saint Death (coming soon)

To LD and FD.

With special thanks to Mike Wright and Ivan Cotter.

PROLOGUE

Southend Harbour
June 1946

SATURDAY NIGHT, three in the morning, and Billy Stavropoulos was making a hell of a racket, kicking and pounding like mad in the boot of the car. Edward Fabian ignored it—they were nearly there—and drove on. Rain lashed the streets, thundering against the roof. The area around the harbour had taken the brunt of a German raid seven years earlier. The rainwater that ran into the gutters was slurry-coloured from brick dust; the tarpaulins that had been nailed over vanished windows flapped incessantly; wild flowers sprouted amongst the ruins. The harbour itself was surrounded by derelict buildings, some of them flattened by the bombs, others looking like they ought to have been. Lines of boats were secured to the moorings, their rigging jangling and rattling as they rose and fell on the tide. There was a strong smell of fish on the wind. Grey streets, blotched and stippled with yellow light, led away into the murky distance.

Edward slowed the car to a stop. It had been given to him by detective inspector Murphy. It was new, probably impounded from some unlucky chap Murphy had arrested, and it still smelt fresh. It was a good car, not as impressive as Edward's Triumph, but good nonetheless. It was almost a pity that Edward was going to have to torch it when he was finished, but there was no sense in leaving forensics that might lead back to him.

Jimmy Stern was sitting next to him in the passenger seat, staring ahead, impassive. Only the almost imperceptible grinding of his teeth revealed his nervousness. "Ready?" he said.

Edward breathed deeply, the cold damp air burning his lungs.

Jimmy put a hand on his arm. "Edward—we've got no choice. We've got to do it."

The cabin's courtesy light illuminated the ugly bruises on his uncle's face. "I know we do," he said.

He opened the car door. There was a dim and economical streetlight at the other end of the harbour but here it was black. It was closer to sleet than to rain, the edged drops seeming to slash their way through the buttonholes of his raincoat. It lashed into him and he was drenched in seconds. He went around to the back of the car and opened the boot. The light clicked on, illuminating the body inside. Billy was curled up in the narrow space, his wrists handcuffed, his knees against his chest, his ankles roped together and with a rough sack tied over his head. He started to moan, the rag that they had stuffed into his mouth turning his protests into an indecipherable mumbling.

Edward slid his hands beneath his shoulders, gripped hard and hauled him out.

PART ONE

Calcutta
May 1945

1

THE TROOPSHIP PASSED THROUGH THE MUDDY ESTUARY of the Hooghly River. Edward Fabian and the rest of the men disembarked amidst the great ships of His Majesty's Navy and were taken by coach through the wide, throbbing, chaotic Calcutta streets. It was a spectacular place that pulsed with life, a place of the most vertiginous contrasts; during the fifteen minute drive to their billet Edward saw a corpse slumped against smoke-stained Victorian statuary, a sparkling American limousine bumping up against a rickshaw pulled by a half-naked tonga-wallah, a blind beggar asking for change from a Naval officer in full regalia, fakirs pushing knock-off suits to men wearing every uniform of the Allies in the Orient. India was poverty cheek-by-jowl with opulence and Calcutta was its apogee. Edward had become accustomed to the rhythm of the jungle: days of monotony between engagements, hours spent in silence broken only by the calls of parakeets and cuckoo-shrikes. Here was its complete opposite: innumerable mendicants, children imploring passers-by for buckshee, slums of swarming multitudes. Plunging into it was a shock to the senses.

They were to be billeted in the vaulted chambers of the Museum, beds jammed among the cabinets and display cases, cool radiating from the marble floor. The welcome was more than Edward could have dared imagine. There were dhobis to launder his clothes and dersis to fix them; after months of sleeping on hard ground or a sodden slop, he had proper rope-and-frame beds; there were baths with unlimited hot water and soap; a spacious canteen with bustling memsahibs fussing over huge pots of curry and dahl. After months of trench foot and pack sores, months of sleep disturbed by threat of Japanese soldiers coming across the wire, months freighted with the constant fear of death; this was absolute luxury.

Edward slept the sleep of the dead for twelve hours. When he awoke he went out to explore. The men were paid eighteen rupees a week and Edward had not drawn anything for the better part of six months; that accumulated into a tidy little sum to spend in a place as cheap as Calcutta. He even looked the part. The men had been given new suits of green fabric, the regimental black cat insignia stitched proudly on the shoulders. He polished his badges and fastened them to his bush hat. He bathed, washed himself with Lifebuoy and slapped Brylcream into his hair. He found his crutch, and, taking the weight off his injured foot, he set out.

He had only paused briefly in India on his way to the front and he was anxious to see the sights. Chowringhee, Calcutta's central avenue, exerted a pull that few serviceman could resist. It was a wide thoroughfare that followed the route of the Maidan, a railway carrying noisy trams laid out between it and the river. The road was jammed with traffic: coolie-drawn rickshaws, military vehicles, battered trucks, countless bicycles. Sacred cows, garlanded with flowers, enjoyed the right of way and wandered wherever they chose. The pavement side of the street bustled with life, the ramshackle shops and stalls promising everything the Empire had to offer. Edward sauntered happily, stopping for a shave from a slender barber who massaged the scalp and shoulders with ridiculously strong fingers. He bought chapatis and curry from roadside shacks, gambling that his guts were up to the challenge. He bought a Conan Doyle compendium for a handful of rupees. He allowed himself to be jostled into the heaving pit of humanity that was the Hogg Market and, by the time he was spat out at the other end, he found himself in possession of a miniature Taj Mahal carved from ivory, a new pair of shoes, a landscape of an Indian sunset in an enamel frame and a much lightened purse.

The light began to fade and Edward threw himself into a headlong bacchanal. He gorged on a steak dinner from Jimmy's Kitchen, ogled the twenty-foot high cut-out of Jeanne Crain in 'Leave Her to Heaven' that had been lashed to the awning above the Tiger cinema, and joined the soldiers in drinking the bars of Chowringhee dry. He eventually found himself in the Nip Inn. The atmosphere was rowdy and febrile, hundreds of drunken soldiers and sailors taking advantage of an opportunity to get drunk and forget the war. As Edward drank his first pint a brawl broke out between a group of naval ratings and half a dozen airmen. Punches were thrown and furniture shattered. The management had long since given up trying to stop the fighting. They let the participants punch themselves out and then ejected those who were still standing.

Edward was standing at the bar with his second pint of warm beer. He looked out at the sea of green and blue uniforms. He was aware of the American airman behind him and tried to back out of the way so that the man could get to the bar to order his drinks. His crutches made moving awkward in such an enclosed space; the man was impatient, edging forwards, his shoulder jarring against Edward's arm and spilling his pint.

"Careful, friend," Edward said.

"What about it?" The man was drunk.

"Pushing and shoving isn't going to get you anywhere."

"Better mind your manners, cripple," he said, indicating the crutches.

"Take it easy," Edward said, trying to placate the man. He was tall and brawny and there were two other flyers in uniform standing behind him. "I don't want any trouble."

"Maybe you're going to get some, anyway."

The man hit him with a straight jab to the nose. Edward's pint smashed against the floor as he staggered back against the bar. The American came forward as Edward dropped his crutch and fired out a right to the body and then a left to the jaw, both blows landing hard and sending the American reeling backwards. The bar was suddenly silent, and then hugely raucous again as the crowd parted, a space forming for the combatants and dozens of drunken soldiers struggling for the best vantage point.

Edward had to half hop on his right leg, but he still managed to stop the man's rush with two straight lefts to the face, and the American, grown wary, responded by drawing the left, then by ducking it and delivering his right in a swinging hook towards the side of the head. Edward absorbed it on his forearms and hobbled forwards, firing out another one-two combination, but he was suddenly cold-cocked by a second man who emerged from the baying crowd from his left. The blow was high up but, when it landed, Edward felt the descent of the black veil of unconsciousness across his mind. For an instant, or for the slightest fraction of an instant, he paused. In the one moment he saw his opponent ducking out of his field of vision and the background of white, watching faces fade away; in the next moment he again saw his opponent and the background of faces. It was as if he had slept for a time and just opened his eyes again, and yet the interval of unconsciousness was so microscopically short that there had been no time for him to fall. The audience saw him totter and his knees give, then saw him recover and tuck his chin deeper into the shelter of his left shoulder. He stumbled into the ring of spectators and was shoved back into the space again, the crowd's bloodlust not nearly sated enough to allow him an easy way out. His foot burned with pain and he shook his head to try and clear away the grogginess. The American came forwards, swinging powerful rights and lefts into Edward's gut, driving the air from his lungs. A low blow followed, way below the belt, and, with Edward's guard down, a powerful right cross connected flush on his jaw. The black veil fell again and this time he dropped to the floor, scrabbling for purchase amid the sawdust, spit and spilt beer.

A moment passed, then another. His awareness returned and found his crutch and struggled to his feet, his knees like water.

The crowd to Edward's left parted as a man in British army uniform shoved his way through.

"Let's be sporting and even the odds, eh?"

The American sized the newcomer up. "More the merrier," he said. His two friends stepped forward with him.

The newcomer fired the first punch, a hook, with the twisted arch of the arm to make it rigid, and with all the weight of his half-pivoted body behind it. The American, caught on the side of the jaw, went down like a bullock hit between the eyes. The raucous audience whooped its appreciation. The new man could drive a blow like a trip-hammer.

One of the others came for Edward. He clinched to save himself, then, going free, allowed the man to get set. This was what he wanted. He feinted with his left, drew the answering duck and swinging upward hook, then made the half-step backward, whipping the crutch in his right hand full across the man's face, the wood catching him against the jaw and crumpling him so that he fell backwards halfway over the bar.

Edward and his new ally stood shoulder-to-shoulder. The final American, facing both of them now, thought better of it. He raised his hands in surrender and helped drag his dazed comrades away.

Edward turned to the new man. "I had it under control," he said, gasping for breath.

"Sure you did," the other said with a hard laugh. He pointed at Edward's face. "Your nose—"

Edward dabbed his fingers. They came back smeared with blood.

He grinned. "Jesus—"

"Here," the other man said, handing him a handkerchief.

"Thanks," Edward said, holding the fabric to his nostrils. "You'd never guess—I'm supposed to be a handy boxer."

"You are?"

"Had a few bouts over here. Army Boxing Association. I was decent—well, until I got shot, anyway."

"Your foot?"

"Jap bullet. Went right through it. I'm on medical leave."

"Didn't stop you then, did it?" the man observed. "That was a hell of a whack you gave him."

"He left his chin open," Edward grinned. "Rude not to take the invitation." He extended his hand. "I'm Edward Fabian."

The other man gripped it firmly. "Joseph Costello. Nice to meet you."

"You want a beer?"

* * *

EDWARD AWOKE EARLY THE NEXT MORNING. He had a terrible hangover and he desperately needed the bathroom. He got out of bed, knowing he was going to be sick yet moving slowly because he knew just when he was going to be sick and that there would be time for him to get to the bathroom. The marble floor was cool against his naked knees as he crouched before the latrine and voided his guts, dunked his head in a sink of cold water and washed. He tried to remember the rest of the night. They had stayed for another few pints and then Joseph had negotiated a discount with a pair of Eurasian prostitutes. Edward remembered seeing Joseph's girl pushing him down an alleyway for a wall job. Then there had been more beer, and he didn't remember much at all after that.

He looked at his reflection in the mirror and couldn't help but grin. His eyes were bleary, bloodshot and crusted with sleep. He imagined he could see a patina of green on his skin. His nose was purple and crusted with dried blood. It had been quite a night. He hadn't had so much fun for months. Joseph was infectious company. A capital chap. He would be very happy to go out with him again that night.

When he eventually found his way to the mess for breakfast it was afire with gossip. The reports were that earlier that morning an American B-29 Superfortress named after the mother of its pilot had been loaded with what was being described as a 'super weapon.' They said that this weapon was an 'atomic' bomb, that it had been dropped onto a city on the southern tip of Japan, and that the city had been scraped from the face of the Earth. Edward did not believe it but, as time passed, gossip was confirmed that made it plain that something momentous had happened. They had heard talk of 'secret weapons' before, of course; Hitler had his V1s and V2s and everyone assumed that the Allied boffins were working on something similar. The concept of an 'atomic bomb' was meaningless to them then but over the next few hours astonishing details were added that made it plain that whatever this weapon was, it was no mere rocket.

The three days after Hiroshima were electric. Edward tried to temper his own excitement. People were talking about the end of hostilities but he limited his enthusiasm in case his hopes were dashed. They all knew that Jap was a ferocious, tenacious foe and they, more than anyone, knew that the word 'surrender' was not in his vocabulary.

But then President Truman gave a second demonstration of his new toy and Nagasaki was flattened. 'Little Boy' and 'Fat Man' erased cities from the map and killed tens of thousands of civilians. They did in seconds what the Allies had struggled to accomplish in years.

Six days later Hirohito sued for peace and the war was over.

The next day a major from logistics was looking for him.

"Sir?" Edward said.

"Corporal Fabian?"

"Yes?"

"You've got twenty minutes to pack."

"They're sending me back? I only just got here."

"You've been reassigned."

"What? To where?"

"London. The boat leaves in an hour."

Edward didn't know what to say. He was excited that his war was over but there was anxiety, too. He had joined the Army to escape his problems. Would seven years have been enough to make them go away? Would the police have closed his file? The Old Bill were not the only ones who were looking for him. Had the others given up, too? They were more dangerous. There was no way of knowing.

After seven years on the run, Edward Fabian was going home.

PART TWO

London
May – June 1945

CALENDAR

— 1945 —

The *Star*, 13th May:

MORE GANG WARFARE IN SOHO

Another three men needed treatment in the hospital on Saturday night after a brawl between rival gangs. The men, who suffered broken limbs and concussion, are not understood to have cooperated with the police who are now powerless to pursue the matter. A spokesman suggested to this reporter that the tussle marks the latest in a series of contretemps between the two rival gangs who are currently vying for control of the London underworld. One of these gangs is reputed to be headed by Mr. Jack Spot, of East Ham, London, a man with a hard-earned reputation for violence. This reporter wonders what it will take for the Commissioner of the Metropolis to take this terrifying threat seriously? A murder? That, surely, is inevitable unless swift and decisive action is taken.

MARK DAWSON

The *Star*, 14th May:

BLACK MARKET GROWS
'ILLICIT SALES OUT OF CONTROL'

News from Ireland that wholesale smuggling is going on across the Eire–Ulster border is just another evidence of slackening morals. In austerity London, the pinch of eggless, milkless, fruitless days has long since twisted morals out of shape. While public morale rode high, toward the end of last year many a Londoner had relaxed his usually rigid code of personal honour sufficiently to treat Government post-war restrictions in much the same way that the mass of U.S. citizens treated prohibition. It looked as though game-loving Britons were inclined to think that outwitting the Government was a sporting proposition.

Scotland Yard optimistically reported a 1 per cent decrease in general crime since 1944. But official figures were unreliable. Police had access only to cases where a complaint has been registered, a culprit booked. The chief evidence of character-loosening was conversation. Topic No. 1 (the war) had been pushed into the background by Topic No. 2 (how to beat the rationing restrictions). From peers to paupers the major chit-chat of Londoners was how to get fugitive eggs, lipstick, fruits, silk stockings, perfume, clothes. At a dinner party recently a peer's daughter triumphantly announced that she had persuaded her dressmaker to sell her a new suit without the required coupons. A politician's wife proudly reported buying a fur coat (18 coupons) with no coupons whatever (she contended the garment was second-hand because it had been worn by a mannequin).

Black markets flourished in Soho streets. Barrow merchants sold silk stockings (probably stolen) with only a pretence of accepting ration coupons. Crates of oranges, strictly restricted to children, passed through a market speculator to his favourite customers. Housewives evaded milk rationing with two companies, thereby getting twice their legal share. Working in gangs—a man or children assisting a woman with a shopping bag—shoplifters raided lingerie, stocking, and sweater counters. Scotland Yard reported a 25 per cent increase in shop-lifting. 'Kerb crawlers' (fences) ferried stolen goods out to the suburbs, sold them couponless to house-wives. A woman reported to the police that she was offered an ebony coat for £16 (half the store price) by a woman black marketeer who had about 20 fur coats in the back of her limousine…

METROPOLITAN POLICE
Criminal Investigation Department
New Scotland Yard

STRICTLY PRIVATE AND CONFIDENTIAL

To Commissioner:
I.O: D.I. Charles Murphy
Submitted at request of: D.A.C. Clarke
Re: Gang Activity in Soho, W.1.

Sir,
You asked me to report upon the state of gang activity in London, specifically as it pertains to the feeding of the black market. I can confirm that the most powerful faction remains the Costello Family, who count among their many activities robbery, extortion, and the operation of illegal drinking and gambling

clubs throughout Soho. The Costellos have been dominant for a generation but there are signs that challengers are beginning to eye their crown. Chief among those is the Jack Spot Mob, led by the eponymous Spot, a powerful brawler from the Upton Park area of East London. He has banded together with several dozen gypsies and my intelligence is that he is extending his influence towards the West. There have already been minor skirmishes between the two gangs and I predict worse is to come if the problem is not tackled.

I understand that this is not what you wanted to hear. My recommendation, as laid out in my separate memorandum to you, remains: the creation of a dedicated "Ghost" Squad to infiltrate the gangs and seek the evidence that will lead to their destruction. Without wishing to appear immodest, I would be happy to put myself forward to lead this Squad.

Sincerely,
D.I. C. Murphy
24th May

2

ENGLAND LOOKED TIRED AND ILL as the train shuffled north-east, picking its way through the blasted suburbs of Basingstoke and then into South London. Particles of brick dust hung in the air, disturbed by the passage of the train. Slag heaps were choked with weeds and thick grass. Whole terraces had been flattened. Long lines of industrial chimneys stood smokeless, stiffly naked against the sky, in huddles over empty workshops. The cellars of demolished houses had been turned into static reservoirs, waters glittering darkly in the fading twilight. A pack of feral dogs, their owners dead or disappeared, clambered onto a pile of rubble and howled at the train as it passed. Familiar roads and streets had been rendered unrecognisable.

The carriage was full of soldiers, loaded down with kitbags, mementoes, trophies. Edward's own bag was jammed into the overhead rack, the curved blade of his kukri tucked into a loop of fabric. The atmosphere was pensive. They could all see it: things had changed. England had changed. There had been female railway porters at Portsmouth, for goodness sake. Edward had heard, like everyone, that women had been working in factories. He assumed things would have quickly settled back down again and returned to normal. But the Axis had been defeated and there they were, women, still doing men's work. And they had gone butch. At all ages and on every social level, they had taken to uniforms. They wore jackets, trousers and sensible shoes. It was a rum lot. Vexed comments were exchanged between boys to whom this was not a welcome development. It was certainly going to take some getting used to.

The door to the compartment opened and a soldier hauled his kitbag inside. "Well, I'll be," he said, a delighted smile upon his face. "It's the brawler from Calcutta."

Edward beamed back at him. "Costello, isn't it?"

"The very same. What are the chances, eh?"

"Did you just come ashore?"

"Yesterday. What about you?"

"A week," Edward said. "There were a few things to tie up and now that's that. Done."

"You're out?"

"Seven years later. You?"

"The same. And not a moment too soon."

Joseph Costello sat down opposite and dropped his kitbag to the floor. He untied the toggle, tugged the mouth of the bag open and reached inside for a bottle of gin. "A little something to celebrate?"

"Where did you get that from?"

"Ways and means. Want to wet your whistle?"

"Don't mind if I do."

They both took their army-issue tin cups and Joseph poured out two large measures. "So what are you looking forward to most?"

"How do you mean?"

He settled back against the seat. "Now we're home—what are you looking forward to?"

Edward sighed expansively. "A chair to sit in for breakfast and the day's paper to read—on the day it was published without people peering over my shoulder. You?"

Joseph tried to light their cigarettes. He had a beautiful silver lighter, but it did not work reliably. Edward finally produced his ugly, flaring lighter, as ugly and efficient as a piece of industrial equipment, and lighted it for him. Joseph passed one to Edward and he lit that, too. Joseph sat back and rested his legs on the bench opposite. "Proper food off a china plate," he suggested, "and tea from a china cup with my own dose of milk and sugar."

"Somebody else to do the washing and make my bed."

"A shirt with a collar and tie, and shoes."

"To go to bed when I like in a room of my own and put the light out when I want to. And no more bloody jungle."

Joseph laughed. "No more jungle. I'll drink to that. Another one?"

Edward proffered his cup and Joseph poured again.

"What are you going to do now?" he asked. "For work, I mean?

"I'll take it as it comes. There's a family business. I'll probably end up there."

"What do they do?"

Joseph paused, as if searching for the right words. He settled for, "A little bit of this, a little bit of that."

"Is it successful?"

"Oh, yes. Big house in the countryside, places in London, a fleet of cars in the garage, more money rolling in than they know what to do with—at least that was what it was like before I left and I shouldn't think much has changed."

"What do they do?"

"Well, I'm not going into details, but let's just say it's the kind of thing that's probably even more popular in an economy like this"—he gestured out at the dishevelled landscape passing by the window—"than what it was like before."

Edward was intrigued but he decided to let it go for fear of appearing too keen.

"What about you?" Joseph said, changing the subject.

Edward's story was well rehearsed and he relayed it naturally and easily. "I studied medicine before the war. Haven't practiced since I graduated, though. I'm sure there'll be refresher exams to take, that sort of thing. And Mr. Beveridge is promising all sorts of changes, isn't he? 'The National Health Service.' Goodness knows how that will affect things."

"Socialism!" Joseph snorted. "My God, we can do without that."

The train started to slow as they drew into Waterloo station. They hoisted their packs over the shoulders and joined the queue of men in the corridor, all of them anxious to disembark. Edward felt his stomach clench as he stepped down from the train. He foresaw figures standing at the end of the platform, near to the barriers, policemen waiting for him, patiently waiting with folded arms and handcuffs hanging from their belts. He grew suddenly tense. He had hoped that seven years would have been time enough for the fear inside his stomach to have been quashed, but it was not. He felt the hairs on the back of his neck prickle. No use thinking about that now. He pulled his shoulders back. No use spoiling his return worrying about imaginary policemen. Even if there were policemen, it wouldn't necessarily mean anything. He had to be realistic—they couldn't still be after him, not after all this time.

As far as they were concerned, he was dead and buried.

Joseph paused on the concourse and shrugged his pack from his shoulders.

"Alright, pal," Joseph said. "This is me. My uncle's coming to pick me up. I'd offer you a lift, but he's not really the friendly type—"

Edward lowered his own pack to the ground. "It's quite alright—I'll get the tube."

"It's been good to get to know you, Doc," he said.

"Doc?"

"Doctor? The medicine?"

Edward had almost tripped up. "Oh yes, of course," he said, remembering to smile. "Doc—very good."

"Listen—I reckon we ought to keep in touch. We've got plenty in common." He shadow-boxed for moment, firing out a gentle combination. "The noble art and all that."

"That's true."

"I'm thinking about keeping it up, doing a bit of sparring. You should come along, once your foot's better."

"It's nearly better now," he said. There had been nothing to do on the voyage home except put his feet up and read and the rest had done wonders for the wound. "I'd love to."

"Here, hold on." He took his travel pass and a pen from his pocket. He scribbled a number on the docket and handed it to him. "You should be able to reach me here. Give me a ring when you're settled. We could have a spar and then go for a pint."

"Capital idea."

"That's settled, then."

Joseph pulled him in and pounded him on the back. "Good to meet you, Doc," he said. "Enjoy being home. And call me—alright?"

Edward said that he would, and he meant it.

3

EDWARD TRANSFERRED ONTO THE UNDERGROUND. When he emerged from Tottenham Court Road station half an hour later it was into a warm dusk. The damage that had been done to the city since his departure was difficult to credit. Even now, with peace a year old, windows were still missing and there were holes in roofs. Some buildings had been pulverised, as if crushed by a giant's fist. Others, the remedial work more advanced, had been removed neatly from the surrounding terrace as one would remove a slice of cake. It was as if they had never even been there, weeds already growing in their foundations. A fine film of dust thickened the city's usual smog, coating everything with a patina of grime.

He passed into Soho. He had grown up on its exciting grill of good-time streets and he retained fond memories of it. It was like a tiny international resort with an ozone of garlic, curry, ceremonious sauces and a hundred far-flung cheeses. The war had not changed it. The carrier cans in the windows were still full of salad and cooking oil and you could still find dozens of Spanish cheeses, snails, octopus and Chinese cheesecake. There was Dijon mustard; Rajah-like Eastern dishes costing pounds or modest four-bob curries; sex books; strip-tease shows; exotic clubs and thirty-odd different kinds of bread.

Edward walked towards his destination and passed a woman reverently dusting bottles of wine, adorned with a whole picture gallery of labels, handing them to her small son who squatted in the shop window arranging them for display. Outside, the father stood, both arms extended, directing the whole operation like a temperamental stage manager.

Eating was still a serious business and there remained sophisticated restaurants that laid on discreet shabbiness like a sort of make-up, knowing that serious gourmets do not bother much about decor. The Shangri-La was one such establishment. It was on Dean Street, one of the bisecting thoroughfares that ran north-to-south, connecting Oxford Street to Shaftesbury Avenue. It had twenty tables offering eighty covers and a small bar. Edward's father had taken out a loan for a hundred pounds in 1936 and had spent it on a thorough refurbishment: wooden panels had been fitted to the walls and intricate stained-glass windows had been installed. The carpet, table clothes and curtains were all in dark colours and a fire burned in the grate. The intention had been to make something that felt exclusive, the kind of cosy clubbable charm that one might find in a Mayfair private members room. It had worked, to a point, but that was back then; now the carpets were tatty and the edges of the curtains had frayed. The room, like the city outside, looked faded and tired, like an elderly relative who had seen better days.

Edward made his way around to the kitchen entrance.

The small kitchen staff was busy. Jimmy Stern was working in front of the range, chopping vegetables, two large saucepans sending clouds of steam up to the ceiling. He was slick with sweat and his whites were slathered with blood and grime.

"Hello, uncle," Edward said.

The old man gaped at him, dropping his knife.

"You want to be careful with that—you'll have your finger off."

Jimmy hugged him and then released him, clutching him by the shoulders so he could look him up and down. "Good lord, Jack—you're a sight for sore eyes."

It was the first time he had been addressed by his real name for seven years. It took a moment for him to reply, "It's not Jack anymore, uncle, remember? It's Edward."

"Hell, I forgot. Edward—?"

"Fabian."

He chuckled. "Edward Fabian—that's right. We really should have found you a better name."

"Beggars can't be choosers. I was in a rush. It wasn't like I could wait around for something better to come along."

The two nodded at the thought of it. Edward Fabian had been the victim of one of the first Luftwaffe bombs of The Blitz. He had been a promising medical student, just graduated from Trinity Hall, Cambridge. Jimmy had a friend in the coroner's office and he had been paid a pound to look out for a casualty who matched Jack's height, build and hair colour. Fabian had been the first to meet the criteria, and they had simply switched papers. The local council was at sixes and sevens as the bombs fell and it had been easy to cover their tracks. Fabian's body had been cremated hastily and that was that: as far as the authorities were concerned, Jack Stern had died in the wreckage of a collapsed terrace. Jack had become Edward.

"What do I call you? Jack or Edward?"

"Edward," he said. "It's been years. I've got used to it now. And Jack's dead. Let's not tempt fate."

"When did you get back?"

"Last week."

"And you're out?"

"I am."

"Properly? For good?"

"I'm officially demobbed. I'm a free man."

Edward noticed a new, manic quality to his uncle. Jimmy had always been highly-strung, prone to mood swings, but it seemed that he was wound even tighter than usual.

"Have you eaten?" Jimmy asked.

"A sandwich on the train."

"'A sandwich on the train.' That's not good enough, is it? Go and find a seat. I'll fetch you something."

Edward was hungry and didn't complain. He made his way through into the restaurant. It was quiet, just a few diners quietly going about their meals, cutlery ringing against the crockery. He checked his watch: it wasn't late. They should have been much busier.

Jimmy brought out a plate of Baked Pig's Cheek and sat down opposite him. "I'm sorry, it's nothing special."

"It'll do fine." Edward sliced a piece of pork and put it into his mouth. He chewed; it was rubbery and dry, barely edible. Jimmy had prepared an excellent apple sauce to mask the poor quality of the meat but there was only so much he could do.

"So? How was it?"

"Up and down" he said. "Some days were good, some were bad. Most of the time it was boring."

"Boring?" Jimmy said.

"You'd be surprised." He had no desire to talk about the war and changed the subject. "How have things been here? It's quiet."

"Slow."

His face showed the signs of strain and worry. "Are you making money?"

"Not really. Not enough."

"What do you mean?"

He dismissed the question with a brush of his hand. "We don't need to talk about that now—you've just got back. It can wait."

This was more than enough to make Edward nervous. "No, tell me."

Jimmy slumped a little. "It's been difficult. Bloody difficult. We've been losing money. The rent, the cost of staff, the ingredients." He pointed at Edward's half-finished plate of food. "I can't charge proper prices for that. The food is the same as a National Restaurant. Worse, probably. It's impossible."

"It's not so bad," Edward said, poking at the remnants of the meal.

"I'm not an idiot, Edward. It's awful. You saw the menu? The beef is horse, we don't have any bread…"

"Bread isn't rationed?"

"It wasn't during the war. Soon as we bloody well get through that, though, and it is. Ridiculous. The vegetables need the mould cutting out of them and the snoek—my God, if there's a worse tasting fish than bloody snoek I haven't had it. Who's going to pay a quid to eat that? Look, I was going to tell you tomorrow but I might as well get it out of the way now. I've had to make some difficult decisions."

"Like what?"

"I sold my house. There was no more money. I would've had to close otherwise."

"When was this?"

"January."

"Why didn't you tell me?"

"There was no point in worrying you about it."

"But—"

"There was no point, Edward," he said firmly. "You were out of the country—what good would it have done, you fretting about it over there?"

"How much did you get?"

"There wasn't that much to be had. I'd already remortgaged twice."

"How much is left?"

"Not much."

"Anything?"

He shrugged disconsolately. "Fifty quid."

Edward could hardly believe what he was hearing. This was not the return he had been expecting. There was more to ask about the state of the restaurant, but it could wait. Jimmy looked tired: blue-black bags bulged beneath his eyes and his skin was pallid and grey.

"Where are you living?"

"Here. It's not so bad." Jimmy stared out of the window, his conviction unpersuasive.

Jimmy fetched a bowl of spotted dick and custard for dessert. Edward felt deflated. He also felt a little shocked. Things were different, and not for the better. The last customers left. Jimmy shut the door and switched off the lights. Edward put on an apron and helped him clean the kitchen. They worked in silence. The news had shaken him, and it was going to take some time to absorb.

"Where do we sleep?"

"In here," Jimmy said, opening the storeroom door and stepping aside to let his nephew pass. A bedroll had been laid out on the floor between shelves of produce, bags of flour and rice. A hurricane lamp rested on the floor. Jimmy knelt down and lit it. He worked his boots off.

Edward lowered himself to the floor. "Did anyone come around for me?"

"After you went? Of course they did. The police were here just about every other day and when I convinced them I didn't know where you are I had the others to deal with. I preferred the police."

"What did you say?"

"That you were dead. I think they believed me in the end."

"And that was that? No-one else?"

"The last one was a private detective. Three or four years ago. I think it was just routine by that point. There hasn't been anyone else since."

Edward extinguished the lamp, lay down and stared into the darkness for a good half an hour, unable to sleep.

"Are you awake?" he whispered.

"Yes," Jimmy said.

"How's my father?"

There was a pause, and then Edward heard his uncle give a long sigh. "Not good. Getting worse. You'll have to go and see him."

The day was a terrible anticlimax and, now, it ended with worry.

4

AFTER SEVEN YEARS IN THE SERVICE Edward's body had become conditioned to rising before first light. It was a habit he would never grow out of and, that second day home, he awoke at four. He had slept fitfully, anyway, waking up and each time finding himself surprised that he was not under the canopy of the jungle and that he couldn't hear the chirping of the crickets. It took him several moments to remember where he was.

His earliest childhood memory was of the kitchen: the clouds of steam, the smells, the clamour and clatter of preparation. The first thing he could remember clearly was an image of his father, wearing an old-fashioned cook's smock with a huge tureen of soup cradled between his elbows. He could see the flour on his arms, his glasses pushed up on his forehead and sweat pasting his thinning hair to his crown; a cleaver brought down onto the bloodied carcass of a pig; his mother going around the dining room to adjust cutlery by infinitesimal degrees; the sound of her calm voice as she explained to a customer why their dinner was delayed; the bitter taste of chocolate that he furtively licked from a bowl. He could remember being taken through the kitchen as a young child, the heat that was as wet as water, the waves that pulsed out of the open ovens, scorching the back of the throat and crisping the hair inside the nostrils each time he took a breath. And, most evocative of all, the smells: roasting meat, the intense aroma of the bread oven, pastry sweetness.

Edward used the customer bathroom and changed into a pair of checked trousers, chef's jacket and clogs. He put on an apron but couldn't remember how to tie it. Jimmy corrected him, crossing the strings at the back, tying it at the front, the bib tucked inside. He paused at the front of house, took the reservation book and thumbed through it. Today promised to be much busier than last night. Perhaps there was hope. Even a broken night's sleep had reinvigorated him and he felt full of determination. He was home now and he wasn't going to let the restaurant fail without a bloody good fight.

It was still dark outside when they got to work. Edward opened the door to the kitchen and switched on the lights. It hadn't changed a bit while he was away: a long, thin space with the service line arranged against one wall with a narrow pass-through opposite it. Six months after acquiring the restaurant, his father had knocked through two of the walls and extended the kitchen into what had once been a store-room. There was a cold station next to the exit door, a row of deep-fryers, two big ranges, a pull-out broiler, a salamander, a brick hearth for charcoal grilling. Opposite, and separated by a slender work space, was a long stainless-steel counter with wooden cutting boards, sinks and a new Frigidaire at the end. He lit the ranges, flames curling up the blackened wall, and Jimmy switched on the steam table. There was no way for the air to circulate in the kitchen and within five minutes the temperature had ticked up to an almost unbearable level: a wall of radiant warmth on one side and clouds of wet steam rising on the other. He remembered his first proper session in the kitchen as a fourteen-year old pot boy: he'd fainted dead away in the broiling swelter.

They went outside to the alleyway where the bins were kept and smoked their first roll-ups of the day. If Jimmy was nervous, he didn't show it. He had always been a brilliant cook, and since Edward had been away he had become as good as Edward's father had been.

"It's going to be hard work today," he warned. "We'd ideally need another two or three in the kitchen but we can't afford it."

"I'm back now. We'll manage."

They went back into the steaming kitchen. Edward opened the Frigidaire to check the ingredients: some mackerel that was beginning to turn, a tray of sickly-looking pigs' livers, a dozen poor quality steaks. He held up a slab of meat. "What in buggery are we supposed to do with this? It's all gristle."

Jimmy looked up from rolling another cigarette. "I had to pay over the odds for that, too. We'll make a nice sauce and hope for the best."

He took out a tray filled with salted water. Two medium-sized birds, de-feathered and skinned, had been left to soak overnight. "What are these?"

"Rooks."

"*Rooks?*"

'Somerset Rook Pie with Figgy Paste. Legs and breast only—get rid of everything else, it's bitter. You make a paste with bacon fat, currants and raisins and serve it with gooseberry jelly."

"And it tastes—?"

"Bloody awful."

The staff drifted in during the half-hour prior to the start of the shift. There was Pauline, a matronly East-Ender who made the fish stew and, during service, doled out the vegetables and side dishes; she had a problem with drink, and the glass at her side was kept topped up with gut-rot gin from a bottle she no longer went to the trouble of hiding. Gordon, the fry chef, had a history of mental illness and plenty of gaol-time. Edward's father had always met him at the prison gates and offered him his job back again although it wasn't purely philanthropic; Gordon was a devil behind the grill with unflagging energy and a high threshold to pain evidenced by the litany of burns and cuts on his arms. He kept a speed pourer topped up with rum in his rack and he sucked at it like a baby with a bottle. Stanley Smith dressed like a pirate with the arms hacked off his chef's coat, lank hair kept out of his eyes with a faded headband and prison tattoos inked onto his forearms. He was the pastry chef, and knocked out row after row of delicate deserts. The kitchen staff had been unchanged for ten years, and it was only the supporting roles—the pot boys, the waiting staff—that were different.

They made their preparations: sharpening knives, folding side-towels into stacks, arranging favourite pans, stockpiling ice and boiling pots of water. Edward took an empty space and arranged his *mise-en-place*. He found a half-bowl of sea salt and cracked pepper, softened some lard, slotted cooking oil and cheap wine into his speed rack. He added breadcrumbs, parsley, brandy, chopped chives, caramelised apple sections, chopped onions and a selection of ladles, spoons and tongs. He arranged the pots and pans into a logical order and slotted his knives into a block so that they could be drawn quickly, as required. The others went about their work, well-practiced routines and roles that complemented each other perfectly. Pauline roasted bones for stock, skinned the pigs' livers and scooped snoek from tins; Gordon blanched carrots, made garlic confit and a mayonnaise sauce with custard powder, powdered eggs and margarine; Stanley caramelised apples, lined dishes with pastry, took the plate of steaks from the larder, separated the worst and turned them into Salade de Boeuf en Vinaigrette, prepared a raspberry vinegar sauce to serve with the livers.

Edward did his best to fit in, aware that he was hopelessly out of practice. He took a bowl of scrapings and made pâté and galantine, boiled off-cuts and knocked up a strong horseradish sauce, caramelized sugar to mask the taste of over-ripe fruit. He filled a huge steam kettle with stock, a darkly simmering mixture of ground beef, meat scraps, chicken bones, turkey carcasses, vegetable trimmings, carrot peelings and egg shells.

It was awful. He wouldn't have given any of it to a dog.

Edward went through and checked the reservation book again. They were busy for both dinner sittings. Twenty tables, four covers per table, two sittings. They would need to put out one hundred and sixty dinners. He knew it was going to be hard, bordering on the impossible, but he kept his doubts to himself.

Soon the kitchen was full of noise: profane yet affectionate insults, curses that would make a navvie blush, the bubbling of boiling water, whisks rattling against the sides of bowls, the rhythmic thudding of knives against chopping boards as vegetables and meat were diced. The ovens were turned to their highest settings and the doors left open; heat ran out of them like liquid until it seemed that the air was scorching the lungs. The temperature soared and it was soon difficult to see from the fryers at one end of the line to the ovens at the other because of the wavy heat-haze, the air squirming, like staring through the water in a fish tank.

Jimmy leant against a tiled corner, drank a beer and smoked a cigarette. He watched through a crack in the door as the diners arrived and were shown to their tables. "Here they come," he called. The first order arrived, Jimmy taking it from Mary, the waitress, and slapping it on the pass. "One Potato Jane, one dried egg omelette, one Marrow Surprise, one Tomato Charlotte."

That was just the first table. Things were fine to begin with but fresh orders arrived at shorter and shorter intervals and it wasn't long before they started to back up. Starters were finished and orders for the main courses began to arrive and Edward was soon up to his wrists in meat and blood, crouching at the locker to pull out stringy steaks that already smelt as if they were on the turn. They yelled at Peter, the thirteen year old runner and pot boy, to bring more margarine and oil, and when they weren't yelling at him they muttered at their stations, cursing, talking to the meat, urging it to cook, begging more fire from the burners, flipping steaks, poking them and prodding them to gauge how well they were done, how much longer they needed.

Jimmy called out a running commentary: 'Sending tables seven, thirteen, twenty, thank you. Table six, two fillets, medium. Four well, two medium, one blue. Hold six, waiting for Rook Pie. Five wants Beef Salad, where's the vinaigrette? Two rare, waiting for potatoes on two, where are the bloody potatoes, Edward? Thank you. Away we go."

The heat got too much for Edward at around half past eight, right in the middle of the rush, the dizziness increasing in frequency and pitch until it felt as if a vice were being tightened around his forehead. He dropped to his knees, unsure of his balance and wary of toppling forward onto the burners. Jimmy yelled at the pot boy to fetch ice buckets for each of them and Edward bent down and dunked his head, the sudden shock chasing away the woozy light-headedness, at least for a few minutes.

The next four hours were a nightmare that he thought would never end. The waitresses cleared the first sitting but the second arrived before they could even catch their breath. A break was out of the question. Fresh orders for starters were delivered and they were plunged back into bedlam again. An oven went down and Jimmy had to attend to it, a bottleneck forming with orders arriving so fast that they couldn't fight their way through it. A thick wad of them built up. The floor was ankle deep in debris: scraps of food, discarded packaging, dropped utensils and dirty towels. Edward ended up drinking the cooking wine to keep himself together, chasing glasses of it with strong black coffee and a cigarette that he stuck behind his ear until it was eaten down to the tip and burnt his skin.

Nine o'clock came and went and they were on the home straight. They cooked everything they had in a mad effort to keep ahead. The wooziness faded in and out, stronger the longer the service went on, the effect of the ice water diminishing each time Edward resorted to it. Burns and calluses marked his hands, his blood felt like it was boiling and salty sweat stung his eyes.

"Rather be in the jungle?" Jimmy called out.

"This is hotter than the jungle," he said, "but at least I'm not being shot at."

"Not yet!"

By the time midnight came Edward had been on his feet for twenty hours with barely any respite. He trembled with fatigue. "Keep going!" Jimmy yelled out.

At a half past twelve the last table cleared the pass. "Finished," Jimmy shouted above the din. "That's it."

* * *

IT WAS GONE TWO BY THE TIME they had finally wiped down, stored the ingredients that they hadn't used and cleaned the kitchen. They had been awake for twenty-two hours. They retired to the side exit, sitting against the wall and bathing in the coolness of the night air. Dog-ends were scattered around and an empty bottle of house wine was smashed in the gutter. Cockroaches skittered around the overflowing bins and hungry mice surfaced from the drains. The smell was overpowering: acidic like ripe tomatoes, yeasty like stale beer, pungent sweat coming off them damply. Edward was tired to the marrow of his bones, light-headed from exhaustion and cheap booze. The cold night air felt wonderful on flesh that was sore, scalded, steam-burned. He rolled two cigarettes and they smoked them in silence. It was a respite from the furnace heat of the kitchen, the yelling of cooks buckling under pressure, the crazy noise and exertion of the line.

Soho wound down around them, illegal shebeens and spielers offering late night drinks but the legitimate trade ending for another night. Drunks staggered through the alley, dragging their feet, wending left and right and somehow maintaining their balance. Neon signs buzzed until they were switched off for the night. A pair of policemen nodded at them as they passed. They looked like casualties of war, or murderers, their whites covered in blood and grime, sweaty hair plastered to their heads, nicks and scrapes covered by hastily applied sticking plasters.

"You need more help," Edward said, finally.

"Can't afford it."

"Can't keep that pace up."

"We have to," he said.

Edward sucked smoke deep into his lungs.

"Is it always like that?"

"More or less." Jimmy grinned, a strained wild-eyed grimace that spoke of how thinly he was stretched. He had been working two shifts in the kitchen every day for eight months straight. His last day off had been imposed on him by Gordon, fearful that he was on the edge of a breakdown. He couldn't have been closer to the edge than he was that night but now, with the kitchen staff at a bare minimum, there was no way that he could be spared.

"How much did you take?"

"Not enough."

"But it was full."

He laughed bitterly. "You know how many people paid?"

Edward shook his head.

"Half. How can I argue with them? The food's not fit for a dog." He sighed out, long and beaten and depressed. "We're busy, yes, but they're only coming because of the reputation the place has. That's your father's legacy, and we're pissing it all away. No-one who came here tonight is coming back. That's obvious. Eventually, word will start to get around. 'I had dinner in the Shangri-La last night—it used to be something special, but now, my goodness, it's a disgrace.' You know what they'll say. If we can still fill that room in three months I'll be surprised. And every seating we don't fill is another step closer to the end of the road. It's pointless, Edward. It's a losing battle."

Edward knew that his uncle was right. Even terrible ingredients were expensive, and they couldn't charge customers the prices they needed to break even. He'd heard about the walk-outs tonight, and the customers who had refused to pay full price. Money was tight and there was the rent to pay, and wages on top of that. Revenue was already insufficient to cover the outgoings. The future promised a long, slow, decline until the funds ran out.

"I'm going to see my father tomorrow," Edward said.

Jimmy nodded quietly.

"How bad is he?"

"Not good. I don't go as often as I should. It's difficult. It's hard to see him now."

Jimmy leaned back against the wall, the two of them laid out like corpses, and blew smoke into the night. Edward closed his eyes and found his thoughts drifting. This was not the return to London that he had been dreaming of. He would help his uncle but he couldn't do it by staying here. He would have to leave the kitchen. Jimmy needed money, and Edward stood more chance of finding it for him if he returned to the things that he was good at. He had a particular talent and he knew that it was the only chance they had to get the things that they needed and the things that he deserved. He was going to have to start from scratch, but that was alright; he had done that before. All he needed to do was to find the right mark.

5

EDWARD CAUGHT THE BUS to Bramley from Victoria. It was a pleasant day, early summer, fresh and bright, and he sat at the front with a sandwich and a thermos of tea and enjoyed the drive. It took a couple of hours to reach the sanatorium. The bus drew up in a quiet lane, the verges bright with spring flowers. It was housed in an old manor house and set within several acres of parkland, a grand old building with seven bays on two floors, with a three-bayed elevation surmounted by a pediment. The light glittered against a grand Venetian window set within the central bay. Edward disembarked and signed in at the gatehouse. He followed the path inside the grounds and paused on the broad terrace, taking it all in: lawns and flower-beds were arranged around the building, rows and avenues of trees set out beyond them. Smaller terraces were bright with flowers, shaded by fruit-laden apple trees, and the facility was surrounded by a high wall, then farm lands and, beyond them, an encircling belt of dark fir. He made his way towards the building, passing the kitchen-garden and the ordered rows of vegetables being tended by a pair of patients. He paused at the door to the main building until it was unlocked and opened. He greeted the guard as he passed inside, and, after asking for directions, made his way directly to his father's room.

The sister was at her desk at the top of the corridor. Two orderlies sat nearby.

"Good afternoon," she said.

"Good afternoon, sister. I'm here to see Richard Stern."

"And you are?"

"I'm a friend of his son."

"Your name?"

"Peter Broom."

"I don't think we knew he had a son."

"He's been in Burma. The war. I served with him. I was demobbed last week."

The nurse warmed visibly. "Bless you," she said. "You boys don't get the credit you deserve."

"Thank you."

Her smile became sad. "I'm afraid your friend's father is not a well man. He has a progressive disease. We do our best to make him comfortable."

"It's his birthday today," Edward said. "His son asked me to bring him a cake. I'll give him a slice now if that's alright and leave the rest next to his bed."

"You know you won't be able to take a knife into his room?"

"Oh, no, of course not—don't worry, I sliced it last night. I wonder if you'd be so kind to ask one of the nurses to give him another slice for his tea?"

"Of course," the sister said. "I'll let the girls know. Here—let me take you to him."

She led the way along the corridor: half a dozen rooms were arranged on each side, the open doors betraying the smells of urine and disinfectant. It was quiet, save for the mumbling of an old man who sat on the edge of his chair, rocking gently. His father's room was at the end. There was a fire in the grate and the remnants of a meal—a dirty bowl, an empty cup—rested on a small table next to an armchair. The walls were painted in pastel shades, the furniture looked comfortable and the early afternoon sunlight poured in through the wide window. His father was in bed, propped up by pillows. His eyes lolled hopelessly, never focussing, and a streamer of drool dripped down from the corner of his mouth. Edward took out his handkerchief and wiped it away.

"It's a side-effect of the drugs," the sister told him. "I'll leave you together."

His father was wearing a dressing gown over a pair of pyjamas. Spilt soup from his lunch had spattered across the fabric. He had not shaved, and his whiskers—white, the same colour as his wild shocks of hair—lent him an unkempt, dishevelled air. He wore a pair of spectacles with thick lenses, the glass magnifying his eyes so that they seemed to bulge from their sockets. The old man looked as if he were about to say something but frowned with confusion again, the thought passing unsaid.

"Happy birthday, father," he said quietly, sitting down in the chair next to the bed. The old man said nothing, chewed, his eyes unfocused.

Edward opened his bag and took out the cake tin and the carton of candles. He opened the tin, and took out the cake; it was a Victoria Sponge, a recipe he had clipped out of the *Sketch*. The first effort had been a failure; he'd used normal flour rather than self-raising and the mixture had failed to rise. The second effort was a little better. He planted a handful of candles around the edge, lit them with his lighter and lifted the cake closer to his father's mouth. The old man looked at it, dumbly, as if unsure what it was; the candles flickered in and out with his breath. He coughed for a moment, his breath thin and reedy. Edward blew the candles out for him, set the cake down on the bedside table, unwrapped the skirt, and took out two slices. He took one and held it to his father's mouth. The old man took a bite, chewed absent-mindedly, crumbs showering onto his day blanket. Edward bit into it. It was brittle and dry, a bit flavourless. He hadn't been able to afford the vanilla essence the recipe suggested and the cake missed it. He was no cook, that was for sure, but it'd have to do.

The old man turned his head and gazed out of the window onto the pretty garden beyond, his eyes glazing and, as Edward watched, bubbles of saliva gathered at the edge of his mouth and slowly trailing their way through the bristles on his chin. Edward took a handkerchief and dabbed the spittle away.

Edward said, "How've you been?" The old man looked at him, nothing in his eyes. "Did you get my letters?" Nothing. "I've been abroad. I've been in Burma, fighting the Japs. Jimmy has been writing to me, though, so I've been kept abreast of how you are. And I sent you cards at Christmas and your birthday. I expect the nurses put them up for you? I'm sorry it's been so long. You don't mind much, do you? I know you understand—you always wanted me to join the army, didn't you? Anyway, I'm getting you a nice new pair of slippers for your present. Good ones they are, proper fur inside, look nice and comfy. They're in the shop, I'll bring them when I've saved up the rest. You can wear them when you go to the bathroom."

The corridor outside was still: the other patients were either asleep or out in the grounds with their relatives. Wan sunlight filtered through dusty windows; Edward watched motes of dust turning in the shafts. He would be his father's only visitor today. Save Jimmy, there was no-one else. It was just the three of them now.

He kept talking. "Things are hard at the restaurant. Ingredients are hard to find what with all this rationing. I think Jimmy has been having a tough time of it. I'm back now, though. I'll find some money for him."

His father sat quietly. The change in him had been rapid: he'd been a big man, before, played prop forward on Sundays, but Jimmy said that within six months of the diagnosis he'd lost his weight and all his muscle. He was just a husk now, unrecognisable. His father turned his head away, nodding. Edward felt bad leaving him stuck here but there was nothing else for it. He had provided Jimmy with a lump sum before he left the country, but that had run out months ago. Jimmy had somehow found enough to keep the hospital sweet, but it was a constant battle. Edward was going to have to find money from somewhere. Better care—a room of his own, more comfortable surroundings—he couldn't even begin to think about things like that yet.

There was a gramophone record on the sideboard. Edward had remitted the money for Jimmy to buy it—his father loved music and it seemed as if it was the least he could do. The old man had always had a particularly fondness for Beethoven, and Edward slipped *Symphony No. 5* from its dust jacket, rested the phonograph on the platter and lowered the tone arm. The ominous First Movement played, the famous main theme opening loud and dynamically, the crescendos and diminuendos putting Edward in mind of tension, stress and a feeling of impending doom. He tried to ignore it but he could not. He needed to hear something optimistic, something creative. He would have chosen something by Vivaldi— the *Four Seasons*, perhaps. He was in a difficult spot. He was in need of optimism.

"Alright, Dad," he said, standing. "Got to run. I'm helping in the kitchen again this evening." He took his jacket and put it on. He took his hat from the hatstand and set it on his head. His father's rheumy eyes wandered across him, flickered to the window. "I've told the sister it's your birthday today, she'll get the nurse to give you another slice for your tea. You'll be alright, won't you? I'll come and see you again on Monday." Edward put the rest of the cake into its tin, replaced the lid and left it in the bedside table. The record kept playing. "Happy birthday," he said as he leaned in, kissing wrinkled skin that smelt of the ointment he had sent two months ago. His father's face suddenly broke out into a wide, open smile. While it lasted, its warmth seemed to peel away the canker of the illness and age and Edward saw him as he remembered him. The moment did not last and he felt an empty feeling of helplessness as he smiled to the nurse on the way out. His father was dying before his eyes, and there was nothing he could do to make it easier for him. Even the meagre comfort that they had managed to find for him was under threat. He needed money.

6

EDWARD SLEPT IN THE STORE CUPBOARD for a week but it was obvious that things could not go on as they were. The restaurant could not afford to pay him a salary and so he drew 15s. 3d. from the taxpayer instead. This required a weekly trip to the Pentonville Labour Exchange, a vast one-storey barn that was permanently surrounded by a four-deep queue of bad-tempered, foul-smelling men. It often took several hours for him to reach the counter where applicants were required to sign the book and make themselves available for the array of menial jobs that required filling. He did not disclose that he was working at the restaurant, for that would have disqualified him from receiving aid. The Exchange put him forward for several unsuitable posts. In order that he might perpetuate the lie that he was actively looking for employment he endured several embarrassing interviews during which he made no effort whatsoever to evince the enthusiasm that might make him attractive to potential employers. He was rejected for positions as a hotel doorman, a cleaner, and then, most embarrassingly of all, as the pot boy in a restaurant around the corner from the Shangri-La. The clerks at the Exchange must surely have realised that he was abusing their best efforts but he wasn't alone in that and, thankfully, his pitiful income was never interrupted.

He took a room for 6s. a week in a boarding house on Brewer Street. It was a terrible, dingy place, a sorting-office and clearing house for the jails, the casual wards, the lunatic asylums and the mortuary slabs. The place belonged to an ancient theatrical agent, a superannuated old queen who, Edward suspected, rented rooms to young ex-soldiers in the hope that a romantic entanglement might ensue, or, more achieveably, so that he might bump into them after they had bathed in one of his two filthy bathrooms.

Edward was allotted the attic. It was reached by way of a bleak staircase with linoleum steps smelling of wax, the grey-striped wallpaper stained with damp and peeling. It smelt of stale frying, with a dirty old gas cooker in what little space there was and a couple of penny-in-the-slot meters. It was long enough to lie down in but would not have been wide enough for that purpose and it was too low for him to stand. There was a narrow single bed, a washstand with a jug and basin on it and a little trunk in which he stored his meagre possessions. The ceiling was painted in a checkerboard of pink and yellow, the colours weighing down on the small space. There was a window through which he could scrabble out onto the roof and he would sit on the foot-wide parapet that ran around it and gaze out across the snaggle-toothed Soho rooftops, smoking a cigarette and miserably contemplating his lot.

If he was careful Edward was able to spread his tiny income to just about cover his vital needs. He would buy a loaf of bread, a pint of milk and a hunk of black chocolate so hard that the confectioner could only break it with a small axe he kept solely for this purpose. He would consume his feast lying down on his tiny bed, sucking each bitter square of chocolate to make it last longer.

* * *

THE SUMMER PASSED SLOWLY. Edward spent his days in the restaurant, arriving at six to begin the day's preparation and often staying until midnight. The work was difficult, tiring and unremunerative. They would tally up the takings after they had closed the doors for the night. A good day would be enough to keep their heads above the water. A bad day would see them sink deeper into the financial mire, relying on the continued goodwill of their bank manager for the restaurant's existence as a going concern and the payment of Dickie Stern's hospital bills. Unfortunately, the bad days came more often than the good ones, and the letters from the bank grew ever more concerned.

Edward settled into this dispiriting routine. The longer it went on, the more difficult it was to escape. He was essentially providing the restaurant with free labour. It allowed Jimmy to save money by trimming the hours of the other staff, something he was loathe to do (for none of the others were earning enough to live comfortably) but it was unavoidable if they were to keep going. As the accounts grew graver and graver, Edward's labour became more valuable. He knew that if he left, the business would fail.

Even with Edward's budget cut back to the bare minimum, his expenses still outweighed his income. The state of his finances worsened until he was left with no recourse but to attempt desperate measures. One afternoon towards the end of June he found himself hauling his only suitcase outside MacCulloch's, an establishment halfway down the Tottenham Court Road. It shared the same characteristics as all pawnshops: austere, with a pitiful collection of goods arranged in the window and a sense of bitterness in the air so thick as to be almost cloying. He paused and regarded the shop front. This one had the usual array: second-hand fountain pens, engagement rings, musical instruments, silver candlesticks and cutlery. There was a doorway for buyers and a doorway for sellers, one grand and the other plain. He opened the shabby door and went inside.

He hauled the suitcase onto the counter. "I wonder if you wouldn't mind lending me as much as you can on this until Friday?" The clerk opened the suitcase and rummaged through the contents. It was, by and large, the sum total of his worldly goods: a pair of trousers, a pair of shoes, a collection of books, a magnifying glass in a real morocco case and a couple of old copper saucepans from the restaurant that they rarely used.

The clerk opened the trousers out and examined them. Edward had prepared them carefully, rubbing out the spots with an old handkerchief and a pennyworth of petrol. But when the clerk brushed his fingers over the cloth the old stains came back. At the touch of a finger the buttonhole disintegrated and then the clerk opened out the cuffs at the ankles and discovered the split lining Edward hoped he might miss. He turned up his nose and shook his head, no doubt disappointed that Edward thought he might be gulled by such elementary deceptions.

The clerk examined the shoes—which were holed—and put them aside, then the magnifying glass, then the books. None of them detained his attention. "I can't give you anything for any of this."

"Nothing?"

He shrugged expressively. "Ten bob, that's the best I can do."

"Ten bob? Those trousers cost four guineas."

"So you say. Ten bob."

"I was hoping for a couple of pounds."

The man laughed harshly. "Out of the question. I can't let you have more than that, and I don't want the saucepans."

"Damn it all, man—just until the end of the week."

"You might drop dead on Thursday and then what would I do?"

"I won't—"

He folded his arms. "Ten bob. That's the best I can do."

Edward paused, his mind flailing around helplessly, and then hitched up his shoulders in what he hoped might be taken for a nonchalant shrug. "Fine," he said. "Take it."

"Do you have tuppence for the ticket?"

"Take it out of what you owe me," he said, exasperated.

Edward took the money and the ticket and made his way back out into the street. He had nine shillings and eleven pence. It was hardly better than nothing: it wouldn't even pay two weeks' rent. He put the silver into his fob pocket and took the fivepence into a Welsh Dai's shop. The dairyman carried sidelines of wrapped bread, canned food, tea and cakes. The publicans, butchers, milkmen and grocers of Soho did not give credit and even the newsagent waited to see the colour of a penny before parting with a daily paper. The serving woman, scoured and starched from hairline to hem, fussed from shelf to shelf as Edward ordered half a pint of milk, a two-ounce packet of tea at two-and-eight a pound, a soft white two-pound loaf of bread in a wax envelope and half a pound of cheddar at eight pence a pound. Impatient at the groaning of his stomach, he ignored his better judgment and added two rounds of toast with dripping and a mug of tea to his bill. He took them, and his shopping, to an empty table and sat down.

"Doc?"

Edward looked up. The man standing by his table was tall and solidly put together, with a striking mop of jet-black hair, dark eyes and strong features. He was smiling broadly.

"Joseph?"

"Doc! Bloody hell!"

He got to his feet and offered his hand. Joseph Costello knocked it aside and drew him into a fierce hug. They disengaged and regarded each other. Joseph looked good; no, Edward corrected himself, he looked better than good, he looked remarkable. "What, this?" Edward said, taking in Joseph's suit with an expansive gesture. "You didn't get that in a Natty Gent's Outfitters."

"Had some luck on the horses," he said, dismissing it with a wave of his hand.

Edward looked terrible in comparison, his backside half-hanging out of his trousers, and he knew it. "Well, you look like a millionaire playboy. I'm inclined to ask you about the seven-and-six you owe me for those beers in Calcutta."

"Good God, man, you've got a memory like an elephant." He pulled out the seat and sat down. "Why haven't you called me?"

Edward smiled wryly. He still had the travel docket with the number scribbled on the back. It was on his dresser, weighed down under a handful of loose change. He had been meaning to call, but something had stayed his hand. He felt awkward about his circumstances, the way he looked, the fact that he could barely afford to buy a pint of milk, let alone a round of beer. "I've been meaning to," he said. "There have been about a million things I've had to do."

"How's it been?"

"Oh, you know," Edward said, putting on a brave front. "Takes some getting used to."

"Don't I know it."

"What are you talking about? You look like you've fallen right on your feet."

He grinned. "You're right—I shouldn't grumble. No, I'm doing alright. It's the getting into a new routine that's the tricky bit."

"Are you working around here?"

"No," he lied. "Out in the sticks."

"Doing what?"

"Bit of this, bit of that." He needed to change the subject. "What about you?"

"The same," he said with the same vagueness.

Edward slid back easily into the persona he had constructed for himself in the Far East. His time away from home had allowed him the opportunity to build an idealised picture of who he was that he wanted others to see. It was impossible for him to tell the truth now, not without fear of the assiduously created illusion being dispelled. That would be embarrassing, perhaps even dangerous. He knew that a lie would lead to another lie, and then a whole series of lies that would spring from the first, and he was comfortable with that. He had been living that way for most of his life and he was good at it.

As he looked at Joseph and his evident good fortune, he wondered whether Joseph might present him with the opportunity he had been looking for.

"Are you living around here?"

"I've got a little place in Camden," Edward lied. He did not want to admit that it was nearby in case Joseph suggested they go to see it. He could not stand the thought of that.

Edward was thankful as Joseph became a little distracted. "Look, Doc," he said, "I can't stay, much as I'd love to. I'm meeting a man about a spot of business. But what are you doing tomorrow?"

"I should think I'll be working."

"Can you slip out for a couple of hours in the afternoon?"

"Yes. Probably."

"Terrific. I'm going to be at the gym. How'd you fancy a spot of sparring? We'll see how well that foot of yours has healed."

"Sparring. Haven't done that for a while."

"So now's the time to get back into it. What do you say?"

"I'd love to. Where is it?"

"On the Hill."

Edward said he didn't know where that was.

"Little Italy. Clerkenwell. We call it The Hill." Joseph wrote the address down on a napkin and pushed it across the table. "You can get the number thirty-eight bus. Two o'clock. Don't be late."

With that, he got to his feet, shook Edward's hand for a second time, and left. Edward looked at the napkin in his hand, the ink blurring at the edges as it was absorbed into the material, and allowed himself a smile.

7

EDWARD WAS WORKING in the kitchen when Jimmy arrived with the first post. It was the usual dreary collection, invoices that they would gamely attempt to put off, paying only those suppliers they could not afford to do without or the ones who were threatening to sue. Jimmy filtered the stack, separating one envelope that didn't fit the usual description. It was a luxurious cream colour and of weighty stock. It was addressed to Edward.

"What's that then?" he cooed. "Look at that—stamped by the War Office. What have you been up to?"

"Haven't got the faintest."

Edward slid his finger inside the envelope and opened it.

"Well?" Jimmy persisted. "What is it?"

Edward realised that he was gawping. "I'm getting the Victoria Cross," he said.

* * *

EDWARD SAT ON THE TOP DECK of the number thirty-eight omnibus, watching the city change as it passed through central London. Tramlines, winding at the bottom of Pentonville Hill, gleamed like silver. The bus passed across them and headed East. It was brown, rather than red, brought up from the coast by the operating company to replace vehicles that had been damaged during the Blitz. The windows were still fixed with cross-hatched lattices of tape to prevent the glass imploding in the event of a bomb detonating nearby. London looked dreary and battered, the view from the top deck disclosing glimpses across fenced-off bomb sites to the rubble, pools of brackish water and scorched walls beyond. The city had taken it very badly at the hands of the Luftwaffe.

He got off the bus at Holborn, turned off the main road and headed up Hatton Garden and into Little Italy. The mongrel district was to the north and south of Clerkenwell Road, hemmed in by Roseberry Avenue on the west and Farringdon Road on its east. To the south, it occupied the area around Saffron Hill, Leather Lane and Hatton Garden. Edward had lived in London all his life yet he had never been here before. The streets were ancient, a baffling maze of narrow and winding cobbled passages that crept between rickety houses and tenement blocks. A number of bombs had fallen and as he walked he passed half a dozen blasted gaps in the terraces where houses had taken direct hits. The evidence of slum clearance and the presence of mechanical machinery suggested Herr Göring had presented the local authorities with the chance to sweep away the old, cramped streets. A row of buildings had been levelled. Barriers had been erected at the end of the road. A sign reading CAUTION – UXB was fixed there. Bomb disposal officers were examining the old wreckage of a house. A hole had bored into the muddy ground, the bomb sunk somewhere at the bottom of it, undisturbed since the end of the war.

Locals passed on bicycles and in horse-drawn carts, thick-wristed men pushing brightly-decorated ice cream carts and mobile barrel organs. The day was warm and the street was busy with pedestrians, Irish and Italian accents merging amidst the clamour. Edward turned onto Saffron Hill and the cobbles became muddy, scattered with ordure from dogs, horses and mules. Small shops offered empty shelves and feral children congregated on corners, eyeing him greedily. The smells grew more pungent and, as he crossed Eyre Street Hill, he had to traverse a plank that had been placed on the stones so he could avoid sewage from blocked drains.

The gym was on Greville Street, situated in one corner of an old bathhouse. It had three full-size rings fitted somewhat haphazardly into the interior. The walls of the gym were covered in chipped, beige tiles plastered over with handbills from ancient fights. There were all sorts there, from bantams to heavies. In one corner, a group of boys were lifting weights, while in the main hall there was a confusion of punch bags and skipping ropes. In one of the rings, two heavily protected youngsters followed each other menacingly, firing out the odd jab and grunt. It was stifling hot and noisy, too: the machine-gun racket of speed bags, the slap of skipping ropes on the hardwood floor, leather gloves thumping into rib cages and sand-filled heavy bags.

Joseph was in a second ring, sparring with a second man: a skinny featherweight. Edward watched him for a moment as they exchanged blows, clouds of dust puffing up from the canvas as they moved, muffled exhalations as they absorbed each other's punches on their gloves. His muscles were taut and prominent and well-defined. Joseph's partner was quick and agile, darting in and out of range effortlessly, his punching speed better than Joseph, too. He feinted with his left to draw Joseph's guard that way and then followed up with a straight right, through the gate and into his mouth. Joseph spat out his bloody mouth guard. "Bugger!" he yelled, frustrated with himself.

Edward collected his duffel bag from the floor and went across to them both. "Joseph," he called out.

Joseph turned. "Doc!" He stepped through the ropes and jumped down from the apron, giving him a firm, sweaty hug. "How are you?"

"Very good. And you?"
"Never better."
"You looked sharp."
"Feel sharp, too."
The second man rested his elbows against the ropes. "Joe? Who's this?"
"My bloody manners—Billy Stavropoulos, this is Edward Fabian. Doc—Billy."
"Pleased to meet you, Billy."
He had a narrow face and teeth that protruded a little over his bottom lip when he smiled. It was rather an unfortunate feature that put Edward in mind of an anxious rabbit. He said, "Likewise," and regarded Edward with what he took to be a lazy ambivalence, a quick up-and-down that said he wasn't going to be an easy fellow to impress.
"Billy's pretty handy in the ring."
"I saw," Edward said. "You're good on your feet. Fast."
Billy shrugged.
"Good?" Joseph said. "He's like greased lightning. Used to be ABA champ."
"What weight?"
"Bantam," Billy said truculently.
"He's got a fight tonight at York Hall. Just giving him a final tune-up. Everyone reckons if he wins he's a dead cert to go professional. Bloody close to making it, aren't you?"
Billy shrugged again, a half-sneer on his face. Edward decided there was something about him that he definitely did not like. He was a hot one alright, this boy, that much was obvious.
"Did you bring your kit?" Joseph asked.
Edward hefted his duffel bag. "I did."
"Billy's done for now. Need to keep his strength. But we could have a bit of a run-around?"
"Capital idea."

Joseph showed Edward through into the changing room. He changed into the same fusty singlet and shorts that he had worn in the army and wrapped bandages around his hands. He returned to the gym and picked up a pair of battered old mitts. He pulled them on. "Let's see what you can do, then," he said.

They went through a couple of three-minute sessions. Joseph showed off, giving it much more than he needed to, firing shot after shot into Edward's mitts, trying to knock him backwards. By the end of the third session he was gasping and his right shoulder was hanging dead from throwing countless jabs. Joseph was more of a boxer than Edward was, but Edward was clever. He knew Joseph would try to impress and would work harder than he needed to. He guessed he wouldn't be able to say no to the offer of more, and so he suggested a fourth session on the mitts and then one on the bag. By the time that was finished Joseph was just about out on his feet.

"Right, then—shall we spar for a few rounds? See if you're as good as you say you are?"

"I'm bushed, Doc."

"Come on. You said you'd give me the run-around. You're here, I'm here, we're ready to have a go—you can't back out now."

Joseph was gassed. Edward leaned on the ropes and flexed his knees a couple of times and then dragged his shoes in the box of rosin.

"Ready?" he said.

"Go on then."

Billy rang the bell and Joseph turned quick and came out towards him. They met in the middle of the ring and touched gloves and as soon as he dropped his hands Edward thrust his left into his face twice. Joseph stumbled back and Edward went after him, going forward all the time with his chin on his chest. Their tactics were obverse: Edward was a dancer, jumping in and out of range, firing out his jab. Joseph was a hooker, a brawler, closing off the ring and slugging, crowding Edward into the ropes so he could do his work in close. All he knew was how to get in there and scrap, and every time Edward stepped into range he had his left hand in his face. Three or four times Joseph brought the right over but Edward managed to take it on the shoulder or high up on the head. Other times he tied him up, getting one hand loose and uppercutting him. When Joseph got his hands free he would belt Edward in the body so hard they could hear it in the street outside.

This went on for three rounds. They didn't talk. They just worked. By the end of the fourth Edward's arm was heavy and his legs were starting to go bad. Sweat ran freely across Joseph's face. Eventually, Edward tied Joseph up, got his right hand loose, turned it, and came up with an uppercut that got his nose with the heel of the glove. Joseph started to bleed instantly. He tried to get away but Edward had him tied up tight, but then, his blood splashing onto both of them, Joseph measured him and then socked a right into his body as hard as he could, as low as he could get it, five inches below the belt. Edward's mouth fell open and his gum shield dropped out. He staggered around as if his insides were going to fall out. He tried to protest, his guard dropping to his waist automatically, and that was that: Joseph feinted with his left and then stepped into a right cross that caught him flush on the jaw.

Edward was out cold for a couple of seconds. When he came around his nose was streaming with blood.

"You alright, Doc?"

Joseph's face swam above him as if heat haze separated them. He couldn't speak. It felt like he was going to be sick.

"Sorry—think I fouled you."

Still he couldn't speak. The ring was spinning.

Joseph helped him through the ropes and into the changing room. Edward undressed and stood under the hot shower for five minutes, letting the water soothe his muscles and, gradually, the sawdust in his head started to slip away. Joseph used the shower next to him.

"Caught you pretty good there."

"Below the belt," he said, still groggy.

"Yeah," he said. "Sorry about that. Still, think I had you anyway."

Edward opened his mouth to let the blood run out. "You what?"

"Had you anyway," he grinned.

Edward looked across at him: his body was muscular and hard, his chest solid. He squeezed the faucet closed and limped back towards the lockers. They rubbed themselves down. Edward put on his shirt and trousers. He took a moment, gathering his strength again. It had been a hard workout.

"You're hobbling," Joseph said. "is it bad?"

"It gets a little sore if I'm standing for too long, but it's much better than it was. Another month or so, it'll be good as new."

"How did it happen?"

"Long story," he said. The time wasn't right for that story, not yet. He needed to work on the details a little, to freshen them up in his mind.

The reference to Edward's injury seemed to prompt Joseph's memories of the jungle. "Be honest, Doc. You've been back a while now. How've you found it?"

He thought of the restaurant and Jimmy, his father and the hospital bills, and the awful situation that they found themselves in. "It's not quite what I was expecting," he admitted.

"It's not having the excitement, that's what I reckon it is. I'm not stupid enough to think that it was all peachy when we were out there, God knows it was boring as sin most of the time, but I can't help thinking that I had scrapes and adventures in the jungle that I'll never get to have again. And part of me misses all that. Does that sound crazy, Doc?"

Edward left a pause and thought about it. It did sound crazy and, yet, he knew exactly what Joseph meant. "I don't know," he mused. "It'd take a lot of money for me to go back there again but I wouldn't mind a bit of that excitement in my life, too."

Joseph towelled off his hair and started to dress. "Got a bit to talk about, haven't we? Why don't you come to Billy's fight tonight?"

"I don't know that I can."

"It'll be well worth it—a few beers, a proper chat. There are some decent fighters on the bill."

"I'm supposed to be working."

Joseph chucked him on the shoulder. "Come on. One night won't do any harm. What do you say?"

Joseph grinned broadly, his teeth shining.

Edward said he would think about it.

8

YORK HALL WAS IN THE MIDDLE OF BETHNAL GREEN. It was a poor area, down-at-heel and often dangerous, and it had suffered badly during the war. Buildings had been flattened, whole terraces erased, and even now there was a dirty, dusty smut that hung in the air. Murphy had decided against driving across from the West End. Hardly anyone owned a motor here, and the last thing he wanted to do was to draw attention to himself. He had taken the underground instead and walked the short distance from the station. He was wearing the cheap set of clothes he used when he wanted to blend in: threadbare suit, crumpled shirt, scuffed shoes. His overcoat was old and fetid but at least it was thick. It was foggy and damp out, and he was glad for its warmth.

The handbills distributed outside the station advertised a night of amateur boxing. Six bouts, six rounds apiece, a motley collection of fighters: youngsters who thought they could fight their way out of the slum, and those who had tried it and knew better. Charlie ran his finger down the sheet until he found Billy Stavropoulos. He was boxing under the name of Bert Gill, going up against a young featherweight from Hackney. Immigrants often chose Anglicised names. Charlie knew it well enough: he'd nicked plenty, and you always had to record both.

A queue of spectators snaked around the corner of the building, stamping their feet against the cold and speculating on the night's entertainment. Charlie paid for a ticket at the door and shuffled inside, following the crowd into the auditorium.

It was a medium sized space, bench seats arranged at a steep rake around a well-lit ring. Charlie spotted Joseph Costello quickly. He was sitting near the front with another man he did not recognise. There was space on the bench next to them but it was filling quickly. Charlie hurried down the steps. "Excuse me," he said as he made his way along the row.

"You're alright, mate," Joseph said to him.

Joseph Costello had never seen Charlie before. He was not concerned that he would be made. He knew all of the mistakes that led to plainclothes men being spotted by the crooks they were observing, and he made sure not to repeat any of them. His only concession to his usual punctilious appearance was the narrow wire-framed spectacles that were his trademark; it was said that he looked more like a don than a policeman. It was an effect he cultivated and it had served him well. Charlie Murphy was the youngest man to make detective inspector in the Met for thirty years. His latest assignment, leading the Ghost Squad, was just the latest in a long line of successes.

The noise in the auditorium built as the first fight got underway. Charlie was close enough to the ring to hear the muffled crump as the leather gloves of the fighters slammed into their targets, heads and torsos, and close enough to see droplets of sweat and blood spray across the canvas. He was close enough to overhear the conversation between Joseph and the man he was with. They discussed the fights knowledgeably. Charlie knew that Joseph had been a keen boxer before leaving for the war. This second, unrecognised, man evidently knew the fight game, too. Joseph called him "Doc," but never used his name. It didn't matter. Charlie filed the information away, and the man's appearance, too. It seemed likely that the two were war buddies, and it ought to be simple enough to cross-check with the War Office and identify him.

The next fighters made their way to the ring.

Charlie eavesdropped as Joseph leant over to his friend. "Fancy a flutter?" he said.

"Can't really afford it."

Charlie glanced across as Joseph reached into his jacket and withdrew a roll of notes, fastened with a gold clip. He thumbed off ten pounds and handed it over. "Don't be daft," the other man protested.

"I want you to have fun. See the fellow in the blue corner—"

"Sorry to interrupt," Charlie said. "Do you have a tip? I could do with some luck."

Joseph looked at him, paused, as if debating whether to be civil or tell him where he could get off. He nodded. "I know him—Battles Rossi. Tough little bugger, from south of the River. If it were me, I'd put a fiver on him to win in the first."

Charlie thanked him. He made his way to the queue for the bookies and was joined by the second man.

"Your mate knows his onions," Charlie said as they waited.

"I certainly hope so," he said. "Go on—after you."

Charlie took a pound and laid it on Rossi.

"Do you box?" he asked.

"Did a bit in the army, but nothing special. Not as young as I used to be."

"I know the feeling." He extended his hand to him. "My name's Kipps."

"Edward Fabian. Good to meet you."

Charlie absorbed everything: the way the man spoke, his attitude, the safety pins that secured frayed double-cuffs. A pair of brogues that had once been decent but now were holed and scuffed. The reference to the army. No sign of an accent. The man was not a local. He did not fit in with the human flotsam of the East End. A soldier who had fallen on hard times? There were plenty of those poor buggers.

The fight was over almost by the time they had returned to the bench. Rossi's opponent was a flashy fighter, dancing in and out of reach and landing a series of crisp jabs that quickly drew blood. The first round was drawing to a close when Rossi, who had evidently been fostering a false sense of confidence in his opponent, pretended to be dazed and lowered his hands. Charlie could see the subterfuge immediately, but Rossi's opponent, sensing a spectacular end to proceedings, launched in at him; and walked straight onto a crunching right-hand uppercut that lifted him onto his tiptoes and sank him to his knees. The referee counted to ten, the crowd bellowed their approval, and, just like that, Edward—who had laid the full five pounds—was twenty pounds better off.

"How's that!" Joseph said.

"Strike me," Edward replied.

"Thanks for the tip," Charlie said. "Got any others?"

"Not tonight."

"The name's Kipps."

Joseph regarded him in cold appraisal. His eyes were blank and soulless, the darkest black, and Charlie felt a shiver pass through him as he was held in his gaze. "Nice to meet you, Kipps," he said, without offering his hand. He turned away, ending the conversation. Charlie was not surprised. Par for the course. It would take more than that to make any headway with someone like Joseph Costello. There was a layer of suspicion to pierce. His type were born with it.

"Reckon I could've taken him?" he heard Joseph asking Edward.

"I should say so."

"Too bloody right."

The next fight was Stavropoulos's. He came to the ring with his opponent, the featherweight from Hackney, and, after they were announced to the crowd, they set to it. The first two rounds passed as the fighters fenced around each other, jabbing harmlessly from range. The fight sparked to life in the third round; the Hackney man came forwards but Stavropoulos repelled him with a series of stiff jabs. He followed with a crunching flurry to the kidneys and then, the man's guard lowered, a hay-maker that twirled the man on his toes and sent him face first to the canvas. The referee could have counted to twenty; it was over. Joseph and Edward went to the apron and congratulated Stavropoulos as he clambered through the ropes and dropped to the floor.

Charlie had seen enough and left the auditorium as the three of them went through to the changing rooms. He needed to write his report and update the other members of the Squad. It had been a productive evening, and he had gathered information on Joseph that would be added to the detailed dossier that was being compiled. He didn't mind the brush off he had received. That didn't bother him at all.

There would be other conversations, ones on his patch, to his rules.

Conversations that were not so easy to avoid.

9

EDWARD DRESSED in his freshly-laundered dress uniform and, as he made his way out of the boarding house, he noticed himself in the dusty mirror that was hung in the hall: he had become the upright, self-respecting young soldier again. He paused. "Hello," he said, smiling into the glass. It didn't look quite right and so he cleared his face and tried again. "Hello," he repeated in the slightly deeper voice he had perfected on the boat to India that first time, part of the routine he adopted as he settled himself into his new persona. "Hello. I'm Edward Fabian. Pleased to meet you." He forced his smile wider, exposing his white teeth. That was better. He felt his shoulders drop a little and the muscles in his cheeks relaxed. He straightened his uniform. He was doing the right thing, behaving the right way. There was no need for anxiety. Edward Fabian, the soldier. It was a role he had played for seven years.

He emerged at Victoria and, after walking the short distance to Buckingham Palace, joined the long queue of military types at the Hyde Park Gate. He handed his invitation to the police officer on duty and crunched across the gravel into the quadrangle beyond the Palace's great façade. A subaltern directed him to the ballroom. It had been arranged with several rows of chairs for the relatives and friends who were invited to witness the investiture. The colours were of red and gold, there were portraits hung in ornate frames, yards of lush drapes and carpets that you sank into, marble floors buffed so bright you could see your reflection in them. The chairs faced a dais where the King received the men who were being honoured. The room was empty at the moment. Edward introduced himself and was ushered into an anteroom for a brief education in royal protocol from a member of the house who remained staid and aloof, as if this teaching these ignorant yahoos how to scrape and bow was below him.

The men were finally led into the ballroom and directed to the reserved seating nearest to the dais. There were men from all three services: the face of a chap from the RAF was deformed by burns and a naval rating had had half of his leg blown off. Edward was in the front row next to those two men. He turned around, scanning the crowd behind him, and saw Joseph. He winked. Joseph grinned back at him. He was wearing a beautiful suit, a shining pair of shoes and he had a trilby in his lap. His clothes were new and obviously expensive, and he looked quite a picture. Joseph was the only person that Edward had invited. He would have asked Jimmy but they could not afford to shut the restaurant and it seemed wrong to have a moment like this and not share it with anyone.

King George, accompanied by a retinue of two Ghurkhas, made his way to the dais and the ceremony began. The men who were receiving the Victoria Cross went first, the rating and the airman among stepping up before Edward. The chamberlain read out their citation, they went forward, the King gave them their medal and said a few rehearsed words, they went back. Edward watched with wide eyes. The whole spectacle was utterly surreal.

"Edward Frederick Fabian."

Edward leant forwards avidly as the chamberlain read out his citation. "Corporal Fabian carried out an individual act of great heroism by which he attacked and killed several of the enemy who had ambushed his own platoon. It was in direct face of the enemy, under intense fire, whilst wounded and at further great personal risk to himself. His valour is worthy of the highest recognition."

Edward took his cue and went forwards, his face stern and impassive. The King shook his hand and held it for a moment. He leant forwards and spoke quietly into his ear. "Congratulations, corporal," he said. When he was finished, Edward stepped back and saluted crisply.

There was an upswelling of applause for the three men. Joseph clapped most of all, beaming a wide grin, and Edward could not resist the explosion of pleasure in his breast. He grinned, too, and, for the moment at least, his reservations were forgotten.

* * *

THEY FOUND A PUB near to the Palace and Joseph bought a couple of beers. "So that's how you got shot?" Joseph said as soon as they were settled in a booth.

"Afraid so," Edward said, feigning reluctance to go into detail.

"How many Japs were there?"

"Eight."

"And they just opened up on you?"

"It was the monsoon—you know what that's like. You couldn't see much further than the front of your nose. Half a dozen of the lads had been hit before the rest of us knew what was going on. I was lucky—I just got the ricochet in the foot before I managed to get into the jungle and get a grenade away. That scattered them, and I picked the survivors off."

"That's a hell of a story." He shook his head. "Stone the crows, Doc. The Victoria Cross. It doesn't get better than that. One of my pals is a war hero."

Edward savoured it. He drank it all in. It could not have been a more successful morning and now every moment to Edward was a pleasure. The ceremony had been tremendously agreeable in itself. And now there was Joseph's acclaim, the way that strangers in the pub looked at him curiously, and the way that fellow servicemen, once they recognised the medal that was still pinned to his breast, would tip their hats or salute. My God, he thought, it all felt amazing. The sense of guilt from earlier had been obliterated. The way that Joseph was looking at him almost persuaded him that he deserved to be decorated. He as good as believed the narrative that he had created for himself.

Edward felt proud for having arranged everything so perfectly. And yet, despite his pride, there was also a curious sense of remoteness. He could not share everything with Joseph, nor with anyone else. He had a feeling that everyone was watching him, as if he had an audience comprised of the entire world, a foreboding that kept him on his mettle, for, if he made a mistake now or in the future, it would be disastrous. Yet he felt absolutely confident that he was a match for the challenge he had presented for himself. He had had a lot of practice over the years, starting even from when he had been a small child, and this was no different. He was quite sure: he was good, and he would not make a mistake.

They finished their pints and ordered another.

"What are you doing this afternoon?" Joseph asked him.

Jimmy had said he could manage all day without him. "I don't have any plans," he said. "We could have a few drinks?"

"Why don't you come with me to The Hill? It's the carnival today—plenty of booze and fun, too. You should come, really, you should. My family will be there. I'd love to introduce you to them."

Edward remembered what Joseph had said to him on the train: there was a successful Costello family business. His interest began to stir. Perhaps there was an opportunity to be had. It had been a good morning. Why not see if he could continue his good luck into the afternoon, too? He looked down at his pristine uniform and the bright new medal that glittered silver against the khaki fabric. He would never have a better chance to make a good first impression.

"Sounds like fun," he said.

* * *

THE TAXI DEPOSITED THEM on Roseberry Avenue and they made their way to Amwell Street where a long line of empty trestle tables had been arranged down the middle of the road, covered with mismatched cloths. An assortment of chairs were set on either side. Women were arranging flowers and greenery around the doorways of the houses and men on step-ladders were hanging yards of colourful bunting from the gas lamps. The Italian tricolore and the Union Jack vied for space from the ledges of first-floor windows. Gay tapestries obscured the dilapidated walls, the street-corners were ornamented by large illuminated frames which bore the statue of the Madonna and windows held statues, votive lights, flowers and candles. Even the narrow courts and alleys had been transformed, blazing with flowers and brilliantly coloured lights. The atmosphere was febrile: in five minutes they passed a spiv selling nylons from a suitcase, a couple embracing with drunken ardour and two men throwing sloppy, half-hearted punches at each other.

Joseph led the way to a table where three women had congregated. "These are my sisters," he said. "Edie, Sophia and Chiara."

"Who's this dish?" Sophia said, making no attempt disguise her lewd up-and-down appraisal of Edward.

"This is my friend, Edward Fabian."

Edward smiled warmly. The women were a strange collection: Evie walked with a stick, was tall and slim with long dark hair and a mischievous sparkle in her eyes. Sophia was shorter, and plumper, with ringlets of copper-coloured hair that spilled across her shoulders in tight coils. Chiara was neither tall nor short, doll-like with slender arms and wrists. Her hair had been carefully water-waved and set, her lips looked soft and shapely with the lip salve she had on them. She wore a brown flannel coat with rabbit collar over an art-silk dress of light blue. Despite their differences it was obvious that they were related. The tone of their skin, the shape of their eyes, their noses and chins; they were evidently poured from the same mould.

He took their offered hands. "Pleasure to meet you."

Sophia turned her hand over and held it before his lips so that he was left with no choice but to kiss it. "Where's he been hiding you?"

Joseph tutted. "Put him down."

Evie kissed Joseph on the cheek. "Bloody hell, you reek. Have you been drinking?"

He grinned at her. "We were celebrating."

"What for?"

"We've just been to Buckingham Palace. Edward has just seen the King."

"Give over."

"It's true. Go on, Doc, show them."

Edward feigned modesty. The medal was still attached to his tunic. He slid his fingers beneath it and held it away from his breast.

"Which one is it?"

Joseph said, "The Victoria Cross."

Evie gawped. "It never is..."

"What'd you have to do to get that?" Sophia asked.

"Nothing much," Edward said. He felt uncharacteristically shy. Sophia had a brash and loud personality and he felt a little cowed by it.

"Don't be coy," Sophia urged with a grin that exposed the wide gap between her front teeth. "Tell us."

Joseph saw Edward was uncomfortable. "Leave it out," he said. "Not everyone wants to crow about the things that they've done. All you need to know is that this man"—he clapped him on the back—"is a bloody hero."

Sophia took Edward's hand again and squeezed it. "It's a pleasure to meet you, Edward," she said. She held her grip a little too long, and, as she gently released it, she trailed her fingertips against the back of his hand. He looked down at her, surprised, and she returned his expression with a cheeky wink.

"Sophia," Chiara chided in a tone of weary exasperation. "I'm so sorry, Mr. Fabian. My sister can be awfully embarrassing sometimes."

Edward knew that the flattery was not just for the benefit of his ego. Sophia and Evie enjoyed embarrassing their brother and they knew exactly how to do it. The more he protested, the more lascivious, and crude, they would become. Chiara did not get involved in their games; she stood silently to the side and observed, taking it all in.

"Where's Billy?" Sophia asked her brother.

"He's meeting us here. Go easy on him, alright?"

"I don't know what you mean," Sophia said with mock outrage.

"You know exactly what I mean. You give him the bloody vapours half the time and you know it. Speak of the devil—there he is."

His face broke out into a smile and Edward turned to see the reason for it: Billy was approaching them. "Billy and me are going to get the drinks. Edward—I'd leave you here but I'm not sure they'll leave you in one piece."

"He's perfectly safe," Sophia said.

"I doubt that. Edward?"

"I'm fine," he said.

There were three pubs in the vicinity. The landlords had rolled barrels out onto the street and groups of happy drunks gathered around them to refill their tankards, a rowdy atmosphere already developing. Joseph led Billy to the Wordsworth and waved the landlord across.

Chiara said, "You're the doctor, aren't you?"

"That's right. How do you know that?"

"Joseph was talking about you."

"He was?"

"He was happy you asked him to come today."

Edward smiled, pleased with himself. He felt very optimistic all of a sudden.

"Have you met Billy yet?" Evie asked him.

"Briefly. I don't think he likes me much."

"He can be like that," Sophia said. "He's awkward around people he's just met. I shouldn't worry about it. He doesn't mean it. His bark's worse than his bite."

"You should know," teased Evie.

The remark was lost on Edward. "Are they good friends?" he asked.

"They've known each other for years. His father and our father worked in the business so the two of them practically grew up together. He's Greek. It used to be one hundred per cent Italian round here when my grandfather came over, but there've been all sorts moving in the last few years—Jews, Irish, Greeks. We call him Bubble when we want to get a rise out of him."

"Why?"

"Bubble and Squeak."

Edward felt foolish for asking. "Oh—I see, Greek."

"He hates it."

Joseph had squeezed three gins between his hands and was coming towards them. Billy was behind him, carrying three pints of beer.

Joseph gave a glass to each of his sisters.

"Go easy on the poor lad," Evie warned her sister as Billy arrived.

"No fear. It's too much fun."

"My sister and Billy used to be—involved," Chiara explained quietly for Edward's benefit, searching for the right word.

"Only when I've been drinking," Sophia said. "I do have standards."

Evie shook her head. "If you say so."

Sophia latched onto Billy at once. "Hello, darling."

"Alright, Sophia," Billy said awkwardly. His demeanour underwent an abrupt and amusing transformation from his usual insouciance. It melted away like an ice cube on a hot day.

"Don't worry, my love, I won't say nothing."

"What you on about? There's nothing *to* say."

"Don't be so hard on yourself."

"That's not what I meant."

"Don't know why you're being so coy."

"Leave him alone," Joseph said, but there was an amused smile on his face.

"I was just being civil."

"You know what you were doing."

Billy hid behind his pint.

Edward enjoyed the exchange. He didn't much like Billy and it was good to see him squirm. Smiling, he drank his beer right away. It was a warm day and he had developed a thirst. The beer was tepid but it didn't matter.

"Violet's waving at us," Evie said.

Edward followed her gesture and saw a woman and a man at one of the large trestles.

"Wonderful," Joseph groaned. "I haven't seen her all week. How is she?"

"The same as ever," Sophia said. "Annoyed you haven't been to see her."

"We better go and see her before we get too lit up."

"You're already lit up."

"More lit up, then."

"Who's Violet?" Edward asked Chiara.

"Our aunt," she explained. "And the fellow next to her is our uncle George."

"We'll leave you to it," Sophia said. "I don't think we need to be subjected to her. We get it every day."

"To what?" Edward said, confused.

"Come on," Joseph said. "You'll see. Let's get it over with."

10

MATRONS FUSSED OVER DISHES that had been arranged on the trestle tables: bowls of pasta, salads, cuts of meat, trifles and cakes, a large tureen filled with punch. Joseph explained that each family had provided a dish, most more than one, the women rising early to start the preparations. The air was freighted with a sweet-smelling aroma: garlic, fried onions, rosemary, tomatoes, roasted vegetables. They picked their way through the crowd until they reached the table. Violet Costello was in her early fifties. She was a handsome woman, dressed elegantly in clothes that were obviously more expensive than those of the women around her. They had the dowdy, homely appearance of the housewife yet she was impressive, bearing herself with a regal air. She obviously had money, and style. If Violet indicated her status with subtle choices, George Costello was altogether more ostentatious. He was tall, over six feet, and his brillantined hair made him look even taller. His shoulders were broad and he was built as powerfully as an ox. He was wearing a fine suit, a clip-on bow tie with changeable paper collars and a loud, checked, belted overcoat. He wore a fresh carnation in his buttonhole. His hair and whiskers had been cut that morning, his grooming punctiliously exact. His head was a little too large for his body and his eyes were a little too small for his face; they glittered darkly, suggesting he was not a man to be crossed.

A steady procession of people approached their table. They acted deferentially, shaking hands with George and kissing Violet's cheek, a few words spoken before they moved away to allow the next person their audience. Most bore gifts: bottles of black, sticky homemade wine, a basket of freshly baked bread. A large collection of bottles, plates and salvers had formed on the table behind them. Young girls removed the gifts and redistributed them around the street to be enjoyed by the revellers.

Edward felt a stirring of excitement. There were opportunities here.

"What's all that about?" he asked Joseph, indicating the well-wishers.

"Violet paid for the party."

"And the gifts?"

"Signs of respect."

Edward did not know what that meant, but he concentrated on his smile as they approached the table. Violet turned. "Joseph," she said warmly, "and Billy. Two of my favourite boys."

"Mrs. Costello," Billy said. His attitude had moved from surliness to close to servility.

"And who's this?"

"This is Edward Fabian," Joseph said. "We served together."

"The man you mentioned?"

"That's right."

Edward extended his hand. "Pleasure to meet you, ma'am."

She took it. Her skin was smooth as porcelain. "Sit," she said, gesturing to the space next to her, and he did as he was told. She spoke in short, curt bursts, with a certainty of tone that suggested she was used to giving instructions and that she was used to those instructions being followed. Her words were inflected with a strong

East London accent that he found surprising, given that her wardrobe was so obviously expensive; she looked like Bond Street but sounded like Bethnal Green. "You all look half-starved. Have something to eat with us."

She reached across the table for a plate and a bowl of pasta. Edward sat next to her, feeling a little awkward, as she dished out a serving and handed him the bowl.

"How have you found being back?" she asked him.

"It's wonderful, obviously, but it's also a bit of a shock."

"Your parents must be glad?"

Edward made sure he looked thoughtful. "Oh, they're both dead, I'm afraid."

"I'm sorry to hear that."

"It's fine," he said. "It was a long time ago."

He could certainly never tell any of them about his father, or about Jimmy, and, despite the ease with which he delivered the lie, he felt a moment of disquiet. It was guilt. He tried to recover himself: what was he so worried about? He had delivered the very same lie a hundred times before and there was no way that these people could possibly tell that it wasn't true.

Violet indicated his uniform. "Is that for a reason?"

"We've just been to Buckingham Palace," Joseph answered for him. "Edward has been decorated."

George Costello flinched, the first break in his rigidity. It was like watching a thick wall shift and lean after a bomb had fallen.

"Really?" he said.

"He got the Victoria Cross."

Violet was visibly impressed. "Is that so?"

"Yes," Edward said, masking the mild unease he felt with a shrug.

"What did you do?" George pressed. He didn't try and hide his dubious tone.

"Nothing really," Edward said. He felt himself begin to sweat, and he tried again to relax.

"No, come on," George pressed irritably. "What did you do?"

"He doesn't like to talk about it," Joseph said.

"You're very modest," Violet commended. "I'd much rather that than some loud-mouthed braggart."

George harrumphed but allowed the conversation to drop.

"How long have you been home?" she asked.

"Just a few weeks."

"And have you found work?"

Edward was about to reply that he had not when a black Wolseley slid to a stop on the side-street opposite. George Costello swore colourfully under his breath. Two men in the front seat took notebooks from the dashboard and, with no attempt at concealment, recorded the number plates of the other cars parked near them.

Joseph regarded them contemptuously. "They just won't give it a bloody rest, will they?"

"Ignore them," Violet said. "It's a free country. They can do what they want. And we've done nothing wrong."

Joseph stared at the two men and, when he was sure that they were looking in his direction, spat theatrically into the gutter.

"Joseph!"

"What? They think they're going to get something today? Here?"

"They're just making a point."

"They're wasting their time," George muttered.

Edward watched the men in the car scribble into their notebooks. "Who are they?"

"Police," Joseph grunted.

Edward stared at the car and the men inside it. Police? The mention of the word made him shiver. He wanted to ask what they were there for but he could see that it was not a subject it would have been wise to pursue. The car dallied for five minutes before reversing away, sliding around a corner and out of sight.

"Good riddance," Joseph said.

The crowd had grown so that there were now hundreds of locals gathered in the street. Plenty of them were drunk, and some had started dancing on the pavement. Others had taken their places at the tables, helping themselves to the piles of food and the gallon jugs of homemade wine. The children were finally quiet, gorging themselves happily from the array of plates and bowls.

Violet laid a hand on Edward's wrist. "What do you think?" she asked, gesturing at the scene.

"It's wonderful."

"It's not what it was. I can remember when there would've been thousands here. The area—it's changing."

"It's the bloody Irish," George said.

Violet ignored her brother. "It wasn't all that long ago when this whole district was completely Italian. I can remember it from when I was a little girl… Italian shops, Italian food, the only language you'd hear was Italian."

"Those days are long gone," her brother muttered.

She nodded sadly. "It's all moved to Soho now."

"Do you live here?" Edward asked.

"No, dear. Not any more. It's so different now, I couldn't bear it." She didn't elaborate. "We were talking about work before—what are your plans now you're back?"

"I'm thinking about a career in medicine."

"He went to University," Joseph explained. "He's clever."

"I hardly think so," Edward said dismissively.

"Where did you go?"

"Cambridge, ma'am." Edward waited, hoping that Violet would ask him something about Cambridge, but she did not. He could have discussed the way they taught medicine, the way the university was divided into colleges, the food at the collegiate dinners, the political tendency of the student body, anything. He had sat next to an officer on a long trip through the Burmese countryside, both of them perched atop the hull of a tank so hot you could have fried eggs on it. The man had been at Cambridge and talked of nothing but Cambridge, so that Edward had pressed him for more and more, devouring it all, predicting a time when he might be able to use the information. By the time the trip was over he felt as if he had gone to Cambridge, too.

"Are you qualified?"

"No, not yet. I enlisted right after I graduated. I still have qualifications I'd need to get before they'll let me practice and then I'm not quite sure what will happen to things with Mr. Beveridge's plans."

"Well, it's a fine profession to be in. We'll always need doctors, however they rearrange things. And until then?"

"I'm keeping my eyes open in case something come up."

Violet frowned thoughtfully. "Perhaps we could help you with that? Our family has several business interests—I expect Joseph has told you. One of them is in motorcars. Second-hand ones, buying and selling. We're always looking for good young salesman. And, someone with your record, the war, your medal and such like—it's the least we can do to thank you for your service and I think that might be a rather good fit."

"I don't know—" he began, pretending to hesitate. Was this it? He thought that he smelled an opening and he knew not to come across as overly eager.

"The offer is there," she said. "Take the weekend to think about it. It can be an excellent job. If you have the gift of the gab the money is very good."

"You should think about it, Doc," Joseph impressed on him.

"Come and have a look on Monday," Violet said. "Joseph can tell you where the showroom is. Have a look, see what you think—there would be no obligations."

"That's very kind of you."

"Nonsense. It's the least we can do."

"I'm grateful."

George frowned at his sister. "We should be going," he said, showing her his pocket watch.

Violet checked the time and nodded her agreement. "We have an appointment. It was a pleasure to meet you, Edward. I'm sure we'll see you again."

The two of them got up and, bidding them farewell, made their way to a parked car. A large, serious-looking man was waiting by the kerb. He opened the rear doors for them, got into the front and drove them away.

"She liked you," Joseph said.

"You think?"

"Certainly."

"This job? What do you think? Was she serious?"

"It's like she said: the family has a lot of business interests," he replied, choosing his words carefully. "The showroom would be a good fit for you—better than a job in a kitchen, anyway." He got up. "Now then," he said. "How about another drink? How about a nice brandy? Doc? Are you listening to me?"

"Sorry," he said. He had been miles away.

"You look like you've got something on your mind."

Edward brushed that off as Joseph went over to the pub but it was true. He had plenty on his mind. Opportunities, openings and main chances. All of them aimed towards the future prosperity of Edward Fabian.

PART THREE

London
June – August 1945

11

DETECTIVE INSPECTOR CHARLIE MURPHY stared out of the window of the car, peering through sheets of rain. He was outside an office building on Upper Street, right in the heart of grotty Islington. There was no sign of a police station, at least not one that could be recognised as such. Charlie got out and trotted through the rain into the building, through a wide door and into a lobby. He took a flight of stairs and passed through another door. The walls were painted green, like all municipal buildings, and the paint was peeling. The windows were tall and narrow and all of them had missing panes, boards covering the gaps. The place was in a state. It looked like it was empty. It looked nothing like a police station and that was exactly what Charlie wanted. If the Ghost Squad was to be effective, it needed to be anonymous, and this was a good start.

Charlie opened a set of double doors. Beyond was an open floor, not all that big, with a couple of offices leading off on one side. The place looked like it used to be a fashion warehouse: a crowd of battered old mannequins were gathered in a corner, dusty armless corpses that had seen better days. There were large industrial windows, a wide door in the wall with a winch outside, the sort of get-up for hoisting gear straight in. Two middle-aged women were working at typewriters and one whole wall was covered with shelves, books, box files and piles of paper. Half a dozen men were working at desks.

Vernon White and Roderick Carlyle, the sergeants who made up the heart of his little team, were waiting in Charlie's office, cups of tea steaming before them. He had hand-picked from uniform all the way back in 1940. They were *his* men. They had been with him since the Ripper case, the arcs of their careers following his own. There had been quick promotions from detective constable to detective sergeant and growing acclaim at the Yard, yet they were loyal and showed no interest in leaving his side. Charlie knew why: he was good, they knew it, and they also knew that they would rise faster with him than without. White was a cold-eyed hatchet-faced man, as lean as a rake and as hard as the manager of a loan office. Carlyle was a fresh-faced, a razor-sharp mind hidden beneath a naïve face. "Morning, lads," Charlie said.

"Morning, guv," they said together.

"Are we ready to go?"

Carlyle nodded. "The men are all here."

"Did we get them all?"

Carlyle shook his head. "We got six. The Commissioner will double it if we can show results."

Charlie grunted. There were hardly mob-handed, and a job like this would only work with a good deal of manpower, but it would have to do. "Get them ready," he said. "I'll get myself a cuppa and then I'll give them the run-through."

Carlyle and White went outside into the main room and Charlie heard them organise the men for the briefing. He made himself a cup of tea and went outside. The six detective constables had arranged their chairs so that they were facing the wall on which Charlie had fixed a pinboard.

"Morning, gents," he said. "My name is detective inspector Charlie Murphy and I will be your C.O. for the next six months. Everything I am going to tell you today must stay in this room. Everything we will do in this building is secret, and nothing must leak out. Nothing." He put his briefcase on the desk before him and popped open the clasps. "You'll all be aware of the problem with the black market. It was bad during the war but it's even worse today. There are shortages of everything and if there's one thing you can say about chummy it's this: he knows how to take advantage of a situation, and he's taking advantage of this one. London has been flooded with criminals looking to make a quick buck. We've got fellows who wouldn't normally have anything to do with crime falling to temptation. Blokes who work in factories leaving the door open so that goods and material can get nicked. Stevedores siphoning off a third of the fuel they've just unloaded and flogging it on. Butchers putting a little extra meat in the packets of their favourite customers for a payment on the side. And, of course, the underworld has reacted. You can't walk down Oxford Street without seeing a spiv flogging nylons. It's everywhere, lads. It's an epidemic. You'll have read some of the stuff in the papers, having a go at the Met for letting it happen. It's got to a point where we can't ignore it any more. The Commissioner has made this a priority. We are going to tackle the black market."

Charlie opened his briefcase and took an envelope. He slid his finger inside and opened it, tipping out a collection of glossy prints onto the desk. He took them and, one by one, tacked them onto the pinboard in the shape of a pyramid.

"It's not going to be an easy job," he admitted, "and it's so big it's difficult to know where to start, but since we've got to start somewhere, we're going to concentrate on this lot. This"—he said, gesturing to the pinboard—"is the Costello Family. They made their name on the racecourses twenty years ago and they expanded into Soho and the West End. Gambling, drinking clubs, prostitution—they have a lot of interests. They've had a harder time of it since the head of the family, Harry, kicked the bucket, and in the last couple of years they've retrenched. They're into the dogs more than horses these days and, even though they still have plenty of other interests, it's the black market that's making their money. They've gone into it in a big way."

He turned to the pinboard and pointed to the picture of George Costello. They had taken it yesterday, at the festival. He was scowling into the camera, frightening even at fifty feet.

"This is George Costello, otherwise known as Georgie the Bull. His real name is Salvatore but since the last person who called him that got knifed in the gut no-one uses it anymore. Early on, one of his relatives said that he reckoned Salvatore looked like his uncle George and that's what they called him from then on. He did badly at school, was expelled at thirteen and started running with the family on the racecourses. He was conscripted in 1917, actually went, which is unusual for a wide boy like him, but managed to stay out of the way before he was discharged. There were plenty of scraps with other men and we think that's where he got his nickname. He's Harry Costello's older brother. Since he got out of the army he's done time for assault and battery, robbery and false imprisonment, and those are just the big ticket items. He quickly made a name for himself for violence and made his way up the chain. The Yard has long suspected him as being an executioner for the family, and there are at least six murders we think he did but we can't prove. For example, it's common knowledge on the street that George participated in the conspiracy to murder Brummy Sage in 1921. And we know that he was involved in the murder of Jock Wyatt after the White Mob murdered Michael McCausland, one of the Costello lieutenants. Those are just two of the men we know he's murdered, but there are more. We can't prove any of it—he's clever enough not to leave evidence and you'd have a better chance of getting blood from a stone than anyone to finger him."

Charlie looked around the room. The men were rapt. He pointed to the picture he had pinned next to George's.

"This lovely is Violet Costello. Also known as Lady Violet on account of her airs and graces and the way she dresses. Also known as Bulletproof Violet on account of the fact that we've never been able to get her for anything and none of her rivals have ever laid a glove on her. Also known as Glorious Violet of Saffron Hill, on account of being a bit of a heart-breaker when she was younger—but she's more likely to break bones now, or at least get her brother to do it for her." The picture had also been taken at the festival. George was next to her, scowling at the camera, and she had a hand on his arm. "If George is the muscle, Violet is the brains. Harry Costello had everything, but since he's been gone the planning and strategy has fallen on her shoulders and, by all accounts, she's good at it. We don't know very much about her save that she's clever and ruthless."

Charlie pointed at the photographs directly below those of George and Violet. There was a row of seven lieutenants. Charlie went through them one at a time.

Bobby "Milkbottle" Minstrel.
Pasqualina Papa.
Paddy "Onions" O'Nione.
Jimmy Brindle.
Stuttery Robinson.
"Mile Away" Johnny Richardson.
Mickey Cornwall.

They were a motley collection of men, some of them in prison, all of them with time on their records at one point or another, all of them dangerous. As Charlie went through them he started to feel a little trepidation at the scale of the task he had undertaken. These were not two-bob dipsters and hoisters, they were proper criminals. Some were clever, others were shrewd, the rest were violent. They had been under investigation for most of their adult lives and yet finding a reason to bring them in was challenging.

The moment of uncertainty did not last long. Charlie dismissed it. He knew he was the man for the job, the best man that the Commissioner had at his disposal. He did not suffer from doubt. He would bring them all down.

"Pay attention," he said. Below the lieutenants came a further five photographs. "This is Joseph Costello. Youngest son of Harry Costello. He's been in borstal for burglary and then he was away in Burma for six years. We don't know much about him except that he's back and up to no good. The chap next to him here is Billy Stavropoulos, otherwise known as Billy Bubble or Billy the Greek. He's a tasty boxer under the name of Bert Gill, borderline professional, with form for assault and burglary. And here we have Edward Fabian. We know less about him than we do any of the others but what we do know is very interesting. He's been away fighting but he seems to be on friendly terms with Joseph—it's possible they met during the war. The only Edward Fabian we can find who would be of the right age was at Cambridge studying medicine until 1938. No criminal record or any suggestion that he is into anything hooky. And this is where it gets really interesting. This photograph was taken two days ago. The reason he's in uniform is because he's just come back from Buckingham Palace where he was given the Victoria Cross. Seems he's a war hero, to boot."

"And he's caught up with this lot?"

"I know it seems unlikely that he's our chap but until we can say for sure we're as interested in him as we are all of the others."

Charlie gave brief mention of Tommy Falco and Jack McVitie, the other two likely lads who were known to associate with Joseph Costello. Joseph and Billy were closest to the family and the most likely be of interest.

Fabian deserved attention because he was so terribly out of place that there had to be something worth knowing.

"So who are we going after, boss?" one of the new men asked.

"There's no point in George or Violet at this point. They're too far from the street, and she's much too clever to do anything that could tie her into anything criminal. The lieutenants are worth a look, but chances are that they're too long in the tooth to make stupid mistakes." He pointed at the lowest row of pictures again. "No. We're more likely to have success here, with these lads. They're young and wet behind the ears. They're all big drinkers and chances are they won't be discrete. Take a look at their faces. Remember them. For the next two weeks I want you to find out everything you can about them, Fabian especially. There must be something we can use: a parking ticket, an overdue library book, something. We bring them in and sweat them for a bit, and then we see what happens."

He looked around the room. They were young and keen. He'd have to work on them, hone them, but there was potential there.

"This is a big job, lads. Important. To the man in the street, it looks like the underworld is giving us the run-around and that's something we can't have happen. People start to think that, they lose respect for what we do. They lose respect for what we do and they start to think, hello, maybe it's not so bad to get a little extra on my ration. And that's just one step away from putting a brick through a window. It can't happen, boys. We can't let it." He pointed up at the rogue's gallery behind him. "We're going to bring these buggers down, boys. This is the Ghost Squad. You're all going undercover. You don't tell anyone about it. Not your wife. Not your girlfriend. Not even your priest, if you're so inclined. We might have to bend the rules a little bit to get what we want but the ends are going the justify the means. I want to know everything there is to know about these lads. The brand of beer they drink. Where they get their clothes. The type of car they prefer. I want to know who they share their beds with. If they fart, I want to know what it smells like. That's what you're going to do, boys. I want these lads here to be the first thing you think about in the morning and the last thing you think about at night. We're going to bring them down. We are. It's just a matter of time." They were looking up at him, avidly. "What are you waiting for? Dismissed. Go and get started."

12

IT WAS JUST AFTER DAWN and a bank of fog was rolling in off the river and creeping, damp and wet and dense, through the streets. This part of town still used gas, and the lamplighter was slowly making his way down the street, extinguishing them one by one as the sun rose. The remaining lights glowed through the smoggy haze, fuzzy globes of gold. Edward emerged from the station and followed the Tottenham Court Road down towards Euston. The area was full of car dealerships, new and used, and the one that Joseph had directed him to was halfway down the road.

He walked onto the forecourt. The floodlights were on, bleeding through the fog. Slogans and signs were hung from the lamp-posts: "over 100 for under £100," they proclaimed, but the fabric banners were tiny compared to the huge mural that had been painted onto the wall at the end of the terrace. There appeared to be plenty of stock: family motors that ran well but were probably on the verge of a serious breakdown; Chryslers and Buicks that had been thrashed too hard by young men who had grown out of them; a handful of sports cars, brightly painted buzz-boxes with plenty of gadgets and chromium lamps and fittings, caned half to death by tearaways with indulgent parents.

He shivered in the damp cold and closed his overcoat more tightly around his body. He passed through the showroom to the back, and followed a painted, pointing hand towards a doorway labelled 'office.' He took a short flight of stairs and passed through another door, this one marked as 'general office.' A final door had 'Mr. Ward' stencilled across its frosted glass panel. Edward heard voices inside. He rapped his fist against the glass and was told to come in.

There was a man sitting behind a desk and another in a chair facing him. The first man was obviously the boss. The first thing Edward noticed was his beautiful suit, and next how well his face was shaved under the faint brush of powder, and then his forehead, where the pale hair receded, which glistened. The man was wide, there could be no doubt about that, but he didn't look like the drones who flogged packets of nylons on the pavement outside Oxford Circus tube station. He was dressed in an understated way that said he knew the value of money but wasn't interested in flaunting it.

"Sorry," Edward said. "I didn't realise I was interrupting."

"Who are you?" the first man said.

"Violet Costello sent me. About a job?"

"Ah yes," he said, nodding with sudden vigour. "I remember. Sit down. We're nearly finished." His voice became harsh as he turned to address the second man. "You've got to pull your socks up, man. I'm fed up to the eye teeth of you and the other blokes let people get away with it. You've got no brains and no ability. You don't ever admit liability, never—do you understand? Giving money to the old fool who brought the Rover back, what were you thinking?"

"But you told me yourself that the guarantee—"

"Guarantee? Nuts! That's just talk. You're a salesman, Ford, you sell things. You leave the business to me. Guarantee? Stone the crows! Guarantee! Unless you can get that into your thick skull you can find yourself a new job. You and all the others. There are plenty of men willing and able to take your job. Take this fellow here." He referred to a pad on the desk. "It's Mr.—Mr.—Mr. Fabian, isn't it?"

Edward nodded that it was.

"Mr. Fabian is only a bona fide war hero, decorated and everything. While you were running around Salisbury Plain finding excuses not to get sent to the front, Mr. Fabian was up to his neck in bloody Japs. Only got the Victoria bleeding Cross, didn't he?"

Edward did not know how to respond to that.

"Do you have anything else to say?"

"No, Mr. Ward."

"No indeed. Now—clear off."

The man stood and, apologising again, shuffled out of the room.

Ruby Ward shook his head and stood up. "Sorry about that," he said. "Half the lads I've got here couldn't sell a car if their life depended on it, and the other half give money back when some old fool complains that the one they've bought isn't running right. They'd have me out of business if I didn't keep an eye on them."

He extended a hand and Edward took it. He noticed that he pressed a knuckle into his palm. A freemason; Edward wondered if returning the pressure would mean favourable treatment.

He smiled brightly at him, revealing two rows of beautifully white teeth. "I'm Ruby Ward. Pleased to meet you."

"Likewise."

"Now then—Violet was telling me you're after a job. She says you're a University man, and that you did well for yourself in the Far East. I can use a person like that. You worked in sales before?"

"I'm afraid not."

"Never mind. If you're as clever as she says you are then you'll pick it up." He took his coat from the back of his chair and slipped it on. "Come on," he said. "I'll give you the tour."

He went down to the garage, passing a battered old Austin-Seven that Ward said he had picked up for a song the previous afternoon. It had certainly seen better days. The motor was over the inspection pit and his man, Joe Buck, was underneath it, shining a light onto the chassis. Ward explained that Buck was his "fixer." He had no formal qualifications as a mechanic but he was an artist when it came to taking beaten up motor cars and making them look halfway decent again. He could only do so much, and even someone with Ruby's patter would struggle to flog a car like that on for more than twenty quid, but it didn't matter because Ruby never bought them for more than a fiver.

"How is it?" Ruby shouted.

"It's in a right mess, boss," Buck called up out of the pit. "If it was a horse, I'd've shot it."

"Lucky I pay you to mend 'em, then. What are you going to do with it?"

Buck hauled himself out of the pit, scrubbing sweat off his forehead with the edge of his dirty sleeve. He looked at the Austin critically and sucked his teeth. "I'll wind the clock a bit, take a few hundred miles off it. The engine ought to run well enough for another six months, maybe a year. The rest of it will be easy enough: the wing stay's loose but I can anchor it with wire and insulating tape; there are rattles in the chassis, but some wet cardboard rolls will dampen them down; I'll tie the battery box to the frame with string and change the oil. We had a delivery yesterday—very cheap. What it lacks in cleanliness it makes up for in heaviness. Perfect for what we need."

"Good man."

Ruby explained that he paid Buck forty-five shillings a week and a bonus of sixpence for every car he saved from the breaker's yard. He took the cars as part-exchange, more of them than he knew what to do with. Some didn't need that much work: a splash of paint, a squirt of oil, a new pair of tyres. The others he reserved for Buck.

They entered the main showroom. Five cars were carefully parked so that the spotlights overhead could sparkle down across their polished bodywork. Another row of similar cars was arranged on the forecourt, visible through the big plate glass windows. Prices had been written on the windshields and a sign overhead proclaimed GOOD CARS WANTED.

Ward poured two cups of tea from a pot on a small table and gave one to Edward. "Here's the deal," he said. "I'll give you a quid a week. Every car you sell is worth another quid to you on top of that. Simple, right?"

"Simple."

"You'll pick it up in an hour or two. If I were you I'd have a look around this morning, see how things get done. Watch the other lads, that'll get you an idea of how they work. Once you're happy with that, you might as well get stuck in. You'll need to pull your weight, mind—Violet's recommendation got you the job, but it won't keep you in it if you can't sell. Understand?"

"Yes, Mr. Ward," he said. "I do."

"Now then, we can't have you dressed like that." Ward looked at Edward's suit with a distasteful expression. He peeled two pound notes from a roll he kept in the pocket of his jacket. "Get down to Marks and Spencer and buy yourself a new suit, a couple of shirts and a pair of shoes. We'll treat that as an advance on your first two weeks, alright?"

Edward took the notes. "Thank you," he said. "I appreciate the opportunity."

"Not a problem," Ward said, turning away. "Just don't make me look like a mug, alright?"

13

EDWARD TURNED UP EVERY MORNING at six for the next week and worked hard. It was a simple enough trade to grasp. Most of the stock was old and near to the end of its useful life. Cars that had been shining and new just a few years earlier would now be bought for a pound or two, touched up by Buck and pushed on to unsuspecting punters for as much as they could get. Where once the motors had been immaculate, now they were battered and bruised: the axles creaked; the gearboxes groaned; the bodywork rattled; the upholstery was stained and torn; the registration books filled, in most cases, with a litany of names.

The other salesmen had little time for Edward or, it seemed, each other. It was a cut-throat way of doing business, the half dozen men circling the forecourt like hyenas, pouncing upon potential customers or, during the quieter periods, trying to round up likely looking prospects from the street. They were loud-mouthed Charlies with oil-slicked hair and faces full of spots, offering oleaginous handshakes and honey-dripped platitudes. They wore check sports-coats and grey trousers, or lounge suits, always completed with an old school tie and shoes polished to a high gloss. Their language was filled with incomprehensible jargon that baffled the punters and yet sounded impressively reassuring and authentic. Edward did not rate any of them in any sense other than the most important: they all had a sixth sense for selling. It was a seeming ease that allowed them to identify and then exploit every customer's foible: vanity, security, reliability. They had a talent for detecting whatever it was to which they needed to pander.

Edward watched them in action. They gathered in groups when times were quiet, scattering at the first sight of a customer. He made to fuss with a nearby car as the man Ruby Ward had chastised on his first day latched onto a young buck who had come in looking for a sports car. He watched as the man smoothly guided him from the one that he had his eye on to another, an unreliable jalopy that Ward had bought for ten pounds and which they were offering for ninety. The salesman was a skilled liar, effortlessly extolling the virtues of a car he knew to be on its last legs, so persuasive that Edward suspected that he almost believed his own pitch. That was a useful attribute, he thought, and one he knew that he also possessed. The salesman summed up the customer in a flash, adapting himself to the man's personality, instinctively knowing which would be the path of least resistance to a sale. After half an hour the sale was concluded. It was an impressive display.

On the second day, he decided to try for himself.

Ruby Ward had something of a name for sports cars and it was another young man who came through the door. Edward had noticed him idling on the forecourt and had positioned himself ahead of the other salesmen so that when the man had plucked up the courage to come inside he was able to smoothly attach himself to his side. The man had paused by a Jaguar XK that Edward knew suffered with a poor carburettor. "This one?" he said to the man with idle charm. "Funny you should notice that. Between you and me, we were going to take it off sale. Mr. Ward himself is rather fond of it, some suggestion he might buy it for his lady friend, but if you want it—provided we move fast—I reckon we could probably have it for you."

"It's nice," the man offered uncertainly. "What's it like?"

Edward assessed the man again: he was young, and, he guessed, this was his first or second car. What would he want? He would want the reassurance that the car was fast. He would want his sense that the car would make him popular with girls confirmed. He was too young to buy the car himself and so he would also need to demonstrate it was a sensible purchase to his parents. "She's a beauty, alright," Edward said, running his fingertips across the chrome bodywork. "Reinforced spring-gaiters. That dummy brake drums help cooling as well as looking good. The engine has unusually high compression, so that makes it extra reliable as well as giving it that little bit of extra poke." He grinned at him. "It's been carefully kept, one owner previous, he always garaged it when it wasn't being used, and just ten thousand miles on the clock. You have good taste—she's a lovely little number."

He noticed Ruby Ward watching him from the side of the showroom as he led the helpless customer around the car, pointing out the particular features that made this model a more attractive proposition than any of the others. He discussed the success of the make on the track, reciting a long list of famous names who had had success behind the wheel: Ted Horn, Rex Mays, Bill Holland. The man requested a test drive and Edward told him that that was fine, he could have one if he liked, but that delay would increase the chances that the car would be withdrawn from sale. The man demurred, negotiated a small discount for cash, and drove away with the car.

"You're a natural," Ruby Ward told him afterwards, shaking him firmly by the hand. "You see what you just did?"

"I'm not sure," Edward said, pretending that he didn't when, of course, he knew exactly.

Ward beamed at him. "You made him think that you were his friend. It's a real art—not everyone can manage it. You have to be an actor, or a born liar, and you've got the gift, alright, Fabian—you, my man, have got a silver tongue."

14

IT WAS HIS FOURTH DAY at the garage, towards the middle of June, when he saw the girl on the forecourt. Edward had been talking to Hynde, the least objectionable of the salesmen. He had thick black hair and a slight paunch, his eyes were bright and greedy and his pleasant smile seemed to be fixed. "Blimey," Hynde said. "Would you look at her?"

He got up quickly but Edward laid a hand on his shoulder. "She's a friend," he said.

"Course she is."

"I'm serious."

"All's fair in love and war," Hynde said with a vulpine grin as he set off. "And motor cars," he added over his shoulder.

"You know Violet Costello?"

He stopped. "Course," he said, frowning.

"That's her niece. Still want to have a go?"

His face fell. "Really? Oh, bollocks to it then. She's all yours."

Edward strolled across the showroom. Chiara was stroking the chrome mirror of a sleek MG and was as beautifully attired as before: a cardigan with padded shoulders, a single pleat plaid skirt with nylons underneath and patent leather Oxfords with a continental heel. She saw Edward's reflection in the MG's windscreen and turned, smiling. "Hello," she said. "I was passing. My Aunt said you had started working here. I thought I'd come and say hello."

"A very pleasant distraction."

"I'm glad you think so. Have you sold any cars today?"

"As a matter of fact, I have—a little Packard Coupe. I sold it to a charming chap just twenty minutes ago for twice what it's worth. If he's not back here complaining that it isn't starting by the end of the week then I shall be most surprised."

She laughed. "Does Ruby still employ the same disreputable types as before?"

"I work here," he said. "I couldn't possibly comment."

"Promise I won't tell anyone."

"Well, then, seeing as you insist. There does seem to be a type." He struck a pose, pretending to spit on his hand and slicking back his hair. "The chaps here all have a certain something about them." Edward did it in pantomime, scooting around the periphery of the MG, pointing out the splendid features, complimenting madam on her excellent taste and, when he learned that she intended to pay in cash, exploding in a little paroxysm of joy and excitement.

"Wonderful!" she clapped.

His tongue rattled on almost independently of his brain. His brain was estimating how high his stock was shooting up with Chiara. He could see it in her face. He smiled, terribly pleased with himself. "Can I tempt you with a cup of tea?" he asked.

"Oh, that would be lovely but I don't want to get you in trouble and I should probably be going, anyway—I'm supposed to be meeting my sisters at Dickens and Jones for lunch."

"Another time, then," Edward said graciously.

"I should probably come clean," she said. "There is ulterior motive for the visit. I don't know if Joseph has mentioned anything to you, but I'm afraid it will be my twenty-first birthday on Friday. My aunt has taken it upon herself to organise a party for me."

Edward sensed an opportunity. "That sounds lovely."

"Oh, it'll probably be dreadful. I'd much rather do something peaceful but everyone is coming and so the best I can do is make sure there are some interesting people there who I can talk to when it all gets a little too much. I was wondering whether I could twist your arm?"

"Friday," he said. He pretended to muse upon it. "I'd like to say I'm busy enough so that I would have to change my plans but that would be a shocking lie."

"So you'll come?"

"I'd be delighted."

Chiara was rollicking on about the party and who was coming and it was not the least bit interesting. Edward said it sounded wonderful, and how he was thrilled to be asked, and as he caught a glimpse of his face in the shining bodywork of the car he saw his mouth turned up at the corners and his eyes shining brightly. He was doing the right thing, behaving in the right way. He suddenly had an unpleasant feeling of dislocation. He had the feeling that he was in a film and that in a moment Chiara or someone else would shout 'cut' and he would be back at the Shangri-La, his hands and apron covered in gore, his eyes stinging with sweat, his prospects narrowed down again from a widening vista into a microscopic, insignificant jot. He mastered the feeling, dismissed it, and the moment passed. Chiara was saying that it was time to leave. They shook hands, hers smooth and cold in his, and he said, again, that he was grateful to be asked and that he was looking forward to it already. She held his hand a moment longer than usual and smiled brightly, right into his face.

"I'm looking forward to it a little more," she said as she collected her bag and made her way back outside.

Edward poured himself a cup of tea and drank it with a smile on his lips. Hynde had watched the episode from the edge of the showroom. Edward held the teacup aloft and nodded in his direction. Hynde wrinkled his nose and shook his head. Edward smiled at him, his mood lifted. This was progress, he thought. He was making excellent, promising progress.

15

THE REST OF THE WEEK followed the same pattern as the days before it: he got to the garage early and left late, selling a car or two every day. It was long and monotonous and Edward distracted himself from the boredom with the promise of the weekend in the country. He had enjoyed his trip to the Hill. It had been, by some considerable margin, his most enjoyable day since he had been demobilised.

Friday was particularly busy and, when, he finished the shift, Edward was exhausted. He brushed down his suit in the bathroom and slicked his hair with pomade that he had purchased in his short lunch break. He bid Ruby Ward goodbye for the week and set off for the underground.

Halewell Close was near Withington. He had arranged with Joseph that he would take the train to Gloucester and be collected from the station. He embarked at Paddington and found an empty carriage. That was fortunate: his mood was tranquil and kindly, but not at all sociable. He wanted his time for thinking and he did not care to meet anyone else, though when a couple entered his carriage he greeted them pleasantly and smiled. As the train cut through the countryside, the sky gradually darkened. They eventually caught up with the storm up and peals of thunder rolled around the low hills.

They reached Gloucester at half past seven. Edward took his suitcase and waited under the station awning for Joseph to collect him. Rain lashed the street and thunder rolled overhead. A car sluiced through puddles of standing water towards him, the lights glittering on the wet asphalt, two long amber slashes. Lightning flashed. The car drew to a halt and Joseph reached across to open the passenger-side door. Edward abandoned the shelter of the doorway and ran for it.

"Alright, Doc," Joseph said as Edward slid inside. "Cats and dogs tonight. How are you?"

"Tired. It's been a long day."

"You need a drink." He offered a hipflask. Edward undid the top and took a swig. It was whisky. He took another slug, the liquid spreading warmth around his chest.

"That's the ticket."

"Course it is. Let's get going."

Joseph put the car into gear and they set off, leaving the lights of the town behind them and cutting out into the darkened countryside. They talked about the war as they drove west, the easy conversation helping to pass the time.

Eventually, Joseph turned off the main road, rumbling across a cattle grid and then passing onto a private drive, the entrance marked by two impressive stone pillars topped by electric lanterns. An engraving in one of the pillars revealed the name of the house beyond: Halewell Close. The evening was growing darker, and Edward could only see what the headlights revealed: the drive was lined by regularly spaced yew trees, and must have been a mile long. Joseph bore right around a shallow turn and the headlights cast out into darkness across a wide lake, the water sparkling. They swung back around to the left and the rough tarmac surface was replaced with gravel. It opened out as it approached a hill and then, as they crested the brow, the house below was revealed.

Joseph explained that Halewell Close was originally a farm, but had been rebuilt and added to over the years. It was set into its own private valley, amongst a sprawling beech wood, and was huge. It was stone-built, and of two and three storeys. Edward's eyes darted across it: he picked out three granges, set into the shape of a U, the steep slate roofs and stone walls the colour of mustard. The granges surrounded a courtyard. The west range was the largest, comprising four bays, the other ranges having been added over the years. Lights blazed in leaded windows all the way across the house, casting a lattice of gold across the wide lawns. A row of stables could be found on the far side of a wide parking area and, at the end of the lawn, was a swimming pool and summer house.

Edward gaped. He had visited houses like this before, in this country and then all across Europe. He felt twitches of excitement in his gut. It was the lifestyle that it promised, rather than the house itself, that stirred him. He had grown accustomed to that, and come to expect it, before everything had changed. The prospect of returning to it excited him as nothing else possibly could. He gazed at the beautiful house and filled it with guests in his imagination, men and women in gorgeous evening clothes, tables full of fine food and wine, the way the light would refract against pieces of jewellery. He could almost smell the mustiness of the rooms, could almost see the light flickering from candles in their sconces. It was all so glorious. Expectation! He sometimes wondered whether it was more pleasant to him than the promise of experiencing it all. It was so pleasant to relish that he suddenly found his nervousness at the idea of a party full of strangers fading away.

"Your family owns this?" he said at last.

"It was my grandfather's originally."

"It's enormous."

"I know," he said with a mixture of pride and embarrassment.

They descended, traversing a small bridge that forded a stream. Wrought-iron lamp-posts were set on either side of the final length of the drive, casting their light across neatly terraced private gardens and the southern shore of the lake, a boathouse built next to a wooden jetty from which a tethered rowing boat bobbed on gentle swells.

"What did he do?"

"He was into gambling," he said vaguely.

"What—bookmaking?"

"The racetracks. Horses, dogs—you know."

It was a vague explanation, and he seemed reluctant to go further. Joseph had explained that the house was occupied by his grandmother, his Aunt Violet and his three sisters. Edward had imagined a large house to accommodate them all, but this was beyond all of his expectations. This was palatial. The gravel crunched under the tyres. Edward could not suppress the buzz of anticipation as Joseph parked in front of the *porte cochère* outside the south façade of the main house. They were at the end of a long row of cars, perhaps a dozen of them, all new and expensive: an American Buick, an Aston Martin, a Daimler.

The summer storm had not abated: thunder boomed and rain slammed onto the gravel. Joseph switched off the motor. "About tonight," he began haltingly. "The party—my aunt and uncle have invited plenty of people. Chaps who work with the family. Some of them are—*characters*, I don't know how else to describe them. They're good lads, solid lads, but a couple can be prickly when they see people they don't know. It's nothing to be bothered about, see, they'll all know you're with me, I'm just saying—if they give you a hard time, don't get the hump, alright? They're like that with everyone."

"Alright," Edward said. It was a strange thing to say, and it helped draw his nervousness back again.

A butler in striped morning trousers hurried out of the house with two umbrellas for them. They dashed quickly inside, leaving their suitcases to be brought after them. The front door entered onto a reception hall, thirty feet across, with a stone fireplace and an oak staircase that led up to the first floor.

The butler appeared behind them with their luggage. He collected their wet umbrellas from them.

"Would you like to settle into your rooms?" he asked. "I've taken the liberty of drawing baths for you both. The party isn't due to start until nine."

"Relax for a bit, Doc," Joseph said. "I'll come and get you when I'm ready."

16

EDWARD HOISTED HIS SUITCASE ONTO THE BED AND OPENED IT. He changed out of his suit, folding it carefully. He had taken Ruby Ward's money and visited a second-hand clothes shop. By spending the two pounds carefully, he had been able to buy two suits, three shirts, a couple of ties and a pair of reasonably decent shoes. The place had held the lingering odours of steam that had passed through tired cloth, the sour whiff of dry-cleaning: the tang of benzine, boot-polish, wax, sweat and cigarette smoke, and some of that atmosphere had been absorbed by the fabric. The suit he unpacked from his suitcase had cost just a few shillings and looked it, although it was not marked or holed. The navy-blue number he wore for work was in slightly better condition, but Chiara had already seen him in it and he didn't want her to think that it was the only one he owned.

The en-suite bathroom held a large free-standing bath and he soaked in it for half an hour, trying to settle his nerves. He stepped out and dried himself, and went back into the bedroom again. It was of a good size, and nicely furnished, although it was freighted with the dusty smell of a room that is only occasionally used. He dressed and stood before the mirror, regarding himself with a mixture of distaste and shame. A cheap second-hand suit in a place like this. It was the best he could manage, but he still felt vulnerable.

He stared into his own eyes and rehearsed his story.

He was an orphan.

His mother died giving birth to him.

His father died in an automobile smash.

He had no siblings.

He was brought up in a children's home.

He won a scholarship to study medicine at Trinity, Cambridge, and he excelled.

His medical career was postponed because he wanted to serve his country.

He had served with distinction and now he was home.

The details had accreted, over time, like layers of silt. He had repeated them so often that the story had became second nature. The lies became truth.

There was a knock on the door. It was Joseph. He was wearing another new suit, perfectly cut, with fabulous creases that looked sharp enough to draw blood. He nodded admiringly in Edward's direction. "Very smart."

"Don't be daft. I look like a dog's dinner."

"You look fine."

"No, I don't. But thanks for saying it."

"What's the matter? You're not nervous, are you?"

"I suppose I am a little."

"There's no need to be. You look fine, and no-one is going to care, anyway. They'll all be rolling around drunk in an hour. We'll go down and have a drink ourselves. Loosen up. That'll help. The lads are there already, I've just been down—you'll like them, you'll see."

"Your sisters?"

"Of course. Come on."

Drinks were being held in the drawing room. Edward looked around, agape. The roof bore three trusses, each with arch-braced collars carrying king posts, double purlins and two tiers of windbraces. A frieze of painted boards with a Latin quotation from the Bible formed part of a central partition, fronting a musician's gallery at the south end of the chamber. The place was grand, yet, as he looked closer, he saw that it was in need of maintenance. Skirting boards were loose, paint was in need of refreshing, woodwork needed polishing, a couple of the sash windows were jammed open and closed off with plastic sheeting. In better times it would have been as impressive as the little châteaux and castellos he had visited as he had travelled south through France and Italy. But those days, he saw, were gone.

The whole house was down-at-heel.

The scuffs and marks did not reduce the effect that the room had on him. If he had felt a sense of his social inadequacy before, now it was multiplied. Where had Joseph's family found the money for a place like this? It was more than inadequacy that was making him anxious. It was the proximity to something that could bring back the life that he had had to throw away. The other guests drank and talked in high spirits, seemingly disregarding their surroundings, the sense of history all around them, the faded glamour, but Edward could not. He knew he had stumbled upon an opportunity. There was money here. He had sensed it, the way a bloodhound tracks a scent. His younger self, so practiced and smooth, would have found his nervousness hilarious. His younger self would have addressed the room and the guests with a rapacious and predatory eye and taken whatever he wanted.

But he was older now and out of practice.

Joseph was talking to him, talking about the room and the house and how it had all felt to him as a small boy. Edward nodded occasionally and made appreciative responses but he was listening with just a fraction of his brain. He was concentrating on his surroundings and the other guests. There were forty or fifty of them ranged around the room, with several groups forming: Violet Costello was smiling beatifically as the focus of a group of women; George Costello was drinking with half a dozen middle-aged men, all of them low-browed, heavy-shouldered and thick-set; Joseph's sisters had attracted a group of similarly aged girls.

Edward made an absent-minded response to Joseph's suggestion that he introduce him to his friends and then, as he led him towards three younger men in the corner of the room, he made an effort to pull himself together and focus his concentration. First impressions were everything and, whomever it was that he was going to meet tonight, he could not allow his dreaminess to set him off on the wrong foot.

"Here's the man himself," one of the men said, fixing Joseph in a hug.

Joseph did the honours, introducing Edward as his "mucker from the jungle." Tommy Falco and Jack McVitie took his hand in turn. Edward guessed that they were a little younger than him, twenty-five or twenty-six, and they both looked wide. Falco was the kind of fellow it would be difficult to forget: big, a muscular man with an expression of brutal simplicity on his face and so much oil on his hair that it almost looked grey. His eyes were prominent, with fair lashes and eyebrows, which made him look perpetually surprised. McVitie was marked by a hat he wore to conceal his thinning hair. It looked out of place, and suggested bad manners, but he showed no inclination to remove it and no-one seemed to mind. He had a strange face, blunt-featured, compact and muscular; a well-constructed, useful-looking face, handsome in spite of the short blunt nose and out-thrust jaw. The two had a relaxed, jaunty confidence, and both were dressed in lovely suits that most certainly were not off the ration. The same could be said of Billy Stavropoulos. He smiled broadly for Joseph but as he saw Edward the expression faded from his face and he gave a nod of dour acknowledgement instead.

The three were already in boisterous good spirits that came, Edward quickly realised, from drink. He felt the fluttering of anxiety again. They were already ahead of him, and relaxed because of it. He knew that if he wanted to take his opportunity he would have to impress. To do that, there was nothing else for it: he would have to catch up, and quickly, and yet there was a careful balance to strike since he could not allow himself to get blind drunk. A waiter appeared with martinis and Edward took one, taking a sip as he looked up at the ceiling, reminding himself that he was quite capable of manipulating people like this. Tonight might be a test of his patience—they were vulgar, with coarse manners and bawdy jokes, and certainly not the type of people that Edward would have chosen to associate with—but the potential was worth the tedium of working them.

The birthday meal was to be held in the Great Hall. It was a large, plush space, decorated with mirrors held up by gilt caryatids. The ceiling was covered in rococo curlicues and a large, elaborate candelabra dripped down. Again, though, were the signs of neglect: there were cobwebs in the candelabra and the wallpaper on the walls was peeling and stained, here and there, by patches of damp.

Edward was in something of a daze as he sat. Two waiters brought out the starter: four large scallops shaped like top hats, sliced into disks and with the overlapping slices arranged like the petals of a flower with an even bigger slice in the centre. It was delicious. He had enjoyed a couple of gins by this stage and was starting to feel a little less self-conscious. Billy Stavropoulos was as truculent as ever, but the others were not as awful as they might have been. Edward had McVitie on the left and Falco on right, with Joseph on the opposite side of the wide table, opposite him. Billy sat next to Joseph.

"Joseph says you're an educated man," McVitie said.

"Well, I went to University. Does that count?"

"He's being modest," Joseph said. "He's a bloody genius—a Doctor."

"That so?"

"I'm certainly not a genius. But he's right that I studied Medicine. What do you both do?"

McVitie chuckled until Joseph gave him a meaningful look.

"What?" Edward pressed, smiling nervously at the private joke.

"Salvage," McVitie said.

"And me," Falco added.

"What—scrap metal?"

"That kind of thing."

The main course was brought out: a galantine of duck and foie gras. Edward's kitchen skills were rudimentary but even an old hand like Jimmy would have been impressed by the gastronomy.

Edward leaned over towards Joseph. "This food—where's it from?"

"A friend of the family."

"Kosher?"

"Not strictly. Let's just say he's into buying and selling."

"A spiv?"

"He'd call himself an entrepreneur."

"But it's the black market?"

Joseph grinned. "He owed my Aunt a favour. Pulled out the stops for us. You're working for him."

"Ruby Ward?"

"He buys and sells a lot of different things. It's not just cars."

"Wherever it came from, it looks delicious."

Edward sliced into the duck. The cross-sectional cut revealed layers of pink meat alternating with meltingly tender foie gras that had been moulded and pressed into the shape of a perfect cylinder. It tasted beautiful.

McVitie spoke up: "What was it like in Burma?"

"Hot," Edward replied.

"I'll say," Joseph agreed.

"And now this," McVitie said, gesturing toward the window, rain lashing against the glass. "Welcome to summer!"

"It makes a change, that's for sure."

"What about the Japs?" Falco asked.

"They were vicious," Joseph said.

"I remember when it all started, the papers were saying it'd be over in a month."

Edward warmed to the subject. "No-one took the Tojos seriously," he said. "Everyone thought a couple of victories and they'd fall over. It didn't happen like that."

"Were you there at the start?"

Edward said that he was. "The early days were brutal—defeat after defeat. It took four years to turn the tide."

"Just as I arrived," Joseph grinned. "I don't think it was a coincidence."

Falco looked impressed. "Joseph said you got a medal."

Edward shrugged. "It was nothing."

"No point going on about it, then," Billy said dismissively.

"Put a sock in it, Bubble," Joseph said, punching him on the shoulder. "Come on, old man, you have to tell us what happened. I still don't know. He won't say."

That was a story that would require a careful telling. Before Edward could begin, George Costello tapped his knife against his glass and the conversation petered away. Slightly relieved, Edward turned his attention to the head of the table. He had blithely assumed that George would deliver the speech in the absence of Chiara's father, but he remained seated as Violet stood instead.

"Family, friends—thank you for coming. Now, as you may have heard, it is my niece's twenty-first birthday today. As you know, her father, my brother, isn't with us any longer and so it falls to me to say a few words." Violet gave a short history of Chiara's life, a few badly phrased jokes that drew compliant laughter from the audience. "Anyone who knows her will tell you that she's always been a headstrong one. I remember, when she was just a girl, how she wouldn't do what her parents wanted. The Italians among us will know what I am talking about—my brother and his wife gave all of their children two Christian names: one Italian, one English. It was just as you'd expect—the Italian to help them remember their history, the English to help them fit in. Chiara was supposed to be known as Clarissa, but even as a five year old she refused to answer to it. It hasn't changed—the last person who tried to call her Clarissa got the rough side of her tongue for their cheek." The diners chuckled, some of them exchanging glances of recognition. "But you can hardly blame her for being proud of her roots," Violet continued, "it's a shame more of us don't share it—but that's a subject for another day." She picked up her glass from the table. "Chiara has become a beautiful young woman. We're all very proud of her. Now then—raise your glasses for a toast. To Chiara."

"Chiara!" the guests repeated lustily.

Violet resumed her seat and, next to her, Chiara kissed her lightly on the cheek. Edward saw her mouth thanks into her ear.

Joseph excused himself from the table. McVitie reached across the table and swiped a full bottle of wine. He gestured towards Edward's empty glass. "Refill, Doc?" Edward had started to feel quite drunk but his half-hearted resistance was ignored. McVitie poured so much that it spilled over the rim. "Cheers."

"Seems like yesterday we were here for Chiara's eighteenth," Falco said.

McVitie nodded. "She's something else now, eh?"

"She always was a good-looking girl."

"I'd give her a lovely birthday present and no mistake," Billy said.

McVitie and Falco both laughed derisively. "Like she'd have anything to do with you."

"Piss off, Jack. I'd stand a better chance than you."

The conversation moved on to Joseph's family. Edward was pleased. He had plenty of questions, and the information would be valuable. "What happened to Joseph's father?" he asked.

"He hasn't mentioned it?"

"Not a word."

McVitie frowned. "Best you ask him about that," he said.

"And his mother?"

"Nothing about her, neither?"

"No."

"That ain't surprising," said Falco.

"What about her?"

He winced. "Best let him bring that up, too. It's—what would you call it, Tommy?"

"Delicate, Jack."

"That's right. A bit delicate."

"Is she alive?"

"Far as I know."

"Where is she, then?"

"Honestly, Doc—best you let him talk about her."

Edward took the hint and didn't pursue it any further. Whatever it was, it was something that both McVitie and Falco were awkward about discussing. They didn't appear to be shy about anything else, and so, whatever it was about Joseph's parents, it could wait until he was ready to talk about it himself.

17

THE MEAL FINISHED and, as the waiters started to clear the debris from the tables, the guests moved back to the drawing room. A gramophone had been uncovered and records were being played, a few of the younger guests dancing to the music unselfconsciously. Edward had been persuaded by the others to move onto spirits, and after two glasses of a very good—and very potent—single malt, he was feeling quite light-headed.

He was standing by the fireplace when Violet Costello came alongside. She was with a heavy-set man who bore the scar from a razor across his right cheek.

Violet smiled pleasantly at him. "Mr. Fabian," she said.

"Please—call me Edward."

"This is Lennie Masters," she said, indicating the man. "He works with the family, too. Lennie—this is Edward Fabian."

"How do you do?" Edward said.

The man regarded him dubiously but took his hand nonetheless.

"This is the one who's working with Ruby?"

"That's right," she said. "And how are you finding the automobile business, Edward?"

"I'm enjoying it," he lied. "Thank you for your help. I'm very grateful."

It was a chore, and he knew he was destined for much better, but the job was serving its purpose well enough. He had made some money, at least. Most of it he had passed to his uncle, who had in turn used it to pay some of the outstanding bills for his father's care. The risk of his being refused treatment, or removed from the sanatorium, had been deferred, and that was a relief.

Violet waved her hand dismissively at his thanks although Edward could tell that she enjoyed it. She was, he concluded, one of those people who took pleasure not so much from being in a position to do another a favour, but from that other person knowing that they are in that position. The perception of status was clearly of importance to her, and being able to dispense favours—so that others might benefit from her munificence—was pleasing to her. Edward was very happy to let her think he was grateful, and, more importantly, impressed.

Lennie Masters excused himself, leaning down so that she could kiss him on his scarred cheek.

Violet explained that the garage was one of several businesses that the family owned and that she was happy to be able to help a returning soldier. "I was thinking about that," she went on. "The family has a connection with a journalist. He's freelance, I believe, but he often has his pieces in the national newspapers. I saw him for lunch yesterday and he said that he was interested in a piece about soldiers returning from the war—how they find things back home, that sort of thing. I think it's disgraceful the way the government is treating you men. You, especially, with the Victoria Cross, it's shocking that even someone like you should find themselves in such difficult circumstances. I happened to mention that to him and he thought it would be a capital idea to write a piece about your experiences."

Edward's stomach turned with panic. "I don't know, Ms Costello," he said. "I'm not really one for publicity."

"Nonsense, Edward. It's shocking that men like you, men who have fought for their country—heroes, for goodness sake—are forgotten as soon as they get home. Shocking. Someone needs to say something about it." She smiled at him. "I'd like you to do this, please. I think it's very important."

Edward knew that he was not being given a choice and he knew that this was nothing about politics or the welfare of soldiers. This was a chance for Violet to be publically lauded for her charity. A terrible, jangling fright went over his shoulders and down his legs. For a moment he felt helpless and weak, too weak to move. He imagined his picture on the front page of the Daily *Graphic* or the Picture Post. A puff piece article, declaiming the way he had been treated and—no doubt—heralding the charity of Violet Costello. The headline would be "Local Businesswoman Helps War Hero," and the article would be more about her that it would about him. But the damage would be done. From there, it was not difficult to imagine what might come next: a knock on the door in the middle of the night, policemen thrusting their way inside, throwing him in the back of a Black Mariah and tossing him into a cell. Or private detectives following him in the street, assembling their cases against him, drawing the net around him until it was so tight that he couldn't move.

"I'll speak to him tomorrow, then," she said with a note of finality that said it was pointless to protest. "It's important, isn't it, Edward? Something needs to be said."

Edward said that he agreed, of course, but when he glimpsed his reflection in the mirror above the mantelpiece he saw the pained, frightened expression on his face. Violet patted him on the arm, enjoined him to have fun, and made her way across the room to where her brother was talking with a couple of glowering toughs.

"Alright, old man?" Joseph put an arm around his shoulders. "What did she want?"

"She wants me to do some press," he replied, setting his jaw in the hope that it would erase the look of vague fright that he felt must still have been on it.

"What for?"

"Something about offering me a job. She says it's a disgrace that men like us come back to nothing."

Joseph laughed knowingly. "That sounds just like her. Violet never misses a chance to get her name in the papers. You'll do it?"

"I don't think she was giving me very much of a choice."

"No," he said. "Probably not. Don't worry, Doc, I sure it'll be painless and she'll be grateful for it. It's always best to keep her happy. Fancy a breath of fresh air?"

The blaring, grating drunken voices pressed into his ears and Edward was pleased of the chance for a little quiet. The rain was still falling as they wandered outside into the formal gardens: low box hedges, ornamental ponds, a gravel path that wound down, eventually, to the lakeshore. It was a little cold and neither had a topcoat, sheltered from the rain by two large umbrellas. Edward enjoyed the fresh air in his lungs. Behind them, golden light spilled out from the French doors, and noise as another record played from the gramophone. They reached the water's edge and, in the shelter of the boathouse, leant against the balustrade. The water beyond shifted and shimmied in the light of the moon, a gentle breeze ruffling across it.

Joseph took two cigars from his pocket and handed one to Edward.

"It's good to see you smiling."

Edward drew on the cigar and quickly felt even more light-headed. "Feels like I haven't had much to smile about recently."

"What do you mean?"

"Life could be better."

"Money?"

"Oh, I shouldn't complain," he said, "the job at the garage has been good, it's made a difference, but I could certainly do with more. You always can, can't you? And your Aunt is right—I can't help thinking the government has forgotten about us—either that or it doesn't care."

Joseph looked dead straight at him. "What if I said I had a way you could lay your hands on some money? Decent money? More than you could make with Ruby."

Edward's interest kindled. "Then I'd say I was keen to hear it."

Joseph regarded him. Edward wondered if it wasn't with something that looked like apprehension. "Do you have an open mind?"

Edward inhaled from the cigar. "As much as the next man."

"You wanted to know how I could afford clobber like this." He indicated his suit with a downwards brush of his fingers. "Nice cigars, a decent motor, a nice place in town."

"You said the horses—"

"What if it was something else?"

"Like what?"

"If I tell you, you mustn't rush to conclusions."

"What, Joseph?"

He paused. "Me and the lads have been turning over houses."

"Very bloody funny," he said, feigning disbelief, because he knew that was what Joseph would expect.

"I'm not messing about, Doc."

"Come on—"

"I'm serious. We've been at it since I got back."

Joseph stared at him: his eyes were flinty, sombre, emotionless.

"Jesus Christ, man," Edward exclaimed with as much indignation as he could manage.

"Don't be like that—all sanctimonious! No-one suffers. The places we go after, they're all high end. Classy. Not people like us, struggling to make ends meet, it's the big boys—bankers, lawyers, professionals—and they're all insured up to the eyeballs. We take what we want, they make their claim, the insurance company makes sure everything gets replaced. We don't threaten no-one, no-one loses out, no-one gets hurt."

"Are you mad?" he said, playing the part as realistically as he could.

Joseph fell for Edward's self-righteousness and pressed on, his conviction blending with anger. "What's the alternative? Say you're one of them poor beggars who finds a steady job. I pity them! Payments on the house, payments on the furniture, endowment policy, burial society. Burial society, Doc!—for fuck's sake—they're buried already." He laughed with sudden cold derision. "Fucking burial society. I've got mates, blokes I know from The Hill, they've never had a house of their own, never had furniture of their own. They've got families, nippers, they can't get credit, they get kicked out onto the street because they can't pay their rent—a few pennies a week and they can't even pay that. They've put everything in hock and now there's nothing else, what the hell are they supposed to do?"

"That's not the point, Joseph. It's stealing."

His tone hardened. "Fuck the law, Doc. Fuck it. We're entitled. We gave this country years in that bloody jungle, we got eaten by leeches and shot up by the Tojos, and what do we get when we come home? A band playing God Save the bloody King, a cheap whistle that don't even fit, a pat on the back and a quid. Thank you very much, boys, welcome home, now piss off. I ain't having that. No, sir, I'm bloody well not—that just ain't good enough. And if it means I have to spin a few drums to get what I reckon I deserve, that's what I'm going to do." He paused for a moment, the surge of annoyance subsiding. "I know you're struggling, Doc. It's obvious. I don't like to see it, and there's no need. And, to be honest, this ain't what you'd call philanthropy. I could use your help—for planning and such like. That brain of yours—it could be a real asset. The better your plan, the less the chance that you'll get your collar felt. What do you say?"

Edward assessed. "Who else is involved?"

Joseph nodded in the direction of the house. "The lads: Billy, Tommy and Jack."

Edward chewed a nail as he stared out at the lake, the undulation as the wind brushed waves across the water, rain lashing into it. "I don't know," he said, pretending to hesitate.

Joseph took his arm urgently. "Come on, Doc," he urged, "it's easy—you force the door, you take what you want, you hop into a motor and you're away. Hardly any risk if it's done right. And we're *entitled*."

"Alright, Joseph. Don't go on—I know." He needed money. Why not this way? The money was as good as if he had earned it. How long could Jimmy keep the restaurant running without his help? A month? Maybe two? No longer than that, surely. What would happen afterwards? Jimmy would have to find something in another kitchen, a job working under someone else, but the loss would cripple him. And, more to the point, what about his father? What would they do if they asked him to leave the sanatorium? How could they cope? It would be the end of him, Edward was quite sure of that. It wasn't what he had in mind but it could be a means to an end. It could be a start. A chance to bring himself closer to Joseph, to the family, and a way to identify and develop the real opportunities. The hesitation was all for Joseph's benefit. Of *course* he was interested.

They stood there quietly, listening to the rain falling onto the water. Beneath them, a tethered rowing boat jostled against the jetty, a steady hollow thump. Edward rolled the cigar end against the balustrade.

"I'm thinking of doing one next week—Thursday or Friday," Joseph said. "That gives us time to have a proper think about it. Sort out a plan."

"I'd want to look at it. Look at the place, look at the area, make some suggestions."

"That's what I want," he said enthusiastically. "Proper planning. That's why I asked you."

Edward stared into the night. He had started to think about how the job might be best carried out, how to minimise risk. "Alright," he said. "I'll have a look at it."

* * *

THE VOICES OF PARTYGOERS who were smoking under his window drifted up distinctly as if they had been in the room with him, and the insistent, cackling laugh of one of them made Edward writhe and twitch. He imagined them talking about him, and how he had not fooled them, how he was different, how he did not fit in with the rest of the guests.

What was he doing here? However was he going to fit in with people like this?

He struggled out of bed, knowing he was going to be sick, the room wobbling as he negotiated it. He knelt before the toilet and brought up his dinner, spitting acrid-tasting phlegm into the bowl, his head hot and woozy. He went back to his bed and fell instantly asleep.

18

CHIARA COSTELLO DID NOT SLEEP WELL THAT NIGHT. She could not settle: her head throbbed from the drink, her mouth was dry and sticky and her mind spun with the memories of the party. She had known that her Aunt would insist that there was an event to mark her twenty-first birthday, and she had been dreading it. She was not an ostentatious girl and did she crave the spotlight. Quite the reverse, she would have been much happier to mark the milestone with a quiet meal with her family and a trip to the theatre. Violet would never have allowed that. She was her niece's exact obverse. Everything was about image and appearance, and a birthday was all the excuse she needed to throw a lavish party. Chiara had protested when she learned how big the party was going to be but Violet had brushed her concerns aside. "Think of it as your coming out," she had said, patting her on the hand. "If they do it in Chelsea, darling, we're fucking well doing it here, too."

Image, status, appearance: they were all that mattered to her. That had been the way of it since the day her Aunt had assumed responsibility for Chiara and her sisters when their father had died. The girls had been bred as socialites, glittering little trophies used to proclaim the family's respectability. What a laugh! Violet obsessed about it. She subscribed to the Tatler and lived by the social diary written by "Jennifer", plotting the key events of the season and doing everything she could to have the girls included. Chiara had witnessed it twice before, with her sisters, and knew it was coming for her, too. The season ran from late spring through to autumn, and included Ascot, the Queen Charlotte Ball and the Dublin horse show. Most mothers put their daughters through the ordeal in the hope of landing an eligible husband. Violet didn't care about that. She toted the sisters as a means to ingratiate herself with high society.

Chiara thought about all of that until dawn broke. She gave up the pretence of sleep, pulled on a robe and went downstairs to find a glass of water. It was cold. Hargreaves always thriftily turned down the heating at night. She heard the sound of movement in the kitchen and tentatively pushed at the door. "Hello?"

Edward Fabian was at the sink, running himself a glass of water. He was wearing pyjamas and one of Joseph's old robes, the yellow material thick and a little worn, full of military frogs and tassels. "Oh—hello," she said. Her face broke into a smile. "Can't sleep?"

"My head—it's a little sore."

"Mine too," she laughed. Edward took a second glass, filled it and handed it to her. "Did you enjoy yourself?"

"Oh, yes. Very much."

"I'm pleased. Thank you for coming. It's lovely to see my family, and George and Violet's friends are very kind, of course, but it's nice to have people my own age."

"That's very kind, but I'm afraid I haven't been twenty-one for rather a long time."

"Nonsense."

"I'm afraid not."

He was standing in the light of the wide window above the sink. She looked him over: he did look rather the worse for wear, unshaven and with red-rimmed eyes, but he was tall and good-looking and he had looked rather dashing last night, even in his tired suit. The fact that he had obviously fallen upon hard times was quite romantic. She would have liked to have sat at the table with him and Joseph. They were the loudest and most raucous, and had obviously had the most fun.

"Do you like the house?"

"What I've seen of it is splendid."

"You haven't had the tour?"

"We arrived a little late for that."

"Would you like to see the rest? I could give you a quick look around, if you have time?"

"That would be lovely."

They started in the hall, with its long run of polished marble, scuffed near the skirting. Chiara led the way to a closed door and opened it, revealing a gloomy room that, once she pulled back the curtains that covered the window at the far end, was revealed as a modest library. The carpet was threadbare, disfigured by worn stretches that revealed the boards beneath. Ghostly pale markings revealed furniture that had once been there but had since been sold. Chiara had forgotten how tired and jaded the room looked and, for a moment, was a little embarrassed by it. Edward was gentlemanly enough not to comment; instead, he pulled aside the sheet that covered a shelf and took out a book. "Dickens," he said. "*Great Expectations*. One of my favourites. This is a lovely room, Chiara."

"It's seen better days," she said. "I remember, when I was a little girl, my father used to spend all of his time in here." She didn't mention that her father couldn't read, but that he just liked to know—and, more importantly, for other people to know—that he owned a room full of books. She closed the curtains again and led the way into the neighbouring room, accessed through an interconnecting door. It was an office, panelled in oak and with ornately carved plasterwork on the ceiling. A large oak desk was set in one corner but it was unused, covered in dust and a confusion of papers that hadn't been disturbed for months.

"The whole house has seen better days," she admitted. "There used to be staff here. We've still got Wilson, just about, and there's a woman who cooks for us and her husband keeps an eye on the gardens, as much as he can manage, but I can remember when we had half a dozen staff."

"What's happened so that you don't?"

"Money. I don't get involved in business but my aunt says that times are difficult. There's a lot of competition— more than there used to be."

Chiara didn't tarry, exiting into the hallway again and leading the way through a curtained arch to a flight of stairs that led down to the basement. She pointed out the fusty-smelling boot-room, a lavatory, the large kitchen with an Aga and rickety wooden dressers.

They returned to the ground floor and Chiara directed them to the vaulted staircase. She pointed out the half dozen portraits that were hung from the wall on the sub-landing.

"Who are they?" Edward asked.

"The owners of the house. The paintings were left behind when my grandfather bought it." That was a polite way of putting it. The Costellos had acquired the house in their usual aggressive fashion and there had been no opportunity for the seller to retrieve any of his furniture or other possessions. What they liked, they kept. The rest was sold or burnt. These paintings, which had appealed to her grandfather's sense of history, had been reprieved from the bonfire.

She pointed to the first, a portrait of a severe-looking cleric. "This is the Bishop of Worcester. The house was built for him in the fourteen-hundreds. This one, I think, is Edmund Lawrence, who leased the house from the manor. This one is Robert Fielding, who married Lawrence's daughter, and he left it to his eldest son, Charles, here.

From the Fieldings it passed to the Roberston Family in the late eighteenth-century. Industrialists. My grandfather bought it from the second Robertson to own it."

"This is him?"

"Yes, that's grandfather."

Edward pointed to the next one along. "Your father?"

"Yes."

"My goodness," Edward said. "Joseph looks like both of them."

That much was indisputable. She looked at her father's portrait and saw, quite clearly, the same thick black hair, cold eyes, the solid lines of the cheekbones and jaw, the same warm complexion. The resemblance was noticeable with their grandfather but it was clear and obvious with their father.

"And these two I recognise."

"Ah," Chiara said. "Yes." The last portrait of the collection was the most recent. George and Violet had been painted together in the library a few months after her father had died and her aunt had moved in. They were sat next to each other, dressed in their Sunday best, both of them presenting stern expressions that came dangerously close to pomposity. The artist was a bit of a hack, despite the price that he had charged, but it wasn't the lack of skill that was embarrassing. It was the presumption of the thing, the notion that, even after a couple of years, their picture should join the other owners of the house. The whole blessed thing was foolish from start to finish and Chiara hated it. She had forgotten it was there and now she was embarrassed to have drawn attention to it.

"Have you seen the gardens?" she said, eager for a chance to draw Edward away.

"Joseph and I took a stroll last night."

"But it was dark then. You should have a look now—they're lovely. Best part of the house if you ask me. Come on, I could do with the fresh air."

A door at the end of the hall opened onto a set of flying stone steps that led down to a terrace. They stopped at the boot room and took a pair of Wellingtons each, pulling them on over the top of their pyjamas. Chiara led them on, down the steps and onto the south lawn. It was trimmed, bordered with shrubbery and low flowers and studded with croquet hoops. Two large English elms, barely under control, stood at the edge of the grass. To the east, around the corner of the house, was the large gravelled space where the cars had been parked. Beyond that were a collection of outbuildings: a barn, the garage and the stable block.

"It's big."

"I know—there are another fifty acres, too. Most of the valley belongs to the house."

"Why is it called Halewell Close?"

"There's a spring in the fields at the back of the house. It's named after that."

They walked on, Chiara looping her arm through Edward's. They passed beneath the elms and onwards to a collection of kitchen gardens that were hemmed in by a low redbrick wall. A cinder path cut between neatly planted rows of vegetables: cauliflowers, potatoes, runner beans arrayed against a pine trellis.

"How long have you lived here?" he asked her.

"All my life—I was born here. My grandfather was still alive then."

"Joseph said he was involved with the racecourses."

"Is that what he said?" she chuckled. "I suppose that's one way to describe it." Edward looked as if he was going to ask her to elaborate, but she didn't permit him the chance. She had no idea what he knew about the family business, and that was not a conversation that she wanted to have. She pressed on quickly. "My aunt moved in a couple of years ago."

"And your uncle George?"

"He stays here a lot, but he doesn't live here. He has an apartment in London. He likes to be right in the middle of things."

"Well, it's a wonderful place. I've never been anywhere like it before."

"I know—we're very lucky." They walked on. "Do you live in London?"

"Yes," he said, a little awkwardly. "I rent a flat."

"What's it like?"

"Oh, nothing special. But I'm getting some money together for a place of my own. Something nice."

"Good for you. I'd love to live in London. We come into town a lot, of course, but it's not the same."

They reached the terrace again and made their way up the steps to the kitchen. Chiara closed the door and fastened the latch. "Oh, dear," she said, "I don't feel very well at all. I think I might go and lie down for another hour."

"Really? You wouldn't guess."

"You're very sweet, Edward."

"Thank you for the tour. I enjoyed it."

She reached across and gently squeezed his arm. "Joseph talks about you a lot, you know. It's very nice to finally get to see what all the fuss is about."

"It's nice to meet you, too."

She looked at him a little shyly. "Will you promise me something?"

"What?"

"I love my brother, but be careful. I wouldn't want you to get caught up in some of the things he does. I know what he's like—he's a rascal, like the rest of the family. I'd hate to see you get in a scrape with him."

Edward started a reply but didn't know what to say.

Chiara laid a hand on his arm and leaned closer. She kissed him gently on the cheek.

"I'll see you again, I hope," she said.

19

THE FIRST HOUSE THEY ROBBED WAS IN MAYFAIR. Rain had started falling at dusk, a gentle sprinkling that strengthened into an angry, drenching deluge. The cold had settled under Edward's skin and as he ran his fingers through his wet hair, a shiver danced across his shoulders. The house was in terrace of stuccoed four-storey houses, most two bays across, joined together in the classical style. Lights were on here and there, the turrets at the top dark against the moving sky. The houses had basements and attics and faced a small square, a private garden that had somehow managed to preserve its iron railings in the face of the war effort. Skeletal trees cast long shadows that swung to and fro in the wind.

They had only ever spoken about planning but Edward had known that he would come along, too. He wanted to. Accepting Joseph's offer had immediately brought him into his confidence. That was necessary, but he needed to bind them closer together, and that would not be possible if he stayed away, leaving him to put the plan into action. It was, he knew, like the army. A shared adventure would be a powerful tonic for their friendship. War stories were more evocative when both parties had experienced them.

Joseph looked up and down the street and, satisfied that they were unobserved, mounted the single step from the pavement and stepped beneath the portico. Edward followed him. He was fizzing with adrenaline, his senses amplified and sensitive to everything. The front door was solid and substantial and he didn't have the first idea how they might open it. Joseph put his hand over the bell for a moment, pretending to ring it, and listened hard. When he was satisfied that all was silent inside, he descended the flight of steps that led down to the basement and the lower entrance. Edward felt as if he had lost the ability to make his own decisions and dumbly followed. The narrow space at the bottom comprised a window and door on one side and a wall beneath the row of railings on the other. His foot crunched against a stray piece of coal and he froze, his heart in his mouth, for what seemed like an age. Joseph cocked his head quizzically, as if he had heard something else, and then pressed them both back against the wall beneath the railings. The sound of slow, deliberate footsteps approached from the street. They drew closer, so close that Edward felt as if his heart were about to stop, and then a circle of torchlight played over the window before them. It was a policeman, it had to be, and he would surely see their reflection in the glass. But the footsteps resumed, absorbed into the storm with the same deliberate rhythm.

"Bloody hell," Edward exhaled.

Joseph shushed him with a stern glare and a finger to his lips.

He took a small six-inch jemmy from his inside pocket and inserted it into the jamb, just below the handle. He gave the jemmy a sharp pull and the lock tore through the wood. He gently pushed the door open and disappeared inside. Edward followed. They were in a kitchen. Joseph took out a small electric torch and shone it around, illuminating a large range, cupboards, a rack of pots and pans. Every creak from settling floorboards or tick from cooling pipes was someone waiting for them around the corner. The steady cadence of the clock on the wall oscillated with Edward's breath and he thought of the jungle, and night-time O.P.s, creeping through the darkness with the morbid certainty that Jap was lying in wait, endlessly patient, a rifle aimed at his heart. He fumbled for his handkerchief and wiped the rain and sweat from his eyes.

Joseph paused to acclimatise himself to the house and then led the way onwards. They passed through the kitchen, along a narrow passageway and up a set of back stairs until they re-emerged in the hallway, the door to the street at one end and, opposite, a wide staircase that was ghostly in the darkness. Joseph flitted silently to a large door and put his ear to it. He turned the handle and the mechanism clicked, the silence of the house seeming to shatter like a bowl of black glass. He opened the door—lifting upwards to take the weight off the hinge—and went through, into what was evidently the sitting-room. Inside was all Regency, with carefully draped curtains and Madame Recamier sofas. They moved through into the drawing-room. As they slipped through the darkened spaces, Edward had the sense of the shadows closing protectively around them and he started to relax a little.

Joseph quietly turned a gilded door knob and led the way into the library. He collected two silver candelabra from the mantelpiece and appraised them, feeling their weight. A nod indicated he was satisfied, and he handed them over. He took a dust sheet from a table and gave it to Edward, too. "Wrap them up," he whispered, his lips brushing his ear, "and stay here."

"Where are you going?"

"Upstairs. I'll have a look around. If I'm not back in ten minutes, get out. Use the front door—you saw where it is?"

"Yes—back there."

Joseph nodded. He paused at the open doorway, listening, before stepping out and fading into the shadows. There was the very slightest creak as, Edward fancied, he ascended a stair, but then there was nothing. The silence was so taut that the slightest creak seemed to stretch it to breaking point.

It was pitch black without Joseph's torch.

Somewhere above, he heard the unmistakeable creak of a floorboard.

Edward felt exposed and vulnerable and yet thrillingly alive. It was a strange combination: fright and a tremendous sense of exhilaration. Here was the adventure that his life had been missing. Cooking dinners and selling cars were for the birds. Edward wanted his life to feel like this.

The door opened again. There was a moment between the handle twisting and the realisation that it was Joseph returning when his heart felt as cold and still as a lump of ice. He was carrying a suitcase. He opened it: jewellery, silver cutlery and plate, a gold watch, some ready money.

"Not bad?" he grinned.

"The suitcase, too?"

"It's useful. It's a prop—you're less likely to get stopped with one."

Joseph unbolted the front door, closing it quietly once they were outside. The rain was still lashing the street and a peel of thunder rattled the glass in the windows. Edward loosened the umbrella and unfurled it above them. Joseph pressed in tight. "Come on," he said with a feral grin, and set off across the pavement. They hurried away.

20

EDWARD ENDURED A NIGHT OF INSOMNIA and, when he did manage to sleep, panicked dreams. He stayed in the bedsitter, trying to come up with a way to avoid the interview that Violet had arranged. He couldn't help it. He was gripped tightly by fear: the fear of having agreed to something that would be irretrievable, the fear of discovery, of capture, of punishment. He gave up the pretence of sleep and stood at the window with the lights turned off, staring across the chimneystacks and rooftops. It was very cold and he had burnt up all the gas. The tap of the fire was up, the broken asbestos elements grey and cold, the air like hot sour cream. Dark clouds swept across the moon and fat drops began to fall. They stroked against the pane to begin with but eventually they strengthened, drumming a relentless beat against the glass. Edward listened to them fall, unable to return to sleep.

* * *

HENRY DRAKE WAS ALREADY WAITING in the Moka coffee bar in Frith Street. Edward paused in the doorway and wondered, yet again, whether there was some neat way that he could extricate himself from this whole sorry mess. But there was not. He had rolled his predicament around and around in his mind but had come up with nothing. He could just flat-out refuse but doing that would have been tantamount to shouting from the rooftops that he had something to hide. He could have cited a desire for privacy, or a tendency towards modesty, but either would have marked him as the kind of shrinking violet that he instinctively knew would repulse the ostentatious Violet. And, more than everything, she would see his saying no as thumbing his nose at her charity. There was nothing else for it: he would just have to do his best to minimise the damage that the interview might do and get on with it. He would have to be smart and watch his step.

The bar was busy, the proprietor—an amiable Italian named Pino Reservato—passing to and from his customers. A pine bar held the till and a neat pile of mugs and saucers, and behind it steamed one of Gaggia's clattering machines. A curving, undulating countertop stretched along the side of the room with cushioned stools set into the floor at regular intervals along it. A mural depicting various styles of ship was fixed to the wall, this theme then repeated on the counter-top. A wire cage fashioned into letters from the Chinese alphabet contained two miserable looking macaws. It was busy: office girls chatted happily with their escorts drinking Grenadilla Juice from the half-shells of coconuts; shoppers and tourists rested and took refreshment; businessmen enjoyed a quick meal, open sandwiches in the Swedish style contained continental savouries. The hubbub was convivial but it did nothing to improve Edward's pensive mood as he made his way to the table.

Drake looked up. "Mr. Fabian?"

"Hello, Mr. Drake."

"Call me Henry, please. Pleasure to meet you—a real pleasure."

"Likewise, I'm sure."

"I've heard a lot about you. What will you have?"

"Just a large black, please."

Drake went to the bar and placed the order. Edward looked him over: he was a plain-looking man in his early middle age, a little shabby around the edges. He wore a stained mackintosh that was fastened with a belt, a battered old trilby and a pair of good-quality trousers that Edward saw had frayed around the cuffs. Nice things that had been allowed to go to seed, not dissimilar to his own things. What did that say about him? Edward had dug into the man's history in preparation for their encounter, spending several hours reading his press cuttings in the National Library. Drake had been a big noise, once, Fleet Street's rising star, but a story he had written had been discredited and he had been cast out. It had been a catastrophic error on his part: Drake had been caught lying, and if Edward had been in a better mood he might have appreciated the irony in that. He had made up ground again with a scoop on the psychopath they called the Black Out Ripper who had terrorised the West End during The Blitz but he was still running, still chasing past glories that, by the looks of things, he would never fully recapture.

Drake brought the coffees to the table and sat down. "As I say, good to meet you. I'm pleased we've been able to sort it out."

"I've read some of your articles, Mr. Drake."

"It's Henry. And how did you find them?"

"Very colourful. The latest one, the 'girl who leads a life of shame'—that one was particularly interesting."

"Just an innocent mill-girl from Sheffield,' Drake intoned as if Edward was about to take dictation for him. "I'm writing her confession in five instalments, a warning to other impressionable young lasses like her. As a matter of fact, I believe I left her being chased down a back street by a seedy stage-door Johnny in a cloth cap. Exciting, I thought. A nice little cliff-hanger, keep them interested."

"What happened to her?"

"She'll be just fine. The Sunday *Graphic* is a family paper, after all."

"You're making the whole thing up?"

"Of course I am. That's the sell—it's life, but hotter, stronger and neater.'

"What a peculiar way to earn a living," Edward said. "Telling untruths. Didn't they cause you problems before?"

"You have been doing your research, Edward. And yes, of course, you're right, but you have to understand that newspapers are all, more or less, in two distinct kinds of business. There's the proper news side. You know: meat will be dearer tomorrow, tax likely to rise, bond-holders beware. That sort of thing's supposed to be true—and you might say I learnt that lesson the hard way, although we could have a long discussion about how half of what they said about me was untrue. The other side of the business is the one the money's in."

"And that's what you're in now?"

"That's right. It's called human interest, although you might as well just call it showbusiness. Non-stop vaudeville, changed every day, and always leave them laughing. If you can write revue sketches and begging letters and you can clean up dirty jokes, you've got what it takes to have a decent little career. That's what people want to read, so that's what I write. It's of no importance that the mill-girl doesn't exist, except that it saves me the trouble of convincing some deluded little thing from up north that the events that have to happen to her really did happen. It also saves my employer some money."

"Do you tell your readers it's all made up?"

Drake sugared his coffee heavily. "Of course not. What they don't know can't hurt them. Or me, come to think about it."

"Whoever said dishonesty didn't pay?"

"I don't know. But it certainly wasn't me." He sipped his coffee. Edward watched his hands carefully, the half-moons of grime caught beneath his fingernails. The man was a shyster, he thought. A confidence trickster. He recognised the signs. It took one to know one, he thought wryly. Drake replaced the cup in its saucer. "Your story, on the other hand, is all true and—from what Violet tells me——so good that it practically writes itself. War hero comes home, cold-shouldered by society, lives in cold garret, barely makes enough to feed himself, *et cetera et cetera*. Tell me some more."

Edward took a breath and told the story. He had run through it a dozen times last night, removing the flourishes and his worst excesses, keeping it neat and simple. He avoided hyperbole and exaggeration, downplaying his own role in the narrative and sticking as close to the regimental history as he could, ensuring that his facts were verifiable and legitimate. Drake took shorthand notes, Edward watching biliously as his charcoal pencil scraped quickly across his notepad, each stroke another step closer to revealing his perfidy. He asked a handful of questions, referring back to his notes and seeking amplification, trying to draw him into more lurid confessions, but Edward stoically resisted. If he neutered the tale then, perhaps, there would be nothing left to tell.

Eventually Edward could see that Drake had realised that he was not going to get the juicy story he had hoped to find. He quickly became bored. After all, what did he have? A bland and inoffensive piece about a soldier coming home from war and gratefully accepting the charity of a local family. If it escaped the editor's spike it would languish deep inside the newspaper, hidden away, soon to be forgotten. Edward noticed that his shoulders were tight and stiff and so he settled back in the seat, loosening his posture. He relaxed and congratulated himself. What was he so worried about? He had done well, handling a difficult situation with confidence and aplomb. He sank into the cushions and pretended to busy himself by spooning another sugar into what was left of his coffee.

"Ah. Here he is. About time," Drake said to the man who had just struggled into the coffee shop with a large camera and a bag of accessories. "This is Trevor. He'll be doing the pictures. I thought here might be nice—war hero not too grand for coffee-shop, that kind of angle. What do you say?"

"Pictures?"

"Of course. We need pictures."

"No-one said anything to me about pictures."

"It's essential, Edward. Put a face to the story. Violet insisted we do it properly. You're not one of these chaps who doesn't like his picture taken are you? Be a shame not to, with those matinee idol looks of yours—you'll have them all going weak at the knees. Fan mail, I shouldn't wonder."

Edward balled his fists so hard that his nails cut into the fleshy part of his palms. He couldn't say no; it would look like he had something to hide. He gritted his teeth as the photographer set up a tripod and slotted his Rolleiflex atop it, inserting the film and winding it through. He tried to persuade them to let him wear his hat, and then tried to angle his head away, but the photographer was persistent and would not take the pictures until he was satisfied with the shot. Edward smiled, thinly and without warmth, as the shutter snapped open and closed.

It sounded final. It sounded like a door slamming shut.

21

IT WAS A PRIVATE JOKE between the chaps that Billy Stavropoulos was particularly well balanced on account having a chip on both shoulders. The subject of his difficult upbringing was one he returned to frequently, a setting against which his subsequent success as a criminal was some sort of underdog's triumphant battle against the odds. He referred to himself as being from 'the gutter', making the assertion so often that it became a sort of catchphrase. The gutter to which he referred was Saffron Hill, yet that was not the beginning of his story. The first five years of his life were spent in Leicester, in one of the sprawling developments built on the city's south side in the 1920s to accommodate the city's expanding work force. His mother, Demetria, found work as a machinist in the city's hosiery factories. His father, Khristos, was a cobbler. The city avoided the worst depredations of the depression and enjoyed growth. Billy's early years were happy, by all accounts. They might not have been rich but they had enough money to get by, and the Stavropoulos family 'villa' was close enough to the factories that Demetria was able to come home to cook lunch for Billy and his two brothers. It was a comfortable first few years: adequate, mediocre, safe.

A fondness for the bottle made Khristos Stavropoulos an unreliable employee and, when it eventually cost him his job, he moved the family to London. They found a house on Saffron Hill and, compared to the relative comfort of life in Leicester, things were difficult. Khristos' alcoholism cost him two other jobs and, as the depression exerted its influence on the city's factories, he found himself unable to find work. He fell in with the Costello brothers and, under their aegis, was persuaded to take to burglary to provide an income for his family. A string of breakings provided a glimmer of hope that he might have finally found something he was able to stick at but, eventually, he failed even at that. He usually got lit-up before a job and one time, his reactions dulled by drink, he fell from a first-floor window, broke his leg and was arrested. He was charged and tried, the judge rubbing salt into the wound by describing him as a 'particularly inept criminal' before gaoling him for a year.

Khristos resorted to the bottle for succour and died a bitter and broken man when Billy was eight years old. Without the income he had provided the family could no longer afford to pay even the meagre rent on their house. Despite the offer of a lighter sentence, Khristos had not named the Costello boys as his accomplices. His loyalty did not go unrewarded and his widow and her three boys were moved into a house the family owned. They had two rooms for the four of them: a front room and a bedroom. The front room looked onto the narrow street below and had a bed that was shared by Billy and his mother. The family's furniture comprised of two beds and a rickety wooden sideboard. The only evidence of Khristos were the mementoes that he had kept from six years as an infantryman in the Great War: a helmet that he had pilfered from the body of a dead German and a beer stein, in which Demetria occasionally kept the flowers that her boys uprooted from the local parks. It was a crushingly depressing existence. The house in which Billy spent the next ten years of his life was low-ceilinged and fetid, thin walls covered with flock wallpaper that stank of fried food and damp.

Demetria became a hoister, raiding stores in the West End and selling her spoils in Clerkenwell's pubs. When times were hard she offered wall-jobs to the local drunks for the pennies in their pockets. Memories of her comfortable life in Leicester must have seemed like cruel taunts and she became bitter and resentful. The bottle found her, too, eventually, and she took her frustrations out on her children. It did not matter. Billy was dedicated to her, and the chaps occasionally spoke of the time they saw a man make a joke about her brassing. He had flown into such a rage they had to restrain him for fear that he would do murder.

* * *

BILLY WRAPPED HIS FIST IN HIS COAT and punched hard through the panel above the door handle. The glass smashed, the fragments shattering as they fell to the floor. He paused for a moment, and heard nothing to suggest that they had been detected. He thrust his arm through the gaping pane and unlocked the door. He went inside, with Jack McVitie close behind. The house was empty, just as Joseph had said it would be. He had been tipped off by a chap from the pub who was seeing one of the maids. The family were off abroad somewhere and the place was vulnerable. Pity for them, Billy thought. The man of the house was a successful businessman, something about the motor trade. He was supposed to be rich and that looked about right, Billy thought, judging by the state of the place.

He flicked on his torch and continued the conversation that the two men had begun as they made their way to the house. "He's lost the plot."

Jack closed the door behind him. "So you keep saying."

"It's true, though, ain't it? Fabian's bad news. Bloody bad news. I mean, ask yourself—what's he doing with us? We don't need him."

"If you say so."

"It was fine, the four of us, before. Me, you, Joseph and Tommy. Does Joseph think we're going to do places five-handed? No thanks. Might as well ring Old Bill up before and tell them what we're up to."

They left the kitchen and climbed the stairs to the first floor. The hallway was wide, wood-panelled and laid with an expensive parquet floor. Billy flipped through the mail that had been stacked on a table next to a telephone.

"What is it with him and Joe?" he said. "Has he said anything to you?"

Jack shrugged. "Nothing you don't already know. Army pals."

"Well, I don't know about that. They only met right at the end, didn't they?"

They went up to the second floor and tried doors until they found the master bedroom. They went inside. It was a large room, with a walk-in wardrobe and a bathroom leading off it. They knew what they were looking for. Billy went to the tallboy and started to turn out the drawers, strewing the clothes on the floor.

"War hero—can you believe that?"

Jack opened a wardrobe and set about emptying it. He shrugged.

"It don't sound that likely, though, does it?—given the evidence, what the man's like. He don't look the type for that kind of thing."

"Who knows?"

"He must have something on him. No other reason why Joe would've let him get into this with us."

"What do you mean?"

"You know—he's got the black on him."

Jack scoffed, "Don't talk rot."

"What, then?"

Jack gave a long, exasperated sigh. "I don't know."

"The last thing we need at the moment is a passenger. From what I've been told things are going to get spicy soon."

"You mean Jack Spot?"

Billy nodded. "You heard he's been telling people that they need to be with him rather than with us?"

"I heard he had a word with a couple of pubs on Shaftesbury Avenue."

"More than that. He's been threatening blokes in Soho, too. He's not someone Violet and George will be able to ignore like he's not there. He's a bloody psychopath, him and his bloody gypsies too. I heard they don't think he's anything to worry about."

They worked in silence for a few minutes until Jack tipped out the cupboards of a chest of drawers. "Here," he said, "found it." He held up a presentation box and, inside, a diamond necklace. There was other jewellery in the drawer—rings and bracelets and necklaces—and Jack tipped them all into his pockets.

The two of them finished in the bedroom and went back downstairs.

"No," Billy said, returning to the same theme, "that Fabian's no good, no good at all."

He had been picking at the same theme for most of the night, and Jack was growing weary of it. "Aye," he said, hoping Billy might let the matter rest.

They exited through the main door and, closing their mackintoshes around them, they walked quickly away from the house.

"He'll get us all nicked, you mark my words."

"Look on the bright side," Jack said, hoping to forestall another tirade. He tapped his pockets so that the diamonds clinked. "Fancy a drink?"

They walked the short distance to the main road. In five minutes they had hailed a taxi and were heading towards Soho.

22

EDWARD AND JOSEPH arranged to meet three days after the burglary at Piccadilly Circus. Joseph was waiting for him beneath the statue of Eros.

They embraced warmly.

"What's the plan?" Edward asked. "We're going for a drink?"

"That's what I was thinking," he said.

"Where? Soho?"

"Actually, I was thinking the Ritz."

Edward looked down at his tatty second-hand suit and scuffed shoes and sighed. "Don't be daft—they're not going to let me in looking like this."

"I was thinking we'd make a stop and get you some new clothes first."

Edward did not complain. They set off, Joseph leading the way. They had to walk past West End Central police station in order to get to the Savile Row tailor's that Joseph had in mind. The station had taken a direct hit during the Blitz and it had only been open again for a few months. A pair of detectives slouched at the bottom of the steps with cigarettes in their mouths and uniformed men emerged for the start of their beats. Edward walked on, eyes down, resolutely aimed towards the pavement.

Joseph chuckled at his discomfort. "Stop being so bloody flighty," he said once they had put the station behind them. "It's been a week."

It wasn't *that* that Edward was worried about. He knew that they were in the clear there but he would allow Joseph to think that he was anxious. He would expect that of him, surely. "Policemen always make me feel guilty," he explained. "But it's not normally with reason."

"We're not getting caught. Nothing's happened, has it?"

"No—not yet. But—"

"So we're fine. Old Bill don't know nothing. Relax, Doc—we're in the clear." They walked on a few steps and Joseph reached into his jacket pocket. "Look, it's natural to be nervous. I'd be lying if I said it didn't put me on edge, too. But you know it was worth it, don't you? Here—this is for you."

He reached across and handed Edward a thick, brown envelope.

He peeled back the seal of the envelope. A thick wedge of banknotes was inside. "How much?"

"Three hundred." Joseph said it with a wide grin. "Not a bad little tickle for your first job, eh?"

Edward could hardly believe it. "You said a hundred, maximum."

"It was worth more than I thought."

Edward put the envelope into his pocket. "Capital," he said.

"Not bad for half an hour's work," Joseph said.

Joseph had arranged a series of appointments for them: a tailor, a shirt-maker, a cobbler. The first appointment was at Dege & Skinner. They were greeted deferentially by a tailor and showed inside. The shop was as quiet as a library and redolent with the dry smell of fresh fabric. There was barely enough space on the wall behind the counter to display the Royal Warrants. George V had been a regular customer, the Duke of Windsor had continued the family tradition and Clark Gable and Tyrone Power represented Hollywood's royalty. It was impossible not to be impressed.

"Good morning, gentlemen. What can we do for you today?"

Joseph said he was going to buy three suits: one off the rack, to wear immediately, and another two that were to be made bespoke. The cost would be around forty pounds, the tailor said, before asking Edward whether he would be ordering the same. He gaped: forty pounds? The most expensive item of clothing he had ever bought was a suit for his interview at Trinity, and that had cost a fiver from Selfridges in the Christmas sales.

"I don't think so," he said.

Joseph intervened, "No, he'll have the same."

"Joseph…"

"You can't wear that thing for another minute more. It's a monstrosity." The tailor must have noticed his awful suit too but he was too discrete to mention it. Joseph tapped his breast pocket knowingly. "We can afford it. Treat yourself."

"Sir?" the tailor prompted.

"Go on, then," Edward said, unable to prevent the self-indulgent grin that broke out across his face. "The same, please."

Another tailor appeared from the back and the two fussed around them, taking measurements and flicking through a book of fabric samples. When they were finished, he chose a suit from the rail, added a new shirt, cufflinks and a pair of shoes, and took it all into the changing room to try on. He shut the door and shrugged off his old jacket, catching sight of the top of the envelope in his inside pocket. He tried on the suit. It was a little long in the leg but adjusting it would be simple. He stepped outside and turned before the big, floor-length mirror. Joseph was waiting for him. They stood alongside and regarded themselves in the glass. His suit was single-breasted, cut from a heavy grey flannel with a waistcoat in a similar colour. It was a traditional English cut, with that combination of style, cutting and craftsmanship that flattered the figure and communicated substance. The shirt was brilliant white and thickly-starched. The brogues were polished to such a high sheen that they reflected the face of the tailor as he knelt down to adjust the fall of the trouser. Joseph took a ninepenny handkerchief, folded it into a neat square and slid it into Edward's breast pocket. He took a grey trilby from a nearby shelf, placed it on Edward's head and adjusted it carefully.

"There," he said. "You look like a new man. What do you reckon? Better?"

Edward turned side-on and regarded himself. He pulled the brim of the trilby down a touch. He amused himself in the mirror. He had always had a malleable face, one that he seemed able to mould to fit the impression that he was trying to portray. He fancied that he looked like an American gangster, the sort of role James Cagney would play in the pictures. He imagined himself with the suitcase full of money and a pistol in his pocket, not long removed from a heist. He liked the way the clothes and the hat made him look.

He shot his cuffs and flexed his shoulders. "Much better," he said.

They took a taxi to the Ritz. Edward had been once or twice, before the war, and had always loved it. He knew all the stories from the newspapers he had read as a little boy: how the Prince of Wales and Mrs. Simpson had dined in The Palm Court, how Charlie Chaplin had needed a retinue of forty policemen to negotiate a passage past his screaming fans, how Anna Pavlova had danced there and how the Aga Khan had permanent suites. He was relieved to see that little had changed. The doormen, dressed in their spotless uniform and with box hats on their heads, ushered them inside with extravagant good manners. "Good afternoon, Mr. Costello," one of them said with a deep tip of his head. Joseph smiled broadly at the recognition and Edward was impressed. They passed through into the Ritz Bar, the gloriously art deco room whose beautiful furnishings and glamorous patrons reminded Edward of an entirely different kind of life. The Merano chandelier gave off a soft, golden light that burnished the tortoiseshell walls and picked out the details in the glistening emblems etched into the Lalique glass. The bar was long and narrow, with the tables arranged as if in the dining car of a particularly opulent train; it had always put Edward in mind of the Orient Express. Joseph took the menu from the bar and handed it to Edward. He scanned it, his eyes widening as he remembered the stratospheric prices that were sensible only if money was of no consequence.

"I don't know about you," Joseph said, "but I'm pushing the boat out."

Edward reminded himself: money was not of so great a consequence today as it had been yesterday and he could afford to be extravagant.

Joseph ordered a Negroni. Edward had ordered one himself, many years earlier, although his had been authentically Italian, ordered in the same Caffé Cassoni bar where Count Camillo Negroni had asked his Florentine bartender to strengthen his Americano by adding gin rather than the normal soda water. The memory promised to lead to others that he preferred to recall alone and so he did not mention it and, instead, ordered quickly for himself. He selected the Cesar Ritz, a cocktail made with Courvoisier l'Esprit, Ruinart Blanc de Blancs champagne and Angostura bitters. The bill for both drinks was two pounds and they were delivered to their table by a tail-coated waiter who fawned over them as if they were royalty or Hollywood stars.

"This is the life," Joseph said, reclining into the generously padded chair. "Ain't it?"

"I'll say it is," Edward agreed.

He looked around at the other patrons. Money was everywhere, almost tangible. The furnishings, the clothes, the exquisite drinks and food, the tiny details that were evocative of the very best quality, he closed his eyes for a moment and allowed himself to sink into it all.

"Are you alright, Doc?"

"Never better," Edward said with a smile. This was what he wanted, he thought. All of it and everything. He wanted it more than anything else in the world.

23

THEY HAD PARKED THE CAR a hundred yards away from the entrance to the depot. It was a stolen drag, taken from Islington earlier that day. Jack McVitie had slipped a flexible strip inside the space between the window and the frame until he found the lock and popped it open. Easy. He had picked up Billy Stavropoulos earlier and now both of them sat waiting, their hands gloved and with their balaclavas in their laps. They were in Dalston, parked beneath a gaslight. Billy was staring at his Pools coupon, referring to the newspaper he had spread across the dashboard, "competitors' hints," his forehead creased with concentration and indecision. What a mug, McVitie thought. Those things never pay out.

"Look at this place," Jack said, glancing out at the desolate streets. "I weren't born too far away from here. What a bloody awful hole. I couldn't wait to get out."

Billy put the coupon down. "It's no bloody good. I can't concentrate."

"Still thinking about him?"

"He's a liability."

Jack chuckled hopelessly.

"Ain't funny. Why's Joseph bringing him out for this?"

"You can't deny he's been better."

"You keep defending him!"

"I'm not, I'm being straight—he's been better."

"Ah, bollocks."

"He has. Admit it, Billy, it won't kill you. I don't know why you've got such a thing for him. He's hardly a bad chap."

Billy grunted. He wasn't going to admit any such thing. He took off his gloves, took a cigarette from the packet on the dash and lit it.

"I reckon we were a bit harsh on him," Jack said. "He's alright. Can't argue he's a bit square. Quiet type. But he's not a bad bloke."

Billy screwed up his nose. "He's a stuck-up bastard."

Jack laughed. "That's a bit unfair."

"He is. That *attitude*."

"He's just quiet—what you'd call a thinker. You can tell."

"He's a thinker, alright—thinks he's better than the rest of us. His head's right up his arse. You know he was at university before the war? *University*." Billy mouthed the word as if it were something distasteful. "Makes sense, though, don't it? He's got that way about him, the way he looks at people like us like we're something to be scraped off the bottom of his shoe. All high and mighty and all that."

Edward was the first bloke Billy had ever met who'd been to University. Like Jack and Joseph, he'd only stayed in school as long as he absolutely had to and, even then, he'd bunked off more than he was there. Life wasn't all about books and blackboards and exams, least not his kind of life. He'd given himself a proper education, taught himself the things he needed to know: how to dip a wallet from a man's pocket without him knowing; how to hide a razorblade in the peak of your cap, how to use it to slash at a man's face; how to smash a window without making a sound; the best way to hoist gear from a shop.

Billy slipped his gloves back on and squeezed the wheel. Fabian. The cowson had been involved in the plotting and planning of this particular job ever since Joseph had suggested it: checking out the route, the best time to go through with it, the fastest way back to the lock-up, mapping it out, working out the traffic lights and the bottlenecks where the traffic might get jammed. Two days solid of sorting everything out. Jack was right: Edward was one of life's planners. Billy was more like Joseph, more of an impetuous type of fellow, the get-in-and-get-out type, more doing, less thinking. He knew his strengths, he knew his weaknesses and he was happy with where the line was drawn.

Jack wound down the window and flicked the dog-end into the breeze. "Can't say I mind him being along. You go on a job with a thinker, you're less likely to get pinched—simple as."

"Don't mean I got to like him."

"No, it doesn't," Jack sighed. There was no point in arguing. The headlights of a van gleamed off the windscreen. "Speak of the devil."

The van parked up the road ahead of them. It flashed its headlights.

"Alright, then? Let's get started."

The two of them went around to the boot of the car and took out a long pair of boltcutters and two crowbars. They pulled their balaclavas down over their faces and jogged briskly to the depot. It was a small warehouse, set back from the road by a narrow yard, access prevented by a solid pair of padlocked iron gates. Joseph, similarly attired, was waiting for them there. Edward was in the van. There was no need to speak; they had been over the plan and they knew what they each had to do. Jack raised the bolt cutters so that the jaws clasped around the padlock and squeezed the arms together. The lock cleaved in two, dropping to the ground, and Joseph pushed the gates apart as Jack hurried through. The depot had a shuttered door for loading and unloading goods, secured with two padlocks that were fixed to clasps on the ground. They took the crowbars and jammed them into the locks, bracing against them until they popped open.

Edward started the van and reversed it into the yard so that the rear was lined up with the shuttered doors that were used for loading and unloading goods.

"Quickly," Joseph called.

Jack ran to the doors and took a key from his pocket. They had been given the original by the member of staff at the depot who had proposed the job—in return for a cut of the profits—and had copied it overnight. Jack unlocked the shutters and heaved them up. The depot was storing fur coats and mink stoles. The place was practically full of them. They were brand new, still wrapped in their plastic dust sheaths.

"Oi!" The shout came from behind them. "What's your game?"

A security guard was shining a torch at Jack. He hadn't seen the others, and so he didn't notice as Billy stalked behind him and swung his crowbar across the back of his knees. His legs buckled beneath him and he fell backwards.

"Alright, alright," he said, raising his hands in surrender.

Joseph knelt next to him and put a hand on his shoulder. "We're helping ourselves to the gear here. Play nice and we'll be on our way. Don't be silly and you'll be fine. There's no need for you to get hurt."

"I won't do nothing," the man said.

"That's good. We'll be as quick as we can."

They hurried into action, taking the coats from their rails and tossing them into the back of the van. Twenty, then twenty-five, then thirty. Eventually, there was no more space. Billy shut the doors.

"Well done," Joseph said to the guard. "That's that—we're finished."

The man looked unhappy.

"What is it?"

"You can't leave me like this."

"What? You ain't hardly even been touched."

"That's what I mean—you have to give me a black eye."

"You *want* a black eye?"

"It can't look like I co-operated with you, can I? The boss needs to think I put up a scrap. He'll think I was in on it and he'll give me my cards. I've got a wife and a nipper to feed. I need this job."

"You want me to hit you?"

"Just—you know, just a black eye."

"If you say so." Joseph struck him, quite hard, a left hook that dropped him to his knees. Billy whooped, laughing, and before any of them could stop him he swung a kick into the man's gut. He fell onto his side, gasping, and Billy kicked him twice more. "How's that?" he said, "good enough for you?"

"Whoah!" Jack laughed, surprised.

Billy kicked him again.

"Billy!"

"No names!" Edward shouted.

"He said he wanted it to be convincing—it's what he wanted. I'm doing him a favour." Billy swung a kick into the man's head and a plume of blood spewed out and splattered across the ground.

"Enough!" Edward said, grabbing him and pulling him back out of range. "Jesus, man—you'll bloody well kill him."

He squared up to Edward. "Get your filthy hands off me."

"Back off," Joseph called sternly.

Billy shrugged Edward aside and laughed.

Edward knelt down by the guard's side. He was bleeding from the mouth but the blood was from a badly cut lip, and not internal. He was conscious, but woozy.

"Is he alright?" Joseph asked.

"He'll live." Edward propped him against the side of the building and followed the others back to the road. "You're a bloody fool!" he called after Billy.

"Ah, piss off." He got into the car and Jack slipped in next to him.

"That was a bit over the top," Jack said.

"Don't you start."

"I'm not having a go—I'm just saying."

"See what I mean, though? About Fabian? The bloke ain't got no balls."

Jack started the engine. He didn't reply.

"Let's get off," Billy said. "I feel like a drink."

24

EDWARD WATCHED AS JACK MCVITIE adjusted his trilby. He was trying not to show his excitement as the dealer dealt another queen on the river. McVitie had played his hand slowly, carefully making sure Billy and Edward followed him to the last round of betting. They had, and he pushed half of his chips into the middle of the table.

Edward paused, making an assessment of the cards and his chances.

"So—what are you doing, Doc?" Jack said. "In or out?"

"I'm in." He pushed the rest of his chips over the line.

McVitie turned to Billy. "You in or out?"

Billy made a show of deliberation. "You're bluffing."

"You best call me then, hadn't you?"

"Fine. I'm all in."

Jack laughed. He pushed the rest of his stack over the line, too.

They were flush, and they were enjoying themselves. This was a Costello place, several large rooms above a shoe-shop. Part-spieler, part-brothel. It was one of the more established joints in Soho. The dividing wall between two rooms had been knocked down and a baccarat table installed. A roulette wheel was next to that, together with a couple of tables for poker and chemin de feu. A mirrored bar had been fitted at one end of the room, with black market spirits hanging upside-down in optics. The bar was crescent-shaped, lit from beneath, with coloured Venetian glasses stacked on glass shelves. A chandelier hung from the ceiling and the windows were covered with thick, expensive Moroccan drapes. The clientele entered through a side-door on the street where they were met by a suited doorman and ushered up a bare staircase into the room. A door at the other end of the room led to three bedrooms. They were reasonably furnished. That was all that was required; after all, the guests did not stay long.

Smoke hung heavy in the gloom. There were ten around the table: Jack, Billy, Tommy, Joseph and Edward, four local businessmen and Lennie Masters, the perpetually-glowering thug that Edward had met the first time he had visited Halewell Close for Chiara's birthday.

Edward settled back into his chair and waited for the last player to fold his hand. He was in an excellent mood. Ruby Ward had visited the lock-up and assessed the coats they had stolen that morning. Edward had discovered that he was much more than the face of the Costello's automobile business: he was their main fence, using the car showroom as a legitimate front to launder their dirty money and to distribute the booty with which they fed the black market. They already knew that the coats cost forty pounds each in Mayfair, and they had thirty of them. Ruby had offered twenty apiece. He would sell them for thirty, but retailing the goods entailed the biggest risk and so no-one begrudged him his mark-up.

The adrenaline of the heist receded and, as it did, the four of them had been filled with exhilaration that they had successfully pulled off the job. It was something different from the burglaries. They were diversifying. Edward, too, felt more optimistic for his own prospects than he had for many years. The afternoon at the Ritz had underlined it for him: he was starting a new life. Goodbye to the deprivations of his return, the ignominy of begging the state for aid, the foul garret and his grasping landlord and the shameful prospect of pawning his things so he could afford to eat. He felt as he imagined emigrants felt when they left their problems behind them in some foreign country, discarded their old friends and relatives and past mistakes, setting sail for Australia, or America, and the promise of something better. He had felt this way before but he had been negligent then and, eventually, he had had no choice but to burn that life and exchange it for another unsatisfactory one. Now he would do it again. It was a chance to clean his slate.

He looked around the table. The five of them looked swell. His ratty old demob suit was a distant memory and now he wore a pale blue silk shirt with a Barrymore roll collar and a burgundy silk tie, the sort worn by Adolphe Menjou, the American actor. His shoes were hand-made from a shop in St. James' that catered to crowned heads. They were made from wild boar, were bright yellow under the instep and they cost ten guineas. His suit was double-breasted, powder blue and cut in the American style. He looked and felt a million dollars.

Billy Stavropoulos had a large cigar clamped between his teeth. Edward looked at him, sitting there like the cock of the walk, and had the same anxious thoughts again. He was not the least bit contrite about his behaviour that morning. He'd made a joke of the beating he had meted out, laughing at the guard's request that he should be marked and suggesting that he would have no trouble now in persuading his employers of his innocence. He'd get a raise, he reckoned, on account of the fight he must have put up. Edward thought Billy was hideous. He was cruel and unpleasant, uneducated even by the standards of the others, untroubled by the faintest shred of culture. If there was a potential impediment to his plan then he, undoubtedly, was it. There was a feral cunning to him, a natural wariness so that Edward knew he would always have to be watchful when he was around. He would never be able to truly relax. Billy made another crack about the morning's work and looked around the table, gawking at the others to ensure that they found it amusing. Add a needy insecurity to his emotional make-up, Edward thought. The man was horrid from his head to his toes.

Lennie Masters chuckled at Billy's joke, baring a yellowed set of teeth. Joseph smiled with a forbearing expression and Edward realised that he had come to accept the extremities of his behaviour. It was "just Billy," he had explained by way of explanation earlier. He had "always been like that." That really was not good enough so far as Edward was concerned. They were already taking significant risks and it made no sense to him to tolerate behaviour that made the risk worse. If he had been in control, that would be something that he would not allow. Billy's behaviour was clumsy, stupid, dangerous and unnecessary. He knew he would have to discuss him with Joseph and he wondered how best to do that without annoying him. Billy was an old friend, after all. His oldest. Edward was new to the scene and knew it. It was difficult.

The bets were called, hands were folded. Billy, Jack and Edward were the last men standing.

"Let's see your hand, then," Billy said to Jack.

Jack gleefully laid the cards on the table. "Three Queens," he said.

Edward had a pair of jacks, and he hadn't played them well at all. Jack's trio beat him. "Damn," he said. "I'm out."

Jack reached across the table for the pile of chips.

Billy raised a hand. "Hold on, my old mate," he said.

"Piss off, Bubble—you ain't never beating that."

"Sorry," he said with a grin that said he wasn't sorry at all. "I am." He put his cards face up on the velvet. "Full boat, kings over tens."

A full house? Edward chuckled. Billy had played them both like a cheap fiddle.

Joseph and Lennie, long since out of the hand and undamaged, could afford to laugh. Jack and Edward were out of chips. It was just Billy, Joseph, Lennie and one of the businessmen left in the game.

Edward and Jack stepped away from the table and delivered their empty glasses to the bar.

Edward had quizzed Joseph about Jack McVitie as they made their way across Soho to the club. He had been involved with Joseph almost as long as Billy had. He had been born in Islington, and had had a difficult childhood, dropping out of school at an early age and falling into petty crime. He met Joseph in borstal in 1936 when both boys were twelve. Joseph had been sent down for burglary, Jack for stabbing another boy in the back with a pair of scissors. The two endured their inside year together, and, when they were released, they started thieving. Then, Joseph had gone to war while Jack had paid a dodgy quack to sign him off with asthma. He had spent the duration robbing whatever he could get his hands on and feeding the black market, but it had been hard graft and he had been glad to get cracking again with Joseph once he got back from the fighting. He was six foot two, heavily built, and crippled by vanity. He kept his balding thatch covered with his ubiquitous hat and had pushed a broken glass into the face of the last bastard who made a joke about it. That had done the trick. The subject hadn't come up since.

"We were fooled," Edward complained. "I could have sworn I had him beaten."

"It's a bad night when you let someone like Bubble gull you. He's as subtle as a slap in the face. I must be drunker than I thought I was."

"Might as well keep drinking then. Another one?"

"Why not. Whisky."

Edward ordered the drinks and they took them to the large, deep-buttoned red leather Chesterfield next to the bar. They touched glasses.

"You've known Joseph for a while, haven't you?"

Jack nodded. "Since we was nippers."
"Do you know his family well?"
"Course."
"You know George?"
"Well enough."
"Everyone seems to be scared of him."
Jack smiled at him as if he was a small child. "Have you met him yet?"
"Only briefly."
"You want to be careful. His temper... Jesus."
"Really?"
"You having a laugh? George Costello? Bloody right. Let me tell you a story." Jack sipped his drink thoughtfully. "There was this one time, last year, just before Christmas, the family was having trouble with a bent slip out of West End Central. This bloke was on the take like they all are but this one was greedy, he wanted more and more, said he'd turn up the heat if he didn't get another few notes when he stuck his hand out each month. So George meets him in the Greek dive on Old Compton Street, says he's going to pay him what he wants but then he goes and pours a boiling hot coffee-urn over his head. In front of everyone. The slip got awful burns. In hospital for a week. They had to peel the skin off him, like an onion. He was bloody horrible to look at after."
"He did that to a policeman?"
Jack nodded.
"And he didn't get nicked?"
"Don't be daft. The slip was out of order—his bosses would've given him a right going over. George has too many of them in his pocket. No-one wants to upset the gravy train."
"And Violet?"
"If anything, she's worse. It was her who set George on the copper. Between you and me, she's a devious bitch and she ain't got no scruples whatsoever. She might pretend to be sweet and light, but that's only if you're on the right

side of her. She don't do the sorting out herself, but then she don't need to, not when she's got a evil swine like George to sic on people."

A shout of indignation signalled the end of the game. Billy had fooled Joseph, too, busting his aces with a trio of fours. They had each put ten pounds into the middle, winner takes all: a tidy amount. The businessman and Billy agreed a split of the pot, Billy gloatingly fanning himself with his winnings.

"Bugger this," Joseph said, disgusted.

"Don't be a sore loser," Billy crowed.

They both joined Edward and Jack at the bar. The proprietor of the spieler was a man in a satin and quilted smoking jacket, of average height and Mediterranean colouring and with a pencil moustache that recalled Clark Gable. He opened a door at the far end of the room and led four girls inside. He brought over a humidor of excellent cigars and offered them around. "Gentlemen," he said, his accent inflected with Latin accents, "allow me to introduce you to these delightful ladies."

The four girls came over to them, each wearing a fine dress that shimmered in the subtle light, each of them smiling a knowing smile as if they were party to an excellent joke of which the poor chaps were hopelessly ignorant. They were superbly dressed, expensively and precisely made-up and with hair arranged in various fashionable cuts: one had a chignon, another the modishly popular Eton crop. Their décolletages were immodest and Jack whistled soft approval.

Billy made a show of sniffing his cigar—they were fine Cohibas—and placed it behind the ruffled handkerchief in his top pocket, patting it, grinning the whole time. "Alright, darling," he said to the nearest girl, grabbing her slender wrist and tugging her closer. "Have a seat." She giggled and allowed herself to be pulled down into his lap.

One of the girls lowered next to Edward. "Hello, honey," she said. She had a fuchsia-coloured cigarette in a long holder, the gold tip barely noticeable. The straps of her expensive dress were pencil-thin, hardly strong enough to support the fabric, framing a long white neck. She crossed a leg, the dress slipping aside to reveal a slender, alabaster ankle and tiny, expensive shoes. Her eyelids were indigo and her lashes were luxuriously long. "You're a good-looking fellow."

Edward smiled at the girl. Yes, this was a life that he could easily get used to, he thought. He allowed her to settle beside him, her fingers playing up and down his arm, her expensive scent filling his nostrils. Justified morally by the luxurious surroundings and the money in his jacket pocket and fortified by the excellent whisky, he felt his mood become reflective. He tried to take an objective look at the past few years. His time in the army had been a waste, a seven year interval during which he had put himself in harm's way, and yet it had been necessary. The funds he had siphoned during his long sojourn through Europe had gradually dissipated. Most had been remitted to Jimmy to look after his father, and then there had been the regular bribes to ensure that his postings were away from the more perilous spots. It was demoralising to watch the reducing balance and know that there was nothing that he could do to replenish it or even staunch the flow. Eventually, it had all been used up.

The men of his battalion were dull philistines for the most part, and he had taken up with them in order not to be lonely and because they could offer him something for a while: conversation, such as it was, and the security of someone to look out for him. There had been moments of joy—watching sun rise above the golden dome of the Shwedagon Pagoda, the freshness of the jungle after the monsoon—but those had been fleeting. It had been a depressing time with his memories the only succour.

Long and tedious marches through the jungle were relieved somewhat by the vivid recollection of his European tour. A trek through France and Italy in search of art and culture, with the nearly unlimited funds of his companion and the benefit of her extensive connections, he perfected his language skills and mingled with the upper class of the continent. They had started in Paris, then moved on to Geneva, then took a trip across the Alps into northern Italy where they visited Turin and Milan. There was a month spent amid the wonderful atmosphere of Florence, a trip to Pisa and then on to Padua, Bologna and Venice. He remembered the sights and sounds of Rome, the masterpieces of painting and sculpture from the Renaissance and Baroque periods, the fabulous architecture. They diverted to Naples to sample Herculaneum and Pompeii, ascended Vesuvius and then, finally, hired a yacht and crossed to Greece before they returned north to Sicily. That was where Edward had made the error that had forced him to abandon the life he had grown to love. He had returned home and accepted his banishment to the Far East.

His reverie was disturbed by muffled shouting from the floor below. There was the sound of a scuffle followed by the unmistakeable retort of a shotgun.

"Old Bill!" Billy shouted, knocking over his chair as he stumbled upright.

The door to the spieler crashed open and a tall, well-built man came through. He was armed with a shotgun, cradling the weapon comfortably in both hands, the smoking barrel held level and aimed into the room.

"Don't do anything stupid, lads," he warned. His voice was deep and sonorous, yet unmistakeably threatening. He glanced around, pitiless eyes beneath a strong brow. Edward looked down. He was afraid of his eyes.

No-one moved. Another three men, these armed with revolvers, fanned around the room. The men were good, first checking that no-one was hiding and then ensuring that everyone was within their arc of fire. It was a routine that Edward had learnt and practised when clearing villages from laggard Tojo soldiers in Burma. These men were smooth and thorough, not a word passing between them.

Lennie Masters did not appear to be afraid. He held his ground and said, "This is a stupid move, Spot, even for you."

"Alright, Lennie. Just take it easy." He toted the shotgun. "No need for me to use this, is there?"

Joseph got to his feet. "Do you know who I am?" he said.

"I don't, lad. Afraid you have my advantage."

"Joseph Costello."

Spot smiled, the corners of his thick lips angling upwards, his white teeth flashing. "The prodigal son," he said. "I've heard a lot about you. You've been in Burma, fighting the nips. Good for you, lad, good for you. I'm Jack Spot. I expect you've heard a lot about me, too."

"I've heard you're a dead man."

Spot's laugh was deep and almost attractive, despite his oversized and discoloured teeth. "I see you have your old man's temper. Pleased to meet you, lad. I'm the new guv'nor around here."

"You've got to be kidding, Jack," Lennie said.

"Like I say, Lennie, don't do anything stupid. Let's keep things nice and cordial, shall we? No-one needs get hurt."

Everyone else was quiet, but Joseph stared Spot right in the eye. "You're robbing from a Costello business, you bloody idiot."

"Less of the salty tongue, lad. You've been away too long—your family's on its uppers. No-one is scared of any of you any more, see? Your old man was something once, but he's brown bread. His name means nothing now and without that—none of you mean nothing. I'll tell you what—you be a good lad and deliver a message to your auntie Violet and uncle George and I'll let you and your mates out of here without touching a hair on your heads. You tell them to clear out of Soho if they know what's good for them. I'd rather you persuaded them to go quietly, but if they need something to help focus their minds, you be sure to tell them how serious I am."

Without another word, Spot aimed the shotgun at Lennie Masters and pulled one of the triggers. The blast took off Lennie's arm at the elbow. He spun around, blood spraying from the frayed stub that dangled from his lacerated jacket. Spot pulled the other trigger and blew Lennie back against the windows, tearing down the old black-out curtain.

There was a moment of shocking silence and then the women started to shriek.

Joseph took a step forward but Spot spun the shotgun around quickly, the barrel pointing directly at him again. "Tut tut, lad," he said, grinning horribly. "You don't want to get fresh with me."

"Like I said—you're a dead man."

"You ain't the one holding the shooter, son. Do me a favour—all that money on the table there, you bag it all up for us, alright?" He threw a canvas sack at him. "And anything else—watches, jewellery, anything behind the bar. All of it, double quick."

Joseph's face flushed the deepest crimson. The girls were crying, trying to stop the sobs and gulping air. One of them fainted. Edward watched carefully, drawing no attention to himself but absorbing everything. Spot flicked the barrel in Joseph's direction and covered him as he dragged the pile of notes from the table and into the mouth of the bag, then went to the bar and emptied the till.

"Chop chop," Spot said, waving the shotgun, "and your watches and jewellery, all of it. Ladies, too."

Edward unclipped his watch and dropped it into the mouth of the bag. The others did the same. Spot was either unaware or uncaring of the deadly looks that were aimed at him.

"There," Joseph said, dropping the bag at the feet of one of the other men. "Done."

"Good lad. We'll be on our way now. No hard feelings, but if I were you I'd keep out of Soho for a while. You and your family aren't welcome here no more. Wouldn't want the same thing to happen to you as poor Lennie there."

25

LENNIE MASTERS'S BODY HAD LAIN THERE, half propped against the wall, the arm missing and blood starting to clot around the horrid, vivid wounds. The proprietor said they should leave, and that he would take care of calling the police. They did not argue. There would be awkward questions asked of those who were present. The place was illegal, for one thing, and there was a dead man slumped against the wall. The patrons and staff dispersed, gathering their belongings and hurrying down the flight of stairs and onto the street. No-one spoke. Billy and Jack went home. Joseph and Edward went straight to the Blue Arabian. George and Violet Costello were in one of the booths, locked in conversation with two beetle-browed heavies and a skinny man with buck teeth who was, Joseph suggested, "a big noise in America." The room was jumping, a large crowd dancing to the Jock Salisbury Quartet, and the music and the smoke-heavy air made Edward's head spin. They approached the booth, Edward waiting a respectful step away as Joseph waited for his uncle and aunt to acknowledge him. He dipped to George's ear and spoke quickly. George's expression darkened and he shared a quick word with his sister. They both made their excuses, leaving the table and hurrying towards the bar.

There was a door to a store room. George shoved it aside roughly and they followed him through: barrels of ale, bottles in crates, rows of empties. Violet looked out of place amid the detritus of the club. She looked glamorous, as always: dressed in a jacket with a high neckline, a knee-length tartan skirt and calfskin pumps with wedge heels. A tiny hat that must have cost a small fortune completed the ensemble. She took a cigarette from her case and screwed it into a holder.

"Not him," George said roughly, pointing to Edward. "Family only."

"He was there," Joseph protested. "And I told you, he's clever—he might be able to help."

Edward stood silently, working out the angles.

"Let him stay," Violet said.

"Fine," George relented. "What happened?"

Joseph spoke quietly. "Jack Spot and three of his gypsies turned over the spieler on Manette Street. And then they shot Lennie. He's dead."

George's face flickered from fury to confusion and then back to fury again. "Why? He wants a war with us?" He slammed his fist into the wall. The confusion and the frustration stayed, and for a moment he looked like a baffled toddler. He appealed to his sister, "Violet—what do we do?"

"What did he say?" she asked.

"That we're finished in Soho. That we should clear out. He says he's the new guv'nor."

"And?"

"That's it. He stole anything worth having and cleared off."

Violet stared at the unlit cigarette but said nothing. She lit the cigarette slowly and carefully. Edward realised that she was as confused as George, but that she was better skilled at masking it. Joseph, too, did not know how to react. Edward had decided when they made their way into the club that he would keep his own counsel, regardless of what Joseph said. He had ideas but he did not want to speak out of turn in case they thought he was being presumptuous. But, watching them flounder, he realised that, in their own ways, they were all paralysed by confusion and doubt. They needed him. He saw the chance and he took it.

"He doesn't want a war," he offered carefully.

"Really?" Violet said acerbically.

"No. He's weighed this up. It might have looked it, but wasn't a spur of the moment thing. He thinks that shooting your friend is all it's going to take to get what he wants. He was going to do that all along, it didn't matter what he did or didn't say. He thinks you're weak. He thinks you'll give up and step away."

"Weak?" In a sudden movement, George was onto Edward, taking him by the lapels and shoving him against the whitewashed brick wall. He was prodigiously strong. "You don't know him and you don't know us," he said, his face so close to Edward that he could see the bubbles of spittle forming on his bottom lip. "I've had people cut into little pieces for saying less than that to me."

"Uncle," Joseph said, his tone calm and even. "He didn't mean it like that."

"Let him go, George," Violet instructed.

George pressed harder for a moment and Edward felt the points of his knuckles burying themselves deeper into the soft flesh beneath his shoulders. He released his grip. "Alright," he said, taking a step back. "Go on then, explain, but watch what you say."

Edward did his best not to patronise them. "Rational people don't want to fight, not if they don't have to. It's messy and no-one ever ends up with everything they want. Spot is sending you a message that it's not in your interests to take him on. There was no need to do what he did—Lennie wasn't doing anything to provoke him and shooting him was gratuitous. That was the message he wanted to deliver—he's saying that he's dangerous and unpredictable, that he'll do anything to get what he wants and if you want to fight him, you'll have to fight on the same level. And he doesn't think you'll be prepared to do that."

George folded his huge arms, his porcine eyes staring dead straight at Edward. "He's wrong," he said. "What a load of old bollocks." Edward could see that it was just bluster.

Violet lit her cigarette, put the holder to her lips and drew in a sharp breath. "Fine," she said, exhaling. "If you think you know what he's doing, why don't you tell us what we should do about it?"

"Start to close your Soho businesses down."

"Shut them down?" George laughed harshly.

"And move out."

"Run away?"

"Let him think he's getting what he wants. Persuade him you've got no stomach for this, a scrap with someone who'll shoot one of your men for no reason. Prove him right—make it look like you *are* weak."

Because you are, Edward thought. Weak and lazy and ripe for the picking.

"And then?" Violet asked.

"And then you plan your next move. All warfare is based on deception. He needs to think that you can't or you won't attack him. You sit down. Plan the correct response. And then carry it out ruthlessly."

"What a load of old bollocks, Violet," George said dismissively. "We start to move out and every Tom, Dick and Harry will be onto us. They're like damn sharks. They smell weakness—real or not—and you're done for. They'd tear us to shreds. Sorry, Joseph, but your mate ain't clever. He's naïve. Wouldn't last five minutes here."

He knew that he did not have to persuade George. When it came down to it, he would do as he was told. It was Violet, shrew-like and wily, whom he had to persuade. She did not speak. She drew down again on her cigarette, her eyes on Edward and yet distant, as if calculating or toying with a difficult problem. She exhaled smoke up into the vaulted ceiling.

"Come on," George said, straightening his jacket. His face was set now, his eyes bulging and the line of his jaw pulsing as he clenched and unclenched. "Best get you somewhere we know is safe. You need to think what we do next. I'll tell you this, and I'll tell you for nothing—Jack bloody Spot will rue the day he thought he could pull a stroke like this. I'll have his eyes before the week is out."

PART FOUR

September – December 1945

CALENDAR

— 1945 —

The *Graphic*, 25th July:

SCANDAL AS RETURNING SOLDIERS
ABANDONED
– NO JOBS, NO ACCOMMODATION, NO MONEY –
By Henry Drake

The leading London hotels are full of well-fed, well-dressed foreign managers, clerks, waiters, porters. In the Piccadilly Hotel I saw only one English employee, a crippled soldier, who ran a lift, and the messenger boys. Yet London is full of disbanded unemployed soldiers. It is pitiful to see hundreds of young Britons, their breasts covered with war medals, turning barrel organs, the organ having an inscription drawing attention to their services and the unfulfilled promises made them. Sometimes they have a wounded mate appealing mutely to the pity of the cruel city; sometimes a wife and children. Others work in parties of crippled men.

That fate nearly befell Lieutenant Edward Fabian, a handsome medical graduate of Cambridge University who served his country with great distinction in the Far East. Lt. Fabian, who is 29, was awarded the Military Cross for conspicuous bravery in battle yet, rather than being clasped to the breast of a grateful nation upon his demobilisation two months ago, he found himself without any money or accommodation. Thank goodness, then, for kind-hearted local businesswoman Violet Costello who took pity on Lt. Fabian and offered him a job selling cars in her West London showroom…

The *Star*, 29th July:

GANG WARFARE IN SOHO

Stern warning was issued to gangland by an Old Bailey judge when he sentenced Patrick Jeremiah Harrigan (25) to 7 years' penal servitude for razor slashing. "If this is gang warfare then let the rest of the gang take notice," said the judge grimly. He was told that Kelly, the man slashed, had asked police to let him "fix this mug my own way."

There was speculation that Harrigan was working for the notorious "Spot Gang", a criminal organisation rumoured to be in conflict with the Costellos, the Italian family alleged to have been in command of the underworld for many years.

The *Star*, 21st August:

YARD HUNTS KILLER GANG

Police and detectives in squad cars today scoured London's underworld haunts for three men who took part in the "Chicago-type" murder last night of a West End gambler. London newspapers said police believed the murder was the result of a sudden flare-up in London's gang land warfare.

The gambler, Leonard Masters, 45-years-old, was shot in front of several women. Newspapers said three men strode into an illegal betting club in Soho, central London, and shot Masters in front of other gamblers and ladies who were found there. The killers ran to a car where another man waited with the engine running and escaped.

26

THE DAYS FOLLOWING THE MURDER of Lennie Masters passed quietly. Edward had no wish to be with Joseph and the others until the immediate aftermath had settled and so he retreated to his bedsitter with a handful of books he had stolen from Foyles and lost himself in their pages. The atmosphere on the street outside his front door appeared normal, unflustered and unchanged, and yet there were signs of discordance if you knew where to look. There were more uniformed police on patrol and Edward had noticed plainclothes men interviewing the owners of the businesses near to the spieler when he went to buy milk from the Welsh Dairy. The Costellos had reacted by bringing more of their muscle into the area, and it quickly became a common sight to see men straight out of Damon Runyan speaking through mouths full of iron filings on the street corners. If Jack Spot had a plan for following the murder then nothing was apparent but then, Edward reasoned, there was little that he needed to do. He had made his point and he would have seen nothing in the Costello's reaction to make him suspect that he had been wrong in his assessment of them: weak, rudderless, and ready to be driven out. Edward tried not to think too much about it. The frustration at Violet and George's inane response—which was hardly a response at all—gnawed at him until it was an almost tangible ache.

Edward received a letter from Joseph on the third day after the murder.

Dear Doc,

I understand that it is necessary given the circumstances but being cooped up like this is driving me mad. To stop me from completely going around the twist, I have arranged an appointment for us both today (Wednesday) in Mayfair. There is a pub on Park Street. I'll meet you there at 3p.m. Don't be late. Bring an open mind.

Regards,
Joseph

Edward was beginning to feel claustrophobic and depressed in his awful garret and did not need much persuasion to leave it. He took the tube to Mayfair and met Joseph at the pub. The rendezvous was not for the drink that Edward had expected. Instead, Joseph suggested that they should go for a walk. They set off, Joseph leading the way until they reached a grand red-brick Gothic mansion block on the corner of Green Street and Park Street. Edward asked what they were doing there. Joseph smiled and told him to follow. He led the way to the pillared entrance and went inside. Edward asked again what was going on. Joseph grinned even more broadly and set off up a grand staircase that wound its way directly up the middle of the building. He stepped onto the landing on the fourth floor. Two doors led off it, numbered ten and twelve. Joseph withdrew a key from his pocket and unlocked the door for number twelve.

Inside was a beautiful apartment. The wide sitting room featured polished wood floors, a large fireplace and wide French doors that opened out onto a terrace that offered views over Hyde Park. Joseph led the way into a generously-proportioned bedroom, and then opened the door to a second. The room had a wide bed and a chest of drawers and wardrobe that were already full of Joseph's lovely clothes. There were several packing crates stacked against the wall and one of them was open, revealing a collection of novels. They were penny-dreadfuls, for the most part, but Edward found them rather surprising. He had assumed that Joseph was a young fellow who was cunning but not particularly intelligent, more likely to be out drinking and womanizing than reading. Perhaps he had misjudged him.

"And the kitchen?"

Joseph showed him through to the spacious kitchen. Edward went back through the rooms again, casting about with hungry eyes.

"What do you think?" Joseph said, beaming proudly.

"It's fabulous. It must cost a fortune."

"It ain't cheap."

He was bubbling with enthusiasm. Edward did not want to think how much a place like that would cost, but he did not want to spoil his mood. "That's capital," he said. He thought about his own place, the malodorous bathroom with the door that did not lock, the grimy attic room that looked like it had been lived in by a thousand different people who had never lifted a hand to clean it, and he felt jealous.

"Big, ain't it?"

"Huge."

"Reckon it's too big just for me. Thought you might like it, too? What do you reckon? Me and you?" For once, Edward did not have to fake his reaction: he spluttered in helpless surprise. Joseph seemed taken aback by his response. "You don't have to, just… you know, if you like?"

He regained his composure. "How much is it?"

"Twenty-five a week."

"I can't afford that," he said, even as he worked out the sums in his head, and wondered whether, if they turned over a few extra houses now again, perhaps, maybe, he could afford it.

"Forget the money. Do you like it?"

"Of course I do. How could you not like it? It's beautiful."

"Perfect spot, too. Right where the action is."

"Joseph—be serious. It's too much."

"You worry too much, Doc. Money's not a problem. We're going to be well off."

"With the nonsense from Jack Spot?"

"That'll get sorted out."

He had expected that that would be how Joseph reacted to the threat from Spot. He was an optimist and he usually assumed the best. That was naïve. Edward was pragmatic and he suspected that this particular problem would require careful solving. He had heard the rumours the same as everyone else: Spot was upping his game, becoming more aggressive and more acquisitive. The newspapers had reported a spate of attacks on businesses aligned to the Costellos.

A restaurant with a brick flung through the window.

A gang of gypsy heavies standing outside the Alhambra, scaring away all the passing trade.

The proprietor of a general store with a knife pressed against his throat, threatened with violence: stop paying the Costellos, start paying Spot.

Edward shelved his concerns for the moment and wandered across the parquet floor to the French doors. He opened them and stepped out onto the stone-flagged terrace. The streets of Mayfair spread out below him and then, beyond that, the green of Hyde Park, its broad fields still scarred in places with the fading green-brown slashes of anti-aircraft trenches. Edward stared across the vista, the hubbub of the city below full of the promise of excitement and opportunity.

"Come on, Doc," Joseph said. "All we went through, the war, getting our arses kicked for the King, and they expect us to live like tramps in dirty bedsitters? That just don't seem right to me. And it'd be fun here, you and me, wouldn't it? We'd have a proper laugh—two bachelors, a bit of gelt to spread around, a nice place to call home. Think of the laughs we could have, think of the judies we could bring back, you can get a whole different class of girl if they think you have something about you. What do you say?"

Edward didn't need much in the way of persuasion. "Alright," he said. "You're on."

Joseph was in boisterous spirits as they emerged onto the busy street. He put his arm around Edward and squeezed. Edward's mood followed his friend's, and he returned the gesture, both of them laughing at a shared realisation: they were young men, with money and the prospect of making much, much more. Life had treated them harshly for too long, but now a corner had been turned, and things would be different.

27

CHARLIE MURPHY MADE his way down Northumberland Avenue to the three buildings that comprised Scotland Yard. It was sunny and cool although not cool enough to be called crisp. The Commissioner's Office and the Receiver's Office were made from old red and white brick, the third from Portland Stone that was mined by convicts down on Dartmoor. He was a little anxious. Deputy Assistant Commissioner Stan Clarke had asked to see him. Urgent, he'd said. Christ. Clarke hadn't said what the meeting was for but the chances were that it was going to be something that Charlie didn't like. Of course, he had seen the papers over the last couple of days. He had stewed over them in the pub with Carlyle and White. They had made glum reading. The front pages all led with reports of the shooting of Lennie Masters and the ruckus in the club. They were comparing it with Chicago and Al Capone. Charlie knew that was asinine nonsense, arrant foolishness of the worst order, but he also knew that excited reporting like that would go down very badly with his senior officers.

That fact of it was that they were losing control of the West End. Jack Spot was there every night, seemingly with more men each time. Charlie received the reports very morning and the coloured pins on his large map demonstrated how his malefic influence was spreading throughout the area, all seemingly unchecked. Businesses that had kicked up to the Costellos for years were being persuaded to change their allegiances. Spielers and shebeens were being attacked, the custom driven away. Two street bookies had been slashed across the faces and driven out. The Maltese, who controlled vice west of Regent Street, were being attacked. And, throughout all of this, there was nothing in the way of retaliation from the Costellos. Charlie could only think of two possible explanations for that: either they were a spent force or they were getting into something else.

The D.A.C.'s office was on the second floor. Charlie knocked and went inside. The office was large, with wide windows that looked out over the Embankment and the iron-grey sweep of the Thames beyond. A couple of olive-green navy pontoons were still lashed to their moorings, bobbing sullenly on the rise and fall of the tide. The D.A.C. was behind his desk, papers spread out before him and a pencil in his mouth.

"Morning, Charles," he said. "Take a seat." He pointed absent-mindedly at the armchair opposite the desk.

Charlie did as he was told. "You wanted to see me, sir?"

Clarke put the pencil down and tidied the desk. "Cost cutting," he explained, indicating the sheaf of papers with a gesture of brusque irritation. "Bane of my bloody life." He settled back in his chair and folded his arms. "Now then, Charles, afraid we have a bit of a problem."

"What's that, sir?"

"Your work on the gangs. The black market and so forth."

"Yes?"

"Not going quite the way we want it to."

Charlie felt defensive. "We're making progress," he protested. "This isn't an easy job, sir. We always knew it would be difficult."

"Appreciate that but you've got to put yourself in the Commissioner's shoes. All this blather in the press, calls for us to be seen to be doing something—it's all about image, Charles. Giving the right impression. And, at the moment, you've not given us anything to show them that we're making a decent fist of it."

"The Commissioner has spoken to you?"

"Course he has, man, course he has. And he's unhappy. The Masters murder is a problem. The *Times* and the *Express* have both been bending his ear about it. And when he can't give them anything useful to print they make up that nonsense they've been coming out with over the last couple of days. He hates that, Charlie, absolutely hates it. He bollocks me and then I have to bollock you. You know how it is."

Charlie spoke with careful patience: "The reason we haven't made any arrests yet is because it's a long and sensitive investigation. I could go in and arrest a dozen men this morning if that's what he wanted me to do."

"So why don't you do that?"

He knew to tread carefully but it was difficult to hide his irritation. "Because it would be a stupid move, sir. As I understood it, the purpose of this investigation is to go after the big fish. We could probably set them back a few weeks by taking the low-ranking men off the street but they'd just replace them. We'd be no nearer solving the problem. All we would have achieved would be to warn them that we're onto them."

"How much longer before you think you can deliver someone impressive?"

"Like who?"

"Jack Spot? One of the Costellos?"

"Hard to say. We're trying to develop a couple of informers. It depends how we get on with that. These are careful people, sir. It's not straightforward."

"Alright, Charlie," Clarke said. "I'll tell him to be patient. But you need to remember that this is a results business. The line that we're working hard and making progress isn't going to wash forever. I'm going to need something tangible."

Charlie got up and smoothed down his trousers. "I understand, sir."

"One of the big fish, Charlie. That's what we need."

28

THE DAWN OF EDWARD'S BIRTHDAY in October found him in circumstances he would not have credited just nine months earlier. The miserable penury that had greeted his return from Asia was now a distant memory. He was well off, with two and a half thousand pounds spread among three bank accounts and two safety deposit boxes, fifty pounds in cash that he kept on his person and another hundred pounds swelling the coffers every week. His wardrobe contained half a dozen bespoke suits, he bought fresh shirts whenever he fancied them and his shoes were handmade by the cobbler who supplied the King.

He still had concerns. The sight of policemen patrolling Soho's streets was still frightening, and there were nights where he would awake in a cold sweat to realise that it was the sound of a passing siren that had disturbed him. And the threat from Jack Spot had still not been addressed. Violet and George had still not taken his advice, nor had they struck back. An uneasy limbo had developed, with the family pressing on as if ignoring the gauntlet that had been thrown down would make it go away. Edward worried about that, too, about their naivety, and worried that Spot would decide there was nothing for it but to make a grander statement of intent. But the worries passed and as the days went by their effect lessened. Life was good.

He regularly had to catch himself. He had been very lucky and, if he played the game skilfully, there was the chance to recover at least some of the extravagant lifestyle that he had enjoyed before. The long years he had spent hiding in the jungle would soon be nothing more than memories. It was difficult to ignore the feeling he had put one over on the rest of the world.

Living with Joseph made a good situation better yet. Joseph was enjoying his company although Edward was careful to keep out of his way when he sensed he wanted time to himself. Joseph was similarly accommodating. They ate out most nights but, on the occasions that they did not, they cooked for each other and then sat around smoking, listening to records on their new gramophone and reading. They both became familiar in the upmarket bars and restaurants in the streets around their apartment, two likely fellows who did not fit the accepted mould— that of the independently rich dilettante, usually funded by a generous trust fund—yet they were clearly well off, too, and Joseph, at least, was not shy about spending. He was frivolously generous, standing drinks and buying dinners with seemingly no concern as to the cost. Edward knew that he was more difficult to assess than his friend, an impression of opacity that he was keen to foster. He was quieter, and less flashy when it came to laying out his money, but his air of reserve helped to increase the mystery that had already settled over the pair. Affluence, mystery; these, together with their good looks, made both popular with the local women and they brought a series of eager debutantes back to their luxurious apartment when the restaurants and night-clubs closed.

As they entered the week leading up to his birthday, Joseph said that he wanted to mark the occasion with a meal. Edward naturally recoiled from drawing too much attention to himself but Joseph would not be persuaded and, eventually, he conceded. Apart from Joseph, Edward had come to know and like Jack McVitie and Tommy Falco. They all made regular jibes about Edward's education but he knew quite well that they appreciated the different approach that he brought to the planning of their jobs. If relations were good between them, his acceptance was far from universal. Billy Stavropoulos remained surly and uncommunicative and, although the outright hostility that had marked the first few weeks of their acquaintance had been reduced to a constant, low buzz of disapproval, he was under no illusions about the way he still regarded him. One had the impression that Billy was good at bearing a grudge, nurturing it just beneath the surface, feeding it, just waiting for the opportunity for it to catch flame again. Outside of what they jokingly called "work", Edward avoided Billy and Billy avoided Edward and, on that basis, they were able to function. But since Edward had invited Joseph and Jack he could not very well ignore him. He had hoped (and expected) that Billy would decline and so it was with surprise and a little dismay that he received the news that he was coming, too.

They chose a restaurant with a small private dining room. The table had been laid with expensive crockery and decorated with party hats and balloons. Joseph, Tommy and Billy arrived together and they were not alone. To Edward's surprise, Joseph's sisters accompanied them. Sophia and Evie were dressed ostentatiously, as before. Sophia wore a three-quarter length evening coat in Shantung silk over a chemise dress with a high belt. Evie wore a Bolero jacket over a chiffon cocktail dress. Chiara was more reserved in a simple dress with a sweetheart neckline, her sleeves puffed up a little with gathers at the top that extended to just below her elbows. They each gave him a kiss on the cheek, Sophia's lips straying dangerously close to the corner of his mouth.

"Happy birthday, handsome," she said, mischief glinting in her eyes.

Edward thanked her. "Good of you to come."

"Wouldn't miss it."

They settled around the table, Joseph taking the place next to Edward. They had robbed a shop two days before and the evening was the first time since that they had all been together. That, at Edward's suggestion, had quickly become their routine. An enforced absence of a few days after the completion of each job would insulate the others should one of them be apprehended by the police. They were all in high spirits. It was a festive occasion, certainly, but their moods had been lifted by the knowledge that Joseph shared as he sat down. The last robbery had been particularly profitable, with a necklace that they had stolen to order worth even more than they had anticipated. They would each make four hundred pounds, comfortably their best haul to date.

Joseph leaned across and whispered into Edward's ear, "Hope you don't mind the girls coming."

"Course not."

"Afraid you've made a bit of an impression."

"Sophia?"

He chuckled. "No, don't worry, not her—she's like that with everyone. Chiara."

Edward looked across the table at the youngest of the Costello girls. She noticed his attention and smiled, a little shyly.

"I don't know what you've said to her. She's always been a bit of a closed book when it comes to chaps."

"I haven't said anything."

"Well, whatever it was, she's taken a shine to you. She's never been like that with any of my mates. It was her who insisted they all come."

Edward told him he was flattered, and he was. Chiara was easily the most attractive of the three sisters. Her quiet reticence—a marked contrast to her boisterous siblings—leant her an enigmatic quality that made her even more beguiling.

"I don't know if it's mutual," Joseph went on, "but, if it is, you know you'd have my blessing. Not that she'd care about that—she never listens to a word I say." He reached into his pocket and took out a wrapped box. "Happy birthday, Doc," he said, laying it on the table.

Edward sliced the paper open with a knife and withdrew the box from within. Inside it was the most beautiful wristwatch he had ever seen. It was a Cartier, made from gilt silver with a rectangular black face, silver Roman numerals and hands and blue cabochon on the stem. He turned it over and saw that Joseph had had it engraved:

TO DOC – A TRUE FRIEND – JOSEPH.

He closed the box before anyone else around the table could notice it.

"Do you like it?"

"Of course I do," he said. His cheeks were beetroot red. "I love it. It must be worth fifty quid. Is it—you know..?"

"Stolen?" Joseph opened his mouth in an exaggerated 'O'. "What do you take me for?" he said, in mock outrage. "You think I'd give you a moody watch for a bloody birthday present? Give it a rest, Doc. I'm hurt."

Buying it with money made from a robbery was just one step removed from reaching into a broken shop window and grabbing it, of course, but it seemed churlish to bring that up. "You shouldn't have," Edward said, taking Joseph's hand and shaking it firmly.

"There's something else," he said, reaching into his inside pocket. He took out a thin envelope and laid it on the table.

Edward picked it up. The envelope was inscribed with the logo of British European Airways. He took up the knife again and carefully sliced it open. Edward took out two tickets to Paris. "I say," he exclaimed.

"It's a bit of a cheeky gift," Joseph explained. "It's almost as much for me as it is for you. You're always going on about how much you want to go to Paris. I thought it might be fun for the two of us to go and have a look. What do you say?"

Edward brimmed with happiness. "You're much too generous," he said.

"I can take them back," Joseph teased.

"No, don't worry," Edward grinned. "It's a splendid idea."

Edward really did think it was splendid. He loved Paris, although it was the kind of city that one could only enjoy properly with a full wallet and the right companion. He was very familiar with the city and his French was excellent. Joseph had no idea that he had been there before and Edward would have to make sure that he kept that quiet. He would just have to pretend that his knowledge was derived from his Baedeker. He would show him all the best spots, mixing the tourist traps with the secret treasures hidden in the back streets, the cafes and little galleries. He grinned with excitement at the thought of it. "When shall we go?"

"I don't know," Joseph said. "They're open tickets. Whenever we feel like it, I suppose." Joseph smiled with pleasure but, as he did, his attention drifted away from Edward and over his shoulder. His mouth dropped open again. Edward turned to follow his gaze. The door to the main restaurant had swung open and the staff had emerged with the starters. He knew immediately who he was looking at.

"I don't believe it," he said. Joseph was staring at one of the waitresses.

"What? You know her?"

"You could say that," he said, grinning. "Her name's Eve. I was seeing her before I went away for the war. We were both kids then—I was seventeen, she was fifteen. Her dad's Old Bill. Nasty, too, a real hard man. Detective inspector Frank Murphy. He didn't approve of me stepping out with her. Told her we had to split up. Next thing I know, she's come around to see me with a suitcase and tells me that he's hit her and she's moving out and we have to run away together. I couldn't do that—I had too much going on and I'd just decided to sign up. Anyway, her old man came around, threw me out of bed and almost broke my arm trying to get me to tell him where she was. She hadn't been home."

"She ran away?"

"That's what it looked like. I haven't seen her since. Well—not until now, anyway. And look at how she's grown up."

Joseph watched as the girl served the next table, his face breaking into a grin as she turned and caught his gaze. She paused, confusion passing across her lovely face, before the wide grin was returned.

"She's lovely," Joseph said.

She certainly was attractive. She had porcelain white skin and the darkest black hair, cut fashionably short into a bob that just reached the base of her neck. Her eyes sparkled, carefully applied purple eye shadow drawing attention to them. Despite her sophisticated appearance, she had still managed to retain that edge of childish innocence that could be so appealing. She attended to the guests with a charming bashfulness that was regularly illuminated by the brightest, most beaming smile imaginable. As she brought around the main courses Edward noticed that Joseph was staring intently at her. She must have noticed it too for she blushed furiously. She did not look up until she was at the doors to the restaurant. Joseph, still grinning at her, gave her a cheeky little wave. Her expression broke into a charming, guileless smile.

The meal was delicious. As the plates were being cleared away Sophia leant across the table and laid both hands atop Edward's. "You never did tell us what you did to win your medal," she said.

Edward feigned reluctance. "Do I have to?" he pleaded.

"Only if you want to shut us up."

"Very well," he said, with mock reluctance. The table quietened as he made a show of considering where he should begin. It was a pretence. He had rehearsed the story so many times that he had memorised it, word for word. He had relayed it several times to men he had met on the troopship bringing him back from India. He had told it to the officer who had demobbed him in Portsmouth and to a pair of wide-eyed squaddies he had met on the train. He had spoken it into the mirror before leaving the flat this evening and had repeated it so often that he had even perfected the expressions—the surprise, fearfulness and relief—that were appropriate for the various beats of the tale.

"Come on, Doc," Joseph said with a expectant look on his face.

Edward looked around the table. They were all waiting for him. "This was in Burma," he began, "I was on patrol with the rest of my platoon. We had the Japs on the run. I can remember it like it was yesterday—it was in the middle of the monsoon, unbelievable amounts of rain, you don't know rain until you've been stuck in one of those"—Joseph nodded his agreement—"and visibility was awful. We were on the approach to a bridge over the Irrawaddy River. The road cut through the jungle and there was dense vegetation on both sides. We wandered right into the middle of an ambush—they had machine guns set up in the trees. They strafed us, most of the boys got hit before we knew what was happening. I took one in the foot of all places, but I managed to get into cover. The firefight must have lasted twenty minutes. I managed to crawl through the shrub to around twenty feet away, maybe a little less, close enough to toss a grenade right into the middle of them. When it was finished, all of my platoon and all of the Japs were dead. I was the last one standing."

"You killed all of them?" Billy asked. He accompanied the question with a tilt of his head that suggested that he found the story dubious.

"Of course not, but I was the only one alive at the end of it. I managed to find my way back to the battalion and they sent scouts to confirm what had happened."

"How incredible," Sophia said.

"Isn't it," Billy said. "Incredible." He barely disguised the sarcasm but gasped in pain just as he was about to continue and, from the steady glare on Sophia's face, Edward guessed that she had kicked him in the shins.

Edward ignored him. "I didn't do it for the medal," he said. "You find yourself in a situation like that, you just react. There isn't really even time to think. I did what any soldier would have done."

"He's too modest," Joseph said. "You know how rare the Victoria Cross is? They only give them out once in a blue moon." He raised his glass and proposed a toast: "To Edward," he said. "Happy birthday."

Edward was fit to burst with happiness. He smiled around the table at all of them. Sophia and Evie giggled at some shared comment. Chiara looked at him with a hopeful look in her eyes. He imagined the speculations of the sisters: Is he single? He can't be single, surely. He's so reserved and private, so mysterious.

The waitress, Eve, returned with clean champagne flutes. She reddened again as she distributed them, Joseph beaming at her the whole time she was at the table. When she finally departed it was with what looked like a mixture of relief and reluctance.

Edward touched glasses with the others and sipped the champagne. His anxiety about the evening looked silly now. Joseph was a natural when it came to directing the mood of a gathering. When he was in this kind of garrulous, easy-going form, it was possible to watch others as they became infected with his good temper. He had an easy charisma and could be completely beguiling when he wanted to be.

Bottles of spirits appeared and the drinking picked up pace. Joseph excused himself from the table and went across to the bar. He poured Eve a drink and they started to talk. It was quickly obvious that they knew each other. There was an easy familiarity to their body language, Joseph resting his fingers on her forearm and Eve touching the back of his hand. She was too shy and he was too garrulous for their conversation to be anything other than one-sided, but it was obvious that he was putting everything into an attempt to impress her and, inevitably, he was meeting with success. It wasn't long before she was laughing freely at his jokes.

Edward was still smiling at it as Chiara Costello came to his side.

"Have you had fun?" she asked him.

"Oh, yes. It was a wonderful evening. And you?"

"I've had a lovely time." Her eyelids lowered elaborately and then rose again languorously, her electric eyes sparkling.

"It was nice of you to come."

"You came to my birthday, didn't you? I had to reciprocate. Only polite." Edward felt himself relaxing into her company. "What have you been getting up to?"

He looked at her sharply, wondering what she knew, but her expression was open and guileless. "This and that," he said.

"Have you thought what you're going to do now you've settled back into things?"

She must have known that he was busy with her brother. It was obvious: the clothes, the fact that they were living together, none of that could possibly be funded by the job with Ruby Ward, no matter how good he might be at it. Of course, he had stopped going to the garage. He had handed in his cards. There didn't seem to be any point now that they were doing so well. Surely she would have been made aware of that? And, yet, despite it all, he did not feel comfortable acknowledging any of that to her. He didn't want her to disapprove and he knew that she would. "I don't really know," he said.

"Medicine, surely?" she said, continuing her wilful blindness. "Could you continue with your studies?"

"I suppose I could."

"But you don't want to?"

"I don't know. I suppose"—he fished for the right words—"I suppose I'm enjoying myself at the moment. Working with your brother."

Working? That was a poor choice of word. Edward realised at once that Chiara would know what kind of "work" Joseph was involved in and pretending it was something else must have been insulting to her. She had warned him against it, too, but if she was offended she didn't show it. She nodded thoughtfully, and said, "I know I mentioned this before, but please do be careful. What Joseph does—it doesn't have a future. It's dangerous. The police might seem hopeless, but they're not. They watch us all the time. They'll get there in the end. They always do. There's nothing I can do about him. He's too set in his ways. You just accept that he'll be caught eventually, and then he'll go away. But I'd hate to see that happen to you. It would be such a shame. You've got so much going for you."

Edward wanted to say something but he felt uncomfortable discussing their criminal exploits with her. Despite her knowledge, it didn't feel right. A question of manners, he supposed. Something as foolish as simple decorum. But that wasn't it, or at least not all of it. There was something else, too: he was feeling the tiniest flicker of guilt. Chiara had been blinded by the false image of himself that he had been peddling and he felt guilty at that. He was surprised. Guilt was not something with which he was familiar.

She saw that he was abashed although she did not realise why. "Goodness, I'm sorry. I hope you don't think I'm lecturing you. I don't mean to."

"No, of course not."

"It's just—well, I wouldn't anything bad to happen to you."

Edward didn't know what to say to that. They both sat, fiddling with their glasses.

"I've put my foot in it again, haven't I?" she said.

"No, no—not at all."

"I was wondering, perhaps we could talk some more—properly, you know, without any distractions. Perhaps you might like a trip up to the house? There's so much I haven't shown you yet. There's plenty of lovely countryside—perhaps we could go for a walk?"

He was a little thrown by her forthrightness, but he was flattered. "That would be lovely."

"Only if you'd like to," she added tentatively.

"I would. Of course. That would be charming, I'm sure."

"Next weekend? Are you available then?"

"I believe I am."

"Well then, that's settled. I'll see you on Saturday?"

They talked for a while longer, Edward listening politely and complimenting her opinions whenever she paused to take a drink. He saw that she was a little drunk and she talked freely, ranging easily across a range of subjects: her schooling, Halewell Close, her family, Joseph and the others, the best shows to see in London, her favourite restaurants. There was very little effort required on his part to keep up and, so, as he sipped the excellent champagne, he allowed himself to daydream about his future. The guilt was easily subsumed within the anticipation of his improved prospects as he planned where he went from here.

29

WHEN EDWARD SET OFF AT SEVEN O'CLOCK the sun was climbing into a powder blue sky. He arranged to borrow Joseph's Humber Super Snipe and as he settled himself behind the wheel he couldn't help but appreciate what a fine motor it was. It was the drophead coupé version and, since the morning was pleasant, he lowered and stowed the canopy. The breeze was pleasantly warm and Edward couldn't stifle the smile as he drove west. The roads were quiet and he was able to put his foot down. He allowed his attention to drift. New billboards bore witness to the flourishing shoots of economic life: Guinness is Good For You, Keep That Schoolgirl Complexion, Try a Worthington. He drove quickly, darting out to overtake slower moving traffic. As he headed further west he passed through slumbering commuter towns, new bungalows springing up on their outskirts like crops of mushrooms.

 A gardener's van was parked outside the entrance to Halewell Close, the man painting the gates. He doffed his cap to Edward as he turned off the road and onto the drive. Edward returned the gesture, rattling across the cattle grid and accelerating away. The house appeared as he crested the final hill and he found himself thinking with something like wistfulness of the poor neglected property, quietly sliding into decay. A place like that needed an owner who would cherish it, who would lavish the kind of attention on it that it deserved, and he could not help but think that the Costellos had allowed it to go to seed.

He pulled up and a large black dog trotted from the *porte cochère* and started to sniff around the car. Chiara followed after it. "Good morning," she called.

Edward stepped out of the car and kissed her on the cheek. She was wearing a simple cotton frock and a pair of leather sandals. The dog ambled over and sniffed his proffered hand. It was an old Labrador, black with grey tufts on its chin. "Who's this fine fellow?" he asked.

"This is Roger," she said. "My old dog. He'd like to come with us on our walk. Is that alright?"

"Of course," he said.

"How was your drive?"

"Lovely. Your brother has a very fine motor."

"He loves it," she said, dismissing the car with a flick of her wrist. "Shall we set off straight away?"

"Where are we going?"

"This way," she said, linking her arm through his.

They made their way through the gardens to the north of the house. There was a wide lawn, then a copse of fir and ash, and then a wild meadow that stretched away over gently undulating hills. There was a rough path trodden into the grass at the edge of the meadow and they followed it, brambles on one side and the open space of the field on the other. The landscape was open for several miles, fringed in the distance by a thick wood. Edward became aware of the treacly weight and torpor of the air. The last few days had heralded the start of an Indian summer, unseasonably hot for October. From across the fields, dulled by heat and distance, there came the grind and crunch of farm machinery, and calling voices.

They walked in companionable silence for half a mile. Roger trotted alongside them, occasionally picking up his pace to scout ahead. He would disappear around a corner and then wait for them, his tongue draping from his wet muzzle.

"How much do you know about the girl Joseph met at the restaurant?" he asked. "Do you know her?"

"I don't know her at all. I believe they were seeing each other before he was conscripted."

"Joseph said they were sweet on each."

She laughed happily. "That poor girl is going to be completely bombarded. My brother can be very single-minded when he thinks he wants something—women especially. I wouldn't be at all surprised if he really goes after this one. He's very keen. It won't matter if she's cool on him. He won't accept no for an answer. He'll try and try and try until she gives in."

"What a coincidence, to see her again after all that time!"

She shook her head. "He won't see it that way. It will be 'providence.' You know how superstitious he is?"

"Is he really?"

"My goodness, yes! It's all nonsense, of course, but he doesn't see it like that. You know he's religious, for example?"

"*Religion?*" he said as they crossed a stile. "Joseph?"

"Oh yes. Catholic. Well—most of the family are, one way or another. Violet is especially keen, but it's only because she thinks it's the right thing for an Italian family to do. Appearances, you know, same as always. Joseph went through a period when he was younger when he was mad about it. It's not so bad since he came back again. I suppose the things that you see and do in war are enough to make anyone doubt that sort of thing."

"Or embrace it more," Edward suggested. "You'd be surprised."

"Well, quite."

She turned her head, as Roger let out two or three sharp yelps. While they had been talking he had been nosing his way through the hedge at the side of the field, but now there was an agitated flapping on the other side of the hedge and he disappeared into a gap in the brambles.

"He's going after a bird," Chiara said. "These used to be our birds once; they're Mr. Austin's now, after we sold the fields and the woods to him. He won't like it if Roger gets hold of a partridge. Roger! Come back! Come here, you idiot dog!"

The dog returned, his head dipped bashfully, his prey uncaught, and they walked on. Edward found that he had relaxed completely into Chiara's company. She was nine years younger than him but there was a quiet, reserved wisdom about her that made her seem older. Her serenity was contagious. Edward typically felt a buzz of nervous anticipation when he was with other people, a constant background stress that derived, he knew, from the need to remember the all lies that he had told or would tell, the continual effort of recalling the correct lie for the appropriate person. He did not feel that way with her. He almost felt as if he could be himself, or at least insofar as that could ever be possible with anyone.

"Can I ask about your parents?" he said. "Joseph has never really spoken about them to me. I was wondering, since they weren't at your party."

She shook her head. "I suppose it's not surprising. Father's dead. It makes him upset—it's upsetting for all of us, of course, but he takes it the worst. It happened while he was away."

"Oh," Edward said awkwardly. "I'm sorry."

"No, really," she said, reassuringly. "It's quite alright." They walked on a little as she worked out how to say what she wanted to say. "Father was killed two years ago. One of Hitler's rockets fell on the house he was in. Rotten luck, really—it was one of the last ones they fired."

"It's none of my business. I shouldn't have asked."

She dismissed his apology with a shake of the head. "It's fine," she said. "Father was with one of his mistresses at the time. It was her house that he was in. They both died. It was too much for my mother. She left us, not that I can really blame her. Father was a bad husband and she stayed with him longer than he had any right to expect. All the other women—he always had one on the go, more than one, usually. The business, he was always out, all hours of the day and night, we never knew where he was most of the time. He tried to keep it secret but mother was always too clever for him. She knew everything. But she never left—I think she got used to the idea that he would always have more than one woman and she accepted it. They argued—she hated that other people knew about what he was getting up to but she still loved him. She knew he'd always come home to her. And I suppose, if I'm being honest, my mother got used to a certain way of life living with my father. He was generous—jewellery, fancy meals, clothes." She pointed towards the house, the chimneys of which had just appeared over the branches of a stand of nearby trees. "She loved it here, too. He knew he treated her badly, and the presents he bought for her were his way of saying sorry. They would have stayed together for ever."

"Joseph's said nothing to me about any of this."

"He's angry with her. He thinks she abandoned us. I don't think he's seen her since he got back. You mustn't bring it up. He'll be furious I mentioned it. Do you promise?"

"Yes, of course."

They idled onwards. "He idolised father," Chiara went on after a short pause. "It's why he joined the army. He could easily have gotten out of it—all of his friends did. Look at Billy and Jack, faking medical conditions. Joseph was desperate for father's approval. The attention was always on my other brothers when we were growing up. Has he mentioned them?"

"No."

"Stan works for the family in Manchester, John is trying to go straight and Paulie is in prison."

"For what?"

"Oh, assault." She relayed this dismissively, as if reporting that he had a nice, safe office job. "They were the ones father thought would follow him into the family business. He groomed them for it—he had them on the races with him early on, they were both up to their necks in it right from the off. But he never wanted it for Joseph––he told my mother once he thought he was too sensitive. There's some truth in that. Father wanted him to go to school, get an education and a proper career—something legitimate. It drove Joseph mad. I can remember the rows they had about it like they were yesterday—Joseph's temper, when he gets going, my goodness, you don't want to be around when he goes off."

"Really?"

"Awful. Frightening, actually. Father was just the same. They were alike in lots of ways." They followed the path into the copse of fir and ash that had grown up at the foot of the house's long gardens. "Father fought in the Great War, got a medal, too, for bravery. Then this last one came around and Joseph said he was going to enlist. Father wouldn't have it. He said he was throwing his life away. They had the biggest argument I can remember—father ended up hitting him and I thought Joseph was going to hit him back. It took Stan and John to keep them apart. After that, the first chance he got to sign up, he took it. You know he lied about his age?"

Edward said that he did not.

"He was sixteen when he went away. He's always been a big lad, I'm not surprised he managed to fool them. He didn't tell any of us about it. He just went."

They walked on in silence, the house appearing as they passed through the last trees.

"And then when he got back father was dead. I can't imagine how badly he must feel about it now—the last time they saw each other—the argument they had—and then to come back and the first thing you find out is that your father has died and you never had the chance to make it all up. It's all horrible. This nonsense he's got himself into now, with Billy and Jack, whatever it is they're doing––it's because of father."

"Trying to prove him wrong."

"Yes, indeed," she nodded. "And trying too hard. His judgment... my brother is not an idiot, Edward, he's cleverer than you'd think, I just think that in certain instances his judgment is wanting." They crossed the scruffy ornamental lawn and stepped over the low hedge onto the gravel drive. "Well, here we are again."

"That was very pleasant," Edward said. "Thank you."

She smiled, a broad and happy smile that showed her perfectly white teeth. It made Edward smile, too. "You must stay for lunch," she insisted, her eyes glowing with an optimism that Edward thought made her look even more attractive. "I told the cook to prepare a picnic. I hope that wasn't presumptuous of me? We could have it on the lawn?"

"That would be lovely," he said, and he could see from her little smile that she had been hoping that he would say yes, that she had been looking forward to lunching with him.

Chiara fetched a picnic blanket from the house and went back inside to speak to the chef. Edward took the blanket and spread it out across the lawn. He sat down and stretched his legs. He was satisfied with himself. The morning had been a complete success. He felt that he had gathered important information about the family and that he had brought himself into Chiara's confidence. That pleased Edward most of all. He knew how useful it would be to have her as an ally. It would be another source of information and, if he developed their relationship with the right amount of care, then it would offer other ways of improving his influence within the family.

Yes, he thought. His satisfaction was justified for he really was making great progress. This talent of his was the only thing that he had ever been good at, but he knew that he was very good at it. He wanted to make himself part of the family and he knew now, for sure, that that was a realistic goal, if he kept working hard at it.

30

THEY ROBBED TWO HOUSES THE WEEK AFTER Edward's visit to the country and both yielded an excellent return. Edward had invited Chiara to dinner in the city on the evening of the second job, booking a table for them at Rules in Covent Garden. He found himself relaxing more and more into her company. She was intelligent, witty and disarmingly honest about her family. She was also often indiscrete, especially when she had enjoyed a drink or two, and that made her an excellent source of information. He listened to her stories, prompting her in the direction that he wanted, and filed the details away. They would all prove useful, later.

This particular evening was no different. As they enjoyed a reasonable meal she told him more about her father and uncle. George Costello was born in 1889 and his brother, Harry, five years later. The boys' father had been a respectable watchmaker from Piedmont. The old man had emigrated to England several years previously. There was a market for his talent and, once he had settled, he sent for the rest of his family. The two boys had quickly taken to Little Italy's natural vocation—crime—and had proven to be very good at it. Petty theft turned to burglary and extortion and, despite their father's best efforts to rein them in, they started to make money. Both brothers grew to be large and intimidating men, with George in particular marked by a cruel streak and a lack of conscience when it came to doling out pain. The two rapidly earned a reputation, frightening men twice their age into doing their bidding. The Great War provided a brief interregnum—Harry fought, George did not—but with the armistice came a renewed onslaught that saw them wage vicious battles across the racecourses of the south. Their opponents were the Brummagem Boys of Birmingham, a motley band of thugs and bullies infamous for their cruelty.

"My father became a bit of a local celebrity," Chiara explained. "Him and George were both tearaways, but he had something extra about him. Some of the stories I heard when I was growing up—there was one time, I think it was just after the War, that everyone started on about him. They were in a pub on the Hill and they saw this chap, Thomas Benneworth—they called him the Trimmer because he was handy with his razor—they saw him bothering one of the barmaids. Benneworth was the leader of the Elephant Boys from the Elephant and Castle, a nasty type with a big reputation. This girl wouldn't have anything to do with him and so he went around the bar and tore her dress off. Just tore it off. My father saw what happened, dragged him outside, beat him black and blue then took his own razor off him and slashed him across his backside—one, two, three, four—noughts and crosses, they called it, you couldn't sit down for weeks afterwards. Anyway, after that, people wanted to work with him—the Elephant Gang ditched Benneworth and joined them, then there was a Jewish gang from the East End, plenty of others."

The skirmishes with the Brummagem Boys became worse. A final confrontation was planned after the Derby, on the outskirts of Epsom. Harry Costello learnt of a plan to ambush them on the way back from the course. He filled their charabanc with stooges and alerted the police.

The Birmingham gang set about the stooges, killing two men and injuring others. The police arrested everyone and, in the trials that followed, the leaders of the gang were imprisoned. The Costellos won out, the remnants of their rivals seen off to the Midland tracks that had always been their redoubt. The south was clear and ripe for the picking.

Harry led the family through prosperous times for the next twenty years. George had always deferred to his younger brother and was ill-equipped to take his place when he was killed. Rival factions within the family that Harry had glued together by the force of his will now sensed the opportunity to break away, and George, despite the threat entailed by his ominous physical presence, was unable to do anything to stem the losses. The racecourses were lost to a police crackdown and ex-allies who changed allegiance, the Alf White gang from King's Cross especially. The in-fighting worsened. Two men were shot and killed and the police—no longer in Harry's pocket—had to act.

As circumstances spun out of control, Violet took a more prominent role in the family's affairs. Under her stewardship, their position was consolidated. The factions were brought into line. Chiara did not elaborate, but Edward was left in no doubt that violent retaliation had been the reward for their presumption. She began a programme of retrenchment. The racecourses might have been lost to them, but they consolidated with the lesser prize of the dogs. Other existing businesses—betting, extortion, spielers, drinking dens, robbery and blackmail—were continued, although times were not nearly as good. Chiara explained the extent of the Costello family empire dispassionately, without varnish or embarrassment. Edward listened intently. She related how business was not what it used to be. The loss of the income from the horses, so long the bedrock of the family finances, had been a crushing blow. The other activities could only go so far to paper over the cracks. The flow of money was stemmed, and Violet had to cut her cloth accordingly. Men were laid off, hired muscle no longer economic, but that meant that they were vulnerable to other gangs who were jostling for position. Tame policemen could no longer be bought off, and so men started to have their collars felt.

"Rationing has been the saving of us," she suggested. The burgeoning black market had bought them a reprieve. As austerity continued, with rationing eventually cutting even deeper than during the war, a voracious appetite for goods had developed that the family was well-placed to exploit. They controlled or intimidated dozens of petty thieves, taxing their profits when they sold their booty to spivs like Ruby Ward and then taxing the spivs when they sold on to the public. The drones were making the real money but the family were able to cream a decent profit from the top. The glory days had gone, but there was enough business so that they could afford to retain a modicum of the lifestyle that they had enjoyed before. The prospect of having to sell Halewell Close—very real at one point—had receded, although they were short of the money to maintain it. They could keep it, but unless there was a significant change in their fortunes, Edward knew they would be just presiding over its slow, crumbling decline.

The evening drew to a pleasant conclusion. As Chiara's cab pulled up to the kerb she put a hand on Edward's elbow, moved in close and angled her face towards his. Edward leant down, and her lips found his. The kiss was brief but the cool confidence in her eyes flickered, just for a moment, occluded by a streak of passion. With her kiss still warm and moist on his lips, Edward watched as she waved to him from the back of the departing taxi. He looked up into the moonlit sky, and watched the silhouette of a couple as they embraced in the lit window of a third floor room. He was trying to decide if there was any way he might have improved on his courtship. He didn't think so. He was controlling the pace, and Chiara's expectations, with an expert touch. He turned and started the walk back towards Hyde Park. He began to plan the next steps. Things were going so well. He wondered whether he might even accelerate a little.

31

JOSEPH ARRANGED FOR FLOWERS to be delivered to the restaurant every day, huge bouquets that Eve couldn't possibly manage to take home with her. With every fresh delivery came a card inviting her to dinner, yet she turned down each invitation. Joseph spoke to Edward and between them they diagnosed the reason for her reluctance. It wasn't a lack of interest, they ascertained, just that she was a traditional girl and her sense of propriety needed to be assuaged. The two of them had been younger when they had first courted and the time and distance since then meant that the prospect of a second romance carried with it the possibility of longer term consequences. Edward ventured that she wanted to do things properly and made the suggestion that he and Chiara could offer to accompany them to dinner. He had been correct and that made all the difference for Eve. The prospect of a chaperone gave her licence her to accede to the request and she duly did.

The night was set for the following Friday. Edward spent an hour preparing himself, shaving and brilliantining his hair until it was neatly slicked. He hadn't seen Chiara for a couple of days and he wanted to make a good impression. He dressed in a new suit that he had purchased earlier that day, matching it with an icy white shirt and a narrow black tie. He was polishing his shoes when Joseph emerged from his room.

"What do you think?" Joseph said.

Edward thought he looked like a prince, and told him so. His suit was sharp and his shoes were from Belgrave. The genuine Vicuna-hair overcoat over his arm cost sixteen guineas. He was wearing a tie-pin that they had seen in a Mayfair shop-window. It was set with a large pearl as big as his little fingernail, shaped like an onion, that looked like it had been blown out of a tiny bubble-pipe. The ticket had said thirty-five pounds and twelve shillings. He had put a brick through the window and had away with it.

It was a gloomy night, the fog thick and damp. Edward drove them into the East End to collect Eve from the small house she rented with a friend. She was waiting behind the door and opened it before Joseph could knock. As she carefully slid into the back of the car, Edward noticed the curtains flicking back and the face of another girl, framed in the gaslight, staring out with a mixture of anxiety and jealousy.

"Where's your sister?" she said to Joseph, a little alarmed.

"Don't worry," Joseph told her.

"You said—"

"You'll still have your virtue. She's meeting us at the restaurant."

They arrived at Claridges at a little after eight. The restaurant was full, with the first seating of diners coming to the end of their meals and their replacements enjoying aperitifs at the bar. Chiara was waiting for them. She kissed Edward and then her brother on the cheek.

"Goodness me," she said. "Look at the two of you."

There was a single empty table and it had been reserved for them. They took their seats and Edward relaxed, looking around the room at the tables full of contented diners. He turned to smile at Chiara. He noticed that her eyes were rimmed with red. And did she look a little pensive?

"Are you alright, Chiara?"

"I'm fine."

"You've been crying."

"I'm probably worrying about nothing but—"

"Worrying about what?"

"Oh, it's Roger. The silly old dog. He's missing."

"How do you mean?" Joseph said.

"Exactly that. It was bright yesterday afternoon so I let him out—he loves to lie in the sun. I watched him trot out to the lawn and settle down and thought nothing else of it. I was distracted, I can't even remember what about, but then I realised I hadn't heard him bark to come back in. I went outside to look. This was six by then, maybe even seven. I looked through the grounds but I couldn't find him anywhere. I went straight across to Mr. Austin—you know how he chases his birds sometimes—but he hadn't seen him. I got back home at ten and he still wasn't there. And I couldn't find him this morning, either."

Joseph was ordering a bottle of Médoc from the waiter. "He'll turn up," he said when he was done.

"But what if he doesn't? He's an old boy now. He never stays outside on his own any more. What if something has happened to him? Maybe he was hit by a car?"

She started to cry. Eve looked worried and confused. Joseph—who could foresee the end of the evening if urgent steps were not made to rescue it—looked pleadingly across the table at Edward.

He took her hand. "It's alright," he said soothingly. "He doesn't strike me as the kind of dog who'd go far. Is that right?"

"No—he never does."

"Exactly. And so maybe he's been shut into a shed or a barn. If you ask me, he'll be home when you get back. And if he isn't, I'll drive straight down to you and we can have a proper look around. How's that?"

"Would you?"

He smiled at her. "Of *course* I would."

She squeezed his hand. "Thank you, Edward. I know it's silly but that dog's been with me since I was a little girl. I've always doted on him a little, haven't I, Joseph?"

"You certainly have," Joseph said, rolling his eyes.

"Don't tease me," she said, managing a smile of her own.

Not wishing to miss the improvement in her mood, Joseph quickly seized his moment, filled their glasses and raised his. "Cheers," he toasted. "To good friends. Let's have a splendid night."

* * *

A LIGHT FALL of rain had slicked the streets as they emerged outside. The fog had lifted and the clouds had moved away. A clear, open sky spread out overhead. Edward was lightly drunk. It had been a delightful evening. Joseph had been in riotous good form, dominating the table with stories from his childhood, from the war, about the host of characters he knew from The Hill. Chiara had painted the detail inside the lines of her brother's broad strokes. They spoke about some of the characters from their childhood, friends of their father: Angelo Ginicoli, Pasquale Papa, a bookmaker called Silvio Massardo whom they called 'shonk' on account of the size of his nose. Joseph recounted a story of how Harry and George were trapped one night in the Fratellanza Club in Clerkenwell, and were saved from being shot by the manager's daughter, a poor girl who was in love with Harry.

Edward was content to sit and listen, enjoying the stories, his friend's high spirits and Chiara's furtive glances in his direction.

The foursome made their way to Piccadilly Circus, the reflections from the advertisements stretching out across the wet pavements in long, neon stripes. A coster offered chrysanthemums at sixpence a punch and Joseph bought five shilling's worth—practically an armful—and gave them all to Eve. She stammered out her thanks but Joseph didn't allow her the chance to finish. He pulled her in close so that the blooms were flattened between their bodies and kissed her on the mouth, the two of them framed for a moment in the light that slanted from the window of a Cypriot café.

Chiara slipped her hand inside Edward's and gave it a squeeze.

"Who wants another drink?" Joseph said.

Eve looked torn, keen to accede yet reluctant at the same time. The hesitation won out. "No, I'd better not," she said. "I'm working tomorrow."

"Then take the day off," he said. "I'll pay you what you would have earned."

"No, that's alright—it's getting late, I'm tired and my friend will be expecting me. And I'd be letting the restaurant down, and that's not fair. Do you mind awfully?"

"What's the matter with you?" Joseph scowled, irritation flickering darkly. "It's been a nice evening. Why would you want to spoil it?"

Eve could see the change in his tone, the stirring of his anger. Perhaps she remembered it from when they were younger? Chiara noticed it, too. "Leave her alone, Joseph," she said. "I'm tired as well, it's past midnight. Do you mind, Edward?"

"No, of course not."

Chiara took Eve's hand. "We can share a cab. Look—here's one now." She flagged the driver and he swung in to park alongside them.

Joseph had no time to react. "Thank you for a lovely evening," Eve said. "Perhaps we could do something together another time?" She added, quietly, but not so quiet that Edward could not hear her, "Just us?"

Joseph was caught between thwarted desire and anticipation. Edward knew that he was not used to being defied, especially when it came to women. Chiara had said as much: he always got his own way. Yet Eve was special and frustrating him just made him even more determined to get what he wanted. "Of course," he said, banishing his scowl with a gorgeous smile as easily as flicking a switch. "We'll go for dinner. Me and you. That sounds lovely. Alright?"

Eve smiled in response, relieved that she had not, after all, offended him.

They bid them farewell and got into the cab. Edward and Joseph watched until it had turned the corner.

Joseph shook his head. "What was that all about, Doc?"

Edward clapped him on the back. "She's shy."

"She never used to be."

"She's older now. Perhaps it means more."

"That was what you and my sister were there to sort out."

"You're going to have to be patient."

"Not one of my strengths." He sighed but then, just as quickly, perked up. "Women! I need a proper drink. You aren't going to turn me down, are you?"

"Certainly not," Edward said. "Lead on."

32

CHARLIE MURPHY tailed the taxi all the way across London. He could hardly believe what he had seen in Piccadilly Circus. He had followed Edward and Joseph to the restaurant but he hadn't noticed the two girls until they all emerged together at the end of the night. He recognised Chiara Costello. She and Fabian had been together several times recently and it seemed likely—if a little improbable——that they were stepping out together.

It was the sight of the other girl that had knocked him for six.

He had had to check and double check and even then it had taken him a little while to be sure that it was Eve. He hadn't seen her for five years. She had been fifteen, then, and now she had grown into a beautiful young woman. The coltish innocence of youth had been replaced by a knowingness that he found difficult to match with his memories of her but there was no question about it.

He was sure.

It was definitely her.

Five years. As he followed the taxi into the East End he thought of the effect that her sudden disappearance had had on his brother. Poor Frank. It had almost destroyed him. It had been at the same time as the murders in the West End and he had been convinced that she had been one of poor doxies who ended up as victims. His single-minded obsession with the case had been driven by his fear. They had cleared that case up and still there had been no sign of her and so he had kept searching. He left the police soon afterwards and set up as a private investigator so that he would have more time to look and less protocol to observe. He had continued the search for five long years but he had found nothing. Frank was not a man prone to speaking about his feelings—and the brothers were not close—but Charlie had spoken to Frank's wife and she had told him how it had torn him apart. Their marriage had failed, he had turned to the bottle and the loss was still tormenting him, even today.

And now this. Charlie thought about it, peering through the smeared rain on his windscreen at the taillights of the taxi in front. He had found her. Here she was, fresh from dinner with Joseph Costello, the presumptive heir of London's most notorious criminal family.

He already knew what he was going to do.

The taxi turned into the Old Ford Road and stopped beside a terrace halfway down. Charlie pulled over too and switched off the engine and the lights. The taxi's door opened and Eve got out, pausing to say something to Chiara Costello before closing it, waving as the cab set off again. She turned and disappeared into one of the houses.

Charlie got out of the car and followed her to the door.

He knocked.

Eve was still in her overcoat.

Her mouth dropped open.

"Eve," Charlie said.

"Oh, God."

"Can I come in?"

She thought about that, her mouth opening and closing, and, for a moment, Charlie wondered if she was about to shut the door on him.

"Uncle—"

"I think we'd better talk, don't you?"

"There's nothing to say."

"I'm not going away, Eve."

She stepped aside and he entered the hallway. It was a simple two-up, two-down. The door ahead of him led to the kitchen. A flight of stairs ascended to the first floor where, he guessed, he would find two bedrooms. The toilet was probably in the yard. She led the way through the door to the left. It was a sitting room: neat and tidy, a table and two chairs and a reasonable sofa arranged in front of the wireless. A bookshelf full of books. A few feminine trinkets here and there: a vase of daffodils on the table; a crocheted blanket folded neatly over the arm of the chair. He trailed his finger over the mantelpiece: no dust. These were the signs of a house-proud occupier. Charlie wondered whether she lived here on her own.

She sat quietly in the armchair, her legs pressed together and her hands clasped tightly on her knees. There was no colour in her face. She seemed unable to speak.

"Eve," he said gently. "Where have you been?"

"Manchester."

"For all this time?"

"Until last Christmas. I was working as a waitress. Then I came back."

"Your father—"

"Please," she said, the mere mention of him seeming to unblock dammed emotions. The entreaty was freighted with desperation. "Please, Uncle Charlie. I don't want to see him."

"He's your father, Eve. You know what this has done to him?"

She looked down at her hands. "I—"

"Eve?"

She looked up, her eyes suddenly fierce with life. "I don't care. I don't want to talk to him. You mustn't tell him you've seen me."

"Why?"

"Because I hate him."

"You don't hate him."

"No, I do."

He sighed. "How can I not tell him? He's my brother."

"Because I'm an adult now. It's my choice whether I see him or not. And I'm asking you to respect that."

He crossed to the bookshelf and ran his finger along the spines of a series of penny-dreadfuls. He knew he had to proceed with a delicate touch if he was going to nudge the situation the way he wanted. "Why did you run away?"

"I was seeing a boy. He told me I couldn't."

"Are you seeing him again now?"

She regarded him suspiciously. "How did you find me?"

"Is it Joseph Costello?"

She looked at him with undisguised panic. "How did you know?"

"You were with him tonight."

"You were following me?"

"No—I was following him."

"Why?"

"Because he's a criminal."

"He's a rogue. That doesn't make him a bad person."

Charlie shook his head. The girl was blinded by emotion. He sat down and took out his cigarettes.

"Give me one of those," she said.

Look at her, all grown up. He shook two out of the packet and handed one over. There was a matchbook on the mantelpiece; she struck a match and lit hers. Charlie lit his own with his lighter.

"You and Joseph. You better tell me what happened."

"Originally? I was young, it was a little bit foolish, but I still loved him. Father and I argued about it. On and on and on. He told me I couldn't see him but how was that fair? I was fifteen years old. Almost a woman. Fifteen is old enough to make your own decisions. He had no right to tell me what to do, where I could go, who I could and couldn't see, and so I ignored him. He found out I'd defied him and we had another row, a big one. He was drunk and he slapped me. He told me I had to do what he told me while I was under his roof and so I decided I wouldn't be under his roof any more."

"And then?"

"I had a friend in Wigan. She used to work down here. I told her what had happened and she said I could go up and stay with her for as long as I wanted. I thought maybe I'd go for a week or two and then contact Joseph. We'd spoken about running away together. I didn't see him before I went and when I tried to get in contact with him again he had enlisted. Burma! It broke my heart. There wasn't any point in moving back to London without him and so I tried to make a life for myself up there."

"Why did you come back?"

"My friend died last year. The cancer. It was different, then—I didn't know anyone else, I was lonely and I missed the city. So I moved back again and got a job waiting on tables. Joseph came into the restaurant just after I started. I could hardly believe it. It's like we were never away from each other. I can't tell you how happy I am."

"You know why your father objects to him, don't you?"

"Yes, and he's wrong. Joseph's a good man. He treats me well. He loves me and I love him. That's all that matters."

"How long has it been going on?"

"A few weeks."

Charlie paused. He needed to work through the angles.

"Please, Uncle Charlie. Please, you mustn't say. He'll ruin everything."

Charlie paused again. He could see it clearly; it really was a simple choice. On the one hand, he could tell Frank and end five years' of misery at a stroke. That would be the right thing to do, the fraternal thing, but then Charlie had never been constrained by morality and he rarely saw his brother, anyway. The alternative was to treat this as divine providence, a means to access the Costello family's affairs. He thought of the difficulty of the investigation so far, the blind alleys and stalled leads, the barely coded warning from the Deputy Assistant Commissioner: bring the black market to heel or we'll take the job away from you and give it to someone else who can. The end of his gilded reputation. It would be as good as dismissal.

And, if he needed further justification, that was a simple enough thing. Was an end to Frank's misery worth more than the public good of bringing dangerous spivs like Joseph Costello and the rest of his family to heel?

Charlie didn't think that it was.

Frank wouldn't understand it like that but, then, he wouldn't know.

He knew what he had to do. He crossed the room, crouched by the armchair and laid his hand atop hers. "You know what you're asking me to do, don't you? Your father is a broken man. Any brother with a heart would tell him that you had come back."

"Please don't—I'm begging you, Uncle."

"If I didn't tell him, you'd have to promise to help me."

She looked at him with pitiful eagerness. "Anything. What do you want?"

"I want information."

33

IT WAS VERY LATE, or, rather, it was very early. Edward and Joseph had ended up in a Costello establishment, a spieler in one of the back doubles near Holborn. A motley collection of gamblers were ranged around a bare wooden table: a couple of faces from the Costello organisation, local businessmen with too much money and too little sense. The talk was of Jack Spot and Lennie Masters, and of what the Costellos would do about it. One of the participants noticed Joseph and the conversation stalled, an awkward silence falling upon the room until a fresh subject was proposed. Edward knew what they had been debating: they had been questioning the lack of response, perhaps even doubting that there would be one. Violet and George had continued to ignore his advice, which, while foolish, need not have been calamitous. Striking back hard and fast was the alternative, but they seemed unable to do that, either. Edward had heard speculation that the Costello soldiers were afraid of Spot's brawny gypsies and their reputation for shocking violence.

Days had passed and still they had done nothing. They had left it too long. Doubt had been allowed to fester and grow and Edward knew that the infection would metastasise and spread. Morale would be the first casualty.

Cracks would start to appear. Questions would be asked, and, eventually, they would not be quashed by the appearance of a Costello in a bar. Hard-won unity would fracture and the family's strength would dissipate. Spot would absorb the remnants or destroy them.

Joseph did not see what Edward saw. He banged his empty glass on the bar. "Another one," he announced.

"What are you going to have?"

"Rum," he said with conviction. "At this hour of the morning, rum is the best thing. Rum for you?"

"Whatever you like. Anything."

"Two rums." The barman poured. "Doubles, man, doubles," Joseph exhorted, and the man poured again.

Joseph took out his wallet and opened it. Normally, it would have been stuffed with banknotes. It was empty.

Edward opened his own wallet. It, too, was empty.

"On the house," the barman said.

Edward put his wallet away. "How did that happen?"

"Bloody women," Joseph chuckled. "Cost you an arm and a leg and you don't get nothing to show for it."

They settled back with their drinks, sipping them as they watched the action on the table. Joseph had told Edward to watch one of the faces, a wiry brawler called Mumbles on account of a pronounced lisp. He had a deft touch when it came to fiddling the hands. His opponents were tired and had imbibed too freely on the booze, and none of them noticed the aces that had a habit of appearing in his hands. He pulled the trick for the third time, corralled the others' banknotes and dragged them across the table.

"See here," Joseph started, nodding at Mumbles' pile of cash. "I could do with a little walking around money myself. What do you say we make a withdrawal?"

"Where were you thinking?"

"What time is it?"

"A little after four."

"There's a house in Chelsea, this businessman owns it––he got rich in the war. Munitions. He's not there at the moment. It's empty."

"Where do you get all this from?"

He tapped the side of his nose and grinned. "Lot of nice stuff there, apparently—some very nice silver. It was going to be the next one I suggested, but I don't see why we can't just do it now, the two of us. What do you say?"

Edward's natural caution had been replaced by drunken bravado. "Why not," he said.

Outside, it was growing light. They were drunk, but not foolish enough to use Joseph's Snipe. They found an MG Y-Type parked on Glasshouse Street. It was a medium saloon, beautifully finished with plenty of leather and wood in the interior. Edward knew the model, and knew that the 1,250cc engine beneath the bonnet packed quite a punch. The drag was more ostentatious than he would normally have liked but he was in drunken high spirits and it seemed perfectly natural to want something fast and swanky. While Edward kept watch, Joseph kicked in the driver's side window, reached in and unlocked the door. Edward got in next to him as he fumbled underneath the dash. The engine started and they pulled out and away.

"That Eve," he said as they drove away. "She's a right cracker, ain't she?"

"Give it a rest—it's Eve this, Eve that, all bloody night."

Joseph laughed. "But she is, ain't she? She was lovely when I was with her before, but she's grown up bloody lovely, hasn't she?"

"She certainly has."

"Can't believe my luck. I've got you to thank. If it wasn't for your birthday party, I'd never have met her again."

They drove across town. Men in wide hats and thigh boots were washing the streets. Bums on the benches in Trafalgar Square shivered in the cold wind that blew up

Whitehall, waiting for the parks to open. In the all-night cafés waiters nipped their cigarettes and swept the floors, their nocturnal trade gradually being replaced by men on their way to work. They reached Chelsea and Joseph parked on a grand residential street. Big houses lined both sides of the road. There was a milk float further down the road, but it was two hundred yards away and the dairyman would never be able to see them from there.

They didn't need to say a word. The routine was second nature by now.

They got out and went down the steps at the front of the house to the basement entrance. Joseph addressed the door, and kicked hard at the spot next to the handle. The door crunched, but held. Joseph kicked it again. It still held.

The shriek of a whistle pierced the early morning quiet.

Edward spun around and climbed the steps: two policemen were sprinting towards them.

"Shit," he cursed. "Joseph, police. Come on!"

They clambered up the steps and threw themselves into the car. Joseph fishtailed it as he stamped on the accelerator. The engine backfired loudly. Ahead of them, the dray horse was spooked by the sudden explosion of noise and pulled against its harness, yanking the milk float across the road until it was parallel to the oncoming traffic, blocking the way ahead. "Bugger!" Joseph cursed, stamping on the brake. The MG was already travelling too fast and they skidded twenty feet until their progress was finally arrested as the car smashed into the side of the float. Edward's head bounced off the veneer panel as bottles rained down on the windscreen with a cacophonous shattering, gallons of spilt milk covering the glass until it was impossible to see out. Joseph swore again and tried to put the car into reverse.

There was an horrendous metallic screeching.

"Come on, you bitch!"

It was futile: the axle of the float was jammed into one of the wheel arches and it was impossible to separate. The MG was going nowhere.

"It's jammed!" Edward's nose had mashed into the dashboard and blood was running freely. He swung around and looked through the rear window: the woodentops were blowing their whistles for all they were worth. They would be there in seconds. "Run for it!"

Edward sprinted but Joseph could not keep pace. Edward stopped and turned back. He was limping badly. He must have injured his leg in the crash. He was trying to run, a pathetic hop and skip, pain written across his face. Edward paused. He could get away but to do so he would have to abandon Joseph, and how would that look? He paused, caught between two competing urges: the desire for self-preservation and the need to remain in Joseph's good graces.

"Dammit!" Joseph spat.

The policemen were two hundred yards away.

Edward ran back to him. "Come on," he urged. "I'll help." He took his elbow and started to drag him along.

"My leg—I've done something to it. It's hopeless."

"Come on!"

"No, Doc, go on. Clear off. No sense us both getting nicked, is there?"

The woodentops were almost on them. Edward started to edge backwards.

"I'll sort it out," Edward said.

Joseph shoved him. "Get going. It'll be fine."

Edward turned and ran. The bobbies shouted out for him to stop but he ignored them. He crossed the road at full pelt and reached the junction. He turned to see Joseph shoved to the pavement, both woodentops on top of him, one with his knee in his back and the other yanking his wrists up towards his shoulder-blades. His face was angled towards Edward and, through the grimace of pain, he thought for a moment that he caught a wink.

34

EDWARD TOOK THE UNDERGROUND and emerged at Embankment. By the time he had reached Victoria Gardens he was as confident as he could be that he was safe. He went across the road, past the fruit-hawkers, and into the park. Not many people were sitting on the benches at that time of the morning and he sat down, joining the anonymous and the dispossessed: the old man feeding sparrows; the woman with a brown-paper parcel marked Swan & Edgar's; the down-and-out blowing a tuneless ditty on a penny whistle. He sat among them with his head bent, staring at his shoes, shivering in cold sweat and trying to regain his breath. He stayed there for ten minutes, watching the grey cumulus passing over the south bank, the eddying throng of people accumulating around the entrance to the underground station. The gulls flew low over the barges and the shot-tower stood black in the cold light among blitzed and ruined warehouses. He thought about what had happened. Their long string of successes had inured him to the prospect of failure, and what that meant, but the consequences were real now.

Joseph had been caught and he had barely escaped. And, if he had been caught, everything would surely have been unravelled. Burglary would be the least of his concerns.

No, he chided himself. No. You're too smart. Clever and resourceful. You can get out of this, and you can get Joseph out of it, too. He told himself to calm down, and, eventually, he did. He stayed there until the man who had fed the sparrows had gone and then, his confidence returning, he retraced his steps, passed the fruit-sellers and went back down into the Underground.

He caught a train towards Holborn, emerged into the sunlight and walked the short distance to the Hill. Billy Stavropoulos still lived with his mother in a two-up, two-down on one of the better streets in the area, but it was still a stone's throw from The Rookery and far from pleasant. He walked down the terrace to number seventeen and rapped on the door.

A raddled woman from whose face dried paint and powder were falling in little flakes opened it. "Yes?" she said, uncovering teeth like mildewed fragments of cheese.

"Is Billy here?"

Her eyes narrowed suspiciously. "No-one called Billy here."

"Please." Edward put his foot between the door and the jamb before she could close it. "I'm not the police."

"No? Who are you, then?"

"I'm a friend. It's about Joseph Costello. It's important."

She wrinkled her nose. "You sure? Our Billy hasn't been up to no good again?"

"No, it's nothing like that. I just need to see him."

She turned, leaving the door open. Edward followed her inside.

"Wait in there."

He followed her instructions, went through into the sitting room and sat on the dusty, unsprung sofa. A goods train rattled and gasped out of a nearby junction and in the distance an engine blew its whistle three times, deliberately. From the street outside came a sudden concert of horns, angry drivers setting off a lugubrious honking that put him in mind of geese. A man shouted. A motorcycle screeched to a stop, its engine turning over impatiently. Edward took the moment's peace to run over what he meant to do.

He knew perfectly well how he would fix the mess.

Billy stood in the door, a cigarette in his mouth. "What do you want?"

"Hello, Billy."

"What is it?"

"Joseph's in trouble."

"What kind?"

"Police. He's been nicked."

Billy shut the door quietly. "Alright—just keep it down, don't want the old dear to overhear. She'll just worry. What happened?"

"We were out last night. We both had a bit too much to drink. There's a place Joseph's had his eye on, we thought it'd be a good idea to do it over."

"Without me?"

"We were drunk. And you weren't there."

"I know I wasn't."

"Well, you couldn't very well—"

"So?"

"You would still have had your cut."

"Too bloody right I would." His hostility fizzed and spat.

Edward didn't have the energy to argue with him. "We were spotted. We crashed the car getting away. Joseph hurt his leg and he couldn't run. They've caught him."

"But not you. You made it off?"

"There was no point both of us getting caught, was there?"

Billy considered the situation.

"What you doing here, then?"

"I need your help."

"Why me? Why not Jack or Tommy?"

"I don't know where they live." The answer was brutal, and any thought Billy might have had that he was suddenly more important was quickly snuffed out. "Look, stop sulking. Are you going to help or not?"

"What do you want me to do?"

35

THE OXFORD EXPRESS DAIRIES operated from premises at 26 Frith Street, Soho. It had been there for more than sixty years, and, during that time, the Welsh had become the cow keepers and dairy suppliers of West London. The business was owned by the Pugh Family, who originally hailed from the county of Cardiganshire. Milk was delivered before dawn every morning on the milk train that collected its freight from farmers on the West Coast of Wales. The milk was excellent, and business was brisk.

Arthur Pugh, oldest of the Pugh boys and presumptive heir to his father's business, cracked the reins and the big dray horse jerked forwards. The dray was loaded with milk bottles, metal cream pitchers and little packets of butter wrapped in greaseproof paper. Larger blocks, forty pounds' worth, were destined for the local restaurant trade. A large blue and white glazed milk crock had been screwed to the front of the dray. It said PURE MILK, and OXFORD EXPRESS DAIRIES, and had been attached there for the purposes of marketing. The bottles were slotted into wooden crates and they rattled loudly as the dray trundled across the cobbles. It was a touch after six and Arthur was just beginning his rounds.

Edward Fabian watched him from the shelter of a parked car.

Pugh was turning onto Old Compton Street when he noticed Edward and Billy idling by the side of the road. Edward knew he would think nothing of them. The streets were always quiet at this time of the day but, even so, it was not unusual to see the odd reveller from the night before still aboard. There were plenty of places where you could enjoy an all-night drink if your face was right and you had money in your pocket. Edward watched as Pugh touched the crop to the dray's flanks and the big horse continued on.

The first stop was at Kettners: the daily delivery of milk and butter. Pugh pulled back on the reins until the horse stopped, then slid down from his seat to the pavement.

Edward grabbed him roughly by the lapels and shoved him hard against the side of the dray. Billy moved in and pressed the edge of the knife he was holding against his throat. Pugh swallowed hard, the bristles above his Adam's apple catching against the blade.

"We're only going to say this once," Edward said, his voice low and even and full of menace. "You saw something yesterday—two chaps being chased by the police. Have you spoken to the police yet?"

"Yes."

"What did they want?"

"Would I recognise them if I saw them again?"

"And?"

"I said I would."

"No," Edward said, slamming him against the wall. "Try again. And?"

"I won't," Pugh said, panicking a little. "I don't."

"They're going to ask you to give evidence at a trial, and they'll ask you to identify the man in the dock, but you won't be able to do it. You'll say you've never seen him before. Do you understand?"

"Yes."

"And you won't mention this to the police, will you?"

"No."

"Because if you do, you'll have a visit from us again. We know where you work. We know where you live. We know about your wife and your daughter. Everything. If you want to make sure nothing happens to your family, or your business, that's all you have to do—you never saw him before. Alright?"

"Yes, yes."

Billy took the knife away and Edward released him. He slumped forward, his knees clashing against the kerb. His head drooped beneath his shoulders and he vomited, his breakfast coming up in chunks. He spat the phlegm from his mouth and turned his head to watch the two men walking briskly away.

36

THE NEON BULBS OF THE ALHAMBRA flickered on and off as they hissed and fizzed in the rain. Red and green light slashed against the damp pavement and low, angry peals of thunder rumbled across the rooftops and through the streets. Clubland's punters scurried from doorway to doorway, umbrellas aloft and hats clasped to heads. It was a Friday evening and, despite the weather, Soho was filled with a humming energy. Drunks reeled across the road, tarts touted for trade and transacted their business in alleyways, couples embraced in doorways, groups of young men hooted and hollered. Edward stopped the cab on Dean Street and paid the driver with a pound note. He opened the door and he hurried beneath the awning of the club.

Billy, Jack, Tommy and Joseph were already at the bar.

"Alright, Doc," Joseph said with a huge grin.

"About time," Billy said.

Joseph clipped him on the top of the head. "Shut it, Billy."

Edward took off his dripping coat. "Sorry I'm late. There was some business I had to attend to."

He had been to see Jimmy. He had given his uncle twenty pounds, more than enough to buy supplies for the next week. He had been making the same payment every

Friday for the last two months. The old man had prepared a meal for them both and they had eaten it in silence while the staff prepared the restaurant for the evening service. Edward had felt a moment of warm satisfaction. He knew that, without him, the restaurant would have closed and his uncle would have been on the street. The knowledge that he was able to help him and his father was the icing on the cake. He was having such fun, and there were such great possibilities, but it was a small practical consequence like that that made it really worthwhile.

He draped his coat on the back of his chair and took off his hat. Joseph had five whiskys lined up on the bar before him and he passed one across.

"Alright then," Tommy said expansively. "We've got some drinking to do." He held up his glass. "Here's to putting one over on Old Bill."

"To milkmen with dodgy memories."

"To friends," Joseph added, smiling broadly at Edward as they touched glasses.

They drank and ordered again.

"Two weeks in Pentonville," Jack said, shaking his head. "What a bloody pain in the arse."

"How was it?" Tommy asked. "I've never been locked up before."

"Bloody horrible, but that's all done with now. I ain't going back there again in a hurry, that's for sure."

They all toasted the sentiment and drank.

He turned to Edward. "You spoke to the milkman, didn't you? Straightened him out?"

"Me and Billy."

"I appreciate it, lads."

"Don't be daft. You would've done the same for us."

"Well, it worked. And you've made an impression on my aunt and uncle."

"Really?"

"They want to see both of us."

"What for?" Edward said.

"Think they've got a bit of business for us."

"And me?" Billy asked with abject hopefulness.

"Just me and Doc for now."

Billy's face clouded angrily. "You've got to be kidding."

"If there's work to be had, you don't need to worry—we'll split it between us, like always."

"That's not fair," Billy said.

"Relax. You'll be involved."

Billy didn't look as if he was ready to relax. He smouldered at the snub.

Edward had to suppress his wide grin.

He had been noticed.

Here was a chance to move up.

"When?" he asked.

"Tonight, actually. They're in the back. Shall we?"

"What about these drinks we're supposed to be having?" Tommy said.

"We won't be long. Order another round. We'll catch up when we get back."

* * *

THE CLUB WAS BUSY: the house band was playing on the small stage at the far end of the room, a crowd of dancing couples swaying across the dancefloor, clubbers gathering around the tables and in the secluded booths that were set around the edge. There was a wall of noise and damp warmth, the smell of alcohol, perfume and pomade. Joseph nodded towards the back and shouldered his way through the heaving crowd. Edward followed him through a door, guarded by a huge man in a dinner jacket, and then up a flight of stairs to another, smaller room on the first floor.

Edward was nervous at the prospect of meeting George and Violet Costello. He had gleaned enough to know that Georgie the Bull was not the sort of fellow that you wanted to cross and Violet, too, was a daunting prospect. The thought of meeting the two of them together was enough to set his nerves on edge. They were at a table in the corner of the room. George looked at home in clubland but his sister was not so easily associated with it. Her expensive wardrobe and air of supercilious disdain suggested other locales: the opera, or tea at the Ritz. Edward suspected that she enjoyed the misapprehension. She had the air of someone who liked to prove people wrong.

Joseph led the way across the room, leant down and kissed his aunt on the cheek. Her hair had been freshly styled, luxuriously bouffant. She offered Edward her hand and he took it. He looked to George but he ignored them, leaning back in the chair and languidly extending his legs. A whiff of cigar smoke wafted across to them. There were two spare chairs on either side of them. Joseph took the one next to George and Edward lowered himself into the one next to Violet. He regarded the two of them. They certainly made for an uncanny couple: Violet was tiny, almost doll-like in her delicacy; George loomed over them all like a Gollum, heavy with muscle and his brows lowered in a seemingly perpetual frown.

"Boys," Violet began. "Do you want a drink?"

"I'll take a whisky," Edward said. Joseph concurred.

The barman delivered two whiskys. Edward took his and sipped, prolonging it. Violet was watching him carefully. "I understand you helped Joseph with his recent situation?"

"I had a word with a witness."

"You must have been very persuasive."

"I suppose I was."

"I'm grateful," she said.

Edward's hand was trembling a little: a mixture of excitement undercut by nerves. Violet held her up her vodka and the others reciprocated. He put the glass to his lips and sipped. The liquid burned his throat.

"Now then, Edward," Violet began. "I want you to know that we appreciated your advice with our friend Mr. Spot. I know that might not have been obvious at the time, but we did. You might also be wondering why we haven't done anything yet. You may rest assured that we will. It's simply a matter of picking the right moment."

"I understand," Edward said. It sounded awfully like an excuse to him but there was no profit for him in pushing the point any further. He had made his point.

"You must be wondering why we want to speak to you?"

"I am."

"Something has come up. A piece of business. It's an interesting proposition and will require significant effort. It's also—potentially—extremely lucrative. It is something the two of you are very well qualified for. You were a corporal in the Army, weren't you?"

"Yes," Edward said.

"And your decoration will stand you in good stead, too."

"I don't understand. How can I help?"

Violet regarded him over the lip of her glass. He was being appraised. "What I'm about to tell you must stay between us," she said, her affability now backed by a warning that didn't have to be said.

"Of course," he said.

"A man has come to our attention. An Army man who works for the government now—a bureaucrat, in the civil service. He comes into one of our spielers now and again. He's a serious betting man, and he has a problem with it. The cards haven't fallen for him recently and he's ended up owing the family a large amount of money. George has had a chat with him." She said that in such a way which left Edward in no doubt as to what she meant: a room out the back, a razor blade held against the throat, a hammer held over splayed fingers. "He says he can't pay but he's been persuaded that he needs to sort out his obligations.

He's made a proposal to do that. Business. I'd like you and Joseph to look into it."

"Why me?"

"You have the background and Joseph says you have the brains for it. You showed initiative in helping Joseph out of his recent situation, too. I like that. It shows initiative. I'd like you both to be involved."

"What do we have to do?"

Violet had finished her vodka. She fitted a cigarette into a holder and allowed George to light it for her. "You'll need to meet him."

37

EDWARD SPENT THE DRIVE INTO THE EAST END wondering how far he could go with the Costellos. Life had been monotonous after demobilisation and now it was thrilling, a series of hair-raising exploits that he found irresistibly addictive. It was about the exhilaration as they sped away from another ransacked house, the excitement that shivered between them in the car, the sheer, undiluted, ineluctable thrill. It was about money. He was being brought closer to the heart of the family. He had proved his mettle with the robberies and then straightening out the milkman and now he was on the way towards being trusted. He had been given an opportunity. He thought of George and Violet, of their money and power, and he wanted all of that for himself. There were other ways to get it, for sure—other scams and tricks—but those would have to be started from scratch and, he knew, none could ever be as promising as this.

Walthamstow was a large track with two large silver-coloured corrugated-iron stands flanking it. Two further banked kops were at either end where you could stand for a penny. The track thronged with people, queues snaking this way and that, and flat-fare taxis formed a single, unbroken, black line. Racegoers made for the wide entrance gates: some ran, the first race due off in ten minutes, desperate punters scrambling before the odds on their favourites shortened. A brass band played at the entrance to the course, drums and trumpets, all the old standards reprised, the crowd joining in. A preacher called for repentance through a loud-speaker. Hawkers sold programmes and form guides. The murmur of excitement grew as dogs paraded before the eight-thirty.

"This place," Joseph said, gesturing around. "It reminds me of being at the horses when I was a boy. I remember it like yesterday. They gave me a bucket of water and a sponge. My dad sent me to rub the odds off the boards of the bookies who wouldn't pay up. My dad and my uncle were like kings. Men tipped their hats to them, no-one wanted to offend them. Everyone knew their reputation—it was enough to guarantee they got what they wanted. A bloke wouldn't play ball and you'd overturn his stall, scare his punters away. That was usually enough."

They passed alongside the track. The overhanging floodlights, glaring down on the track, made the grass unnaturally green, the white paint of the starting traps unnaturally white. A long line of bookies called out for bets and advertised odds like fairground barkers. Tic-tac men fluttered their hands, passing messages around the course. "Marshall Plan, ten to one, ten to one for Marshall Plan." Losing tickets lay scattered around, trampled underfoot. Teenagers stood on wooden stools and paid out money. Men jostled for space, elbowing each other in their haste to give away their cash, notes held out in proffered fists. The bugle went and the kennel men shoved their dogs into the traps. The lights in the stands went out, the grass still more brilliant under the floodlights. The hare rumbled around the circuit, rounded the corner, the traps flew up, the dogs exploded away in a blur of colour. They sped by, feet thudding like drumbeats on the dry ground, cheers rising from the half-crown enclosure, forming a tight pack as the commentator called the race over the course's loud-speakers, the pitch of the crowd winding up as they turned onto the final straight, cheers mixed with groans as the favourite was overhauled, a long-odds chancer winning by a nose.

They climbed the steps to the members' bar. Major Herbert Butler was waiting for them at a table. Butler was a man of considerable girth. His hairline had retreated to the top of his crown and what wispy remnants of hair were left he kept plastered to his scalp with handfuls of Brylcream. His eyes were porcine nuggets, his nose a fleshy button and his jowls so pendulous that they spilled over the collar of his shirt, dragging the corners of his mouth with them so that he wore a permanent expression of sour distaste. He was dressed in clothes that would once have been expensive but had not been cared for properly, the jacket and corduroy trousers frayed at the cuffs, the fabric with a dull shine. A packet of cheap cigarettes sat before him. It looked like he was on his uppers.

Joseph approached. "Major Butler."

The man swung around anxiously at the salutation. "Costello?" He was nervous: his nails were bitten to the quick and he swept regular glances around the room as if he expected to be observed. "You're late," he said with the attitude of a man used to giving orders.

"Traffic was murder," Joseph said with a cool smile.

"You were supposed to be here half an hour ago."

Joseph held his smile patiently. "Well, we're here now––what do you say we have a chat?"

"Yes, yes."

They sat down at the table and Joseph began. "My uncle says you have a way to pay back the debt you owe." His choice of words was deliberate. It would do Butler no good at all to think that his age, experience or rank gave him any kind of authority over them. He needed to remember that he was in hock to them.

"It'll do more than pay him back."

"So you say. You better tell me about it."

"Aren't you a little young? I thought it'd be George Costello I was dealing with?"

"You've been given a chance, Major, and you're dealing with us. You'd do well to take us seriously. We can leave if you like, but you won't get another chance."

He ground his teeth. "Fine. I'm sorry, it's just—it's just—"

"It's just what?"

He paused. Edward could almost see his mind turning. "No, it's fine," he said eventually. "I'm based at Honeybourne. Do you know it?"

"The big base near Evesham? I passed through it briefly during my training."

"You're Army?"

"We both are."

"Where?"

"Burma."

That helped the man to relax. "I was there, too. Bloody place. Took a Jap bullet in the shoulder when we pulled out of Rangoon and that was the bloody war over for me. They transferred me to logistics when I got out of hospital."

"To Honeybourne?"

"Eventually. The Americans took it over during the war but when they left they handed it back to us. Ministry of Supply runs it now, and we look after it for them. It'll be bigger now than when you were there—a thousand huts over five hundred acres. Small town, really. They had shops, playing fields, everything."

"And there's an opportunity there?"

He laughed dryly. "Bloody right there is. Biggest opportunity I've ever seen in my life. When the Yanks went they left all their gear behind. All sorts—you can't imagine it unless you see it: cars, jeeps, trucks, radios, medical supplies, refrigerators, washing machines. Then there's gear that's still on the ration: tinned food, fuel, bedding, towels. They even left half a dozen Sherman tanks. Two bloody Dakotas, for Christ's sake. Dakotas! Everything's brand spanking new. A fellow from the Ministry came down to try and put a value on it all. He took one look at the stores and gave up—there's too much to inventory. But he reckoned it was worth hundreds of thousands."

"And there's no record of what's there?"

"Nothing precise. I doubt even the Yanks know, but even if they did it wouldn't matter—they're gone, and they're not interested in any of it. They wouldn't care if we dropped it in the sea."

"Is it guarded?"

"They've got chaps on the gate, like at any camp. You couldn't just walk in off the street and help yourself."

"But?"

"But it's lightly guarded and they've all been bought off. Between us, we've already disposed of a few lorry loads."

"So why do you need us? Why not take it all yourself?"

"That's the problem—we can manage small loads but that's missing the opportunity. It's scale. We don't have the means to get enough of the stuff off the base and even if we did we wouldn't have a clue how to sell it. We need someone who knows the black market. George Costello said—"

"Fine," Joseph interrupted him. "What's your plan?"

"It's all worked out. I can get you onto the base, that's easy, but it's too risky to take the gear straight to a warehouse or to customers. If it got traced back to us we'd all be buggered. But a captain who used to work with me has just been transferred to an OS Depot at Barry. And we can write transfer orders to move anything we want. We load the gear up at Honeybourne, consign it to the Barry depot and *then* we move it where it needs to go. The chaps at Barry won't miss it because they weren't expecting it in the first place. My mate supervises the arrival and departure of the goods in Wales. And if they ever get trouble at Honeybourne, they'll have the paperwork to show where the goods went. It'll all look above board. We'll just say that it must have gone missing there. Call it bureaucratic mismanagement—Christ knows there's enough of that going on. By the time the Ministry tracks the goods to Wales, the trail will have gone cold. It's foolproof."

"Who else knows about this?"

"There are four of us. The lieutenant colonel, me, my mate and a lieutenant. "

"The C.O.'s involved?"

"It's his idea."

They sat in silence. Edward could tell at once that the scheme had enormous potential but he knew better than to say anything. Better to let Butler think they were hesitant. Joseph had evidently reached the same conclusion and sat silently. He almost looked bored.

"What do you say?" Butler asked anxiously.

Joseph spoke speculatively. "Let's say for the sake of this discussion that we could be interested. What do you expect to get out of it?"

"To pay off what I owe and then a share of the profits."

"What kind of share?"

"Half."

"Don't be daft, mate. We're doing all the work."

"You can't do it without me."

"No, but you owe my uncle a small bloody fortune and he's been generous with you so far. I wouldn't recommend trying to drive too hard a bargain. Being greedy won't end well for you."

"Forty per cent."

Joseph shook his head firmly. "More like twenty."

"Twenty? Christ, man—that's ridiculous."

Joseph got up. "Come on, Edward," he said. "We're finished here."

"Thirty."

"Good night, Major. Enjoy the races."

"Damn it all," he spluttered. "Alright. Twenty. Twenty."

"Good. My uncle will be pleased."

He spluttered something about daylight robbery and Edward noticed, for the first time, that Butler's hands were trembling. He saw Edward looking at them and slid them beneath the table. "So what do we do next?" he said, aiming for brusqueness but coming up short.

"We'll come and have a look."

"When?"

"No time like the present. How's tomorrow?"

"Fine."

"Tomorrow, then."

They bid him farewell and made their way back to the table for a drink.

"What do you think?" Edward said. "Sounds good?"

"I'll say," Joseph grinned. "I think this sounds very bloody good indeed."

38

EDWARD DECIDED TO treat himself to a meal out. Joseph was going out to see Eve and so it would have to be alone, but, he thought, that suited him best. He enjoyed his own company and it would be an opportunity to assess how far he had travelled in achieving his objectives. He went home and shaved, changed his suit for an understated grey pinstripe that he matched with a white shirt and black tie and brown brogues. There were plenty of new establishments opening up all around Soho but he was in the mood for something with a little more history and class. He had enjoyed Claridges when he and Joseph had taken Chiara and Eve but the foolishness that had followed that night—despite the nimble extrication that he had orchestrated—had soured the memory a little. If he was going to fix a trip there in his memory, it would have to be one without blemish. He would return, just by himself, and do things properly. It would be a pure experience, as it should have been before.

The maitre d' recognised him and showed him to an excellent table in the corner of the restaurant. He sat and ordered a gin and tonic, looking around, enjoying the almost palpable sense of tradition and the ambience. These were normal people; people of a particular class, certainly, but people who led normal lives. Bankers and salesmen and their wives and lovers. Most would never have been stolen from and most would never steal. Most would never have experienced physical violence, or the raw, visceral thrill of a robbery. They would live out their lives, one day after the other with the predictability of a fine, Swiss watch. All as regular as clockwork: home, the train, the office, the train, home. All the money in the world was no compensation for a life like that. Edward would have the money but he would not sacrifice the joy in his life to get it.

He was lost in a dreamy reverie when he became aware of a man standing next to the table, looking down at him.

He looked up. The man was medium height and medium build, salt-and-pepper hair and a pair of wire-framed glasses that made him look ascetic and studious. He was reasonably well dressed although not, Edward concluded with a note of satisfaction, anywhere nearly as well as him. He recognised him from somewhere, too, although he couldn't place where.

"Good evening, Edward. Do you mind if I call you Edward?"

He was a little wrong-footed. "Do I know you?"

"We met."

"We did?"

"The boxing—your friend Billy Stavropoulos was fighting."

Edward recalled him and their brief encounter at the bout in Bethnal Green. "Kipps? We laid a bet together?"

"I'm afraid I was a little duplicitous. My name isn't Kipps."

"No? Then what is it?"

"It's detective inspector Murphy."

Edward felt his own face pass from the friendly smile that was always ready and available to a frowning wariness that was one step removed from panic. "I see."

"But call me Charlie, please."

"I think I'd rather call you detective inspector, if that's alright."

"Really? That'd be a shame. I'd like us to be friends, Edward. The kind of friends that can dispense with formality."

"I don't think so, detective inspector."

He smiled and shrugged. "Whatever you prefer."

Edward worked on recovering his composure. He sipped his gin, the ice cubes bumping against his top lip. The policeman regarded him sharply, his cold eyes articulate with intelligence. Policeman, individually, did not tend to concern Edward. They were typically dull and stupid, unthinking automatons who followed protocol without question. This man did not seem to fit the pattern and Edward was suddenly quite sure that he was on dangerous ground. He had no idea what Murphy was doing here. He had no idea what he knew and what he didn't know.

"I'm guessing this isn't a coincidence," he said, a gentle gambit that he hoped might have him tip his hand a little.

"I don't believe in coincidences in my business, Edward."

"And what is your business?"

"Closing down the black market."

He set the glass down on the table. "How could I possibly help you with that?"

He pointed at the empty chair opposite him. "Do you mind?"

"It's a free country."

Murphy sat down. He took out a box of Senior Service and handed it to him. Edward tapped out a cigarette and lit up. He sucked down on it greedily, feeling the nicotine hit his lungs, exhaled and gazed through the fuzzy smoke at Murphy.

"You're a mysterious one, Edward, I don't mind admitting it. Let me tell you what I know about you—and don't worry about stepping in and correcting me if I've got any of this wrong. Alright?" He put his cigarette to his lips and took a long drag. "We know you enlisted in 1938. We know you had two tours in Burma and that you have an enviable record: cited for valour six times and then you top that with the Victoria Cross. A bona fide, gold-plated war hero. Very impressive. You're given your demob papers in 1945, you land at Portsmouth and then it's up to London where you can't seem to find employment. You sign on at the Labour Exchange. The next thing we know, you're turning up with the most notorious mob in London."

Edward said nothing. He felt a prickly sensation running down between his shoulder blades.

"Not what I would expect from a man with your record. You're observed in Little Italy, in Soho and at Lennie Master's funeral. We're reasonably confident that you were the other man when Joseph was arrested on suspicion of burglary, and that makes us think that you were responsible for straightening out the witness. We know you've been to their place in the Cotswolds and we think you've been stepping out with Chiara Costello. How am I doing so far?"

"Please—this is fascinating. Go on."

"You seem to have found your way right to the heart of the family. The problem I have, Edward, is that none of what you've being doing fits with what we know about you from before. I like to have as much information on the men I'm looking into as I can. I've had detectives going through the records with a fine-tooth comb: we've checked the Criminal Records Office at Scotland Yard, and Edward Fabian has never been in trouble—you've never so much as stolen a bon-bon from a sweetshop. You studied medicine at Cambridge. You did well and when we asked them your tutors seemed to think you'll have a fine career as a doctor. Your parents are both dead, but they were both respectable members of the community—Rotary Club, Women's Institute, et cetera. Getting yourself involved with the Costellos is about as far from what you'd expect for a man like you as it's possible to get."

Edward tapped the dead cigarette into the ashtray, trying to hide his nervousness. The knowledge that the police had been looking into his background made him tense. He had no idea that Edward Fabian's parents were dead. That was a lucky break; what if they had been alive? What if the police spoke to friends that they might track down? They would tell them that they hadn't seen him since the start of the Blitz, and that would have raised more questions than he would have been able to answer.

"I'm really nothing special, inspector," he said off-handedly. "I doubt there's very much to find. Give me another, would you?" Murphy offered the packet and Edward tapped a cigarette out. He put it to his lips and allowed Murphy to light it for him. "The attention is all very flattering but I don't see how any of it is relevant and I'm afraid I am rather hungry."

Murphy grinned. "Not relevant?"

The waiter paused at the table and Edward held his tongue. The man smiled at them both with an attitude of perfect servility. "Will you be dining with us tonight, sir?"

"No," Edward said before Murphy could answer. "My friend is just leaving."

"Very good, sir."

Edward waited until the waiter moved away and then said, "No, it's not relevant. None of what you are saying makes any sense. I met Joseph Costello while I was in Burma. We saw action together and we became good friends—but that's as far as it goes. Really, inspector, I'd like to eat and none of this has anything to do with me. It's a flight of fantasy, at best, and outright harassment at worst. I don't see any way that I can help you. I mean, do I look like the kind of chump you'd normally be chasing?"

"You mean men like Joseph?"

"If you like."

"You've got the money and the clothes. But apart from that? No. You're not like him at all."

"Right."

"But criminals come in all shapes and sizes." He screwed his cigarette into the ashtray and stared at him, his eyes steeled and humourless. "You might not see it now but I'm trying to do you a good turn. This might be the only chance you get to save your neck. I don't know who you are but I do know that a man like you has no place with the Costellos. I can understand some of it: you come home from the fighting and everything seems tame by comparison. The excitement in your life has suddenly been taken away. You don't have any money, either, and the idea of getting involved in something illicit has a certain charm. Really, Edward, it's not an original reaction. You're not the first serviceman I've met who's felt that way."

Edward fixed him in a cold, magisterial gaze. "Did you serve, detective?"

"No. The police was a reserved—"

"Yes," he interrupted impatiently, "a reserved occupation, I know. As far as I'm concerned, that's just one step removed from wearing a white feather. Very convenient if you don't want to do your duty. If you want me to take you seriously it would be better if you didn't presume to talk about something of which you have no knowledge. I find that offensive."

Murphy smiled at that, his jaw tight. The barb had found its mark; was he sensitive to accusations of cowardice? "Seems to me I have your advantage," he said, maintaining the tone of friendly threat. "I know plenty about you. It's only fair you know something about me before I leave you to your dinner."

"Please."

"You need to know that I'm the most driven and ambitious man you'll ever meet. I'm the youngest policeman to make detective inspector in the history of the Metropolitan Police. My father was a policeman, too, and I found out that he was involved in corruption so deep that the stink could've stuck to me, too. I could have ignored it—it would have been safer for my reputation to do that—–but I brought him down. I sent him to prison where he will die an old and lonely man. And I didn't think twice about it, Edward. I don't have a wife or children. I don't even have a woman. I have no interests outside of the law. And do you know why that is? Every waking moment I'm chasing fellows like you."

"Sounds like a awful kind of life."

"It's the only life I know. I don't want another one. I don't know how to do anything else."

Murphy stared at him, across the table and right into his eyes, and Edward felt a momentary connection between them. "Neither do I," he said quietly, almost in spite of himself.

Murphy fixed on the momentary connection, too. "It's not too late for you, Edward," he said, evenly. "I don't know what you've done, but there's not much I won't be able to ignore if you'll work with me. Give me the Costellos. That's all I want. Help me put an end to the black market. All this"—he indicated around the room— "all this money and the smart clothes and the fine dining, it'll all be irrelevant if you get caught."

"Who said I'll get caught?"

Murphy got up. He tapped out another cigarette and left it on the table for him. "You'll get caught, Edward. I'll catch you. We'll see each other again, you can count on that. It would be better for you if it wasn't with you in handcuffs."

He straightened his shoulders and, with a single nod of farewell, made his way across the room to the exit.

Edward watched him go. He put his drink to his lips and finished it. His hand was trembling. He tipped the ice cubes into his mouth and crunched them, the cold making his teeth ache. The encounter had shaken him. There would have to be a recalibration. He thought about it for a moment and realised that perhaps there was something positive to be drawn from the meeting: it was new intelligence, a warning that the police were not just looking at the black market, they were looking at them specifically. Everything he suggested from this point on would have to be with that at the front of his mind. He would give them chances. Murphy might have been better keeping himself to himself.

The knowledge was a positive, certainly, but the evening had still been spoiled. He signalled the waiter.

"Yes, sir?"

"Could I have the bill, please?"

"Is everything alright?"

"It's fine. It's just—well, I'm afraid I've rather lost my appetite."

39

JOSEPH DROVE THEM to George Costello's scrapyard on Charlton Marshes and swung the car into the entrance to the yard. The sign above the gate said "John Williams' Scrap". Joseph had explained that it was one of the family's kosher businesses. They had several, scattered across London, and used them to hide the family's illegitimate operations and wash their dirty money. George had established it with Harry Costello at the start of the Blitz. The Costello boys had bought three second-hand Bedford trucks from the army, the big two-tonne monsters with plenty of space in the back. They would send them to bomb-sites, remove re-usable scrap and sell it on. Joseph said that he had worked in the business for a couple of months before he enlisted. He admitted that he had found it "too much like hard work", lugging iron girders and other bits of wreckage into the back of the lorry, threw it all up as a bad lot and went back to screwing places instead. "Stick to what you're good at," he conceded. "I could make made ten times as much spinning drums than he could breaking his back with that malarkey."

The family had wound the business down at the end of the war. George mothballed the lorries and still used the yard for storage, but Edward had heard the rumours about what he really kept the place for. It was quiet and off the beaten track, perfect for "business meetings" with fellows who needed persuasion to see things the right way.

Pliers, red-hot pokers, electric shocks.

None of it was very pleasant.

Edward looked around as the car bumped across the uneven ground. The yard was in a state. Beaten-up cars had been left to corrode, cannibalised for parts until there was nothing left of them but rusting, rotting husks. There was a small hut at the side of the yard. They parked and went inside. Tommy Falco had his feet on the single desk, eyes closed as he tried to grab a little extra sleep. Ruby Ward was writing in the small ledger that he always carried. Jack the Hat proffered a bottle of whisky and poured Edward a generous measure into a chipped china mug. Billy was there, too. "Alright, Joe," he said.

"Mr. Fabian," Ruby Ward said. "I was wondering where I'd lost you to."

"No sore feelings?"

"None whatsoever," he chuckled. "You'll make me more money with this than you would flogging cars, believe me."

Tommy had a kettle on the gas ring. He brewed up mugs of tea and handed them around with a plate of biscuits.

"Alright," Joseph said. "Settle down. Let's get cracking." The men fell silent. "This new job—it's a big one. Very big, and lots of dough to be made. My uncle knows this fellow in the army. He looks after the base at Honeybourne, old Yank place, they used to have a battalion based there. Now they've gone it's just about empty—thing is, they've left all kinds of stuff behind. Me and Edward went and looked at it yesterday. Loads of stuff, brand new gear—cars, food, clothes, ammunition, fuel, domestic stuff. They never inventoried any of it so they don't know what they've got. God knows what it's all worth. Thousands. Millions, probably."

"You two went to see it?" Billy said trenchantly. "You and him?"

"That's what I just said, Billy. What's wrong?"

He shook his head. "Nothing."

Joseph paused, a sour expression on his face, and then continued. "The fellow is going to let us onto the base. We're going to pretend to be shifting gear for the MOD. We're going to move it to a base in Barry."

The men quietly absorbed the information. There were a few questions—how would they get onto the base, why was it necessary to make a second trip to Barry—but Joseph handled them all confidently.

"We just drive into the base and load up?"

"We're going to be cleverer than that. Doc's set up a kosher company. It'll all look above board."

Billy exhaled loudly.

"What *is* it, Billy?"

"Nothing."

"No—what?"

"Can we have a chat—after?"

Joseph looked at him, with curiosity and irritation, but let it go. "It'll be easy," he said, pressing on. "There's hardly any risk and it'll pay bloody well. Who's interested?"

"Are you kidding?" Jack said. "Course I am."

"Count me in," Tommy said.

"Ruby? You'll be shifting it all on."

"I like the sound of it already."

"Billy?"

"Course," he said.

"Alright then. Doc?"

Edward had worked late into the night. It seemed to him that the scheme needed meticulous planning if it was to proceed as they intended and, in his opinion, only he had the intelligence and forethought to do the job properly. So he had taken over their sitting room, brewing a pot of strong tea and sketching out an itinerary and a division of labour. He didn't stop until a dozen Senior

Service had been stubbed out in the ashtray and the tea pot was exhausted. Now he went through the list, assigning each of them a task. When he was finished he was satisfied that everyone knew what they had to do.

The men dispersed. Edward watched with wary curiosity as Joseph beckoned Billy across to him. The two went outside into the yard, moving a few feet away from the entrance hut. Edward moved a little to the left so that he could see them through the open doorway. They were too far away for him to hear what they were discussing but it was evidently heated. He could hear an angry tone in Joseph's voice and Billy's monosyllabic answers. Billy started speaking and then Joseph interrupted him angrily, his posture slumping as Joseph spoke, his finger jabbing in angry punctuation. Edward fussed with his shoelaces, casually observing the conversation as it became less fraught and then, finally, ended with Joseph placing a hand on Billy's shoulder. Edward did not know what they had said. Had they been talking about him? It seemed likely. He heard a laugh rising from the yard, and, as he looked back outside again, he saw Billy's happy face as he turned to face him. What had Billy said about him? He fretted about that, the sudden weight of worry making him sweat. He would have to keep a close eye on him, he thought. He had made such good progress with the others. Billy, though, was proving to be more difficult to persuade.

40

THE FIRST JOB WAS SET FOR FRIDAY AFTERNOON. They agreed to meet at the scrapyard. Joseph picked Edward up and they drove down to Charlton Marshes and parked behind George Costello's Daimler, chocolate and cream with the prominent chrome grille. The driver was running a chamois over the windscreen, his peaked cap resting on the canopy. It was a beautiful motor and it looked out of place, parked there in front of stacks of salvaged metal and debris. They made their way into the yard. The trucks were parked alongside the hut, freshly painted with "DRAGON TRANSPORT" written across the sides. Tommy Falco was a whizz with mechanics and had broken down and then reassembled the engines, replacing worn out parts and changing the oil, filling the tanks with moody petrol that Ruby Ward had provided. By the time he was finished they were running nicely.

The others were idling outside the hut, dressed in the blue overalls that Ruby had procured. George Costello gave them the once-over like a sergeant major inspecting a line of men. Georgie the Bull looked as out of place as his car. He was wearing a tie with a fist-sized knot and shoes so polished you could see your face in them. He wore a panama hat and carried a gold-headed Malacca cane. He walked past one of the trucks and rapped his knuckles against the side. "Good job," he said. "You've done well, lads. Looks authentic. I hardly recognise them."

Joseph followed him. "They just need to pass muster."

"Aye." George sauntered back towards them, running the palm of his hand over slicked-back hair. "How are you, Bubble? You alright?"

"Yes, Mr. Costello," Billy said. The nickname suddenly didn't seem to bother him so much when George used it.

"Fabian?"

Edward looked from George to the hut and his mind lingered on the stories he had heard of the things that had happened here. Had Butler been brought here, perhaps? An evening of 'persuasion?' It made him feel frightened and uncomfortable. "Very good, sir," he managed to say.

He eyed him carefully. "You look nervous."

"Just keen to get started."

"Ready to make some money?"

"Of course."

George said, with a noticeable sneer, "Not the two-bob you lot were making spinning drums. This'll be proper dough."

"Yes, sir."

George looked again at Edward in that hungry, lazy fashion he had. He couldn't help but think of the way the big cats in London Zoo address the dead sheep that are tossed into their cage. He didn't say anything else and turned back to Joseph instead. "You know what you're doing?"

Joseph was calm and collected. "We've been planning it all week. Driven up on a dry run, scouted the base, we all know what we're up to. It'll run like clockwork."

"What are you taking?"

"Refrigerators today. Big ones—for hotels and restaurants."

"You've got buyers?"

"Ruby's sorted it."

"Won't be hard to move," Ruby Ward confirmed. "People will pay top whack—couple of hundred each. Can't get them otherwise."

"You lot best get going, then—go on, bugger off. I'll see you tomorrow. And bring the money."

Joseph had divided them into teams. There were three trucks and five men. Jack McVitie and Tommy Falco were paired in one cab and Joseph had the middle one. That left Billy and Edward to bring up the rear. Edward was not keen on the arrangement, far from it, and it was obvious that Billy shared the sentiment, but Joseph had insisted. He said that it was important that they took the chance to get to know each other better. Edward couldn't argue with the logic—they couldn't afford ill-will—but the prospect of a long drive with him and his monotonous, tiring attitude was not something he faced with any sense of anticipation.

He cranked the starting handle, opened the door and hauled himself into the cab. Billy slid into the passenger's seat. Edward made a great mental effort to be as friendly as he could be. "Alright, Billy," he said. "Me and you, eh?"

"Looks like it," Billy said glumly as Edward released the brake. He pulled out of the scrapyard, crunching through the gearbox, careful to leave plenty of space between the wagon and George's DB18.

Edward turned onto the road and settled back into the seat. He grasped the gearstick awkwardly and tried to start a conversation. "Got any more bouts coming up?"

"Yeah," Billy said.

"Really?"

He shrugged. "Couple."

Edward persevered. "Who against?"

"Couple of chumps."

"And when you beat them?"

"What?"

"When you beat them, you still plan to go professional?"

He gazed out of the window and said, in a faraway tone, "Eventually."

The conversation was awkward, clumsy and unsatisfactory. Billy made no attempt to join in. He sat there, making no effort to hide his boredom, staring glumly out of the window. The atmosphere was tense and strained and there was no point in pretending otherwise. Edward gave up and they drove on in silence. The traffic was light and they quickly made their way beyond the suburbs and out into the countryside. Buildings give way to villages, fields and woods. He made sure they kept in touch with the others, maintaining their nose-to-tail formation. They made good time.

They were just outside Oxford when Edward noticed a change in the atmosphere. The feeling of awkwardness had become something more tense and, when he turned his head to look at Billy, he found that he was already looking at him. "All this," Billy said vaguely, "you going to be alright with it all?"

"How do you mean?"

"The job. You ain't going to be milky when they get there? Not going to piss your pants? We're going to be able to count on you?"

Edward was nervous, certainly, but the suggestion that he might not be reliable was irritating and he let it get the better of him. "I'm not milky," he snapped angrily.

"I wouldn't normally say it, but there ain't going to be no way we can afford it if you ain't right in control."

Edward hesitated while his mind ran over the welter of things he might have said: bitter things, recriminatory things, hostile. His mind went back to a similar question that had been put to him during the war, during a patrol in the middle of the monsoon, and to the way that the rest of the men had laughed at him. Richard Watson had joked that Edward was scared and he had been indignant, but the other men had found his reaction even more amusing, and eventually he had ignored them all and kept his own company. Watson and the others had died during the ambush that followed and Edward had been decorated so who was laughing now?

Billy was staring at him, his eyebrows raised, and so Edward said, "Jesus, man," loading it with resentment, "compared to what we got up to in the jungle, this is nothing. This is child's play."

"Really?" Billy said, dubiously.

He laughed dryly, without humour. "You have no idea."

There was silence for a minute. Edward stared at the road.

"Those Japs you topped—what was it like?"

Edward looked over at him severely. "I'm not going to talk about it."

"Come on. Tell me. What was it like?"

"You don't think about it. You just do it."

"But what was it *like*? Shooting the buggers. Taking another fellow's life?"

"You do your duty and that's that."

"This modesty, Doc, it don't suit you."

"Take the hint, Billy. I'm not going to talk about it."

He sneered. "You ask me, it's all bloody bollocks. You want us to think you're some kind of war hero, but you ain't. You ain't nothing special at all. No better than any of us. You might've pulled the wool over Joe's eyes, but you ain't fooling me."

The sudden outburst was shocking. Edward shook his head and gripped the wheel a little tighter. Billy put his feet on the dash and started to drum his fingers on his bent knees, making a show of his contentedness. They didn't speak after that. Billy knew he had got under Edward's skin, and he wanted him to know that he knew.

* * *

IT TOOK LONGER THAN THEY HAD PLANNED, nearer three and a half hours than two. There was a diversion and they approached the base from a different direction than they had when they had scouted it before. The new perspective emphasised how enormous it was. There were rows and rows and rows of huts, all organised with geometrical precision. They drove for a whole ten minutes alongside the wire fence until they came to the gatehouse. Edward pulled the truck off the road and stopped. A private approached the passenger side with a rifle. His nervousness reached a crescendo and he found himself holding his breath.

Billy wound down his window.

"What's your business, sir?" the guard asked.

"Moving surplus goods."

"Where are your papers?"

"Here." Billy handed down the requisition form that Butler had faked for them.

The soldier squinted at it dubiously. "What are you here for? It don't say."

"Surplus goods." Billy's tone was brusque.

"For who?"

Edward leaned across the cab. "Major Butler," he said.

"Butler?" The man was doubtful. "No-one's mentioned it to me."

Edward started to get very nervous indeed. They were vulnerable. The other two trucks had pulled off the road and were parked behind them, pinning them against the gate. There were another two men in the guardhouse and he knew each of them would have a Lee Enfield. If the sentry didn't believe their story, there would be nothing for it. Their truck certainly wasn't going anywhere.

They were helpless.

Edward leant over again. "Why don't you speak with him?" he suggested brightly. "Get him on the phone."

As he spoke, Billy reached into the bag by his side. In the corner of his eye Edward watched as he started to withdraw the butt of a Webley revolver. There was nothing he could say without alerting the soldier's attention so he reached across the seat and rested his hand across Billy's, gently holding it against the bag.

The guard returned the credentials. "I haven't heard about nothing getting moved but that'd be par for the course. They don't tell us nothing. Sorry to keep you waiting, chaps—it all looks in order. Do you know where you're going?" Edward did, but he allowed the guard to provide directions. "On your way, then," he said when he was finished. He lifted the gate for them. Edward hurriedly put the truck into gear and motored through before the man could change his mind. The others followed close behind.

"What the hell is that?" he muttered tightly.

Billy slipped the gun back into his bag. He smirked at Edward's dismay, calmly fastening the bag again. "Shooter. What's it look like?"

"No-one said anything about guns."

"You never know, do you?—looked like we might need it for a moment."

"What are you talking about?

"Tight spot, could've been important."

Edward was incredulous. "You were going to shoot him? How long do you think we would've lasted? This is an army base, you bloody fool. It's full of soldiers."

"Calm down," he said in a gloating tone. "We're inside now, aren't we? No need to panic."

His tone was patronising, the way you would talk to a child. Edward clenched his jaw, refusing to look at him for fear of further losing his temper. "I'm not panicking," he said.

Billy saw how much he had rattled him and didn't let up. "I knew you was milky," he leered. "I bloody well knew it. The first sign of trouble and you're all over the bloody shop. What the hell Joe was thinking getting you involved, God only knows."

Edward turned away from him. He was sweating and shaking. For a moment he heard his voice denying that he was scared but then he realised that he hadn't spoken, that the words were like a phonograph playing in his head, and that Billy was looking out of the window again, carelessly, and that he needed to pay more attention to driving the lorry.

He gathered himself. The private's directions took them along the main road through the base. Edward had been there before but the place was larger than he remembered. It had been a small staging post for two or three thousand men when he had passed through on the way to India, seven years earlier. It had grown out of all proportion since then and fifteen thousand Americans had been stationed there during the preparations for D-Day. Nissen and Maycrete huts were arranged in neat rows, radiating out from a central hub. The accommodation was arranged end-to-end, prefabricated corrugated iron walls and asbestos roofs. The Americans had built basketball courts and a baseball diamond and advertisements for Lucky Strike cigarettes and Oreo cookies could still be found in the windows of the stores. He imagined that the United States must look like this.

Butler was waiting for them on the hard-standing outside the administration block.

"What did he want on the gate?" Joseph said to Edward once they had parked.

"They didn't know we were coming."

Butler shook his head. "What?"

"They had no idea."

"I told them—"

"Never mind," Edward said. "We're in now. Make sure it's sorted out next time. Now—where's the gear?"

"Follow me."

Butler jumped into a jeep and they trailed him through the quiet base, the huts stretching away in neat, symmetrical lines, hardly a soul about. Butler parked in a space next to the stores and Edward slotted the truck alongside, reversing in to make loading up as easy as possible. The other trucks followed suit.

He switched off the engine, jumped down from the cab and went around to Joseph's wagon. It would have been better to have it out with him later, when they were safely away, but he couldn't wait; that, and he was still seething with anger. He took Joseph by the elbow and tugged him around to the back of the truck where they would be shielded from Butler.

"What's the matter?" Joseph said.

"Billy's got a *gun*."

Joseph put a hand on his arm, trying to calm him down. "It's just in case."

"You know?"

"I told him to bring it. We don't know Butler. We don't know anything about him. And you never know when you might find yourself in a bind."

"You didn't tell me."

"I didn't think it was necessary."

"Not necessary? He was halfway to shooting him!"

"Everything alright?" Billy had followed him over.

"It's fine, Bubble," Joseph replied. "Get the truck ready."

"You sure he's got the gumption for this, Joe?"

"Go back to the truck."

"Right you are," he said, making sure Edward caught his grin.

"You didn't tell me," Edward repeated. "You asked me to plan this, and I did. But that only works if I know absolutely everything that's going on. No surprises. Bringing along a gun was not something on my list. Giving it to Billy makes it worse. You can do that if you want too, but, just so everything is clear between us, you'll be doing it without me."

Joseph put his hand on Edward's shoulder. "Come on, Doc—we're inside now. Alright? Now's not the time.

There's plenty to do and we're going to look like amateurs if he catches us arguing. We can talk about this later. Let's get cracking. Alright?"

"Fine," Edward said, far from happy. He stalked back to the truck. The chaps were busy, lowering the flaps at the rear of the vehicles and taking down the pallet-trolleys and loading equipment.

Butler was at the entrance to the nearest store. "You've gone the extra mile, haven't you? Looking the part and all that."

"Ready to start?" Joseph said to him. "The sooner we get going, the sooner we'll be out the way."

"Hold up, men," Butler said, looking behind them. "Here comes the cavalry."

A group of six soldiers pulled up in two extra jeeps.

"What's this?" Edward said warily.

"Thought you could do with some help. They're good lads. Speed things up a bit."

"Do they—"

"Not a thing," Butler said. "As far as they know, this is all as it should be."

It got worse, Edward thought. He was unhappy with this late addition to the plan but there was nothing for it now but to trust Butler. They swung open the big doors of the nearest store and stood there with their mouths hanging open. The store held twenty or thirty brand new industrial refrigerators. They were stacked two-high and crammed in all the way to the back of the room. Edward couldn't help but be impressed. He had never seen a fridge before; only a few businesses could afford them. It was certainly beyond Jimmy's means at the Shangri-La.

They got cracking. Each refrigerator weighed half a ton. They manhandled them onto the hand-drawn fork-lift and then rolled them out to the trucks. That was the easy part. Loading them into the trucks was much more difficult. It took half a dozen of them to manage it: three to raise one end so that the refrigerator rested on the lip of the truckbed and another three to push, shouldering the big units until they were far enough inside for gravity to make the rest of the job a little easier. The Bedfords were large enough to manage five units each. It took them two hours to load all fifteen. By the time they were finished, the suspensions sagged heavily and they were drenched in sweat.

"Your pal in Barry's expecting us, then?" Joseph asked Butler after he had dismissed the other soldiers.

"You won't have a problem."

"You said that before."

"I'll call ahead to make sure. Have you arranged buyers?"

"Don't worry about that," Joseph said brusquely. "You just leave it to me."

"When can I expect to be paid?"

"Later."

"When?"

Joseph smiled tightly. "You get your cut right at the end, pal, once everyone else has been sorted. You just do as you're told and be patient, and everything will turn out just fine."

41

THEY SET OFF AGAIN. Edward had been ready to refuse to ride with Billy but Joseph had rearranged the order before he could complain, taking Billy off his hands so that he could drive alone. That suited Edward perfectly well. The prospect of spending more time with him was almost more than he could bear and he was quite content to use the time thinking about how the day had gone and how it could be improved. Getting Bubble out of the way would be a good place to start, he thought. He settled behind the wheel and wondered how that might be done.

The journey from Honeybourne to Barry took another three hours. They headed west towards Gloucester and turned south at Cinderford, following the coastline the rest of the way. It was a pleasant ride and Edward found that the scenery lifted his mood. The truck was sluggish because of the heavy load in the back and he had to concentrate, nudging the wheel back to the centre and correcting the small errors in the handling. Joseph led the way, scrupulously observing the rules of the road, maintaining a steady forty miles an hour. Edward had laboured the point that good driving was essential. It was important to avoid the attention of the police. The last thing they needed was to be pulled over with a haul of moody goods. Major Butler had given them transfer notices for the refrigerators but Edward did not think that they would stand up to much scrutiny. The paper trail would eventually lead back to Butler and he was not the sort of fellow to make one feel confident about things.

They arrived a little after seven. The base at Barry was smaller than Honeybourne. Butler's contact was an officious captain named Williams. He had remembered to tell the guardhouse that they were coming and this time they passed inside without a hitch. They parked up at an empty warehouse and got to work again. There was no help this time and so they unloaded the trucks themselves. The fridges seemed twice as heavy now and it took two hours to lower them from the trucks and transfer them to the stores. By the time they were finished it was after nine. They had already driven over two hundred miles and they were all dog tired. Edward had been fighting heavy eyelids for the last half an hour of the drive and now all he could think about was a pint, something to eat and bed. Joseph evidently felt the same way and suggested a change of plan: rather than attempting the return trip to London they should find somewhere to stay overnight instead. They could have a meal and a drink and make an early start in the morning. No-one objected.

Edward remembered a roadside inn that they had passed outside Gloucester and led the way north again, pulling into an empty car park next to the hotel. Petrol was still rationed and the days of going out for leisurely drives were long gone. Businesses like this struggled to stay afloat without passing trade and the proprietor gladly welcomed them when they asked whether he had any vacancies. They took four rooms: two doubles and two singles. Edward was thankful for the peace and quiet of one of the singles, and, stripping out of his overalls, he soothed his muscles in the tub.

When he awoke an hour and a half had passed. Feeling partially refreshed, he dressed and went down to the dining room. He needed a beer and something to eat. The others were already there and the empty pint pots on the table suggested that they had made a start without him.

"Perfect timing," Joseph said, nodding at the empties. Edward ordered beers from the bar and passed them round. He sat down in the spare seat, Billy to his left and Joseph to his right. There was a strange atmosphere around the table, a mixture of relief and fatigue. There was an edge of hysteria to it, too, a manic quality that was exacerbated by the alcohol. They had been up early, on edge all day and all of them were tired. They were living off nervous energy.

"Well done, chaps," Joseph said, holding up his pint. "A good day's work."

Edward couldn't disagree with that. They all touched glasses and he drank off half of his beer in one thirsty gulp. It felt good, so he finished the rest and got another.

"How long are we going to leave the fridges down there?" Jack McVitie was asking when Edward returned to the table.

Joseph deferred to Edward. "A week should do it," he said. "Plenty of time to make sure it's safe. We'll leave earlier next time—pick up another load, drop it off and take the fridges back with us. It'll be easier. We'll know what we're doing. We'll have a routine."

Joseph had already ordered the food—gammon and chips five times—and the proprietor appeared with the plates, setting them down on the table. The smell reminded Edward how famished he was. They ate in silence for five minutes, shovelling the food into empty stomachs, in the meantime finishing their pints and ordering replacements.

"I needed that," Tommy said with a satisfied pat of his belly as he handed around a packet of Lucky Strikes he had taken from the store at Honeybourne. Edward took a cigarette and lit up.

"Remember the Lucky Strikes in Calcutta?" Joseph said to him, drawing deeply on the fag. "Remember that, Doc?

Playing poker with that Yank corporal?" Edward laughed at the memory and Joseph explained: "There was this American soldier we met in Calcutta. This was the night I met Doc—he'd just got his arse kicked, as I remember."

"I don't remember it like that at all," Edward chuckled.

"We got falling down drunk and ended up persuading this Yank to play poker. He told us he was an expert."

"He was completely boozed," Edward said. "By the end of the game Joseph had gulled him out of an entire evening's worth of drinks for us both, six packets of US army issue Lucky Strikes and a quart of rum."

The others laughed, all except Billy.

"You two must have got up to all sorts," Tommy Falco said.

Billy deliberately hurled a derisory sneer at Edward. "He was talking about all that in the truck earlier," he said. "Burma and so forth. I was trying to get him to tell me about shooting all those Nips, the ones he said he topped to get his medal. All I wanted to know is what it was like and he wouldn't tell me."

Edward was startled by his own nervousness. "And I told you," he said sharply, "that it's not something I'm fond of talking about."

"You say that, but it makes me wonder whether any of it is even true. Do you know what I mean, lads?"

"Of course it's true," he said, doing his best to keep the anxious tremor from his voice.

"Leave it alone, Billy," Joseph warned.

Edward's palms were damp with sweat. He rubbed them against his thighs.

"I'm just saying."

"And I'm telling you to put a sock in it."

Billy went on, "I'm just saying, I bet he don't have the balls for it. You should've seen his face when he saw my hand on the shooter today. Thought he was going to wet himself, like it was the first time he'd seen one. A proper soldier wouldn't never have reacted like that, Joseph, would he? I mean, he wouldn't have nearly shit himself."

Billy started to laugh, looking around at the others in the expectation that they would join in. It choked in his throat as he saw that Joseph was staring grimly at him. "I've already told you once—that's enough."

"But he—"

Joseph spoke harshly. "Shut it, Billy. If you're so interested in what it was like you should've signed up rather than ducking out." Joseph's voice was clipped, as if he was a teacher chastising a naughty child. Billy's cheeks flushed and he looked down at his empty plate.

"Bubble's jealous of you," Jack explained to Edward. "He likes to think he'd make a grand soldier but he didn't have the bottle to go out and actually get shot at."

"Piss off, you Scotch twat," Billy spat out. "I've got more bottle in my little finger than you'll ever have."

They all laughed at the sudden vehemence. Edward knew he should have let it go. He saw that Billy had reacted badly to being chided, and prodding at him further could only make things worse. But he had suffered his jibes and taunts all day. The others were laughing at him and he couldn't resist the opportunity to laugh along with them. Billy deserved it. He could see that Jack's comment had found its mark and probed a little further. "You must have been eligible to go, Billy? You're a young man. There's nothing wrong with you, is there? Not psychologically, I mean—well, it's obvious you're not the full ticket—but medically, I mean. You look fit. How did you get out of it?"

"That's where you're wrong, see," he muttered, not looking at him. "I'm not well."

"Oh, aye," Jack said, 'that's right." He faked a long, wheezing cough and the others laughed along with him.

"Piss off, the lot of you."

"George has a doctor on the books," Tommy explained. "He had him doing fake medicals during the war. He did Billy's for him."

"Terrible asthma, wasn't it, Bubble?" Jack said. "Can't hardly run five minutes without getting the vapours."

Billy glowered across the table. "Didn't see *you* volunteering."

"I never wanted to go. At least I don't pretend that I did."

"Billy comes from a long line of cowards," Jack said. "His old man was all talk and no trousers. The apple didn't fall far from the tree."

The laughter continued.

Joseph frowned but Edward laughed along with the others. Billy stared at him, seemingly transfixed. He banged his fist on the table. "What do you bloody well know?" he said to him. "You don't know me. You don't know none of us. You swan around here, pretending you're one of the lads but you ain't and you never will be."

"Billy," Joseph said sharply.

"Piss off, Joe." Billy was furious now. "I don't know what happened to you, you can't see nothing straight no more. You only met him once, you don't know him either! He goes around with his bloody university education, his airs and graces, but he ain't got nothing in common with any of us and he needn't think he does. He don't belong here."

"There's no need for that," Edward said. "You want to calm down."

"Is that right? I want to calm down, do I? You want a kick in the slats, you patronising bastard." He stood up so suddenly that his chair clattered behind him and, before Edward could even get his hands up, he swung a right-hander and stitched him square on the chin. It was the shock of it more than anything else. Edward toppled backwards off his chair like a skittle. The punch was decent but he was too far away to put any power into it and he hadn't connected with enough force to do more than dizzy him for a moment. Edward bounced up and tackled him into the table and then onto the floor, firing in two quick punches of his own before Tommy and Joseph pulled him away.

The proprietor hovered by the door. "It's alright," Joseph said. "Just a little argument. Bit too much to drink." He put his palm against Edward's shoulder. "Right then, chaps. No more nonsense. We'll have a drink and forget all about it, alright? Alright?"

"I'm fine," Edward said, his temper tamping down. He wiped bloody saliva from his mouth.

"Billy?"

Tommy was between them. Billy did not say a word.

"Bubble?"

"Don't call me that!" He shoved Tommy away and headed for the door.

"Let him go," Joseph said. "He needs to calm down. I'll sort him out later."

Outside, one of the trucks growled into life.

"Joseph—?"

"Bugger. He's got the key."

They went outside. Billy jerked the truck backwards and crashed into a bollard that marked the boundary of the car park and the hotel's ornamental garden. He crunched the gearbox into first and pulled out onto the road. They watched as the headlights painted the dark trees at the side of the road, the red glow of the tail-lights dimming as he turned through corners and, eventually, disappearing completely as he crested the brow of a hill.

The four of them stood there, the sound of the engine gradually fading away.

"I didn't even know he could drive," Jack said.

"He can't," Joseph said.

"What if he gets stopped?"

"It's late, the roads are empty. He'll be fine. I'll speak to him tomorrow."

Edward stood shivering in the cold. He was imagining the worst. He pictured Joseph and Billy together, Billy persuading him that the story behind Edward's medal did not bear weight. He imagined Billy checking the regimental history, somehow knowing to ask questions about the injury to his foot. He tried to remember everything that he had told them at his birthday dinner, tried to remember the expression on Joseph's face as he recounted his adventure. It was no good. He suddenly felt insecure about what he had told them. The story needed more detail. The more detail it had, the easier it was for him to believe it himself. He began to invent. He was imagining himself back in the jungle, the rain lashing into his face. He imagined himself in the middle of the formation, sweeping across a paddy field towards a road and, beyond that, a river and a bridge.

42

THE ROAD STRETCHED on endlessly to the east. The windscreen was not fully flush with the chassis and cold air whipped through the gaps. Billy turned up the collar of his overcoat and tried to ignore how cold he was feeling. All he wanted was to get back to London. He did not want to stop. He sat bolt upright, his eyes fixed on the road. Occasionally, a row of flickering lights to his right or left revealed the locations of the towns and villages that he passed. He had been driving for half an hour when he saw the lights of another all-night café approaching. Half a dozen laden lorries had drawn up in a wide car park next to a filling station and, beyond them, advertised by a bright neon sign, was the café: WATSON'S.

He gave up. He needed a hot drink. He rolled the lorry between two others, jumped down from the cab and went inside.

"Shut the door, mate, it's brass monkeys out there."

Billy did as he was asked and looked around. The café was down at heel, redolent with the smell of sweaty bodies, an open coke fire, damp clothes that were drying in the warmth and the cheap fat they used to fry the eggs. Most of the floor was sanded, and stairs led up to a second storey where a bed in a dormitory could be had for a few pennies. A handful of drivers were gathered around a pin-table, gambling. Others sat around the open fire, one of them cutting up plug tobacco with the blackened blade of his knife. Billy went up to the counter, paid three ha'pence for a cup of tea and went over to the fire to get some warmth.

A woman had been observing the action at the pin-table. She came across and took the seat next to Billy. "Alright, handsome?"

Billy looked over at her. She was wearing patent-leather slippers with worn heels. Her cheap stockings had been darned one too many times. Too much make-up, cheap perfume that smelt sickly. He nodded in her direction.

She took a dog-end out of her pocket and lit it. "Where are you headed?"

"What you want? A ride?"

"Yeah. Can you give us one?"

"Where to?"

"London. Give a girl a lift?"

Billy thought about it. He didn't have much truck with pushers but he could do with some company, help him keep his eyes open. "Go on then," he told her. "Get your coat."

Billy finished his tea and led the way back out to the lorry. The wind was up, slicing through his clothes like a knife. The girl was hardly dressed for the weather. Billy opened the cab for her, cranked the starting handle until the engine caught, then pulled himself up into the cab.

"Bloody freezing in here," the girl said. Her imitation fur collar was turned up but it couldn't have made much of a difference. She crouched forwards towards the engine, trying to keep warm, and opened her battered old handbag. She fumbled through it: old letters, a handful of change, a box of cheap powder. "What a bloody turn-up."

"What's the matter?"

"Can't find my bleeding smokes."

"Here." Billy passed over his packet of Players.

"Got a match?"

Billy handed her his lighter and she thumbed flame, her sallow flour-coated cheeks hollowing as she drew hard on the fag. They roared through a sleepy market town. In the market square, across from the church, was a brightly lit café. It looked cosy.

"I've been in that bloody place all night," she said. "Ended up spending half a crown on grub and tea. None of them lorry sheiks even staked me a cup, right mingy lot of bastards they were. None of them would give me a ride, neither. Never thought I was going to touch lucky, not until you came in. You can't deny the Old Bill are right mustard about lorry girls these days but how many plod do you reckon are going to be out on this toby on a night like this?"

Billy stared resolutely ahead, hardly hearing her. His mind was racing.

"I'm just trying to get myself a bit of money together. Just a little—get my hair permed, just the ends, mind, that ought to do me nicely. You can get off alright if your hair looks nice under your hat. Riding in wagons you don't need to take your hat off." He didn't pay her any heed. "You a London bloke, then?"

"Yes."

"Which part?"

"Here and there."

"I'm from the Angel. Originally, that is—on the road most of the time these days."

"Yeah?"

"Don't say much, do you?"

"Not as much as you."

"Right charmer, you are."

"Got something on my mind."

"Go on then—a problem shared's a problem halved, or whatever it is they say."

Billy tried to relax but it was no good. He needed to get it off his chest. "You ever been let down before?"

"How'd you mean?"

"By a friend. Someone you thought you knew. Not like a misunderstanding, more than that—someone really disappointing you."

"I ain't really got that many friends. My line of work—"

Billy wasn't listening to her. He just wanted to talk and she was in the cab: she would have to do. "I'm pals with this bloke, right? Been chums for years, ever since we was nippers. Best mate, that's what I always thought. He goes off to the war and I didn't and when he comes back he's got this new mucker, this bloke he met out there. Not my type, he ain't—he's been to University, thinks he's a right clever sort, looks down at the likes of me like I'm the shit off the bottom of his shoe. Joseph don't see it, though. This is my mate. He don't see it at all. Thick as thieves, the two of them are. Living together now and all. I try and tell him something ain't right but he ain't listening. Next thing I know, this bloke's been brought into our business."

"What business is that, dear?"

"Doesn't matter what business it is. You need certain- -certain *qualities*—to be any good at what we do, and this bloke don't have none of them. There was this time, a couple of weeks ago, my pal gets himself arrested and he'll never go and say it but I know for sure that the only reason he got pinched is because of this bloody cowson he's been dragging around with him. Bad luck, straight he is." A private car rushed past without dimming its lights. "I don't know why that cowson gets under my skin so much, but he does. I've been working hard for years to make a name for myself, carve out a reputation. My chum gets back and I seen my chance. I'm no mug, see—my mate's going to be a big noise, a proper face, like his old man was before him, like his uncle is now. I know I'm not like him- -I don't have his brains, and I know I'll never make as much of myself if I work alone. That's why I've tried to work on our friendship, tried to make myself what you'd call indispensible. By rights, I should be his right-hand man—he's known me for years, he knows he can trust me, it's obvious, right? And then this Fabian comes along—bloody Fabian, his head up his bloody arse—and it all goes wrong. And I don't know what to do about it."

They rode in silence after that, mile after mile ticking off on the speedometer. Billy had said what he wanted to say and neither had anything else worth mentioning, certainly nothing that was worth shouting over the noise of the engine.

Eventually, the girl looked bored. "Come on then, mate," she said. "You got a present for me?"

"You what?"

"I'm not here for the good of my health, you know. How's a girl supposed to eat? I could be very nice to you."

"I'm not after any of that."

"What you mean? You don't like me?"

"I just want to talk."

"Talking ain't going to pay my bleeding rent, is it?"

"I'm giving you a lift…"

"Bloody hell, mate, don't talk silly. Give me half a dollar."

They were approaching London, the lights of the city glowing beyond the rim of the North Circular. A filling station was on the road ahead. Billy changed down through the gears and swung into the forecourt. He reached into his pocket and took out a handful of loose coins: half a crown, a florin and six-pennorth worth of coppers. "Here you go," he said, giving the coins to the girl. "Out you get."

"We ain't in London yet," she protested. "I'll never get a ride here."

"Not my problem. Go on. Get."

She muttered darkly but opened the door and stepped down. Billy cranked the lorry into gear again and pulled away. He glanced in the mirror, the woman stamping her feet against the cold, and then turned his gaze to the road ahead and, beyond that, the lights of London. His thoughts turned back to Joseph, and then to Edward. Talking about it hadn't helped at all.

He needed to do something.

43

TOMMY FALCO ROLLED THE AUSTIN A40 to the kerb and killed the engine. Two in the morning and it was still busy out. Drunks, poofs and perverts: par for the course. Tommy gave it a swift East to West. Nothing out of the ordinary. He sat back in the seat and relaxed. The car was only a month old and still smelled new. It was the Sports model, a four seater coupé with the 1200cc engine. Joseph had promised him a new motor and he had been true to his word. His parents wouldn't have believed it. Wouldn't have approved of his line of work, but that didn't matter now, both of them long since dead and gone. The wheels, the fancy clobber, the gelt. The old man would have choked: thirty years in the rag trade hadn't got him the kind of dough Tommy was making now. The last thing he'd said to him before he died was that he needed to get a job, to get ink on his fingers, but the old bastard had been boracic when he went so what kind of example was that? Tommy looked in the mirror and stroked his pomaded hair. Wasn't going to happen to him, no fear. Twenty-seven years old and he felt like a prince, driving a car worth more than his parents' house. No doubt about it. He was on the up.

They had made another run with the trucks yesterday. They had stopped at Honeybourne and loaded up with silk parachutes, delivered them to Barry and returned with the refrigerators. Ruby Ward had nearly fallen off his chair when he had seen them. He had said they would be worth more than he had originally thought, the condition and quality of them, quite a bit more than he had thought. Joseph had promised him a tidy sum from the job in any event and now it looked like there was going to be more. Tommy wouldn't complain at that, not at all.

He clicked off the headlights and opened the door. It was chilly out. He draped his coat over the Remington .12 bore, reached down for the bag, got out of the car and walked across the pavement to the club. REGAL BRIDGE AND BILLIARDS said the long vertical sign stretching between the second and third floors. That always made him chuckle. One battered old table, the baize ripped to buggery and the balls rolled up against one cushion because of the sloping floor. It hadn't seen a game for donkey's years. It was all just for show. The Regal was a spieler, the jewel in what was left of the Costello crown. George Costello ran it like a military operation together with the rest of the betting clubs, drinking dens and whorehouses they'd managed to keep since Jack Spot had been coming around.

Tommy knocked on the door.

No answer. He knocked again.

The peephole opened.

"What are you—deaf? It's me, cloth ears. Open the bloody door."

The bolts slid back.

"Alright, Tommy?" Alfredo DeNina said, opening the door.

"Everyone back?"

"Upstairs."

"Any trouble?"

"They never said so."

Tommy was relieved. The last few weeks had been difficult. The trouble with Spot was common knowledge on the street now, and so was the fact that George and Violet had sat on their hands and done nothing. He had been knocking off their businesses and they hadn't lifted a finger. People were starting to think that they were soft touches. Reckoned that gave them licence to have a bit of a go. There'd been an example of that tonight: a bolshie barrow boy was into them for thirty quid, debts piled up at their faro tables. The bloke had asked for an extension, demanded it almost, and then got lippy when Tommy told him where to get off. There was nothing else for it: he pistol-whipped the mouthy bugger, knocked out a couple of teeth and put him to the floor, gave him a shoeing while he was at it. An example to the others. You couldn't afford to show weakness. Give them an inch and they'd take a bloody mile. You had to be strong. One of the rules of the game. George Costello had taught him that himself. Tommy didn't understand why he had stopped following his own advice.

He went inside, DeNina double-locking the door behind him. He took the stairs to the first floor. Four members of the Costello gang were drinking and smoking. They were the collectors. Their job was to fan out around the family's interests and bring the takings back to be counted. George had put him on the strength at Chiara's birthday party. Tommy had been well chuffed to be asked. It meant they were taking him seriously, that the reputation he'd been working on was starting to have the right effect. He wanted them to see him as trustworthy, reliable and hard, able to cut up rough when that was required. George had told him that he knew he was good for the job and that meant a lot.

The others were older. Bert Thomas was nursing a whisky sour. Eddie Bennett and Paulie Spano were at the table working on the cut-up, sorting a pile of money into neat stacks. George Taylor was peering between old black-out curtains into the street.

"Alright, Tommy," he said, letting the curtains fall back into place.

He nodded. They were all tense and tired. The only things he could think about were a couple of whiskys and his bed. He dropped the bag of money at Bennett's feet.

Eddie hefted it. "Full?"

He nodded. "Punters everywhere. Turning them away."

Eddie gestured to the money on the table. "Same for everyone."

Spano riffled a stack of notes. "Been a good week. Can't remember a better one."

Tommy undid his jacket and fixed himself a drink. He was all done in. He'd driven the Austin across north London all night, visiting the spielers and liquor dens. He'd had the Jimmies all the way, the old nerves on edge: keeping an eye out for Jack Spot's lads, the bagful of cash under the seat and the shotgun across his lap. George Costello had warned them about the rumours that Spot was plotting something, and you couldn't be too careful, not with that devious Jew.

He checked the time: half past two. He picked up the tumbler, the ice jangling against the glass, and drained it. He poured another double measure, shook a cigarette from a pack and lit up. No need to worry, he reminded himself. The club was locked tighter than a nun's knickers. The street door was two-inches thick and Alfredo DeNina was behind it with a sawn-off and a machete like the stevedores at the docks used. The windows were two storeys up, impossible to reach without ladders. The fire escape was chained and bolted shut. The place was nigh-on impregnable. Tommy got up, twitched the curtain aside and looked down into Wardour Street. Nothing. He stood and watched. Nothing out of the ordinary. He a glass of whisky that he didn't really want and went back to the window. He folded his hands across his chest. Ten minutes passed. He shook a cigarette from a pack and lit up. Georgie the Bull would be along soon enough to collect the takings.

Two men in overcoats walked to the outside door. He squinted down at them. Trilbys covered their faces.

One of the men knocked on the door.

Tommy cradled the shotgun.

"Who is it?" he called down.

The sound of a muffled conversation came from downstairs.

"It's alright," Alfredo shouted up. "Punters. Sent them away."

A shotgun blast, loud, close range. Tommy spun around. Bert Thomas staggered towards him, half of his head gone. Tommy turned his head at the blow-back as he went down, spun the shotgun around and ducked. A puff of blue smoke from the stairs. DeNina pushed the curtain aside, ejected shells and reloaded. Damned turncoat! The sound of feet taking the stairs two at a time. DeNina aimed, fired again. George Taylor took one in the face, an arc of white bone and grey-green brain splattering the black-outs. Bastards! Tommy swung the shotgun around, triggered a spread. DeNina caught buckshot, staggered back against the wall, slid behind a table. Tommy dived for cover as two other men came up the stairs. He pressed himself behind a stack of chairs, recognised the thin one: Archie Eyebrows, Jack Spot's first lieutenant.

Eddie Bennett got a shot off, missed, pellets perforating the black-out, smashing windows. Archie fired back and Bennett blew up, thrown backwards onto the billiard table. Balls rumbled across the floor. How many were there? Paulie Spano ran for the fire exit. He didn't get far. A buckshot spread peppered him across the neck and shoulders. He slammed into the wall, not moving. Tommy popped up, fired again.

He wiped something warm from his cheek, pumped the shotgun and stayed low, scrambling for the fire exit. The only way out. He dived out, another shot rang out—

shit shit shit—and pain lit him up, his knees buckling inside-out as he landed chin-first. He saw lights, reached out for a chair leg, yanked. A few inches. Reached for Paulie Spano's ankle, yanked. Half a foot closer to a locked door, crawling through a stew of blood and brain.

A kick to the ribs, hard. A foot slid beneath his chest and flipped him up and over on his back.

Jack Spot stood over him in a vicuna coat and trilby, a smoking .12-guage pointing down at his face.

Tommy tried to shuffle away, got nothing but useless scuffles. He looked down: his right leg was wrecked, gone from the knee down.

"Evening, lad," Spot said.

"My leg…"

"I warned your boss."

The pain was unbelievable. "You don't have to do this."

"I told him—you Ice Creamers aren't welcome around here no more. All of this is mine now."

"How much do you want? The takings are over there——take it all."

Spot laughed. "Don't worry, lad. I'm going to."

"Please."

"It too late for please and thank you. Should've buggered off home when you had the chance."

Tommy went for his .38 as Spot pulled the trigger. He took both barrels in the chest from twelve inches away. Spot slotted extra shells and finished him off, his patent leather loafers—bloody and gore-streaked—the last things that Tommy Falco ever saw.

PART FIVE

London
January – March 1946

CALENDAR

—1946—

The *Star*, 25th January:

GANG WARFARE IN SOHO
MAN DIES VIOLENTLY IN SUSPECTED FEUD

A murder investigation has begun after the bodies of four men were discovered in a property in Soho, W1. Thomas Falco, Albert Thomas, George Taylor, Edward Bennett and Paul Spano were found in the Regal Bridge and Billiards Club, a well-known gambling den, on Friday. While police were not prepared to be drawn on the motives for the mens' deaths, this reporter has been informed that it is the latest in the escalating blood feud between rival gangs in London's West End.

MARK DAWSON

STRICTLY PRIVATE AND CONFIDENTIAL

To: Commissioner
I.O: D.I. Charles Murphy
Submitted at request of: D.A.C. Clarke
Re: Gang Activity in Soho, W.1.

Sir,
You asked me to provide up-to-date information on the spate of killings in the West End. I can confirm the speculation in the press: these murders are certainly inspired by the increasing violence that has erupted between the Spot and Costello gangs. The recent victims were all Costello men, and it is a curiosity to both my men and myself as to why there have been no reprisals. Of course, we must assume that retaliation will be forthcoming and the delay makes it more likely that, when it does finally come, it will amount to a serious escalation.

Our investigations to date have concentrated on the Costello Family. While we have made some progress with that, it is not as fast as I would have liked. With that in mind, I am considering novel approaches to the enquiry. The methods I am considering might be considered radical, or perhaps even dangerous. I will, of course, keep you abreast with developments.

Sincerely,
D.I. C. Murphy
2nd February 1946

44

THE COMMISSIONER'S OFFICE was the grandest in the whole of Scotland Yard: a large bookcase against one wall carried law reports and criminal treatises; a chandelier hung down from the high ceiling; a framed portrait of Lord Trenchard hung over the fireplace; wide windows offered a view of the Embankment and Waterloo Bridge. The Commissioner, Harold Scott, was behind his desk and Deputy Assistant Commissioner Stanley Clarke was sat in the armchair against the left wall. The atmosphere was tense, freighted with a dull foreboding that did not augur well. Charlie thought it felt like an inquest. He stepped forward, removed his hat and hung it, together with his coat, on the oak hatstand next to the door. The Commissioner invited him to sit and he did so.

Charlie had never been particularly impressed with Scott. The man was a civil servant. His background was in the Civil Defence Administration and something to do with aircraft production—nothing to do with policing or police. His face was long and sombre, marked by the deep lines that ran from his nose to the edges of his mouth, and he rarely smiled. He wore wire-rimmed glasses that made him look like an accountant. He did not suit his uniform.

"Good morning, detective inspector."

"Morning, sir."

"You know what this is about, don't you?"

"Yes, sir, I believe I do—the murders in Soho."

"Five men. A massacre would be a more appropriate way to describe it."

"I think that's fair."

"Yes, inspector, quite fair. What can you tell me about it?"

"The five were all Costello men. It is a safe assumption, therefore, that the shooters were from the Spot Gang."

"You're just assuming?"

"They left no evidence and no witnesses, sir. I can't offer any more certainty than that at the moment."

"This isn't good enough, inspector. It really isn't. There was the murder in August, too, I believe."

"That's right. Leonard Masters."

"We've got nowhere with that case, either?"

"We know it was Spot—"

"—then bloody well arrest him!"

"I could bring him in, sir, but it would be a waste of time. No-one will go on the record against him. We don't have a case yet."

"Do you understand the pressure this is putting me under, detective inspector? A massacre, right on our doorstep? This isn't America, for God's sake. It's bloody London! And the black market, too." He held up a report. "This is from the government. Home Office. They say the black market is totally out of control. Rampant, they say. Getting that sorted was the whole reason behind your investigation. You said you could do it and, yet, all I can conclude is that things are worse now than before you started."

Charlie took a deep breath. "I understand your frustration, sir. It's frustrating for us, too. These gangs are well organised and professional. They are held together by the promise of significant reward and the threat of violence. It might not look like it from your position"—from behind your comfortable desk, he felt like adding—

"but we are making progress. We're developing our understanding of how these groups are comprised and how they function. We are gathering intelligence. We're probing for weaknesses, and for potential informants."

"Do you have any?"

"Potentially."

"'Potentially?' What does that mean, inspector?"

Charlie felt a flash of anger but he smothered it. "It means, sir, that we are developing two particular ways into the Costello family that could be very fruitful for us."

"Details, man!"

He took a deep breath before he spoke again. "There's an ex-soldier who's working with them," he said. "He doesn't fit the usual type. I've spoken with him. Put the screws to him a little. There's something that makes me think he could be a weakness for them."

"And the other one?"

He thought of Eve. How could he mention her to them? His brother was not a policeman any longer but he was still a liked and respected man, well connected, and everyone knew about Eve's disappearance during the war. Charlie knew that they were aware of his ruthlessness—he had to believe it was one of the reasons why he had been promoted so quickly—but withholding the information that his brother's daughter was alive and well and, what was more, consorting with a known criminal in the hope that he could turn her into an informant? They would see that as a step too far, even for him? Frank would find out, they would clash again, Eve would be pulled back from the brink and he would lose one of the two levers he had worked so hard to find. No. That wouldn't do at all.

"And," he said, "The other one I'd rather keep to myself for the moment, sir."

There was grumbling and shaking of heads but they did not press him.

"I'll admit that progress is slow," Charlie said, "slower than I would have liked, but I remain completely confident that I'm the best man for the job and that if given sufficient time I'll deliver the results that you want."

"Yes," Scott said. "Time. That comes down to the nub of it."

"We have to set a deadline on this, Charles," Clarke offered from the side. "If you can't present us with tangible progress—and by that we mean reliable arrests—then we've decided that we are going to have to close the investigation down and try something else."

"I see, sir. How much longer do I have?"

"Three months," Scott said. "Not a day longer."

"Very well, sir. I understand." Charlie stood. "Will there be anything else?"

Scott steepled his fingers and looked over them at Charlie, his eyes cold and blank. "Sit down, Murphy. I'm not finished yet."

Charlie sat. He felt his heart hammering in his chest.

"The press is bad enough, detective inspector, but it's more than that. The Minister was in here yesterday. Two hours. He was complaining that we're not doing enough to get our house in order. And he can make ultimatums, too. He can assign blame. Just think about it for a minute: there are thousands of hard young men who have just returned home after fighting in the war. Many of these men have been unable to find work. After five or six years of service abroad, some of them might think that they have been abandoned by their government. Many of them will be tempted by the quick cash they might think they can make outside of the legitimate economy. Those men are not likely to be dissuaded from that course by a police force that is trumpeted as inept all the way across the national press. It was made very clear to me that something will be done unless we start to bring things under control." He paused. "I know your reputation, Murphy. My predecessor and the deputy assistant commissioner here speak very highly about what you did during the war and, I'll admit, your record is particularly impressive. But none of us can live on past glories. This is a results business and, to put it simply, you are not getting results. Your reputation and your career depend upon you doing your job and bringing these animals to justice. You understand me?"

"Yes sir," Charlie said. "Perfectly well."

"See that you do. Dismissed."

45

EDWARD CROSSED PICCADILLY AT THE RITZ and headed west, then north, following Hyde Park up. They still had searchlights from the war hidden amongst copper-beeches and sycamores. St Johns was on Hyde Park Crescent. An empty hearse was already parked at the kerb. Edward parked behind it, checking his reflection in the hearse's window before going around to the cemetery, a narrow space bounded by fir trees and box-cut hedges. Twenty-five men were gathered around the freshly dug grave. He slid through the throng until he was between Joseph and Jack. They each acknowledged him with a silent nod. They were dressed in black suits, white shirts and black ties, just as he was.

The atmosphere was palpable: sadness and anger in equal measure.

Tommy's girlfriend stood alone on the other side of the grave. The chaplain delivered the sermon and she started to weep. Violet Costello put her arm around her shoulders. They sang a hymn before the eulogy, sang another hymn afterwards. Edward stared at the coffin. The vicar recited the committal as Tommy was lowered into the ground, the family and a few of the men casting flowers and handfuls of dirt down onto his coffin.

THE IMPOSTER

* * *

THE WAKE WAS IN THE ALHAMBRA. The club looked tattered and worn in the daylight, the imperfections that could be hidden in the darkness now more easily displayed. George and Violet Costello stayed for a drink, paid their respects to Tommy's girlfriend, then quietly left. Edward necked a couple of jars then went up onto the roof to smoke and get a lungful of fresh air. When he went down again, the women were all gone. The chaps were gathered at the bar, talking. Edward went over.

"Something's got to be done," Jack McVitie said. "Another bloody funeral. My mate was shot dead by that bastard, and what are we doing about it?"

"Nothing."

"That evil Jew must be laughing his bloody socks off at us."

"You heard what happened in Soho last night? Fucking liberty! They hit three restaurants that have been paying up to us for donkey's years. You know Da Vinci's on Brewer Street? I went in there this morning, and they're sweeping the glass up from all the windows they smashed, and I ask him for the weekly payment and he says he ain't going to pay it no more. He says what kind of protection am I getting for my money when this kind of thing can happen? I gave him a thick lip, fair enough, I ain't having him talking to me like that, but then I got thinking and you have to admit—end of the day, he's got a bloody point."

"And I can't get the bookies on my patch to pay me my points. They're more scared of Spot than they are of us. He's nabbing all of them."

"What's happened to George's bollocks? If this was a couple of years ago, he would've strung the greasy kike up on the nearest lamp-post weeks ago. He's making us look like a bloody laughing stock, that's what he's doing. I used to be able to walk around the manor and people would treat me with respect. Blokes would either tip their hat to me or cross over to the other side. That don't happen no more. They don't give two shits about us. They all think he's going soft."

Joseph had been listening with a deepening scowl. He had no answer to that. Edward could see the colour rising above his collar and into his cheeks and decided it was better to intervene. He stood everyone a round. "To Tommy," he said. "A good mate."

"To Tommy."

He drained his glass and ordered two more. He took Joseph by the arm and turned him away from the others.

He handed Joseph one of the fresh pints. "You can see the way this is going, can't you?"

"I know," Joseph said, fixing his stare into the bottom of his glass.

"If George and Violet don't do something, they'll start to lose the men."

"Thank you, Doc," Joseph said, his voice a tight slap. "I know that."

Edward realised that Joseph didn't want to pursue the conversation, but he there were things that had to be said and, he thought, he was the best man to say them. "Maybe I could speak to them? Your sister has invited me down to the house at the weekend. I could have a word with Violet?"

He snorted. "You saw how they reacted the last time you tried that. You're not family, Edward. It wouldn't go down well at all."

Edward gritted his teeth. *You're not family*. He did not respond to that, even though the truth of it stung. It was a reminder that that would always stand between them, a gap he could not cross. Joseph stood with his arms folded, staring out of the window behind them. Edward fumbled for the right thing to say, unable to find the words, his attention switching from the smell of the Senior Service between Joseph's fingertips, to the curlycued grain in the wood of the bar beneath his hand, to the tight pressure in his stomach as if someone was holding their palm against his navel. The sense of frustration and inarticulateness was agony to him and, helpless to stop himself, he said, "Jesus, man, *someone* has got to do *something*."

Joseph snapped. "Leave it out, Doc, alright? For God's sake—on and on and on, every bloody day. I don't need your advice. We don't need it. You're starting to be a bore." Joseph started to say something else, his eyes flicking away as he considered better of it. He took a breath and said, instead, "Violet is sharp and she doesn't mess about. You think she got to be where she is now by sitting around and letting things happen? She'll have something in mind for Spot. We're just going to have to trust her and brazen it out."

There was no point in pressing him and so Edward reluctantly let the matter drop. He drank quickly, his mind working. He had been presented with an opportunity to make something of himself. A chance, and he had only really scratched the surface of it so far. To be stood at the side, watching impotently as the family slowly imploded, crippled by fear or inertia or laziness at the very moment that he arrived, was torture. He felt sick at the thought of it. It was almost more than he could bear.

46

EDWARD WAS IN THE SAME ROOM as the last time he stayed at Halewell Close. He laid his suitcase on the bed and changed out of the comfortable clothes he had worn for the drive from London, choosing one of his new suits instead. He applied pomade to his hair, shaved, and then regarded himself in the mirror: he looked very fine. He crossed the room and opened the window, lighting a cigarette and blowing the smoke out into the cool night air beyond. It was eight o'clock and the light had faded, replaced by a gloaming that made strange shapes of the lines of trees and made the landscape beyond the garden murky and indistinguishable. He saw his new car, next to Violet Costello's Packard. It was a Triumph Roadster, the lights of the house reflecting on the highly polished, blood red bodywork. It had an 1800cc engine and a four speed gearbox with synchromesh on the top three ratios. There were large headlamps at the front and the radiator was set back between large "coal scuttle" wings. He was always taking taxis or relying on Joseph to drive him around and, now that money was less of a problem, he had decided to splash out. Ruby Ward had arranged the car for him. It had been enjoyable to return to the showroom. He was not fond of the other salesmen, and he knew that they would be jealous to see how far he had travelled in so short a time. It was brand new, not second-hand, and he had paid for it in cash. It had been a pleasurable way to spend an hour. Their gawping incredulity had been worth it all on its own.

The car was a beauty, and he loved it. He loved to own things, carefully selected items that he could cherish. He was not materialistic, but he liked the kind of things that said something about a man and his standing in the world. Excellent clothes and fine shoes, well-chosen pieces of jewellery, cultural artefacts that spoke of taste, tables at the best restaurants and seats at the opera. They gave a man a sense of self-worth. They spoke of his substance. It was more than just the impression they projected to others, although Edward was aware enough to know that that was a part of their appeal to him. They provided him with ratification. They were the proof that he had done well and that, despite the rotten cards he had been dealt so often in his life, he had still made a success of himself on anyone's terms. They made a mockery of the self-doubt that sometimes whispered in his ear. He had owned those things before and, together with the lavish lifestyle that he had arranged for himself, they had made him as happy as he had ever been. He had had to abandon it all when he had stopped being Jack Stern. All he had taken with him into the jungle were his memories, and they had been just enough to make the worst moments bearable. It would never have been possible to make a beginning of reacquiring those things on the pitiful fifteen shillings a week that the Labour Exchange paid to him. It would have taken him a decade, even if he lived frugally, to buy the things he wanted. Joseph and his family had given him the opportunity to acquire them more quickly. The money would allow him to travel to Paris with Joseph and to do the trip properly, to fly first class, to stay in the best hotel and to enjoy the best restaurants. Paris would only be the beginning: he was already planning a trip to Athens and Rome, he wanted to return to Venice and he had heard that the Adriatic Coast was spectacular. His circumstances would allow him to begin his book collection again and, to that end, he had spoken to a dealer on the Charing Cross Road who said he would be able to source the first edition Dickens, Dostoyevskys and Conan Doyles to replace the volumes that he had had to sell. It would grant him the leisure to attend the Opera or to wander without direction through the sober halls of the Tate or the Royal Academy or even to find a struggling artist and to serve as their patron. It allowed him the opportunity to demonstrate his taste and the aesthetic discretion that set him aside from the likes of Joseph and Billy and all the others. They simply could not have been any more different to him. They were plebeians, ignorant and unappreciative of the things they were lucky enough to possess. It would allow him to support his father and uncle, too.

He looked down from the high window onto the Triumph below, on the voluptuous curves of its bodywork with the chrome details, and he smiled happily.

He sucked down on the Senior Service and exhaled into the darkness. Chiara had written to him and invited him to spend the weekend at the house. He was flattered, and had happily accepted. A break from London would be good for him, and it was an excellent chance to improve his relationship with the rest of Joseph's family. He had hoped that Violet would be at the house and yet, when that was confirmed by the sight of her car as he pulled up earlier that night, the prospect had made him anxious, too. He knew that there was an opportunity to impress her, and that that was essential if he was to continue to ingratiate himself with the family, yet subjecting himself to her waspish temper filled him with apprehension. He wanted to speak to her, too, despite Joseph's warnings. Spot was a problem and yet he was also an opportunity. If Edward could propose a solution he knew it would be good for him.

He finished the cigarette and lit another, smoking that until he had his equilibrium properly under control. He found his way down to the drawing room. Chiara was standing before the hearth, a fire burning in the grate.

"Hello," she said, leaning up to kiss him on the cheek.

"You look lovely," Edward told her, and she did. She was wearing a pleated skirt and a contrasting jacket. The colour of her face was warm in the glow of the flames.

"Thank you," she said.

"Is your aunt joining us?"

"I'm afraid so. Is that alright?"

He smiled. "Of course."

"I think she's in a good mood, if that's any help."

"It's quite alright, Chiara. It'll be good to get to know her properly."

They spoke for a few moments until Violet Costello entered. She was wearing a midnight blue cowl neck dress. Her hair was meticulously styled, as ever. Joseph had not considered her age before then, but, as he assessed her, he guessed that she must have been in her late fifties. She looked younger than that tonight.

She came to the hearth and kissed him on the cheek. "Edward," she said. "It's a pleasure to see you again."

"And you, Miss Costello."

"Please—it's Violet." The butler brought over three glasses of champagne. Violet raised hers and proposed a toast: "To friends and family," she said, "the only things that really matter."

Edward touched glasses with Violet and her niece. *Friends and family*. Chiara winked at him from behind the glass.

"It's good that we are able to do this," she said, "during such difficult times."

"Very," Edward agreed.

"Did you know Tommy Falco very well?"

"A little—through Joseph. He was a good chap, I thought."

"I knew his mother and father," she said sadly. "I remember him as a youngster. He always was a bit of a tearaway, he used to give them both fits. His heart was in the right place, though. He was always good to his mother. He knew what was important." She smiled a tight smile. "Never mind. We won't worry about it tonight."

Chiara excused herself for a moment as the butler returned with a tray of canapés.

Violet regarded him with carefully. "There's one thing I have to say, Edward, while we're alone—you should know that I'm very protective of my nieces and nephews, the girls in particular. When my brother, their father—when he died"—she paused thoughtfully—"well, there wasn't anything else for it. I've treated them as my own ever since. It's flesh and blood, isn't it?"

"I understand," Edward said.

"You said you were an orphan," she said. "Do you mind me asking what happened to your parents?"

The lies were at the front of his mind and came easily. "My mother died when I was a child and my father just after the Great War."

"How were you brought up?"

"In an orphanage."

"How dreadful!"

"It wasn't ideal, but you manage, don't you?—you do your best with what you have."

"Was your family from London?"

"Yes," he said, although they were not. Practice lubricated his lies. He had anticipated questions about his background and had rehearsed the story in the car until he was confident that he could deliver it as if it was the truth. He adjusted his stance, and made it more relaxed by resting his hand against the mantelpiece. Violet's posture was open and friendly. Edward found he was able to relax.

Chiara returned and Violet insisted that they all have another glass of champagne. Edward sipped his, careful not to finish it too quickly because he knew that she would insist he have another. He was happy to drink enough to quieten his self-consciousness but he did not want to drink so much so that he would become drunk. After half an hour Violet suggested that they should eat and led the way into the dining room. The table had been laid for three, with expensive cutlery and crockery, polished glasses and two large candlesticks with lit candles. They moved across to the table and took their seats. Violet kept returning to the subject of Edward's childhood. "How did you manage to get to University with such a start? It's very impressive."

"Hard work and a bit of good fortune, I suppose. I've always been rather bookish and I did well at school, well enough to sit the entrance exam and pass it. The rest took care of itself from then."

"And what will you do for your career—you don't intend to knock around with Joseph forever, I'm sure? Will it be medicine?"

He sensed that Violet wanted to hear that he was ambitious, and that his ambitions were legitimate. He was happy to oblige her. "I should think so," he said and then, as he noticed her approval, he added, "Yes, I think, eventually, it will be medicine."

The conversation was dull and unchallenging, and Edward was able to navigate it without incident. Violet seemed fascinated by his background and asked what he could remember about the orphanage, and how he had managed to transport himself to the cusp of a career in medicine. She seemed especially impressed with that, and kept returning to it. Edward answered her questions with a combination of modesty and bashfulness, feigning awkwardness at being the centre of attention but, in truth, the evening could not have proceeded any better if he had planned it.

"Did you know I have a son?" she mentioned without preamble.

"I didn't."

"Joseph's never said anything?"

"Not that I remember."

"I'm not surprised," she said.

"Joseph and Victor never really got on," Chiara explained.

"Victor found him a little—limited. Would that be fair to say, darling?"

"I suppose so," Chiara replied. She rolled her eyes when Violet looked away into the fire.

"Where is he?"

"Italy. He was in the Army, like you. Egypt to start with, then Greece and back to Egypt again. They didn't know what they were doing at the start of things. Victor was captured at Tobruk and then shipped to Porto St Georgio. And then when the Italians capitulated in 1943 he led the escape from the camp."

"And then the Germans arrived," Edward said.

"Of course. I don't know all the details—lots of secrecy, obviously—but Victor has been fighting as one of the Partisans. Italy is our home and he is a very patriotic boy—to be honest, I wouldn't have expected anything else from him."

"Where is he now?"

"A place called Rassa, in the Borgosesia valley. He's been helping with the rebuilding. And I believe there has been work to do with regard to the Fascists who were left behind, too. Trials and executions."

"I'd like to meet him," Edward said.

"I'm sure you will." Violet smiled absently and stared into the fire again. Chiara raised her eyebrows in mild amusement.

The main course of chicken was brought out. They ate quietly for a while, just the sound of cutlery against their plates breaking the silence. "You have a beautiful house here," Edward said eventually.

"Thank you."

"The first time I saw it—my goodness, it took my breath away."

"We're very lucky to have it."

He cast a hand around, gesturing to the room. "I can't imagine what it must cost to maintain."

He had made a mistake and he realised it immediately. "What do you mean by that?" she said, her voice suddenly tight and clipped.

He felt Chiara tense next to him. "Just that it's so big," he said, "the repairs, the staff—it must cost a fortune."

"It's not a problem," she said. "Why would that be a problem?"

Chiara glanced at him, a warning in her eyes. He began to sweat. He smiled at Violet, trying to recover his poise. "I'm sure it isn't."

"Then why would you say that? Do we look like we're short of cash?"

"No, no," he said, backtracking furiously, although he could see it *was* a problem—that much was obvious from the shabbiness of the furniture, the scuffed paint, the leaks and spills that had discoloured the plaster—and he had offended her by suggesting, however obliquely, that they might not have the funds to do the house justice. Why had he said that? What had he been thinking? It was a foolish error.

"I don't think Edward meant that, Aunt," Chiara said.

"I think it's absolutely splendid," he followed quickly, "I've never been anywhere like it before. Spectacular—really quite spectacular."

Violet allowed herself to be placated. The embers of her temper flickered, then abated. "My brother bought it twenty years ago. Has Chiara told you about him?"

"Yes, Aunt," she said. "I've given him all the stories. I expect he's heartily bored of all of them."

Edward smiled at her and said that he was not.

Violet did not catch Chiara's hint and seemed determined to speak about her family's past. "Harry was quite a man. Strong and decisive—he wouldn't stand for some of what goes on these days. He had no time for weakness." She spoke haughtily. "I don't know what you think of things these days, Edward. Society. Young people, they don't have any respect for anything. Some of them seem to think they should be given everything on a plate. Nothing is for free, is it? They need to get their sleeves rolled up and work for what they want. You agree, I'm sure?"

He thought about how difficult it had been to find any money, the humiliation of the Labour Exchange, the scarcity of accommodation, the deprivations that he only managed to save himself by falling in with Joseph. He thought of it all, and decided it was better not to mention it. "I do," he said, instead. "I think there are always opportunities if you are prepared to go out and look for them."

She nodded enthusiastically. "Quite so. Just as you have done."

Wasn't it ironic that Violet should agree with him when he was looking for opportunities right at this very moment? That was amusing, he thought, but, as he considered it, he suddenly felt vulnerable. Surely she could see his agenda? Wasn't it obvious? The confidence rushed out of him and shivers of fear ran up and down his spine. He told himself that it was irrational. He had convinced them of his story and so there was no need to be afraid, no need at all. He was too clever for her, for all of them.

"A penny for your thoughts?" Violet was asking him.

"I was just thinking about my parents." The lie slipped from his mouth without him even thinking about it.

A tray with a bottle of brandy and three glasses was delivered to the table and Edward took it upon himself to pour. They repaired to the drawing room where they enjoyed another glass each, Violet becoming increasingly mellow as she reminisced about Little Italy, Chiara smiling contentedly to herself and Edward struggling to tamp down the fear that he had said something he ought not to have said and was about to be discovered. He wished the dinner was over and that he could get back to his room. He got up from the comfortable sofa several times, taking his drink to the fireplace, fretting with a loose button on his jacket, and, when he looked into the mirror, he watched a tic jerking in his cheek. He toyed with the button for too long and the thread snapped. He slipped the button into his pocket and undid the others to obscure the damage. He felt dreadful.

Chiara rested a hand on his wrist. "Edward and Joseph are going to Paris next week," she said.

"Is that so?"

He managed to relax again. "Yes," he said. "It's a birthday treat. I'm looking forward to it very much."

"Have you been before?"

"No, never."

"I've never been either," she admitted.

"It'll be interesting to see it now. I doubt the Germans were all that respectful."

"You must tell me everything about it."

"I'm hoping I might persuade Edward to take me one day," Chiara said, smiling at him warmly. "I can't think of anywhere I'd rather go."

Chiara excused herself after the second whisky, saying she was tired and needed her sleep. She kissed Edward on the cheek, her hand brushing down the top of his arm as she leant in closer. Edward was minded to do the same but Violet wouldn't hear it, and poured him a third drink before he had a chance to demur.

"Actually," Violet said over a genteel sip of her whisky, "Chiara not being here gives us a chance to talk about other things. I try to keep her away from business as much as I can. Ruby Ward telephoned me this morning. He's sold the refrigerators you collected from Honeybourne for a tidy sum. I'll make sure that Joseph gets your cut of the profits—he can distribute it among the men."

"That's excellent news."

"What did you make of the goods at the base?"

He pictured the wide storage sheds, filled with booty. "There's a lot. It will take several trips to empty. Even if we are selective with what we take—the high value items first, then we can look at what's left—even then, I'd estimate fifteen or twenty lorryloads of quality merchandise. Maybe more if we're less picky."

"And the Major?" Violet said as she lit a cigarette. "How was he?"

"There was an issue with our clearance at the gate but I think we've sorted that out, now. He'll certainly see the benefits of working with us when he gets paid."

"Tell Joseph to keep an eye on him. He's not family. I'm not convinced he'll be reliable."

There it was again, that word, another reference to family. It caught like a torn fingernail. Edward was beginning to see how the Costellos were obsessed by the idea of it, that blood was the only thing that they ever really trusted. He tightened his grip around his glass. "I'll be sure to tell him."

"There was another thing," she said. "I know my brother and I were a little short with you when we spoke about Jack Spot before, after what happened to Lennie. I hope you understand why—that we were upset."

"Yes, of course."

"Things have worsened since then, obviously. What happened at the Regal was awful and unnecessary. I know you have your own ideas about how we should deal with Spot, but I'm afraid they're just not right. Soho is too hot. There's Spot, obviously, but he isn't the only one. There are other men, other gangs, trying to move into areas that we have traditionally controlled. The Maltese have always had their brothels but they are starting to expand East of Regent Street, and to open shops selling dirty books. New spielers and shebeens open every day. Ten years ago, we had the manpower to stop that from happening but it isn't the same today. It's all competition, and it makes it more difficult to bring in the same profits. And the cost of buying police support is rising—Spot wants them too, and that puts the price up. Two of our oldest friends have switched sides in the last week. Supply and demand, you see?" She smoked for a moment, her eyes fixed on Edward. "We could fight him, but it would be bloody and long and I can't be sure that we'd win. I only fight when I know the odds are in my favour."

"But all the business he's taking from you?"

"We'll wait him out."

He felt impatient at hearing the same excuses again. "And in the meantime?"

She seemed vaguely amused at his curt response. "There are other avenues that we have started to explore. We were involved in the black market throughout the war but it's even more profitable now than it was then. Honeybourne is a good example, but there are others. It's criminalised whole sections of society. Housewives who pay a little extra for more cheese than they are entitled to. Extra cuts of beef slipped into the bag. Oranges and bananas selling for fifty times more than before. The goods have to come from somewhere, and we have a network of suppliers and dealers who can service the demand. Ruby isn't the only one. We are in a fortunate position, Edward, and we've decided that that will be our focus from now on."

"You're leaving Soho for good?"

"Perhaps not for good, but for now."

An irritation boiled in his blood that made him tremble. He was furious at her foolish inaction, and he could not hide his dismay. "That wasn't what I meant when I told you what I thought," he said sharply. "I said you should make Spot think you were giving up—I didn't mean you should really do it."

"I know what you meant," she said, her tone growing firmer. "We decided that the old way of doing things doesn't make sense any more. The sums don't add up. It isn't worth the aggravation."

The atmosphere seemed to be cooling. Edward wasn't sure if it was the drink, or the turn of the conversation, or the fractiousness that often came at the end of an evening, or a combination of all them, but Violet's mood was certainly blackening. He knew he should have smiled politely, acknowledged that surely she was right, thanked her for a lovely evening and excused himself, but he did not. He felt stifled and he could not hold his tongue. "And Spot?" he said. "You're going to just let him continue on as if nothing has happened?"

She replaced her tumbler firmly, the glass thunking against the wood of the side table. "Be careful with your tone, Edward," she warned acidly. "You needn't think we've forgotten what he did. He will be taken care of. He'll be visited by someone when he isn't expecting it. He'll be paid back what he's owed."

Edward could not help himself. "I'm sorry," he said, "but I just don't think it's sensible. The black market won't last forever. You must read the papers—the government are going to crack down on it harder and harder, and then, eventually, things won't be so scarce. Things will get back to normal. The money you're making now can only be temporary. A year or two, at best, and then it all dries up—and then what?"

She regarded him coolly, her tight little smile disappearing as her lips pursed. "And then we'll concentrate on new areas," she said, as if she was speaking to a child.

He pressed on. "Such as?"

"Building. There's a lot of money to be made repairing all the damage the Germans caused. We have some interests in that direction." She raised her hands in a conciliatory gesture. "You strike me as a practical man. What's the point in starting a war when the profits don't justify it? We'll make hay while the sun shines and pick our moment to settle the score with Spot."

Edward found that he could barely open his mouth to speak. "I think you're making a dreadful mistake," he said.

"I don't really care whether you agree or not," she snapped. "I'm only telling you this because Joseph speaks highly of you. I'm not looking for your approval."

A look of puzzlement and suspicion had fallen over Violet's face. Edward could see that she was perplexed at his reaction, and irritated by it, but, at that moment, he did not care. Violet and George were making a foolish error and someone had to tell them before they lost everything. Wasn't it obvious? He wanted to explain himself, to break through to Violet so that she could understand him, see that he was right, and feel the same way. "Think about it," he urged. "If you don't stamp on him now, it will be harder the longer you wait."

Her eyebrows lowered into a stern, unforgiving frown. "You've only been working with us for a few months. You might have ideas, but you have no experience. You don't know the West End, you don't know anything about it. You have no idea how the business works—you'd do well to remember that."

Edward realised, too late, that he had gone too far. "I'm sorry," he said contritely. "I know, you're right. I get ahead of myself sometimes." He laughed a little, tried to make his objections look silly. Violet did not respond, only put the cigarette holder in her mouth and poured herself yet another whisky. Edward felt himself beginning to sweat. He wanted her to say something to him, to tell him that she wasn't offended, perhaps even to say that she appreciated his candour, even if she disagreed with his sentiments, but instead she said nothing. She was indifferent, looking at him across the table through the long exhalations of smoke.

He sat up, thinking that he had heard a car on the gravel outside, but there was no car. He looked back at Violet but his eyes were blurred. He blinked, trying to bring her into focus, feeling a sudden dread of her. His thoughts turned to her brother, Georgie the Bull, and the things that he had heard about him. Edward took up his glass and, sipping down the last of his whisky, he jumped up so suddenly that he knocked the chair backwards. "Sorry," he said, setting it back in place again. "Thank you for a super evening," he managed.

She got up and took his hand in hers, squeezing it gently. He dipped so that she could press her lips to his cheek. They were pursed, hard and cold. "Good night, Edward," she said. Edward's knees felt like water and, as he passed out into the hallway and took the wide stairs up to the first floor, he felt an overwhelming surge of relief. It was over. He closed and locked the door of his room behind him and sat on the edge of the bed, working off his shoes and then loosening his tie. There was a tall dressing mirror in the corner and he caught his reflection in its glass: he was pale, a little sweaty, and his eyes bore a frightened look. He took off his tie and his shirt and ran the cold tap, cupping the water in his hands and dunking his face into it. He felt thwarted, and sick with fear that he had taken too many drinks and spoken too freely. He dried his face, finished undressing, and slipped between the cold sheets. He knew he would find it difficult to sleep but he closed his eyes anyway, experiencing the conversation again despite trying to think of something—anything—else.

47

EDWARD GRIPPED BOTH ARMRESTS as the Douglas DC-3 accelerated down the runway and, after what seemed like an eternity, took to the air. He had always been a poor flyer and the double gin he had quickly swallowed in the departure lounge had done very little to soothe his nerves. He glanced out of the window and watched as Northolt Aerodrome shrank away, the propellers blurring through the early morning sunshine as they ascended into a low bank of cloud. He watched as the hostesses unhooked their safety belts and made their way back to the galley to prepare breakfast. It was early, just after eight, but he hoped he could order another drink. His nerves were shot to pieces.

They rose into the clouds and then, abruptly, passed through them and into a bright, blue sky. He could see the ground through the jagged gaps in the white below: the tiny houses, the miniature cars passing along ribbon-like roads. It looked so peaceful from up here. It looked unreal.

His thoughts settled again on the events of the last few weeks. The operation was running smoothly, and, as far as he could tell, no-one was wise to what they were doing. He should have felt like one of the heroes in the tuppenny bloods he used to read when he was a boy—illicit, outside the law, putting one up against the world—and yet he did not. He felt awkward and nervous. It was Joseph who was causing his trepidation. Edward could not shift the awful sensation that something had fallen between them. He could not precisely define it, yet he worried that some decision had been made of which he had not yet been made aware. It was a sense of finality that, perhaps, once the last lorryload of goods had been removed from the depot there would be nothing else for him to do. Surely his own lies would come to stand against him. The family would expect him to go back to his medical 'career'; delaying it again so that he could continue with them would appear perverse and suspicious. Why would he do that? He was an educated man, highly qualified, and medicine promised to be lucrative without any of the risks that they had to run. Why would he put that to one side? Edward could not shift the terrible feeling that there were one or two more trips to make but that when the base was empty of the most saleable goods it would all be over, and then what would he do?

Their relationship was troubling him, too. Edward had always been prone to insecurity and he knew that his insecurity could easily run to paranoia, but, to him, Joseph's polite cheerfulness on the drive to the airport had been forced, like the good manners of a host who has loathed his guest and is afraid the guest realises it, and who tries to make it up with last minute good humour. Things had not been good between them for several weeks. They had argued regularly since Tommy Falco's funeral. Edward continued to insist that they must persuade his aunt and uncle that their course was wrong and Joseph had seemingly grown weary of it. Edward knew he should keep his own counsel but he could see them make mistake after mistake and he just could not do it. And if he did not say something, then who would? No-one. They would continue to totter down the road to disaster, oblivious, helpless, and then where would that leave him?

Edward looked across at Joseph. Pretending to be sleepy, he had put a sleeping mask over his eyes, folded his arms across his chest and settled back in the reclining seat. Edward took frequent glances at him, staring at his dark skin, and the thick black hair with the comma that fell across his left eye. Edward knew with a sick sense of certainty that he was failing with Joseph, the knots of his plan fraying and splitting, that careful latticework that he had worked so very hard to weave slowly coming apart. A riot of emotion swelled within him, of anger, impatience and frustration. Joseph had been different when they met in Calcutta. He had been relaxed there, carefree, willing to take risks and damn the consequences. That night they met, when he had come to his aid; what had happened to him since then? The longer he spent in this benighted country, the more he was drawn closer to the bosom of his lunatic family and his lunatic friends, the more different he became. Edward had failed, in every way, but it was not his fault. It was Joseph's stubbornness, his lack of independent spirit, his unthinking reversion to what he had been used to before. Edward had offered him his respect, his intelligence, his companionship, and Joseph had replied with indifference and now, it seemed, the beginnings of hostility. Edward could see into his future and he knew, as certainly as he had ever known anything in his life, that it held nothing for him. He would be politely nudged to the side and then left out in the cold. He would have to return to the kitchen, to the Labour Exchange, to insignificance.

A pretty hostess rested her hand on the seat in front and dipped her head. "A cup of tea, sir?" she asked quietly for fear of disturbing Joseph.

"I'm sorry to be terribly difficult," he said, "but I'm an awful flyer. Do you have any gin?"

If the hostess disapproved she did not show it. "Of course," she said, smiling, and went back towards the galley.

No, Edward chided himself. He needed to pull himself together. It did not serve to brood on things that had not even happened. And, of course, he reminded himself, there was a chance he was over-reacting. That was another of his faults. He concentrated on being optimistic. He had taught himself, long ago, that one could summon the desired mood by simply acting in the fashion that best evoked that mood. If you wanted to be thoughtful, or cautious, or hearty, or joyous, then you simply had to act those emotions with every gesture. So, he would summon optimism: he forced himself to smile, straightened his back and squared his shoulders. If he was correct and there was a problem between them, then surely this trip would be the perfect opportunity to iron it out. It was Paris, for goodness sake! The City of Lights! Edward was confident that his memory of it was good. Joseph had never been to France, let alone Paris, and there would be ample opportunity to enjoy it. There would be museums, galleries, and excellent food and wine. That was the way to look at it: this was an opportunity. They had two days together with no distractions. There was no need to worry about Billy Stavropoulos, there would be no Eve to divert Joseph's attention, they had no need to discuss Jack Spot or the folly of the Costellos' appalling response. Two days. That ought to be ample for him to remind Joseph of why he had invited him into the family business. Optimism. This was an opportunity and he would take advantage of it.

* * *

THEY TOOK TWO ROOMS in a splendid little pension on the Left Bank and spent the day exploring. Edward was filled with anticipation for a day of culture and good living but Joseph seemed distracted and refused to be vigorous about anything. He showed no interest as Edward read him passages from his Baedeker, did not seem impressed as he spoke in deliberately bad French (his French was excellent, but that would be difficult to explain) and practically had to be dragged into the Louvre. He complained of boredom as Edward led the way through the narrow streets and sulked until Edward gave up and found a pavement bar where they could drink Bieres Excelsior and watch the mademoiselles go by. Joseph said that he was tired and wanted to sleep before dinner and, in the end, Edward suggested they go their separate ways and rendezvous later in the hotel bar. Edward walked all the way to Notre Dame and back and, by the time he reached the hotel with a half an hour to spare, his feet ached and he was in a bitter and resentful mood.

He reminded himself to be cheerful and, as Joseph came down the stairs to meet him, he popped up with a wide smile on his face. "I've read about a great place for dinner," he proposed, tapping the cover of his Baedeker. "Do you like French food?"

"I don't know," Joseph said. "I've never had it."

They took a taxi to Montmartre. The restaurant was off the beaten track, with ten tables, cheap bottles of excellent wine and wonderful food. They took a table on the terrace that offered a view of the white-domed Basilica of the Sacré Coeur. Edward explained the history of the district as they waited for their starters to arrive, telling Joseph about Dali, Modigliani, Monet, Mondrian, Picasso and van Gogh. Joseph was still preoccupied. Edward gritted his teeth with frustration. There they were, in the middle of Paris with a chance to drink in the atmosphere, and all Joseph could do was to ogle the women and make crass jokes at the expense of the French, usually at how they had been occupied by "Fritz." Edward had known that Joseph was not predisposed towards culture but he had hoped that he might be swayed by all the art and the history that he would be able show him. That had not been the case. His conversation tonight was also tedious. Joseph had been pensive at first but, once the drink had loosened his tongue, he went on and on about what it had been like growing up in Little Italy, telling stories about the trouble that he and Billy had caused, and Edward had found the whole thing disinteresting and frustrating. It was ancient history and it betrayed narrow horizons. He seemed unable or unwilling to think about what he could achieve if he really put his mind to it.

Edward eventually persuaded him that they should book tickets to a music-hall show but their taxi driver took them through the Ninth Arrondissement so that they passed alongside Le Folies Bergère and Joseph told him to stop, and told Edward that he had heard about the women inside and that it would be a much more enjoyable way to spend the evening. Edward felt jaded and did not have the energy to argue. Why not, he conceded. They booked tickets for the midnight show and were allotted an excellent table near to the front. Joseph was quickly in buoyant spirits but Edward struggled to lift himself out of a despondent slough. The show was tedious and he was pleased when it was over. The day had not gone as he had planned. He wrote it off and tried to forget it. They had another day tomorrow. He would try harder then.

They took a taxi back to their hotel.

Joseph settled back and stretched out his legs. He looked to be drifting away to sleep when his eyes suddenly flicked open. "Damn!" he said. "I nearly forgot. I saw Billy before we came away. He said the strangest thing happened to him yesterday. He'd gone to the showroom to see Ruby about some business and he says this chap came in looking for you while he was there."

Edward had a sick, empty feeling in the pit of his stomach. "For me?" he said in a deep voice, trying to hide his tremulousness.

"So he says. Billy said this bloke said he was your brother. I didn't even know you *had* a brother."

He thought rapidly. He did not have a brother or sister but perhaps the real Edward Fabian did? He had no idea.

What would be the safest thing to say? There was no way of knowing. He wet his lips. "I do," he said quickly. He prayed that Billy did not have a name, or that, if he did, he had not told Joseph.

"You never mentioned him."

"We don't get on. I haven't seen him for years. What else did Billy say?"

"Not much. He said this fellow had seen your picture in the paper—that story that you did about the showroom. He wants to see you."

Edward felt weak and helpless and before he could do anything to prevent it his mind was picturing policemen waiting for him on the runway when they disembarked at Northolt. He forced himself to calm down. He was running ahead of himself. He began to plan his story and then what he would have to do when he returned. He would need to rehearse it all in his head, a hundred times over so that it became substantial, and that therefore he would have to believe it himself. He had a brother but they were estranged. He hadn't seen him since before the war and he had no idea what he wanted now. He would have to meet him and find out. It was nothing unusual. Family business, the sort that all families have.

"Are you alright? You've gone pale."

"It's my stomach," Edward explained. "I must've eaten something bad."

"Those oysters," Joseph suggested. "French rubbish. I told you they were a bad idea."

* * *

THEY HAD ONE MORE DAY before their return flight at eight o'clock. Edward was determined to spend it well. He had tried to put the news of the previous night out of his mind. There was no sense in worrying about it now and Joseph had not mentioned it again.

They checked out of the pension and took a taxi to the Eiffel Tower, walked to the Hôtel Royal des Invalides, and then spent two hours wandering the Champs-Elysées, pausing at the luxury shops and eventually stopping at a café with tables that spilled out onto the pavement. The Arc de Triomphe was blindingly white in the harsh sunlight. They ordered Americanos and croissants. Joseph had been quiet that morning, a little reserved, and Edward had the unshakeable feeling that whatever it was that had come between them was about to reach its inevitable conclusion. He did not wish to precipitate it but he could not stand the pensive atmosphere. "Is everything alright?" he said, trying to be cheerful.

Joseph hesitated. "There's something I want to say, Doc—and I hate to say it if it's going to cause any fuss."

Edward went cold. "Well, I won't know until you tell me what it is."

He looked uncomfortable. "I was thinking that perhaps we should look at getting our own places." He paused, a quizzical expression on his face that Edward ignored, forcing himself to stare blankly out into the busy street. "It's been great fun," he went on, choosing his words carefully, "but it was only ever going to be a short-term thing, wasn't it? Until you had enough money to stand on your own two feet. And you do now, don't you? You've done well out of all this."

He reply was a curt, "Yes, of course."

"Don't be like that. Wouldn't you rather get your own place? A bit more space to breathe?"

"Isn't this all a bit sudden?"

"I've been thinking about it for the last few days."

"I can't say that I have. I thought you were enjoying living together?"

"I have enjoyed it. But I'm getting more serious with Eve, now. It's not fair on her, bringing her back and you're there in the flat. You can see that, can't you? She needs a bit of privacy. I suppose we both do."

"I'll start to look around then."

"Doesn't have to be right away. Take a couple of days to find somewhere nice."

A couple of days, Edward thought bitterly. How generous! "No, I'll start when we get back. You've obviously made up your mind. I don't want to outstay my welcome."

"Don't be like that, Doc. There's something else that's made me think about this. I'd rather we kept it between us for now, but I'm thinking of proposing."

"Proposing?" he spluttered. "You've only been seeing her for a few months."

There was hurt confusion on his face. "What difference does that make?"

"Each to his own, I suppose."

"What does that mean? Oh, never mind—I was going to get the ring out here. I thought maybe you could help?"

It was a bit late to draw the sting, Edward thought. "I don't know."

Joseph grimaced a little. Edward watched him in the reflection in the café window and knew there was still worse to come.

"While we're at it, I'm afraid you've upset my aunt. I told you not to go on at her, about Spot and how they've chosen to do things, didn't I, but she says you gave it to her when you went down to the house last week."

"I didn't 'give it to her,' as you say," Edward protested with a laugh that sounded horribly false. "She brought the subject up and told me what she proposed to do about it. I told her I didn't agree. It was perfectly civilised, no more than that."

"She didn't see it that way. Her temper—"

"I was trying to be helpful, Joseph. I happen to think she's making a mistake. You agree with me, I know you do."

"I don't know what I think, so I've no idea how you'd presume to know."

"I don't see how I can be responsible if someone misinterprets what I say." The sense of frustration was agony to Edward. He forced himself to concentrate on the bitter coffee, trying to wrestle back some equanimity. He looked across the table: the annoyance was evident in Joseph's face, and Edward knew that he was irritated with his presuming to know best, even though Edward knew that he was right. He wanted to explain himself better, wanted to show Joseph that he was right, break through the suspicion and reluctance so that he would understand and they would feel the same way. "I wish you could see my point of view," he said. "Doing nothing is the worst thing that you could do."

"You don't know what you're talking about!" Joseph retorted angrily. "On and on and on. Jesus, Doc, you want to listen to yourself sometimes! You've only been involved for a few months, you don't know Soho, you don't know my family and you don't know Jack Spot. You don't really know anything and despite that you seem to think you know best about *everything*. I'm starting to think it was a bad idea asking you to get involved in the first place."

His expression had changed quickly from confusion to blackened anger. Edward had seen that switch in him before. His temper was finely balanced at the best of times, teetering between precipitous extremes: his good nature could curdle to fury before you knew where you were and it was frightening to see. Edward knew he should stop before he made things worse, but he could not. The frustration had been building in him for days until it was like an ache in his stomach. He should have said, "Alright, Joseph," to put an end to it, to tell Joseph he understood, that he knew he was being presumptuous and that he would keep his own counsel from now on, that they could move past their disagreement. But he couldn't say that, he just couldn't.

Joseph paused, and calmed his temper. They had bought a packet of French cigarettes that morning and he tore it open. He gave one to Edward and reached across to light it for him. Edward felt in the grip of an enervating weakness, as if his knees would buckle and he would fall to the ground. It was all too much to bear: his failure, Joseph's attitude, the fact that he obviously hated him. Edward suddenly saw it for exactly what it was. They were not friends, and they never had been. He did not know Joseph, not really. They had met, briefly, far away, drunk on whisky and elation at the end of the war. Burma and India were all they had in common, the only memories that were special to them, and, even then, those memories were limited to a drunken brawl in a bar and a drunken carouse afterwards. Those memories were fading fast, like photographs that had been left out in the sun. It was too much. He looked around at the café, at the tourists gathered at the tables and booths. He felt surrounded by strangeness, by hostility. He could see what would happen. It was all so awfully obvious. Only yesterday Joseph had said, "Are you planning a holiday soon" in an offhand way in the middle of a conversation, and now that made sense. So terribly transparent. Joseph and the rest of the family would very quietly, very politely, leave him out. Every convivial thing that they would say to him from now on would be an effort for them. It would all be insincere and Edward couldn't bear to imagine it.

"Look, Doc," Joseph said as he lit his own cigarette, "I might as well come out with it. Once this job is finished, Violet wants us to knock it all on the head."

Joseph's tone was conciliatory, friendly, but what he said gave Edward a painful wrench in his breast. "What does that mean?" he said.

"My aunt doesn't want you to work with the family any more."

"This is ridiculous!"

"That's how it has to be."

"You agree with her?"

He shrugged. "Maybe she's right. Maybe it's for the best. You've got the medicine to go to. I shouldn't have asked you to do that house with me. It was selfish of me. You should've worked on being a doctor when you got back. It would have made a lot more sense. It still does. Think about it. You know she's right."

Edward gripped the edge of the table until his knuckles showed white. He stared at Joseph's black eyes, at the clench of his eyebrows, the severe folds that creased his brow, and back to the eyes again, dark and black and unsmiling. There was no life there, no sparkle, nothing more than if Edward had been peering into the bloodless surface of a mirror. He felt as if he had been punched in his chest and his breath came fast, through his mouth. It was as if Joseph had suddenly been snatched from him and, at that, the boundless possibilities that he represented had been blown away like smoke. Edward didn't care about Joseph. It was the injustice that made him so angry.

"Say something, Doc," Joseph prompted, a little gingerly.

Edward got up, threw a handful of francs onto the table and set off. Joseph took his coat from the back of the chair and hurried after him. "If I knew you were going to take it so badly—"

A burning fury boiled in his blood and made him quiver. "You've got some nerve," he said in a cold voice that was flat despite the crazy anger that he was struggling to contain. "You're an ungrateful, spineless fool." Edward stopped in the middle of the pavement and stared at him. "Do you think we would have made so much money at Honeybourne if it wasn't for me? You wouldn't have known where to start. You're fine if things are simple, forcing a door or cutting rough with a guard so you can rob his depot. But if it's complicated, if it needs careful planning? It'd be you and your friends, blundering around with no idea, not a clue, with no plan and no sense. The same goes for your bloody stupid family, too. You wouldn't have lasted a week before the police got wise. You talk a good game, Joseph, all that lip, the silver tongue, but up here"—he stabbed a finger against his temple—"there's nothing inside that pretty head, is there? It's empty."

"Watch what you say," Joseph warned him.

"Or what? You'll hit me below the belt again?" They had raised their voices and people had stopped to watch them. That made Edward angrier still. Joseph set off, striding purposefully towards the bone-white monument.

Edward followed him. He turned his head to see confusion and something else—fear, or suspicion?—in Joseph's face. That made it worse. Edward wanted to explain to him, to persuade him that there was no need to behave like this, but he knew now with a sickening sense of certainty that he had been right: he was on his way out of the family. Events had gathered their own momentum now and he wouldn't be able to stop them. The thought of that was like agony to him. The frustration, to be thwarted when he was so close, when he had finally found such possibilities for his future. The tension rose higher and, suddenly, it snapped. "I pity you sometimes, Joseph, I do––the way you can't see how people like Billy Stavropoulos are dragging you down, and I think, without me, all you'd ever do is rob the odd house, turn over a warehouse or two, but all it would ever be is just a wait until you get your collar felt and sent down." He went on furiously, unable to stop. "Asking me to help you wasn't a mistake—it was the most sensible thing I've ever known you to do. And now you think you can just tell me it's all over? Just like that? Toss me aside like a piece of rubbish?" He laughed caustically. "You've got to be joking."

Joseph picked up his pace and so Edward reached out and grasped him around the shoulder. Joseph spun on his heel and, the angle changing so that his face became visible, Edward could see that he had prodded him too far. It was choked with fury. Joseph shucked his hand from his shoulder, closed his right fist and hooked at him. The blow was thrown carelessly and glanced Edward on the right temple. Again, he knew he should have stopped, that there were lines still to cross, but his own anger had him in a tight grip. He replied with a left-right-left combination, more accurate than Joseph, who took the first punch on his chin and the second and third on his quickly raised forearms. He ducked his head and tackled Edward into the doorway of a boutique. They rolled back into the street, each trying to hold the other down, using their elbows and heads and shoulders to wrest an advantage that they could not hold. They were of similar height and weight and equally matched.

Eventually, both with bloodied lips and noses, they broke apart.

More pedestrians had stopped to watch. A man approaching on the pavement took a step forward as if he were going to help, but stopped.

Edward rested his hand against the wall and breathed heavily. Joseph wiped the blood from his face with the back of his hand, then cleaned that with his handkerchief. The top four or five buttons of his shirt had been ripped out and the shirt gaped untidily. Edward's jacket had gashed beneath the shoulder, the sleeve hanging loose and the lining exposed, and his trousers were ripped above the knee. They stared at each other for five or six seconds. Joseph looked at Edward with disgust. Edward's sudden avalanche of anger was spent and he suddenly felt hollowed out and desperate. He started to say something but Joseph eyed him with open contempt and the words were stopped by a tight twist of despair in his throat. He felt a sudden loss and a sense of helplessness.

Joseph straightened his ruined shirt, trying—futilely—to close it. He flagged a passing cab. Edward stayed where he was, propped against the wall, and watched Joseph's long legs as he trotted over to where the driver had stopped and got in. The cab merged with the traffic and disappeared around a corner.

Edward found a bar and ordered a drink. His hands were still shaking. He bought a carton of untipped Gauloises. He remembered something that Joseph had said to him as they waited in the first class lounge at Northolt yesterday. He had mentioned, very casually in the middle of some conversation, that Edward had been more patient than he deserved in light of his slovenly attitude to keeping the flat clean and most people would have abandoned him by now. "I'd understand if that's how you felt," he'd added, trying to be guileless. It had been a clumsy hint so that he wouldn't have to come out with what he wanted to say more directly today. Edward had ignored it but now he wished he had not. It would have made things easier, and he would have been better able to control the conversation and, therefore, his temper. Things might have been salvaged but now he knew that serious damage had been done. He knocked back his drink. All right, he would find somewhere else. He knew when he wasn't wanted.

48

EVE MURPHY LOOKED AT HER REFLECTION in the mirror. She was in the Ladies' Powder Room at Vincanto, the chic new restaurant that had opened in Theatreland. She turned: front to the side. She was wearing the dress that Joseph had given her. He was very sweet like that, with all the presents and the surprises. It had been a Valentine's gift, wrapped in expensive paper, sealed with ribbons and a huge bow. She could hardly believe the dress inside: a black rayon crepe with beaded and studded bodice, a modified sweetheart neckline, sleeves with darted headers and shirred elbows and a self belt. Her friend had actually gasped when Eve held it up for her. She had gone on and on about how much a dress like that must have cost, and how could Joseph afford it, and what about all the coupons you'd need, where had he got those from, and what would people *think*? Eve had explained it the same way Joseph had explained it to her when he had given her the watch, the necklace, the broach: he said he had been lucky on the dogs.

    She knew that wasn't true. Eve was the daughter of a policeman and she was not a stupid girl. She did not know exactly how Joseph came by these things, but she knew it wasn't legitimate. She had considered giving the first gift back to him, but they were so nice and she didn't want to hurt his feelings and she couldn't see the harm in accepting them. One gift had led to the other and then to the next and by that time she had decided it would have been churlish to hand them back and so she had kept them. And why shouldn't she have some of the nicer things in life?

She thought of her Uncle Charlie. She had been worried about his proposal for the first few days but he hadn't asked much of her—so far, at least—and she had allowed herself to relax about it a little. He had arranged to meet her three times and they had chatted about things, usually over a coffee in one of the new coffee bars that were springing up in Mayfair and Kensington. It was just little pieces of information every now and again: who Joseph was going out with, what had she heard about his aunt and uncle, his friends and the other members of his family? None of it seemed dangerous or damaging and she had started to believe that perhaps she could manage her uncle, give him just enough to keep him satisfied but no more. It wasn't as if Joseph told her very much about his business, after all. How could she be expected to tell him things that she didn't know? She had told him that and he had appeared to believe it.

She checked her make-up in the glass. She looked lovely. As she collected her handbag she realised that she was a little drunk. She was a very moderate drinker and she had allowed Joseph to pour her a second glass of wine with dinner. It was all going to her head. She would have to put a stop to that.

Vincanto was especially nice. They had been to plenty of other places, fancy establishments, but they usually ended up here. She felt special as she made her way back into the dining room. She knew she was pretty, she was beautifully dressed and waiting for her at the table was her beau, and wasn't he a cracker?

"You took your time," he said, grinning at her.

"Had to make sure my make-up looked alright."

"What are you on about, girl? You look a million dollars."

The table was lit by a candle and the warm golden light flickered across his face. She felt the familiar flutter in her stomach. The light danced in his dark eyes, his olive skin framed by his jet black hair with that errant strand that curled above his left eye. He was so handsome. Such a *dish*. He could have had anyone he wanted and she had no idea why he was interested in her.

Their waiter arrived at the table with an ice bucket, a bottle of champagne and two flutes.

"This is our best bottle, sir," he said. "Bollinger Extra Quality Brut, 1943."

Joseph took the bottle and turned it in his hand. "Looks blinding," he said. "Thank you. I'll do the honours myself."

"Yes, of course, sir." He took the hint and backed away.

"I'm not sure I can manage another glass," Eve said.

"Nonsense," he told her. "Just the one. If you don't want it all, you don't have to drink it."

"It looks too expensive to waste." She screwed up her nose. "Is it?"

"It's not cheap, but that don't matter. We need a splash to celebrate." He shifted awkwardly in his chair. "We've been serious for ages now, ain't we? Five months, and then all the time from before. I haven't been out with anyone for as long as I've been with you. I wasn't planning it, you know. Out where I was, with no women for so long, I had it in my mind that I'd stay a single lad for a while."

"Why didn't you?"

"I met you again, didn't I? It's got me thinking—I've never been with someone like you before. I'm serious, Eve—I can't hardly stop thinking about you."

"Joseph—"

"Hold on. I've been building myself up to say this all day and I want to get it out straight. It's like I said, see, I'm serious about us. You and me. I want to prove it."

"You don't have to prove anything."

Joseph ignored her. He stood and then lowered himself to one knee.

"What are you doing?" she almost squealed.

He took a box from his pocket and opened it. "What do you think about us getting married?"

She looked: inside the box was a diamond ring. It had a large oval stone in the centre, set in platinum, and accented with smaller pear-shaped stones all the way around.

She gaped at him. "Oh, my goodness. I—I—" She took the ring and turned it in her fingers. Her mouth opened and closed as she searched for words.

"So what do you say?"

"I don't know *what* to say."

"Well say something, girl! You're not going to leave me here like this, are you?—I feel like a right bloody lemon."

She slipped the ring onto her finger. "Yes," she said with sudden impetuousness. "Oh, yes, of course!"

"Terrific."

Eve hadn't noticed, but the other diners had stopped their conversations to observe them. With her happy acceptance, several of them started to applaud. It quickly spread around the room until, finally, Joseph stood and declared that everyone should have a glass of champagne on him and, then, once the drink had been poured and he had popped the cork on their bottle, he orchestrated a toast. Eve knew that he was enjoying the spectacle, barely able to keep the grin off his face. He waited until the hubbub died down and the other customers returned their attention to their plates.

"I've been thinking about how we ought to go about things. I'm not one for a long engagement. The way I see it, you get engaged to someone, that's that, there's no sense in waiting ages to make it official. Best get cracking, right?"

"If that's what you think is best."

"I do. There are some things we'll have to sort out. We'll need to book the church and a place for the knees up after. And then there's where to go afterwards. A nice little honeymoon. We'll have a think about that."

"Where would we live?"

"My place, I reckon. Doc's moving out, anyway—he wouldn't want to share the gaff with a couple of lovebirds, would he? Eventually we'll get ourselves a place in the country."

Eve removed the ring from her finger. She twisted and turned it, the light refracting against the diamond. How much must it have cost? She had no idea. Her life had moved so quickly over the last few weeks. She had no idea how she had managed to snare someone like Joseph Costello, but, as she watched him laughing and joking with the waiter, she replaced the ring on her finger and shivered with a warm, excited tingling.

She was still aglow with happiness when the four men came inside. At first, she thought that they must be a party of diners but then Joseph saw them too, and she noticed tension stiffening his body, and then she wondered whether they might be here for something else. Two went to the bar. The manager followed after them, his voice fraught, and then she noticed that they were both holding short metal bars. The man opened the bar and stepped behind it, held his jemmy up behind his shoulder and then swung it, like a cricket bat, straight through the rack of bottles.

The colourful glass smashed. Some of the other diners screamed.

"What's going on?" she said, her throat closing with panic.

His dark eyes glittered coldly. "Don't look at them. They're not here for us."

"What are they here for?"

"They work for a man I know."

The men made their way through the restaurant. They each carried a large paper bag and, as they passed from table to table, they ordered the frightened diners to remove their valuables and deposit them into the bags. Wallets, watches, jewellery—it all went inside until the paper bulged.

"Well, look here," said one of the men as he reached their table. "I know you, don't I?"

"I don't know—do you?"

The man was large and dressed neatly in an Edwardian suit with many buttons and velvet facings. "You're Joseph Costello."

"That's right. Don't recognise you, though."

"No. But you know who we work for."

"I can guess."

"Sure you can, Joseph. Mind if I call you Joseph?"

"Where is he?"

"He ain't here. But he sends his best regards."

"Good of him."

The man's eye fell to the table and settled on the empty box. "Been buying some tomfoolery, Joseph?" He picked up the box and turned it over. He saw the logo and whistled appreciatively. "Tiffany? My word. *Expensive* tomfoolery. Let's have a butcher's at it then."

The colour leeched out of Joseph's face. "I don't think so."

Eve self-consciously covered her left hand with her right. Slowly, she moved them both towards the lip of the table and was about to drop them beneath the tablecloth before the man noticed her doing it and tutted, shaking his head. "Not so fast, darling," he grinned at her. He pulled back his jacket to reveal the butt of a revolver stuffed into the front of his trousers. "Let's stay best friends when this is all said and done, alright? Best to avoid unpleasantness, I always say. You'd agree with that, wouldn't you, Joseph? We don't want a nasty argument."

"Just show him," he said to her through gritted teeth.

She reluctantly raised her right hand, uncovering the left. The diamonds glittered on her finger, refracting the candlelight.

"Stone the bleeding crows. Will you look at that? The size of it! How much that set you back, then?"

"Enough."

"You two lovebirds getting engaged?"

Joseph glared up at him. "If you're going to do it, do it. Get on with it."

"Easy there, pal. Mind your place. You ain't the one with the shooter, remember. Let's have it, then, darling. Take it off. Chop chop. And your watch and wallet, Joseph. Quick as you like."

Eve fought back the tears. Joseph did as he was told, his eyes half-closed, the line of his jaw set straight and firm as he clenched his teeth. She knew about his temper but she had never seen him as dead in the eyes as this before and it frightened her. He was a prideful man and this—to be emasculated before his fiancée on the night of their engagement—it must have been the purest, most dreadful humiliation for him. The man didn't seem concerned with that, nor with the murderous look on Joseph's face; he took the watch and wallet and dropped them into the bag, draping his fingers over the stippled butt as a reminder that he should be civil as he turned his attention to her. She choked a sob as she worked the ring off her finger and gave it to him. "There you go," he said, the diamonds glittering in his palm. He dropped the ring into the paper bag with everything else. "That wasn't so hard. I'll leave you the box."

"Just go," Joseph muttered.

"Patience, sport. We will—just as soon as we've done everything we came here to do. This place is one of your family's, isn't it? Under Costello protection. The fellow over there needs to pay attention to that. Your lot are finished in Soho, china. If he wants to avoid unnecessary accidents in the future he really needs to speak to Jack. Know what I mean? The alternatives just ain't so reliable no more."

The man looked up at his colleagues and gave a curt nod. They took their jemmies and swung them into the windows, slammed them down on the stacked piles of crockery, stabbed them into the paintings that had been hung on the wall. It was a concentrated orgy of violence that lasted no more than thirty seconds but when they had finished the place had been completely wrecked. No-one spoke. It was silent save for the gasped sobs of the diners and the crunch of shattered crockery and glass as it was trodden underfoot.

"Alright then. That'll do. As I say, Jack sends his warmest regards. Goodnight."

Joseph did not look at them. He stared at Eve instead. His eyes were black orbs, without warmth or life, more frightening than the men and their threats and their violence and anything else that she had ever seen. She reached out across the table and took his hand in hers. He did not flinch. His flesh was cold to the touch.

49

EDWARD DISTRACTED himself with an hour or two of shopping. He visited a haberdashery where he bought a pair of yellow silk pyjamas, as close as possible to the pair that he had borrowed from Joseph when he had visited Halewell Close. He bought a pair of narrow satin-like trousers and, for Chiara, flared hipsters of black wool, waist twenty-six. He added a gold tie-pin and settled the twenty pound bill from his money roll, making a show of taking it out of his pocket and counting off the notes. It made him feel much better, as did emerging from the shop with his purchases in crisp paper bags. After that he descended into Bond Street station for the short trip to Soho. He could have taken a taxi but he preferred the anonymity of the Underground, a chance to lose himself amidst all the other Londoners going about their business. He went to a pavement telephone box and asked the operator to place a call to Jimmy Stern's number. They spoke briefly and Edward said that he would be around to discuss business in a half an hour. There was a homeless man begging on the pavement next to the telephone box. Edward stopped and gave him a pound note.

He had given Jimmy the money to rent a small flat on Bateman Street, just around the corner from the Shangri-La. He knocked on the door. The sound of barking came at once, close at hand, then Jimmy's voice, ordering the dog to be quiet. The barking did not stop. The door opened.

Jimmy was exasperated. "This bloody dog—"

"You're doing a fine job, uncle."

"How much longer?"

Edward stepped inside and shut the door before Roger could get out. "I don't know. Not yet. A few more weeks."

"You must be joking. I'll have strangled him by then."

The flat was small: one bedroom, a tiny kitchen and a sitting room. It had come with its own furniture, none of which was in particularly good condition. The carpets were threadbare, the underlay visible in patches, and the paint was peeling from the damp that crawled up the walls. The dog's bowl was pushed into a corner of the kitchen, scraps of food from the restaurant spilling out of it and all over the floor.

Roger reached up, his paws on his chest. Edward sat down on the flea-bitten sofa and scrubbed the dog's ears. "Just don't get too attached, alright?" He stretched out his legs. "Well?"

"They were there. Intimate, the lads said. He'd just given her this."

Jimmy dropped a diamond ring onto Edward's open palm.

Edward nodded. "Nice."

"Expensive."

"He doesn't do things by halves."

Edward had had Joseph followed for the better part of two days. Jimmy found the lads through a friend of a friend—Mancunian hard-men who wouldn't be recognised in the smoke, who could be in and out of town in the space of a week.

"How did he take it?"

"How'd you think he took it? Johnny said he thought he was going to blow his top."

"And they made it obvious they were with Spot?"

"Told him than once. He got the message."

Edward held the ring up so that the light from the bare electric bulb sparkled through all the different facets. It was a shame to have to spoil Joseph's big night but hadn't he brought it upon himself? What choice had he left Edward? He had none. The Costellos given him no other options at all. They were blundering into a dreadful mistake and they just needed to be able to see it: he was the only one who could help them. There was no way he could just sit by and watch them destroy themselves.

He slipped the ring into his pocket. "How much did it cost us?"

"Fifty notes."

He took a wedge of notes from his pocket and handed them to Jimmy. "Cheap at half the price. This should cover it. They've all left town?"

"Yes." Jimmy went through to the kitchen and filled the kettle. "Straight back up north. They won't come back down. You want a cup of tea?"

"Please. Definitely best for them they stay away. I know what Joseph is like. I'm telling you, he'll top them if he sees them again."

"You had any improvement with him?"

"Haven't seen him since Paris."

"And you're sure this is going to help?"

The dog nudged his knee with his head and he scratched him behind the ears again. "They need me. They just need to see how much."

50

EDWARD MOVED OUT the next day. He had waited outside the apartment until he was sure that Joseph was not there and then he had quickly packed a suitcase with his best clothes and hurried away. He took a room at a smart hotel in Covent Garden and took long walks so that he might have the thinking time to decide upon what to do. He spent hours composing a letter in his head, apologising for losing his temper and trying to make a joke out of it, but the right words would not come and he could not satisfy himself that he had found the right tone. Eventually, he sent a note on the hotel's headed paper suggesting that they go for a drink to mend the damage that had been done. Joseph had not replied. Edward spent a sleepless night, and then a day, of pacing the hotel room while he tried to work out the best way to fix the situation. The stark contrast between his happy confidence of just a few weeks previously and his present fearfulness was awful to him. The rift with Joseph was at the forefront of his mind but he recognised clearly that he was obsessing with it so that he could pretend to ignore the other awful development: the man whom Billy had met who said he was Edward Fabian's brother. That, he knew, was a more dangerous situation. He expected the man, or a private detective, or, worst still, the police, to come knocking at his door at any hour of the night or day. They would have questions for him and he would not have the time to prepare the right answers. The thought of it terrified him. He could neither sleep nor eat nor sit still. He seemed barely able to function at all. The whole awful situation was pure agony.

On the second day in the hotel he started to plan an escape. His luck had held for too long and now it was beginning to turn. What was to stop him making a run for it? Nothing at all. He had a decent amount of money. He could sell his car and empty his accounts and make off with it all. Where would he go? Europe seemed suddenly too hot for him but what about America? How was that? He would drive to Liverpool, sell the car there and board a transatlantic liner. What better place to make a clean break and start afresh? He had so nearly succeeded with the Costellos. Who was to say he would not be more successful the second time?

Something stopped him. He could not abandon his father again. There was also a sense of unfinished business. He did not want to run. The realisation helped him to settle his thoughts. In the end, his thoughts settled on Chiara. He wrote to invite her to London so that they might have dinner together. She replied by return, her enthusiasm obvious, saying that she would be delighted. In a postscript she admitted to feeling claustrophobic at Halewell Close and that a night out was just the tonic she needed. Edward had counted upon as much.

He checked out of the hotel and took a lease on a furnished apartment. He planned the evening carefully. He booked a table at the Ritz, went to his barber for a shave, a trim and a vibro-massage, and then picked out his best suit, matching it with a crisp new shirt and tie that he had bought for the occasion. He dressed and regarded himself in the mirror that he had hung on his bedroom wall. There was no question about it: he looked absolutely splendid. He looked, he thought, like he had money and knew how to spend it tastefully. The years had been kind to him, he thought, lending him an air of sophistication that had not been there before. He was the kind of man who looked best when he had a little money. He had worked hard to get it. It took talent to notice the right opportunities, and then skill and great patience to exploit them. He had invested time and effort in the family and he would not allow Violet or Joseph or anyone else to prevent him from getting what he deserved.

He met Chiara at the restaurant, the *maitre d'* greeting them and showing them to a prime table. He slipped a pound note into the man's hand as he shook it and went around the table to remove the chair for Chiara to sit down.

"This is a rare treat," she said. "To be honest, I couldn't wait to get away."

"What's the matter?"

"You haven't heard about what's happening at the house?"

"No."

"It's that nonsense with Jack Spot. Violet has put two of George's best men in the gatehouse at the end of the drive. She's worried he's going to try and do something. She hasn't let me out for the last week."

"What about tonight?"

"She thinks I'm with Joseph."

"Oh dear," he said. "Best it stays that way—she's not very fond of me."

"She won't admit it, but this whole situation is getting to her."

There was a short pause as Edward decided how to start the conversation he knew that they must have. It was the reason that he had invited her to dinner and there was no point in delaying it but yet the thought of what she might tell him in response made it difficult to begin. He had the sense that this moment was important and, as it assumed more and more gravity, it became correspondingly more difficult to address. He started to speak and then, suddenly fearful, he stopped.

Chiara noticed his awkwardness and smiled sweetly at him. "I know about you and Joseph," she said. "Your silly tiff in Paris."

Edward gaped. "Have you spoken to him?" he asked anxiously.

"I have. And he feels absolutely awful about it."

"So do I," Edward confessed urgently. "What did he say?"

"That it was a foolish argument and that he regrets it very much."

Edward was surprised by the sudden rush of relief that washed over him. "I wrote to him," he said. "He didn't reply."

"He was still angry when you sent it. And now that he isn't angry, he doesn't know what to say to fix it all up and then, on top of everything else, he's had Eve to think about."

"Think about what?"

"Oh," she said, blushing a little. "Of course—you don't know." The waiter delivered the menus and Chiara was silent. Edward found that he was avid for the news, his stomach churning as the man described the specials and until he left the table. "This is probably about as foolish as your argument," she continued, "especially since they've only known each other again for half a minute, but he proposed to her the other night and she said yes."

"My goodness!" he said.

"They're talking about getting married at the end of the month. The service would be in the local church and then there'll be a big party at the house."

"It's all very sudden."

"I know. It's lunacy. But it will give the two of you a chance to make it up. He's planning a thing"—she fluttered her hand as if it were something amusingly distasteful—"with his friends. Last night of freedom, I suppose, something along those lines. I suspect it will involve all the pubs and clubs in Soho. I can't think of anything worse but, anyway, he asked me to apologise for what happened and to tell you that you have to go."

Edward's mind went blank with relief. He felt the surge of his old confidence. It wasn't too late, after all. He had made a dreadful error and yet he had not been punished for it. He had been given a second chance.

He became aware of some people waving at them from a table on the other side of the room. Chiara noticed them too. "Who are they?"

"I've no idea," Edward replied, making a vague sign of greeting in return.

"Well, they certainly seem to know you." She folded her napkin, laid it on the table and stood. "I'll just be a moment. Would you order me a drink?"

"What will you have?"

"A gin, please. I shan't be a moment."

Edward watched her cross the restaurant to the corridor that led to the bathrooms. He caught sight of his own reflection in the mirror that hung from the opposite wall and seeing again how swell he looked helped to restore his mood. He was still gazing at himself when he noticed the man who had waved at him get up and leave his table. His stomach fell. He took up the menu and pretended to be absorbed by it but it was no use. The man approached and stopped by his table.

"Pardon me, are you Jack Stern?"

Edward smothered a frightened gasp. The man was next to him, crouching, his left hand resting on the table and his body turned at an angle to face him. He had him trapped against the table. Edward stared at him, paralysed. He didn't look like a policeman but perhaps that was the point of it. He had heard of the Ghost Squad, after all, and perhaps it was their tactic to send someone who looked anonymous, to give that man the best chance of apprehending him before he could flee. Or perhaps he was a private detective. There had been others but not for many years. The man was well-dressed, like all the others in the restaurant, sporting a beautiful dinner jacket, his generous belly constrained by a scarlet cummerbund and his hair swept backwards across his head, a little grey at the edges. He smiled at him, a happy beam of greeting, and now Edward's frantic brain groped for the right thing to say.

"It *is* you," the man said, not waiting for his reply. He looked a little tipsy. "I knew it. I saw you when we came in—I said to my wife, 'That's Jackie Stern or I'm a Chinaman' and I was right, wasn't I? I wasn't sure but then I realised, you're not wearing your glasses. How are you, old chap?"

"I'm sorry, I—"

"Goodness, my manners. It's Bert? Albert Whitchurch? We met in Cannes. I'm not surprised you can't remember. My God, it must've been thirty-eight or thirty-nine—before the war, in any event. I was down there with Clara, my wife—look, she's over there."

Edward followed his gesture across the crowded room where a woman in a black dress and pearls was waving broadly at him. He cast his mind back to the time he had spent in France and found that the name was faintly familiar. Albert and Clara Whitchurch. That's right, he thought, he *did* remember them. A well-spoken chap, a polished wife, quite a bit of money. Was he an industrialist? It was something like that. They had met next to the pool at the Carlton and shared a couple of meals together. They had aroused his interest.

"Do you remember?" he pressed. "You were going to Venice."

"I'm sorry," he said, speaking in a deep voice to master the quaver in it. "I'm afraid I'm not who you think I am."

"You're not Jackie?"

"I'm afraid not. My name is Fabian."

"Well, I'll be damned. I could've sworn you were someone I met in Cannes. You're his doppelganger, old boy, his absolute spit."

The conversation was awkward and uncomfortable. He thought of Chiara and he turned towards the corridor that led to the bathrooms. He could not see her, but he couldn't wait for her to come back. It was too dangerous.

"Well," Edward said. "I'm extremely sorry to disappoint you."

The man nodded, a slightly vacant expression on his face. Edward could see that he did not know what else to say. "No," he said. "I'm sorry for disturbing you. Enjoy your evening."

Edward waited for the man to wander back to his own table and then laid his napkin down and stood. Whitchurch was talking to his wife, and she looked over at him with a confused expression. He hurried to the cloakroom, collected their coats and took them to a spot where he could intercept Chiara before she returned to the restaurant.

"Whatever are you doing?" she said.

"I've changed my mind," he said breathlessly. "Let's take a cab and look at the moon."

"You're crazy! It's freezing out there."

"I want to show you my new place."

"What—now? What about dinner?"

"I'll cook for you at home. Really, I can't wait to show you. I'll be terribly distracted all evening unless we go right now. What do you say?"

She grinned at him. "Well, then," she said happily. "Why not."

* * *

EDWARD FUMBLED IN HIS POCKET for the key to his apartment. They had diverted to a bar on the way back and had enjoyed a bottle of champagne. Chiara swayed a little as she stood by his side. She was the worse for wear.

"Hold on," he said to Chiara. "It's in here somewhere."

The apartment was in a large Victorian red-brick building on Wimpole Street. It was of decent size and it had been expensive. He wanted his apartment to be elegant, to be at least comparable to Joseph's, and he intended to spend a generous sum furnishing it. The apartment had one bedroom, a sitting room with a small interconnecting study, a compact bathroom and a kitchen. The expensive furniture suited the neighbourhood, he felt, and contributed to the image that he wanted to present.

"I'd love a smoke," she said. "Do you have any?"

"Certainly." Edward took out a packet of filched Lucky Strikes and tapped out two cigarettes. Their fingertips touched, briefly, as he handed her the cigarette. He took the match and used it to light the two large candles on the table. Warm, flickering light was cast around the room.

Chiara took a greedy pull on the cigarette. "I had a lovely evening. I enjoy spending time with you."

"And me with you." He smiled at her. She sat down on the edge of the settee. She gestured that he should join her and he did, sitting next to her.

She rested the cigarette in the ashtray, took his hand and leant towards him. She closed off the distance until her lips brushed against his.

Slowly she pulled his head towards her.

Edward put out a hand to her left breast and held it softly. He lifted her hand and put it round his neck. Their mouths met and clung, exploring. A small night wind rose up outside and moaned round the building, giving an extra sweetness, an extra warmth. The candles began to dance in the breeze from the open window, the golden light flickering against the ceiling and the walls. A pigeon landed on the balcony outside, its wings clattering through the air. Chiara shrieked, her closed eyes opening. She looked at the window, saw the fat-breasted bird strutting along the balustrade, and laughed. Her mouth drew away. She smoothed Edward's hair and got up, and without saying anything, opened the window and clapped her hands. The bird flapped away. She stood away from the window and turned back to him. She undid her blouse and dropped it on the floor, then her skirt. Under the glint of moonlight from the open windows she was a pale figure, her soft pastel shadow extending forwards. She came to Edward, took him by the hand and led him into the bedroom. She undid his shirt and slowly, carefully took it off. Her hair smelt of new-mown summer grass, her mouth of champagne, and her body of baby powder. She lay down beside him. The filtering moonlight shone down on them both as he leant across, bridging the distance and touching his lips to hers.

* * *

THEY AWOKE AT EIGHT O'CLOCK and it was the same glorious thing again. This time she held him to her with tenderness, kissed him not only with passion but also with affection. He lay back down on the bed and rested his head beside hers on the pillow. He leaned across to kiss her, at first softly, and then more fiercely. Her body stirred. Her mouth yielded to his and when his left hand began its exploration she put her arms round him. "I'm catching cold," she complained. Edward pulled the single sheet away from under him and covered them both with it. He lay against her and drew the fingernails of his right hand softly down her flat stomach. The velvety skin fluttered. She gave a gasp and reached down for his hand and held it still.

She looked into his eyes. "You do love me a little bit?" she said. Her tone was playfully pleading but her vulnerability was unmistakeable, as if his answer was very important indeed.

Edward whispered, "I think you're the most adorable, beautiful girl. I can't believe that you're Joseph's sister. I wish I'd met you as soon as I got back." There was at least a little sincerity in his sentiment, but he amplified it for her benefit it. The stale words seemed to be enough. She removed her restraining hand.

When it was over and they lay quietly in each other's arms, Edward knew that she was his.

51

BILLY STAVROPOULOS PARKED HIS CAR a little way down the road. He was close enough to observe the comings and goings from the apartment block but not so close so as to be noticed. He looked around critically. Fabian had moved to a posh area, he thought. Wimpole Street was to the north of Oxford Street, and adjacent to Harley Street. It was lined with red-brick Victorian apartment buildings, elegant four and five-storey blocks that sheltered behind the curtillage of the ash trees on either side of the street. Billy had strolled along the road twenty minutes ago, pausing at the steps that led up to the wooden front door of number two-two-one. A glass-fronted panel next to the door announced five apartments, with a neat FABIAN written alongside apartment 'B'.

He had returned to the car and did not have long to wait. The sun had sunk behind the building when the door opened and Edward Fabian appeared, framed in the light from the lobby behind. He paused at the top of the stairs, holding the door for a second person. Billy squinted through the gloaming. Unbelievable, he thought, shaking his head. He cursed quietly as he recognised Chiara Costello. She linked arms with Fabian and they walked down to the street together. He was wearing a dinner jacket and she was wearing an elegant dress and a fur stole.

They were together? Who would have thought it. They were going for an evening out. That was good, Billy thought, putting his jealousy aside. That was perfect. He would have plenty of time. He reached across to the passenger seat and picked up his leather gloves. He put them on and picked up a small jemmy, hiding it inside a folded copy of the morning's *Times*. He stepped out of the car, locked the door and strolled towards Fabian's building.

He trotted up the steps and made to tie his shoelace as he inspected the door. It was not substantial. He checked up and down the street and, satisfied that he was not observed, he inserted the tip of the jemmy into the narrow space between the door and the frame, right below the lock, and gave it a sharp backwards yank. The frame splintered and the door swung open. Billy went inside and quickly made his way up to the second floor. The door to apartment 'B' was off the landing. Checking again that he was alone, Billy tried the handle. To his surprise, it had been left unlocked. He opened it and went inside.

The flat was dark. Billy took out a torch and worked quickly from room to room. There was an empty champagne bottle and two flutes in the kitchen. A dress had been neatly folded across the back of one of the dining table chairs. There were two toothbrushes in the bathroom, together with a compact, a bottle of Italian Stradivari cologne, two lipsticks and a blusher. Billy picked up the lipstick and absent-mindedly twisted it, then took the bottle of cologne, held it beneath his nose and sniffed it. He replaced it on the stand and went into the bedroom. The bed was unmade, the sheets ruffled and a pillow dislodged onto the floor. Billy shook his head. Fabian was a good-looking fellow, he supposed, but Chiara Costello was something else, and he'd been having it away with her. Lucky bastard. Another reason to stitch the lying cowson up.

Billy went back to the sitting room and opened the only door that had been left closed. It gave onto a small study: a desk and a single chair, a standard lamp, a gramophone, neat piles of stationery. He turned on the lamp and sat in the chair. He opened the desk drawers, one by one, reading through the papers inside and tossing them behind him when he was done. There was nothing of interest. The final drawer was locked. He took a metal ruler from the desk and inserted it between drawer and pedestal. A solid yank: the lock shattered and the drawer slid open. An unsealed envelope was inside. He took it out. It was fat and heavy. He slipped his fingers inside and withdrew a wad of pound notes, fifty or sixty of them. There was a letter attached to the envelope with a paper clip. Billy unfolded it and read:

Dear Jack,

Your father's account at the hospital is overdrawn and I do not have the ready funds to meet it. I realise that it was only the other day that you made your last remittance, but there any possibility that you could make another? I would gladly pay myself, but I have paid the money you gave me to the builders so that they can begin work on the restaurant and I am not sure how easy it would be to get it back.

Regards,
Jimmy

And the unsent reply, marked with today's date.

Dear Jimmy,

I'm afraid this might be the last payment, at least for a little while. I trust it is sufficient to put father's account back into credit. Things are not going quite as well as I had expected, although I am taking steps to rectify them. In the meantime, I hope that the refurbishment is proceeding to plan. I will be in touch.

Jack

Billy turned took the envelope and turned it over.

It was addressed to the Shangri-La Restaurant, Dean Street, London.

He went through the rest of the drawer. He found three passports and flicked through them with a growing sense of disbelief. The first was for Edward Fabian, the second was for Jack Stern and the third was for Roger Artis. The photograph in each was of Fabian. He found different Registration Cards, different Ration Books and another hundred or so pound notes. Billy laid them all out on the desk.

He had known something was wrong as soon as the man had said Fabian was his brother. The poor fellow had said that he hadn't seen him for years, since the start of the Blitz, that they had been close up until then and that he just couldn't understand what had happened so that he had just vanished into thin air. In the end, the family had assumed that he must have been killed in the bombings. But then he had seen the story in the paper and he hadn't been able to believe it. The picture was of a different person, that was true, but everything else was exactly right: the name, his age, the university at Cambridge, the degree in medicine. Perhaps the picture was a mistake? He had wanted to speak to him and Billy had taken his details and promised to pass them on. He wouldn't do that, of course, there would be no point. He had known, then, what Fabian must have done and, if he was right, there wouldn't be much of anything left for the fellow after Billy was finished with him.

He pulled the drawer all the way out and turned it over, shaking everything that was left out onto the floor. A packet of cigarettes. Pens. A stapler. Some paper clips. Scraps of paper. Army documents. When the drawer was finally empty, he traced the toe of his shoe through the debris on the floor. Something glittered back up at him. He knelt down and sorted through the rubbish with his hands until he found it.

A platinum ring. A large oval diamond set in the centre. Smaller pear-shaped stones all the way around.

Billy recognised it at once. He had been there with Joseph when he bought it. Tiffany on New Bond Street. It was the same day that he had asked him to be his best man. The day after he came back from Paris.

He thought for a moment; it didn't make sense. He sat down in the chair and thought about it some more. He cleared a way through the confusion to leave just one possible reason why Fabian would have the ring.

Fabian was working for Jack Spot.

And Fabian wasn't really Fabian at all.

He laughed, unable to stop himself, the laughter driven by the anticipation at what he would now be able to do. He looked again at the passports and documents and the ring. It was too good to be true. He would finally be able to balance the ledger. All those frustrations, those sneers and snide remarks, so much to pay him back for. This was quite a haul. It was better than he could ever have hoped for.

52

EDWARD STIRRED GROGGILY at the early morning sun shone through the open window, motes of dust drifting lazily though the golden shafts. He settled back against the mattress, allowing himself the luxury of waking gradually. He had a hangover, he discovered, a dull throb in his temples and an insistent ache in his bones. He and Chiara had enjoyed a splendid night, returning to the Ritz for the meal that Edward had originally promised and then drinking at the hotel's bar until two in the morning. He had drunkenly suggested they take a room there rather than return to his apartment but she had chided him for his extravagance, and they had taken a taxi home and gone straight to bed. He felt her weight beside him, and the warmth from her body against his skin.

He got out of bed gently, so as not to wake her. Chiara had bought him a gift as they wandered around the West End yesterday: a luxurious Egyptian cotton dressing gown from Dickins & Jones. Edward pulled it on and went through into the living room. They had barely paused there the night before, removing their coats and shoes before repairing to the bedroom. Now, with the full light of the morning blazing through the uncovered window, he could see that something was wrong. The door to his study was ajar and he always kept it closed. He crossed the room and touched it with careful fingertips, then pushed it open. The room beyond was in a mess: papers had been removed from the desk drawers and strewn around the room, books had been tipped from the shelves, the standard lamp was lit, the chair was overturned. Edward stepped inside and quietly shut the door behind him. He went to the desk; the most important drawer had been forced, the wood splintered and torn around the lock. He pulled it all the way open and searched inside. Edward felt the blood go out of his face. He felt faint. His passports, his correspondence, his money; it had all been taken.

He stood in the middle of the small room, his hands braced against the desk to stop him from falling. He stared vacantly out of the window at the jagged horizon of rooftops and chimneypots, feeling nothing except a faint, dreamlike panic. Chiara was sleeping in the next room but she suddenly seemed hopelessly far away. He was friendless and alone, that was the thing he had to remember. He always had been, and nothing had changed. A cold shiver ran up and down his spine and then, much too suddenly for him to react, he vomited. The first gout fell across the papers on the carpet but the second, more powerful, he managed to direct into the wastepaper basket. His head began ringing as if he were about to faint, and the absurdity of his faintness, plus the danger of collapsing and having Chiara find him dazed and prostrate on the floor amid all this mess, made him gather his strength and walk slowly and carefully back into the sitting room, then into the kitchen, and then to drink a pint of cold water.

He opened the window and breathed in the fresh air deeply. He wasn't going to faint, he told himself. He was going to compose himself, recover his equanimity and think rationally about what he had to do. He went back into the sitting room and quietly closed the door to the study, then he went into the bathroom and stood under a cold shower for ten minutes, letting the water run all over his body, scrubbing it into his scalp and face, the icy cold driving away the dazed panic so that he could think clearly. He turned off the shower, dried himself and, after quietly collecting his clothes from the bedroom so as not to disturb Chiara, dressed in the lounge.

He wanted to go out and take a walk but he knew he couldn't leave Chiara in the flat. He stood looking at the disorganised clutter on the desk, the acrid tang of his own vomit starting to fill his nostrils. For a moment, he wondered if he had the strength or the energy to straighten it all out. It annoyed him how foolish he had been. Those things should have been hidden properly, under the floorboards or put away in a safety deposit box. He had meant to, too, but he had continually put it off. Lazy and stupid, he cursed himself. He banged his fist against the desk. Lazy and stupid and now he was going to have to pay for it.

He heard the sound of the mattress as Chiara shifted her weight on it, and then the creak of the floorboards. He closed the door to the study, took the bin into the kitchen and washed it out. He splashed his face with cold water, scrubbed it dry with a tea towel and took a deep breath, preparing himself to start the day.

53

THE SHANGRI-LA WAS EASY TO FIND. It was on Dean Street, towards Theatreland and Shaftesbury Avenue. A great spot, Billy thought. Slap bang in the middle of the action. Just the kind of place that out-of-town theatregoers would visit before their shows, a little bit of authentic Soho atmosphere but not *too* much. The place was shut at the moment. The windows were covered with paper but Billy found a gap that he could peer through. The place was in the middle of a redecoration: the tables were covered with drop sheets, pots of opened paint were lined up, a step-ladder rested against the wall. There was a man inside, spreading out another sheet over the bar. Billy knocked on the window. The man shook his head and mouthed that he was closed. Billy knocked again, smiling, and pointed to the door. The man weighed down the ends of the cloth with a pot of paint, rubbed his dirty hands against the apron he was wearing, came over and opened up.

"Sorry, pal, we're closed. We'll be open again next week." The man was old, in his early sixties perhaps. He was thin, with wispy greyish-black hair and large grey eyes that seemed to wobble in his head as if he was cockeyed. He wore a pair of square glasses that were marked with tiny flecks of white paint.

"Are you the proprietor?"

"Yes."

"It's Jimmy, isn't it?"

"Yes," he said carefully. A flicker of suspicion passed across the man's face and there was a natural wariness in his eyes. "Who's asking?"

"Can I come in for a moment?"

"I said we're closed."

Billy looked straight at him. "It's about Jack. Jack Stern? It's important."

He watched as the man's face clouded with a wariness that was quickly cleared by a shrug and a shake of the head. "Afraid I don't know anyone by that name," he said, breezily. "You must have me mistaken for someone else. Good day to you."

He smiled and started to close the door but Billy was too quick. He jerked his body forwards, catching the frame against his shoulder and bouncing it backwards. It thudded into the man's chest and he staggered into the restaurant. Billy followed inside, shutting the door behind him. He slid the bolt across and pulled down the blind.

"Look here," the man protested angrily. "What's your game, mate?"

Billy looked around. There was a small, framed picture on the wall above the bar. It was of the man, Jimmy, and a young boy. Billy recognised him. He was much younger then, wearing chef's whites. Billy guessed the photograph must have been ten years old. The younger man was Fabian. The shape of the face, the hair, the same knowing look in his eyes; there was no doubt about it.

"That's him," he said, chin-nodding towards the photograph. "He calls himself Edward now, but I know that ain't his real name. He's been lying to me for weeks."

"That's a friend of the family," the man said. "Really, sir, I don't know what you're talking about. Please, just leave—I don't want any trouble."

"'I don't know what you're talking about,'" Billy mimicked. "They always say that." He reached into his pocket and slipped the fingers of his right hand into a pair of brass knucks. "They don't say it for long, though." He closed his fist, took his hand out of his pocket and, without any other warning, rabbit-punched the old man. He went down, wheezing and gasping, falling to his knees. "Now then," Billy said as he stood above him. "I want me and you to have a little chat, alright? You're going to tell me everything about Jack Stern. Everything. I won't lie and say I'd rather we could keep it civil. Your boy's caused me a lot of problems. I've got what you might call a lot of frustration—I need to work it all out."

54

SO JOSEPH HAD ASKED BILLY to be his best man. Edward knew that the two of them had grown up together, and that they had history, but he wanted to tell Joseph that that had been years ago, when they were both boys, that they hadn't seen each other all the while he had been fighting and that, most of all, couldn't he see, after all that time apart, that Billy was no good? Couldn't he see that he was impetuous, unreliable, prone to jealousy, violent, and, most damning of all, that he was dull and stupid and just so awfully boring?

He had been irritated by the predictability of the news but he had quickly reminded himself that it did not really matter. He had been a little surprised to have been invited to the evening at all. He was grateful for that. He knew that he had very nearly lost his chance with Joseph altogether, and that he had been given a reprieve.

It had fallen to Billy to organise the stag party. The group had gathered for dinner at Claridges and, after enjoying the meal, they had taken a drunken tour of their favourite Soho haunts. The evening had been especially raucous. There had been a dozen of them at the start of the night and they had collected hangers-on as they stumbled around Soho's streets and alleys. By the time they reached the Alhambra they were nearer thirty. They arrived at a little after midnight, everyone drunk except Edward. He was keeping a careful eye on the amount that he drank. He felt as if he was negotiating a high-wire above a precipitous chasm and he couldn't risk losing control.

The upstairs room had been reserved for the party and the most attractive of the barmaids were deputed to serve them for as long as they had a thirst. Jack McVitie had spoken to the Malts and arranged for three strippers to provide the entertainment and a temporary stage had been erected at one end of the room for them. The first of the girls, a busty redhead who teetered on vertiginous heels, had just negotiated the shallow step up to the stage and was beginning her routine. Joseph, Jack and Billy were sat at a table that offered the best view of the performance. Joseph had been identified as the groom and the redhead was lavishing her attention on him. The girl finished her routine, festooning her underwear around Joseph's head. He stood and kissed her on the lips, the men hollering their approval, and pressed a note in her hand.

Edward stood with his back against the bar and took it all in. Billy twisted around, craning his neck until he found him. He smiled at him for the third or fourth time that night: a cold smile laced with enmity and hatred.

Edward had not seen Joseph since Paris. They had shared a slightly rueful greeting at the start of the evening but they had not yet had the opportunity to speak properly. Now, though, he disengaged himself from the others and made his way across the room to the bar. Edward was suddenly nervous. He had the strange feeling that his brain remained calm and rational but that his body was out of control and that, unless he held himself tight, he would be unable to stop his muscles from trembling. He thrust his hands into his pockets, his fists clenched, and then took them out again, moulding his fingers around the shape of his glass.

Joseph sat next to him. "Keeping yourself to yourself, Doc. Having fun?"

"Just catching my breath. Are you enjoying yourself?"

"I'll say. You lads have done me proud."

Edward looked over at where Billy was standing with Jack McVitie. "Billy's done a grand job," he forced himself to say.

Joseph looked thoughtful, his knees splayed and a hand pressed against his knee. "I know you don't like him," he said, "and I know he can be a right pain in the arse, but you've got to remember I've known him since we were nippers, and, when you think about it, what is the best man, anyway? It's just a symbolic thing. Doesn't actually mean anything. I thought it would be the right thing to do. He has his problems but I've treated him badly lately. I want him to see this as an olive branch."

"You don't think I've done anything to make matters worse?"

"No, nothing deliberate, but I think you probably need to cut him some more slack. You intimidate him—Jesus, Doc, you intimidate me some of the time. You're an educated man, a University man, Billy knows you're clever, more than he is, I think it makes him feel very self-conscious. Me too, sometimes, if I'm honest."

"I'm sorry," Edward said. This was all very annoying but there was little he could do about it now. He felt a moment of awkwardness but Joseph alleviated it by putting his arm around him and hugging him close. "Look, Doc, I'm sorry about what happened in Paris. It was bloody ridiculous. I said some awful things. I don't know what came over me."

"I'm sorry, too," Edward admitted. "There's been such a lot going on, it's been difficult."

"That's no excuse."

"No. But I'm sorry if you think I was interfering."

"You weren't. You're frustrated. I am, too."

"But I shan't mention it again." He paused. "What about what you said about us working together?"

"No," Joseph said, shaking his head. "We'll finish Honeybourne and then call it quits." He noticed Edward's irritation and clapped him firmly on the shoulder. "Look, Doc, you just need to think about it for a moment. You're a clever bloke, you know what the right thing to do is—it's annoying but you know it's for the best. You don't really want to get involved with all that, do you? Not really. It's got no future. I'm not daft, I know we'll get nicked eventually. And I've been inside, Doc, remember: it's bloody awful. Why would you want to take that chance when you've got all that other stuff going for you? If you get nicked, and you get yourself a record, that'll be that for you, won't it? There'll be no medicine then. You don't get doctors who are ex-cons, do you? You'll have thrown away everything that you've worked for." He paused again, and took a drink. "Don't look be so glum. You know you'll always be a good pal to me, don't you?"

"You're drunk," Edward said, managing to smile all the same.

"Maybe a bit."

"As you should be."

They stood side-by-side for a moment, each of them taking a drink. Edward was satisfied. His apology had been accepted and, it seemed, the rift between them had closed. He wasn't concerned about all the rest. Everything else would follow in time.

Joseph grinned at him. "How are things with my sister?"

"You know?"

He grinned. "You think I wouldn't find out? My sisters have never been able to keep a secret. It's all they've been talking about."

"You don't mind?"

"You say the strangest things sometimes, Doc. Of course I don't bloody mind! You're one of my best pals. You and her? It's good, saves me having to worry about straightening out the dirty cowson I thought she'd end up bringing home. She's a feisty one, though, much more than the other two. She'll keep you on your toes."

"And your aunt? She doesn't mind?"

"I haven't spoken to her. As long as you treat her well, you'll be alright. If you mess her around, though, she'll have your balls." He said this with a bright smile but Edward knew that there was truth, and a gentle warning, in his words.

* * *

BILLY WAITED UNTIL EDWARD WAS ALONE. He was sitting at the bar, taking a whisky and smoking a very good cigar. It had been a decent evening, all things considered. The nonsense with Joseph had been put behind them and Edward had started to feel more optimistic. He felt more comfortable. With a little luck, he would be able to restore things to the right footing, the way he saw them in his more optimistic moments: he would bring himself closer to Joseph, he would demonstrate his value and then, over time, he would make them realise that they needed him. He was working on that. It was going very well.

There was Chiara, too. He would be around the family all the time and they would grow to accept him; to like him, even. Violet and George would see the error of their foolish assumptions. He had paced himself carefully through the evening and, although he was starting to feel the effects of the alcohol, he was still reasonably clear-headed. He felt suddenly hopeful and strong and, allowing himself a little scope for celebration, he downed the remnants of the whisky and enthusiastically ordered another.

Billy took the stool next to him. He smelt of alcohol and cigarette smoke. "Having fun?" he said.

"I am," Edward replied, managing to smile at him. "Good party."

"I want a word."

"Oh yes?"

"It's about you, actually."

"Not now, old chap," he said, nervously looking down at the tumbler in his hand. "It's late and I'm tired. I don't have the energy."

"No, you want to have this conversation, you really do."

"What is it?"

"I know about you."

Anxiety flared and he rubbed his palms together anxiously. "Don't be tedious," he said gruffly.

"I *know*."

"What are you on about? I'm not in the mood."

"See, I'm not sure what I should call you any more. Why don't you tell me? What do you prefer: Edward Fabian or Jack Stern or Roger Artis? There are probably others, too, right? Other people you pretend to be."

Edward felt his eyes stretch wide, terrified, and though he knew his fear was just what Billy would want to see, and that it would encourage him, there was nothing he could do to hide it away. He put out a hand, resting it against the cold brass rail that was fixed to the bar. A moment of intense dizziness washed over him and, for a moment he thought he would fall from his stool. He had known it was Billy who had broken into the flat. "I don't know what you mean," he managed to say, but it was a pitiful denial and Billy grinned wolfishly at it.

"You've had us all fooled, haven't you? All this stuff about being a doctor. None of it's true. I couldn't believe it when I found out. It's all moonshine."

"Billy—" He saw his own face in the mirror behind the bar: he had a wall-eyed stare that made him look rather idiotic and frightened.

Billy sniggered. "It was that bloke who came into the garage that started me thinking. He swore blind that you were his brother. I said he must have been wrong but he was so sure, eventually I had to take him seriously. And then I thought about it a bit more. There's always been something about you that's been a bit off. So I had a look around your place the other day. Found all sorts of interesting stuff." He reached into his pocket and laid a passport on the bar. Edward looked down at it fearfully: it was for Jack Stern, his real passport. "There's another couple of these, plus Registration Cards and all sorts of other things you probably don't want people knowing about. I've just borrowed them for a bit. Letters, too. I had a good read of all of them. It was your uncle who put me in the picture. Uncle Jimmy. I went to see him the other day. Lovely chap. He said I didn't know what I was talking about at first, just like you, but I can be persuasive when I want to be. You know that, though. That's why you asked me to help with the milkman."

Edward rose so quickly that the stool clattered against the bar. He closed the distance between them but Billy did not flinch, raising a hand and holding it lightly against Edward's sternum. Joseph had turned at the sound of the stool. Billy smiled at him, took his arm and put it around Edward's shoulders and turned him away to face the bar. In the mirror, he saw that the colour had drained from his face. He was as white as a ghost. "Don't do anything silly," he advised quietly. "You'd rather we kept this between ourselves, right?"

He reached into his pocket again, took out the engagement ring and dropped it onto the bar.

Edward reached impulsively but Billy cupped his hand over it.

"Wouldn't want Joe to see that, would you?"

"If you've hurt him I'll—"

"You'll what? You'll do *nothing*, mate. Sweet fuck all. Me and good old uncle Jimmy just had a friendly little chat and it all came out. Every last detail. And you're not in a position to make threats, are you? I've got everything I need. The ring you stole from him, the passports, pictures of you when you were younger, letters, and—I nearly forgot—I know where your old man is. Jimmy told me all about it. Basket case, ain't he? Dribbling into his soup. From now on, see, when I tell you to do something, you're going to do it. Understand? Because if you don't, I'll pay your Dad a little visit like I did with Jimmy. And when I've finished with him I'll go to Joseph and explain how you've led us all up the garden path since you got on the scene. How you've been working for Spot. And then I'll tell Violet, I'll tell George and I'll tell Joseph's sister, too. That's the best of all, how you've pulled the wool over that poor little bitch's eyes. How do you reckon she'll feel, learning that she's been spreading her legs for a con artist like you? I reckon she'll want to be the first in line to watch what her brother and her uncle does."

Edward flinched at Billy's arm across his shoulders. "What do you want?" he said, his voice knotted.

"We'll get to that but you can answer a few questions first. I was wondering—the real Edward Fabian—did you top him?"

Edward gritted his teeth. "He was already dead. He was killed by a German bomb."

"So you made it look like Jack Stern died instead? Just took his papers and off you went?"

"Very good, Billy. You always were sharp."

"Mind your tongue. You don't want to upset me no more, do you? How'd you do it?"

"I had a friend working in the mortuary. He doctored the papers."

"Clever. It was all going so well, too."

"How much do you want to keep quiet?"

"We'll start at a ton and see how we go from there. Every Friday. No exceptions. Mess up and"—he lifted his cupped hand for a moment, the ring sparkling beneath, and then replaced it—"everyone knows about your dirty little secrets."

"Alright," Edward said. "Fine."

"You know what?—I always knew there was something wrong about you, Jack. I had a feeling in my gut. But it's all over now, isn't it? Now that I know." He tightened his arm, squeezing him closer to his body. He leant closer, breath that reeked of alcohol on Edward's ear. "And unless you want everyone else to know, you'll do exactly what I say."

55

EDWARD LEFT THE CLUB and walked hurriedly to the Shangri-La. This was a nightmare, he thought. The worst nightmare he could have imagined. Billy had him in a terrible spot. Everything was suddenly put back at risk again but it was worse this time. It was not just his place with the family that was at risk. It was everything: his clothes, his car, his apartment, his lifestyle. His freedom. Billy could go to the police and take his liberty from him. Everything would be revealed. Something awful was going to happen now, he knew it. He had been lucky for too long and now the world was going to mete out his just desserts. He had been lucky for nearly seven years in avoiding detection for what he had done but his luck had finally run out. They would find out who he really was and, from there, it would be a simple enough matter to tie him to what had happened in Sicily. His mind became fixated on his fate. He would be hung. The life he wanted to lead, the things he wanted to see, and to own, the places he wanted to visit, all of it would be denied to him. A fatalistic premonition of his own doom settled over him and he felt that there was no way that it could ever be lifted.

He reached the restaurant. The paper sheets that obscured most of the windows had been pulled away in one corner and he cupped his hands around the aperture, staring into the darkened room. He could see the brighter white of fresh paint on some of the walls, paint pots and brushes arranged neatly on the floor, and then, beyond them, two chairs had been overturned. A cold fear ran across Edward's body and he knocked loudly on the door, then, when there was no response, he crouched down and pushed open the flap of the letterbox with his fingers, calling into it.

He went to the flat, let himself in and knocked on the inside door. The dog barked again. There was nothing for several minutes until, finally, a light came on and Edward heard Jimmy's voice asking who it was. He sounded frail.

"It's me—Jack," he said.

Jimmy unlocked the door and opened it and Edward came inside. There was enough silvered light from the street outside to see that Jimmy's face was puffed and bruised. Both eyes were blackened and livid contusions marked his cheeks and forehead. Edward felt the beginnings of an awful fury at what had been done to his uncle. He slipped his arm beneath the older man's shoulders and helped him to the settee. He set him carefully down and switched on the light. Jimmy's injuries looked much worse. One eye socket had swollen so badly that the eye was shut, dried blood had collected beneath his right ear and, when he smiled painfully at him, Edward saw that two teeth had been knocked out.

"I'm sorry," he said, because that was all he could think to say.

"I tried to telephone," Jimmy said, his voice weak. "I couldn't get through."

"I've not been around. I've been busy. Oh, Jesus, Jimmy, look at you—I'm sorry."

His uncle dismissed his apology with a feeble wave of his hand. "Looks worse than it is," he said, his laugh whistling through the gap in his teeth. Edward didn't believe him. "Who was he?"

"His name is Billy Stavropoulos."

"I'm sorry, Jack—I told him everything."

"It's not your fault. It's my fault. I was stupid." Edward thought of the blasted newspaper article, and was conscious of a certain sense of annoyance as he recalled it, because it had been an awful, amateurish error.

"What's he going to do?"

"He means trouble. He knows about father."

"Don't worry," Jimmy said. "I spoke to the sanatorium. They won't let him have any new visitors."

That, at least, was a relief. Edward thanked him for it.

"What are you going to do?" Jimmy said.

Edward thought about that. What *was* he going to do? He realised, then, that he had already decided. He had been considering what to do ever since Paris. There was a line that he had thought he would not need to cross. It was funny, he thought, just two hours ago he still thought that. Now, though, he saw that it would be necessary, and much more besides. "I'll sort it out," he said. He waited until Jimmy had settled himself back into bed and then spent the rest of the night in the front room, sitting at a table with a bottle of whisky and a single glass. He spent the next hour running through what he knew he had to do. He would have to amend his plan a little to take Billy into account, but that should be possible. He plotted out his next steps, considered the two alliances that he would have to form. His timetable would need to be accelerated a little. He built the story that he would have to tell and planned where he went from here.

He would fix it all.

Joseph.

The family.

Billy.

He would take care of everything.

56

IT WAS JUST before dawn. Ruby Ward stood by the side of the street as George Costello's driver stepped out of the Bentley and handed him the keys. "Can't get it started most mornings," he complained. "If you ask me the engine's shot. He wants you to have a look at it."

"Of course," he said. "Leave it with me."

Ruby had sold that car to him—well, he said 'sold', but George had made it clear that he wanted it and Ruby had ended up practically giving it to him. It had been a very nice motor then, a top of the range Mark V1, but that was nearly five years ago and it was beginning to show its age. The motor sounded throaty, the paint was fading, the leather upholstery was cracked and weathered. It had seen better days, Ruby thought, and that was just about right; the car was like George and the rest of his insane family.

He watched as the chauffeur disappeared down the street towards the Underground. Ruby had known them for years. He had started doing business with George's younger brother, Harry, taking nicked cars, filing off the registrations and flogging them on. Harry Costello: now there was a man. Astute, ruthless, all the angles covered, nothing ever got past him. His siblings weren't a patch on what he had been: Violet was shrewd, for sure, but you didn't want a bleeding judy at the head of the family;

George could be a frightening bastard but he was too simple to be really dangerous. Neither of them—not even when they put their heads together—could match up to old Harry. He had been the real ticket.

He wasn't foolish enough to bring it up—not with anyone—but Ruby could see an end to it for the Costellos. They'd had a good run at the top, coming up to twenty years, but the last two or three had been difficult. Harry's death had started it. They had been kicked off the racecourses, swapping their action there for the same kind of scams at the dog tracks. Like George's car, that, too, summed up their plight: from private boxes at Ascot to chicken-in-a-basket at Walthamstow and Wimbledon. The gee-gees had always been their bread and butter, that was Harry's father had started out, and without that action; well, Ruby thought, things looked bleak. He had been over to the big house in the Cotswolds for Chiara Costello's birthday and the place was starting to look tatty, unloved, nothing like what it had been like before the war. That was a sign, and now George couldn't afford to replace a five year old motor that was well past its best; as far as Ruby was concerned, the writing was on the wall.

A case in point: the five hundred pounds he had given George were for the lorry-load of stolen whiskey he'd bought from him the previous month. Ruby had turned the booze around the next day for a grand, so he was laughing. It wasn't going to be so good for George; he'd have to split his gelt, passing the right amount down the line to the blokes who'd hijacked the truck; more to the geezer from the hauliers who'd passed on the inventory and shipping timetable; more to his dodgy coppers down at West End Central so they'd let him know if the Swedes were barking up the right trees. By the time he was done with settling all of that little lot the most he'd be left with was a hundred, two if he was lucky.

No, Ruby Ward was not a stupid man. He had started to hedge his bets, started to cast around for other people to work with. He didn't want to get caught with all his eggs in one basket.

He shivered in the damp cold and closed his overcoat more tightly around his body. He went through the garage to get back to his office. This business had been his career once, but times had changed. He still made plenty from it, but the black market paid more. Ruby washed his illicit profits through the garage and the two pubs he owned south of the river; there was a lot of money to hide. He bought this place ten years ago, selling his first dealership and funding the difference with a loan he had inveigled out of the bank against trumped-up accounts they must have known were moody. He had worked hard for the first three or four years, but it hadn't taken long for him to realise that, when it came down to it, his old man had been right: 'only mugs work.' There was more to be made on the fringes of things, in the margins between legal trade and the black market. The war had been the best thing that had ever happened to him.

He first saw the smoke as he passed the inspection pit. It was coming from the showroom. He reached for the door and recoiled: the doorknob was burning to the touch. He wrapped his hand in the sleeve of his coat and opened the door, a cloud of smoke billowing out, curling up against the ceiling. He covered his mouth and went inside. There was a slick of petrol all the way across the floor and he watched, in confused fascination that quickly became horror, as a blue wick of flame spread avidly across it. The flames crackled hungrily, racing across the showroom, high enough in places to start to blacken the ceiling. He was backing away when he saw the rag that had been stuffed into the fuel tank of the Packard nearest to the door. The fuel cap had been taken off and the rag was pushed all the way inside. It was alight, burnt almost all the way down, and as Ruby dumbly realised what was about to happen he also realised that it was too late to do anything about it. A moment later and the tank exploded, lifting the car off its rear wheels and then crashing it down again. The blast flung Ruby off his feet and tossed him back outside again. He landed heavily on his back, his head whiplashing back against the floor. His vision swam with woozy filters as consciousness ebbed away. He would wonder, later, if the hooded figure he saw was real or a tattered figment of his imagination, a concussion dream.

57

EDWARD BRACED HIS ARMS against the sides of the wooden-panelled corridor as the train rumbled around a sharp bend. He continued along the carriage, checking through the windows of the compartments on the left of the corridor. The train was on the fringes of the metropolis now, and most of the compartments had emptied out as commuters disembarked at the end of their journey home. He made his way along to the end of the corridor and the final compartment. He had checked earlier; it had been full, and he had decided to wait. Now, it had emptied out. The lone occupant was sitting facing the direction of travel, a copy of the *Times* held open before him. A glass of gin rested on the small table fixed to the wall of the carriage, ice clinking against the sides as it moved with the motion of the train.

Edward had done his research. Everything Charles Murphy had said to him in the dining room at Claridges had been true. He was the youngest detective chief inspector at the Metropolitan Police in living memory. Hugely ambitious and ruthless to a fault. His career had been made by the apprehension of a serial murderer during The Blitz but he had built on those strong foundations in the years that had passed. His own father had been one of his victims. The newspapers called him the "Scourge of the

Underworld" and said he was spearheading the Commissioner's public promise to root out black marketeers and put an end to gangsterism.

It was all true.

Edward wanted to speak to him somewhere quiet to reduce the chance that they would be seen together as much as possible. He paused at the door, his eyes on the man, and then on the landscape rolling past the window. The world keeps turning, Edward thought, and here I am, about to make myself a grass, the lowest of the low. But it was necessary, he told himself. There was no question about it any longer: it was what he needed to do.

The last few days had been miserable. His time with Chiara had been uncomfortable, undermined by a persistent chill of anxiety that he could not dismiss. It was the same with Joseph. Had Billy said anything about him, he wondered? Every cross word, every disagreement, and Edward convinced himself that the cause was Joseph's knowledge that he had deceived them all. The sudden weight of guilt made Edward sweat, droplets on his forehead and on his back, his palms slick and damp. He needed to act. It would remove a dangerous threat and provide him with an opportunity to put his career with the family into its natural and proper place. He had wrestled with his decision and was happy with it. It needed to be done. Without it, he would probably have to leave, to flee, to go abroad.

He would never get what he deserved.

No. He knew he was doing the right thing. He had no choice.

He slid the door aside and stepped into the compartment.

"Detective inspector," he said.

Murphy looked up, unable to prevent the expression of surprise that broke across his face. "Edward."

He pointed at the bench on the opposite side of the compartment. "Do you mind?"

"It's a free country."

It was a knowing reference to their first meeting in the restaurant. Edward pretended a smile—he hoped that it might mask his nerves—and sat.

"How did you know this was my train?"

"I've been following you."

"You didn't think to make an appointment?"

He laughed derisively. "Really? You know what would happen to me if they found out we were talking, don't you?"

"Yes, of course—foolish of me. George would cut you up into tiny little bits and throw you into the Thames. What can I do for you?"

"I've been thinking about what you said to me."

"I'm glad to hear it. And?"

"And perhaps we can work together." The train's horn sounded, up and down, long and short and short again. "This situation in Soho—I'm no expert, but, the way I see it, it's completely out of control. There are the Costellos on the one side, not as powerful as they were but still heavily involved. And then, on the other side, you've got Jack Spot. Ambitious, ruthless, not clever enough to be subtle but very dangerous—he has his eye on what the Costellos have managed to hang on to and he wants it all for himself. And, as you say, men have already died: Lennie Masters, Tommy Falco and the others. And they won't be the last, will they? How am I doing so far?"

Edward wanted to make him recall their previous conversation and see how the boot was on the other foot now. Murphy knew what he was trying to do and glared at his impudence. "Not too bad," he said, tightly. "Please—go on."

"You know Ruby Ward?"

"Of course."

"You know about the fire at his garage this morning?"

"Yes."

"The whole place—burned to the ground." He shook his head solemnly. "From what I heard, he was lucky not to have been killed. Can't have been an accident, can it? Spot knows Ward works with the Costellos. He fences all their stuff. If you ask me, that was Jack upping the ante again."

"Maybe."

He leant closer. "Inspector, you've staked your reputation on being able to clean up the West End and, with respect, none of this is making you look very good. More bloodshed makes you look even worse. I don't know what it's like to be in the police, but I do know the army. Let's say we had the Tojos causing trouble in a particular area and my commanding officer ordered me to put a lid on them, only it gets worse before it gets better. I reckon, in a case like that, odds are I'm going to get a bollocking and given something else to do. It's definitely not the way I'm going to get myself that promotion I've been hankering after. Like I say, I don't know how you work all that out in the police but I reckon it's got to be similar."

A muscle twitched in his cheek. "As you say—you don't know."

Murphy's weakness was his ambition and the screw only needed to be tightened just a little more so that the bait Edward was laying down became impossible for him to resist. "Just for the sake of argument, we can agree it'll be better for you to get on top of this, right? Before it gets worse."

"And what can you do to make that happen?"

"How long have you been chasing George Costello?"

"Long enough."

"What if I said I could deliver him and a dozen of the family's men?"

"I'd wonder if you had a death wish. George Costello is not someone I'd want to cross."

"No, he isn't. Me neither. But I know what I'm doing."

"Fine—then I'd say I'm interested. And I'd ask you how you could do it."

The light disappeared as the train thundered into the mouth of a tunnel. The noise of the engine reverberated against the walls, smoke gathering against the brick, and Murphy reached up to close the window.

"The Costellos have been running a very large black market scam for the last four months. They're stealing goods and Ruby Ward has been flooding the market with them. It's lucrative—immensely so, worth thousands and thousands of pounds. It'll make what you've been looking into look like small change in comparison. How much do you know about that?"

"A little."

"But not enough?"

"No."

"I can tell you everything: how it's operated and where they're getting the goods from. I can tell you the next time they'll be collecting the merchandise, and I can make sure that George Costello is there. Red-handed. You'd just need to be there and mop them all up. Sentencing is stiff for black marketeering these days, isn't it?"

"A couple of years. Maybe more." He leant back and, regarding him shrewdly, he pursed his lips. "I'd be interested in that. In principle. But that's only half of the problem. What about Spot?"

"What if I told you that I could make sure that he was sorted out, too? That he and his men wouldn't be a problem in the West End any longer?"

"How?"

He shook his head. "You'd have to leave that one with me."

"Alright—assume for the sake of argument you can do all that. But you wouldn't be doing it out of a sense of altruism, would you?"

"We'll call it self-preservation. You were very persuasive."

"What do you want? Immunity?"

"That, and something else. Just remember what you'd get in return: the Costellos and the Spot Gang out of commission. Peace on the streets that you can take the credit for. None of it at any risk to you. It'll be my head on the block, not yours."

"Out with it, then—what do you want, Fabian?"

The train cleared the tunnel and the moonlight returned, bathing the landscape in silvers and greys.

Edward leaned closer and looked Murphy dead in the eye. "Billy Stavropoulos."

"You want him arrested?"

He nodded. "I tell you where and when. Arrest him, keep him out of the way for a day or two and then bring him to me."

Murphy sucked his teeth. "And then?"

"And then you leave."

"And then what happens to him?"

"Not your concern."

"What's he done?"

"Doesn't matter."

He shook his head. "You know I can't possibly do that."

"Those are my terms. They aren't negotiable."

"Then I think we're finished here. Good night, Fabian."

Edward smiled at him. "Just think about it. Those things you said before—about how ruthless you are. I believe you. I recognise your character. I went back and read those newspaper reports from the Blitz, the murders you solved, what you did to catch that man. Your father, too. I read about that. You knew it in the restaurant—we both did—we're cut from the same cloth. Ambition. I can tell—it drives you as much as it drives me. And we're both ruthless. We don't allow people to get in our way. I'm offering you the chance to *decimate* the gangs. Think of your reputation. All I want in return is Billy Stavropoulos–

—a nasty, murderous little crook who would cut your throat as soon as look at you. It's a small thing in comparison and it's not up for debate. You can take it or leave it. But if you turn it down, think of how many more men are going to die until Jack Spot finally gets what he wants. How many more Lennie Masters and Tommy Falcos will there be? Think of the bloodshed. The chaos. How will that make you look? Really, inspector, you must weigh it all up. Is Billy worth that? My terms are reasonable."

The drinks trolley clattered along the corridor outside. Murphy was quiet, his expression opaque. "I'll think about it," he said at last.

"Don't take too long. My information will only be good for another few days. If you don't move soon, the chance will be lost."

"Give me until tomorrow."

"How will I know?"

"I'll be on this train. Be on it again."

58

FIVE IN THE EVENING AND THICK, choking smog hung over the landscape in a cloying pall. The streets huddled close, geometrically and depressingly perfect, lines of identical workers' terraces built for the docks, a thousand chimneys sending smoke to thicken the miasma. The gardens in this particular street were, like all the others, small and prim at the front and unkempt at the back. Edward had observed the view as he drove East: row after row of barren grey streets, straggled allotments, derelict waste ground. Litter blowing in the gardens. Bomb sites and overflowing bins. Cars rusting against the kerb with no petrol to run them. Children out late in rationed clothes that had been patched and repatched until there was nothing original left. The streets were busy: men, alone and in pairs and in small groups, shuffled forwards in the wan light, all of them slouching home, away from the same location: the docks, and the unending trainloads of goods that needed to be unloaded and dispatched.

He had been busy. Spot had seen him before, albeit briefly, and he did not want to take the chance that he might be recognised. He had visited his uncle. They had drawn a bowl of water in the tiny bathroom and Jimmy had treated his hair with a rinse to make it darker. He had combed his hair across his scalp and then moved to the tray in his lap. It held what looked like barbershop floor sweepings but Jimmy shook it out and revealed it as a beard fastened to an almost invisible, flesh-coloured gauze. Jimmy fitted the moustache first and then the beard, fixing it in place with a light glue. It felt odd to have hair on his cheeks and lip but the effect was adequate. He had stuffed his cheeks with cotton wool to adapt the shape of his cheekbones, added a pair of heavy spectacles with plain glass lenses and then smiled at his reflection in the mirror, just gently so as not to disturb the still setting glue. His face was barely recognisable and he was pleased with how it looked. It would be good enough.

Edward parked the car near to the Boleyn Ground. This was deep in Jack Spot's manor, the heartland of the criminal empire that he knew, with sombre conviction, was inexorably spreading west. Edward had made discreet enquiries and had learnt that Spot generally took his dinner in the working men's club on Green Street, next to the Boleyn Ground where West Ham played. It was said to be his headquarters, a collection point for the mixture of East End toughs, Jewish heavies and gypsies who made up the majority of his strength. Edward got out of the car, shivering in the damp cold, and walked the few hundred yards to the club. The door was open and he went inside. The room was large, and thick with smoke. There was a bar at the opposite end, a series of tables scattered in between and two or three dozen men: some were drinking and eating, others were talking, others were playing darts or bar billiards. Edward paused at the entrance, his stomach seething with nerves. He was in unfamiliar territory and, suddenly, he felt out of his depth. The men at the nearest table had noticed him, pausing to regard him with unveiled hostility. Edward gathered his courage and went to the bar.

"I'm looking for Jack Spot."

The barman was wiping a cloth over a dirty glass. He looked him over. "Who's asking?"

He raised his chin and spoke firmly: "Dick MacCulloch."

"What do you want?"

"That's for me and Mr. Spot to talk about. Is he here? Can I speak to him?"

The barman put down the glass and stared at Edward for a long moment. Edward held his eye, the nerves still fluttering in his stomach. "Wait here," the man said.

Edward stood at the bar and started to fret with the edges of a towel that had been spread over a spillage. He knew that he was taking a risk by coming here, a big one, but there had been no alternative. There was Spot's reputation for violence, for one thing, but he was less concerned about that than he was about the Costellos. If he was spotted, and the news got back to them... well, that didn't bear thinking about. He would have preferred to send someone else but who was there? Jimmy would have been a possibility, but he was still black and blue from the beating that Billy had dished out, and who else was there after him? No-one. It had to be him.

The barman returned. "This way," he said. He led the way to a room at the back of the club. It was plain, furnished with a table and two chairs and a filing cabinet. Crates of beer were stacked against the wall. Edward recognised Jack Spot. He was alone at the table, eating a plate of liver and onions and drinking from a cup of tea.

"Sit down," he said to Edward pointing to the empty chair opposite him.

Edward did as he was told. Spot was dressed impeccably, in an expensive suit with a bright red handkerchief folded in the pocket. A crombie had been hung from a hook on the wall and a trilby rested on the crates of ale. Spot himself was an impressive figure. Although he was sitting, Edward estimated that he must have been well over six feet tall. His face was ponderous and heavy, full of flesh, somewhat ruddy—his face might have been stone to Edward. He had large grey-green eyes that flicked and darted, or perhaps he was one of those people who never looked at anyone they were talking to. His shoulders were wide and his hands enormous.

He picked up the tea and sipped at it.

"Thank you for seeing me, Mr. Spot."

"Eric says you have something you would like to discuss?"

He flinched and touched his moustache with his finger. "I do. Business."

He replaced the cup in its saucer. "I'll let you have a minute. I don't normally appreciate my dinner being interrupted, so you better make it interesting."

"Thank you."

"Fifty seconds. Get to it."

"I work for a freight company."

"Doing what?"

"Driving trucks."

"I see. Freight?"

"That's right."

"Valuable?"

"Sometimes."

"And the opportunity?"

"There's a consignment of whisky being delivered to the depot in the next couple of days. Very good stuff, Mr. Spot—it's worth hundreds of quid, especially with the way things are."

Spot stabbed a piece of liver and inserted it into his mouth. He chewed thoughtfully for a moment. "And what does that have to do with me?"

"I heard that you were the man to speak to about opportunities like that?"

Spot looked at him with a faintly amused expression, gazing at him as if he were some kind of animal which interested him, and which he could kill if he decided to. "And who told you that?"

Edward feigned to fluster. Spot was the kind of man who would beat up someone he thought was wasting his time, and here, alone with him in his club, in the middle of the East End, there could not have been a more propitious place. "I know some chaps who gamble in one of your spielers," he explained, "they said it was right up your street."

Spot noticed his anxiety and a smile spread slowly across the man's red, fat lips. "I might be interested, Mr.—?"

"MacCulloch. Dick MacCulloch."

"Mr. MacCulloch." Spot put another piece of liver into his mouth and chewed. "But how do I know you're not a stool pigeon or a detective?"

"Do I look like a detective?"

"No, Mr. MacCulloch, you don't, but I didn't get to be where I am by taking unnecessary chances and you can't be too careful these days." He watched him with the same neutral smile. Edward knew he was weighing up his proposal. "When will you have the goods?"

"I'm taking the truck to Scotland to pick it up on Sunday. I should be back down again with it a week tomorrow."

Spot tapped his fork against the side of the plate. "And how much would you want for doing this?"

"Fifty notes. I'll probably get my cards over losing the load, so it's got to be worth my while."

The neutral smile flickered and then disappeared. Spot's eyes snapped into close focus, and Edward felt drawn into them. They were dark and unfeeling, with no suggestion of compassion or empathy, and impossible to read. "Alright, then, Mr. MacCulloch. Speak to Eric again on the way out. He'll give you a telephone number. Call it when you are three hours away from London. I'll have a think, maybe ask a few questions about you. If it is something I think I might be interested in, and if I think you can be trusted, you'll be told where to go. If not, you will have needlessly interrupted my dinner."

"Thank you, Mr. Spot."

Spot nodded and concentrated on his half-finished plate. Edward took that to mean he was dismissed and, nodding his head deferentially, he backed out of the room and into the smoke and noise of the bar.

59

MONDAY MORNING. The hands of Edward's wristwatch moved towards eight o'clock. It was cold and overcast, with wispy tendrils of river mist creeping across the breakers' yard. It was to be the last run to Honeybourne, although only Edward knew that. He grabbed the rails with both hands and hauled himself up into the cab of the lorry. Joseph was waiting in the passenger seat, his feet propped on the dashboard and a selection of holiday brochures spread out across his lap. Jack McVitie was behind the wheel of the Commer Express delivery van parked ahead of them and behind them came the other lorries. Everything was as it normally would be.

Edward had spent the last few days refining the plan. He had persuaded Joseph that they should have George come with them this time. There was a lot of merchandise, he had explained, and it would make sense for him to see it all for himself. Edward had been wary of making too big a thing of the suggestion for he knew it was essential that it was not so obvious as to be remembered later, after everything, nor that it was something that he had proposed. Joseph did not seem to make very much of it, and, after a little persuading, George had agreed to come.

He was behind the wheel of the third lorry, the one directly behind theirs.

"What about the south of France, then?" Joseph was saying, stabbing his finger at the open brochure. "Still full of the French, no doubt. What about Eve? Think she'd like it? Her cup of tea?"

"The weather's splendid, I've heard there are some spectacular beaches, the hotels are luxurious, the food will be out-of-this world. I should think she'd love it."

Joseph looked at the brochure again. "We could fly direct from London Airport on BOAC—they have planes that go all the way down. It ain't cheap, though, none of it. The whole thing's a great big racket. You get them a ring when you get married, you pay for the wedding they've always dreamed of, then you have to stump up for a holiday. I ain't even thinking about a house, clothes, a nice car. As soon as your woman realises you've got a little bit of folding about you, their taste gets expensive all of a sudden, and then there's babies and the whole thing starts all over again. Chiara won't be any different—believe me, I know. That one's been brought up to expect the good life, always has. You better have plenty saved up if you're planning on making an honest woman of her, that's all I'm saying."

Jack McVitie hauled himself into the open doorway. "Where's Billy?" he asked.

Joseph tossed the brochures down into the footwell and frowned. "No idea. He's a bloody fool half the time, but it's not like him to be late like this."

"Strange," Jack said. "We were supposed to be having a drink last night and he never turned up."

"He's not ill, is he?" Edward asked innocently.

"I saw him yesterday morning," Joseph offered. "He was fine."

Edward found a look of concern. "You don't think—it couldn't be Spot?"

"What? How?"

"I'm just saying—the fire at the garage, the attacks on the family's business. And then there's Lennie and Tommy, what happened at the Regal. I mean, let's not ignore it, it's not like he's been shy of violence before, is it?"

Joseph dismissed the suggestion. "I can't see it," he said. "Billy's too careful to get caught up in something like that."

Edward did not want to press it. He knew very well what had happened to Billy. "Well, we can't really wait for him. The longer we're here, the less time we'll have at the other end."

"We'll have to go without him," Joseph said, his irritation obvious. "Go on—let's get started."

Jack McVitie jumped down and clambered into the truck ahead of them. He gunned the engine.

"What's he playing at?" Joseph said.

"Billy? No idea," Edward said. He felt a flutter of nerves despite himself as he cranked the ignition. "Away we go then."

It started to rain as they pulled out. Edward switched on the wireless and tuned to the Light Programme. The forecaster warned that storms were expected across the country.

60

CHARLIE MURPHY CHECKED HIS WATCH. Eight-thirty. Four hours had passed already and no villains. Not anyone, just the occasional military policeman walking his lonely beat around the perimeter. The two lads he'd borrowed from uniform looked nervous. Charlie had seen the two of them around the nick before and could guess what they were thinking: probably reckoned this was their chance to impress, get themselves transferred into plainclothes. The C.I.D. lot looked sharp in their dark suits, white shirts, understated ties, polished leather shoes. Nothing too flashy. You didn't want to attract chummy's attention when you were on the job but you didn't want to look like a two-bob steamer, either. The woodentops were awkward out of their blues, wearing their Sunday best, trying too hard.

Charlie had been receiving intelligence all day. He had left two of his best men behind to keep the salvage yard under surveillance. Because of them, he knew that four trucks had driven out at six that morning. They had been followed, heading west, until there could be no doubt that they were on their way to Honeybourne. The unmarked car that had tailed them all the way had dropped one of the constables at a telephone so that Charlie could be forewarned. That had been the cue for them to take up their positions.

They couldn't be far away now.

The men were tightly squeezed into the small Nissen hut. Charlie's space was bounded by the legs and feet of the two coppers opposite him. The air was hot and clammy. The men were grumbling. The two uniforms were the worst, whispering away with the aides as if they'd already been made C.I.D. Fat chance if they keep that up. They had a lot to learn. One thing they could bet their lives on was that a career in the Met would include plenty of sitting around in cold, ill-appointed surroundings waiting for chummy to make his move. That was the job.

"Gawd's sake," one of them said. "Who farted?"

"Should've brought your gas mask. Stop bellyaching."

"Shut it!" Charlie hissed. The men quieted down

Charlie tapped Alloway on the shoulder again and took his place at the peephole. Cold air blew against his eyeball as he looked out, up and down the road that ran through the middle of the base. He could see the hut opposite that the Military Police had taken; another dozen men, some of them armed with Sten guns.

Apart from that: nothing.

He tried to keep his mind occupied. The busier the mind, the less the chance he'd fall asleep and bugger up the collar. He'd done that before—nodded off—back when he was a Winter Patrol, years ago, as green as the aides in the van. Forty hours freezing his arse off on the roof of a shop because his guv'nor had information it was going to be cracked. Chummy pulled the job while he was kipping. He woke up with the door open, the alarm going, the place ransacked. Copped a serious bollocking.

It was a good lesson to learn.

He heard the sound of an engine, and then another.

He squinted.

A lorry was coming towards them.

Charlie held his breath. Another lorry turned onto the road, and then a fourth. Four of them. The lorries drove slowly, carefully, drawing to a halt as they reached the long row of storage huts.

He moved slowly to the door, lifted the latch and opened it. The door of the MPs' hut opened, too, and he saw an anxious face poke out.

The door to the nearest lorry opened and George Costello dropped to the ground. He was smoking a large cigar.

"Now!"

Shouts of anger and shock filled the air as the two huts emptied out, streams of men springing at the crooks from both sides. Charlie led his men, tackling George Costello to the ground. He took a fearsome wallop to the eye, rolled onto his side. The villain tried to get his feet underneath him, getting ready to run. Charlie threw himself at him again, looping his arms around his torso and hugging tight. His grip loosened and his arms dragged down to his knees. He squeezed tight, encircling his legs, and they both went down. The man was as strong as an ox; Charlie could feel his muscles through his clothes, solid, hard. Costello bucked beneath him, twisting his trunk around so that their positions were reversed so that he was on top, scraping Charlie's crown against the asphalt. He hung on for dear life, trying to link his fingers but the man's shoulders were too broad. He was a beast. Costello clenched his fist, his eyes boiling with anger, and he drew back his hand. "Help!" Charlie called out.

Both of the aides flung themselves onto Costello and he toppled away and against the wheel of the lorry. The brawnier of the two punched down with right-handers until Costello stopped struggling. A second man jumped over the mêlée, started to run; a detective constable laid into him, clobbering him with a right-hander that took his legs out from under him.

A volley of automatic fire cracked through the air.

Charlie scrambled to his feet and looked around. The tussle was almost at an end. The Costello lads had been unarmed and taken completely by surprise. Most of them had dropped to the ground with the volley from the machine gun. The villains were eating concrete, men with knees pressed into their backs and arms twisted around and halfway up to their necks.

A scuffle was taking place at the edge of the huts, two men fighting with two of his lads. He recognised Edward Fabian and Joseph Costello and, as he watched, Fabian knocked down his opponent and turned to help Joseph. The two of them quickly overpowered the policeman, breaking the hold he had around Costello's neck and sending him to the floor.

Fabian paused, just for a moment, and Charlie locked eyes with him.

"Guv?" his sergeant said, pointing at the two of them.

Fabian was backing away, still looking at him. "They're too far," he said. "Let them go. We'll pick them up later."

The Aide yanked George Costello upright. He could feel the belligerence growing in him as surely as if his huge body was boiling with a heat that could be felt from yards away. "George Costello," Charlie recited between ragged breaths, "I'm arresting you for theft, fraud, breaches of the defence regulations, resisting arrest and assaulting a police officer. You, my friend, are well and truly nicked."

61

THE LORRY'S ENGINE ROARED.

"Doc!" Joseph yelled from the open cab. "Doc, come on, let's go!"

Edward turned and ran. Joseph stamped on the gas as he leapt for the door, swinging from the handle as they picked up speed. The truck rushed at the gatepost at thirty miles an hour, pulverising the wooden barrier and then slicing through the wire mesh gates beyond. They made it out onto the road losing barely any speed, Joseph spinning the wheel so that the rear end fishtailed, spinning it back again to correct the skid. Edward opened the door and slid into the cab.

"We've been set up!" Joseph spat.

"Best worry about that later," Edward said, hanging out of the open window to look behind them.

"They coming after us?"

"Not yet. We'll never get away in this. It's too slow and too easy to spot. We need to dump it." He stared up the road ahead. "There," he said, pointing towards a narrow track that led away from the main road. Joseph pumped on the brake to slow them enough to take the sharp left hand turn. The road was paved for fifty yards and then unfinished: a farmer's track, used to get into the fields, rutted with deep ridges from heavy machinery. They bumped around, the suspension groaning in protest until the track turned to the right and entered a dense copse of trees and then petered out. Joseph brought the truck to a halt.

They sat in silence, trying to regain a measure of composure.

Joseph looked hopeless. "What are we going to do? We can't stay here."

Edward waited until his heart slowed a little.

"We'll leave the truck and go on foot until we can find something else." He opened the door and jumped down. "Come on."

The main road cut through the fields two hundred yards to the north. The copse hid the truck from sight, but they would be visible as soon as they left its shelter. They had no choice. They set off, following the line of a low hedge, both of them alert to the sounds of traffic. The terrain was wet and muddy, with long swathes composed of ankle-deep sludge that clung to their feet and plastered their legs. There was a gentle slope that led up to an elevated point. They followed it.

"What happened?" Joseph said out as they ran.

"Someone grassed."

"Who?"

"I don't know. Butler? Who else?"

"You think?"

"They must've got to him."

They clambered up the incline, the view opening wide as they gained height. The top offered them an elevated vantage point and, from there, they could see over the valley and into the facility, onto the rows of storage huts arranged beyond. The wide parking area where they had collected the merchandise was visible: the three remaining trucks had been blocked in by two green-painted military police lorries and two dozen police, several of them armed, were guarding a line of men prostrate on the ground before them. The prisoners had their hands behind their backs as two detectives worked up and down the line, securing their wrists with handcuffs.

Joseph looked over the scene, and Edward watched as the colour drained away from his face. "What is it?" he asked.

"It's bloody Billy," Joseph said. "It's him, isn't it?"

Edward paused, taking the opportunity to catch his breath. "Really?"

"He grassed us up."

"Don't be daft," Edward said, because that was what Joseph would have expected him to say.

"I know, but where is he? He wasn't here this morning. The only one of the chaps who didn't turn up the morning we all get tumbled by the Old Bill. Don't you think that's odd?"

"Just a coincidence." Edward did not want to push any harder than that. He had left the dots. It was not his place to join them, too.

The wind suddenly picked up, bending the tops of the nearby poplars like sword-tips. Branches—small and dead—were blown from the trees and rattled as they fell to the ground.

"Get down!"

A road ran twenty yards below them, cresting the hill half a mile ahead. A police car suddenly sped from around a hidden corner, its lights flashing and siren blaring loudly. The car roared around the bend and down towards the base. They dropped down, landing in a thick puddle of mud. They stayed there until the sound of the siren faded into silence. When they stood, fearfully checking the road to make sure it was clear, they were covered head to foot in muck.

Edward tried to wipe it from his clothes but it was wet and adhesive, and the attempt just made matters worse.

Joseph looked lost. "I don't know what to do, Doc," he said helplessly.

This was it, then. Everything Edward had worked towards was approaching a conclusion. He just had to approach it carefully, make it all seem natural and easy. The first thing he needed was Joseph's support. The speech of reassurance and persuasion sprang full-blown to his mind. "First of all, we don't panic," he said. "We got out. If we're careful and we move quickly, they won't be able to find us. It's not like we've never done this before."

"This ain't the jungle, Doc."

"No, it's not, but we know what we're doing. How far to Halewell Close from here?"

"Fifty miles—maybe a little less."

"That's where we should go."

"You want to walk fifty miles?"

"Do you have a better idea?"

"Why there?"

"We need to speak to your Aunt. This has gone on long enough."

62

VIOLET COSTELLO MUST HAVE SEEN them as they loped across the fields at the back of the house. They were covered in mud, scratched from clambering through brambles and almost completely spent. They had struck out for Evesham, then followed the route of the A438 to Pershore, Upton-upon-Severn, Welland and Ledbury. They had seen several police cars, and had navigated around a road-block on the road outside Bradlow. It took them eleven hours to cover the fifty miles and they were exhausted.

The storm had gathered strength and now it lashed the countryside with wind and rain. It was dusk and the lantern that had been lit and hung under the *porte cochère* swung to and fro in the intensifying wind.

Violet opened the front door and came to them. "What's happened?"

"The police—they were waiting. They arrested everyone."

"George?"

"Everyone."

"What about you?"

"Lucky. We were at the back."

Violet stiffened the line of her jaw. "Get inside," she said. She called for Hargreaves and told the butler to draw two baths. "You need to clean yourselves up."

Joseph pointed dumbly at the candles that had been lit.

"The storm's put the electricity out," she explained. "It's been on the wireless. It's supposed to be quite fierce tonight." She shook her head in weary resignation. "The perfect end to a perfect day."

Joseph paused. "Is there something else?"

"It's Chiara."

Edward stepped forward. "Is she alright?" he said quickly.

She sighed. "It's that bloody dog. You might as well see it now."

"He's come back?"

"In a manner of speaking. In the back yard."

Joseph led Edward through the house to the rear entrance. There was a wide courtyard, catching and amplifying the wind as it swooped around the house. A crate had been placed next to the wall. It was three feet long by two feet wide. The lid had been prised free with a chisel, the wood splintered around the nails as Joseph flipped it upside-down with the toe of his shoe. Edward looked down. The body of the old dog was inside, resting on a bed of balled-up newspaper. The dog's fur was damp in the rain. A wreath had been laid on top of him.

* * *

EDWARD WENT UPSTAIRS to his usual room. A set of Joseph's clothes had been laid out for him—a suit, a shirt, even a new pair of shoes—and a bath was running in the bathroom. He stripped off his muddy clothes and looked at his body in the mirror: his skin was streaked with mud, and his legs had been shredded by brambles and thorns, dried blood running down from the scratches.

He reclined in the hot water, closed his eyes and listened to the rain beating against the window panes. For the first time all day, he had no audience to persuade, no performance to give. He allowed himself to relax. The day had been perfect. He had ensured that they were last into the base, and then had stalled the engine so that the other lorries could draw further ahead. There had been enough distance between them and the others for escape to be possible and then, when detective inspector Murphy had had the opportunity to renege on their deal, he had chosen not to. He must have removed Billy from the street. Those were the main strokes, but even the details had been better than he could have expected. He had expected that he would have to prompt Joseph to the conclusion that Billy might have been involved but that hadn't been necessary. He had sown the seed himself. It would be a simple matter to help him nurture that doubt into the certainty that it was Billy who had sold them out. After all, where was he? Who was the only man who hadn't turned up today? Yes, he thought happily, it really was perfect. He spread soapsuds luxuriously up and down his arms and across his chest, closing his eyes and sinking his head beneath the surface so that he could scrub the dirt from his hair. He emerged again, blinking water away, and chuckled at how it could not have gone any better.

He giggled again, and then sobered himself by deliberately concentrating on the one problem that he still had to solve: how to persuade Violet and Joseph to follow his advice and take the fight to Jack Spot. He had brought them to a desperate pass, removed the threat of Billy from the equation, removed George and his enmity and cynicism, and deftly manoeuvred events so that he could persuade them that Spot had orchestrated the family's demise. Raiding the restaurant. Burning down Ruby Ward's garage. The dog. They were hopeless. They would listen to him now. He would have what he wanted.

But was he ever tired! He allowed himself to relax and tried to concentrate on the things he had to do. He thought of Joseph, a few rooms down the corridor, bathing himself at this very moment, his legs as sore and weak as his own, his body covered with mud. He would be confused and angry. He could see the frown across his brow, the hurt in his eyes as he sat brooding about his oldest friend and what he might have done. He would still be doubtful but those doubts would become suspicions when Billy failed to show up. He imagined him tomorrow, setting off for the Hill, knocking on the door of Mrs. Stavropoulos, but she wouldn't know where her son was, either. He pictured him in Soho, trying the Alhambra, the French, the Caves de France, the Colony, the Mandrake and the Gargoyle and finding no sign of him anywhere… what else was he to think, under the circumstances?

So tired.

A sense of grogginess overcame him and he closed his heavy eyes. The scene dissolved in a wash of greys and blacks and then it was all green and brown, the greens of bamboo and delphiniums and hostas, the browns of teak and mangrove trees, the colours of the jungle, and, overhead, the grey and black spectrum of the monsoon. The air was still and heavy, pregnant with static, and then the rains came. Big, fat, ponderous globules that grew heavier and heavier and then, as if at the press of a celestial switch, fell as a deluge, a great roar of water, thundering against the trees and the earth and river and the mountains. Edward saw himself, at the rear of his platoon, dressed in his khaki fatigues and with his Sten gun aimed out ahead of him, sweeping the vegetation on either side of the narrow road as they progressed towards the bridge across the Irrawaddy. He was scared. Rain washed across his face, blurring his vision. He watched the muzzle flashes from either side of the road, a Japanese platoon lying in ambush, hidden behind screens of bamboo and obscured by the curtain of rain, two type 92 heavy machine guns set on tripods on either side of the road, a lethal firing zone that they were already deep within. The machine guns were 'woodpeckers' because of the noise they made, the whirring rat-tat-tat calling out, the men at the front taking the first barrage. Their weapons splashed into muddy puddles as they staggered backwards, arms flailing. The other men got their weapons up and started to fire, shredding the bamboo as they emptied their clips. Edward threw himself into the mud, shuddering as the body of one of the privates collapsed across him, then another falling across the first. He closed his eyes and prayed, his bowels loosening as a third and then fourth soldier was picked off. The woodpeckers fired for thirty seconds straight and then stopped. Eleven soldiers were left dead on the road. The only noise was the thunder and the rain, the cycling down of the guns and the whooped celebration of the Japs. Edward lay still, feeling the thick, warm tick of another man's blood as it dripped down onto his forehead, onto his lips, into his mouth. Four Japs approached, firing single shots into the fallen bodies, one by one, but not Edward. They missed him. The Japanese paused for a minute, sharing a prayer to their Emperor or whoever the hell it was that they worshipped, and began to fold up the machine guns. It took ten minutes, twenty minutes, then thirty, the guns dismantled and hoisted onto their backs. A banded krait slithered out of the envelope of grass at the side of the road and curled itself into the warm cavity between Edward and the dead man beside him. A snub-nosed *meh nwoah* monkey sneezed in the overhanging branches. Edward did not move. Finally, the Japanese turned towards the bridge. He shouldered the bodies aside, the snake slithering away as he burrowed out from amid the outflung arms and legs, swiping rain and blood from his eyes. He stooped to collect a Sten gun, pressed in the box magazine with shaking fingers and held the trigger, spraying the platoon with bullets. The six men were close, and too encumbered with the woodpeckers to defend themselves, and Edward fired until the magazine ran dry, replaced it with his spare and emptied that, too. Sixty-four shots. He went over to where they had fallen, took a Nambu pistol from the holster of one of the men, and shot them in the head, one after the other. Then, one bullet left in the chamber, he aimed the muzzle downwards, at his foot. He pulled the trigger.

Edward looked around the bathroom, looking for the dead bodies and the Japanese soldiers in the corners, in the laundry cupboard, beneath the bath. He felt his own eyes stretched wide, terrified, and although he knew his fear was senseless he kept looking for them, in the dusky windows and in the mirror above the sink. He lifted his leg out of the water and stared at his foot. He saw the corresponding scars where the bullet had punched its way in and out. He held his breath and dunked his head beneath the water again, letting the warmth envelop him, and then pushed himself up. His body felt leaden and slow, as if he were trying to raise himself out of deep water.

A peal of thunder brought him back to himself again. He got out of the bath and towelled himself dry. He had let his imagination run away with him. They were all dead. The grogginess was just fatigue and hunger. He just needed to manage for another hour, or maybe two, and then he could sleep. There would be more to do tomorrow and then the days that followed, much more, and he would need to be rested to do it, but, for now, he bounced on his heels with satisfaction. He was inordinately proud of himself. The day had been all he could have expected, and more.

63

EDWARD DRESSED AND, putting himself back into character again, made his way down to the study. The storm had grown bigger, and now lightning crackled overhead with thunderclaps, still distant, booming in response. The electricity was still out and it had made the house unnaturally dark, pools of darkness gathered around every corner. He paused to compose himself at the foot of the stairs, his hand on the gilt angel that formed the newel post, and then he went through into the library. Violet and Chiara were sitting in high-backed chairs next to the fire. Joseph was pacing anxiously in front of them. The room was lit with the orange and red of the flickering fire and the warm amber from candles that had been placed around the room.

Chiara got up and hurried to him. "Oh, Edward," she sobbed. She had been crying. Her eyes were red and her face was ashen.

He held her in his arms. "I'm sorry."

She held her hand up against her mouth. "Did you see him?"

"Yes. I'm truly sorry, Chiara. It's horrible."

"Poor Roger."

"It's Spot," Joseph said. "All of it."

Chiara buried her face in Edward's neck. "Poor dog. Poor boy."

"Are you sure, Joseph? The wreath didn't say—"

Joseph interrupted him angrily. "Of course it's him. He's making it personal: what he did to me, Ruby's garage, the dog."

"And this morning," Edward added.

"Yes, and this morning. It must have been him. Aunt?"

"I don't know," she said wearily. "I need a drink. We can talk about it over dinner."

They repaired to the dining room. It was one of the worst dinners Edward had ever endured. The food and wine were superb, the cuisine of such excellence that would normally have provided him with satisfaction, even happiness, but the quality of the meal was lost on him today. Chiara was heartbroken, Violet's mood was ambiguous and Joseph seethed with fury. This was all as it should be, of course, but the effort of balancing their responses and then adjusting his own—sympathy where required, then umbrage, then shocked affront—was debilitating. He straightened his back and breathed, his chest aching with tension. They sat in awkward silence as they struggled through the main course. Edward chased the last morsels of sole and butter around his plate, soaking the juice with the last slices of potato, and took a mental stock of the situation. Yes, he thought. Everything was good. He was satisfied.

Hargreaves cleared the plates away and, as if that was the signal to resume the conversation, Joseph brought the conversation straight back to Jack Spot. "You think he spoke to the police?" he said, finishing the last of his glass of wine and pouring again.

"Who else would've done that?"

It was all becoming such an effort. Edward recognised the fatigue very well—the languor of a player who, in the furtherance of a difficult performance, has given his all.

But he was in the last Act now, and he knew he must persevere. "I agree, for what it's worth," he concurred.

Hargreaves returned with soufflés and coffee. Edward attempted to finish his, and failed.

Violet dabbed her spoon through the delicate crust. "But how did he know you would be there?"

Thunder boomed overhead, rattling the glass in the windows.

Edward spoke calmly and carefully. "That's it, isn't it? Someone has betrayed you. Someone who's been involved. They told Spot about Honeybourne and Spot tipped off the police. He wants the family off the street, doesn't he?––can you think of a better way to do it than this? There's no risk to him and no more bloodshed. It gets George out of the way, too. The police have done his work for him. It's perfect. He'll take his chance and take all of Soho now." He stopped to let his words register. "If you don't act now, there won't be another chance."

"What about Roger?"

"That must have been someone who knew you had a dog. Someone who knew the house, too, so that they could get in, take him, and get out again. Spot wouldn't know that without help. And you, Joseph, unless it was all a complete coincidence, he must have been told by someone who knew what you were going to do that night."

"I feel sick," Chiara said.

Joseph pushed his untouched soufflé to the side. "Where was Billy today?"

"I'm wondering that too," Edward allowed. He spoke with elaborate care—the very essence of probity—he would let them draw their conclusions themselves.

"He did all this?" Violet said.

"Who else?"

Violet's cup made three distinct clicks against the saucer as she set it down. "It can't be him. I knew his mother and father."

"Then where was he this morning?" Joseph's face was redder, and a nerve in his cheek trembled. He set his empty wine glass down rather hard on the table.

Violet went across to the drinks cabinet and poured four brandies. Chiara sipped hers and then, putting it down, pushed away from the table and stood. "This is just pointless talk!" she said indignantly, walking towards the fire. "Talk got us into this mess. There's no more time for talk. We need to *do* something." Her alabaster cheeks had turned to a pale olive colour and her dark eyes flashed at Violet. "Who cares if it was Billy? I don't. We can deal with that later. Whoever betrayed us, that damage has already been done. It's what comes next that is important. Look at us, sitting here, eating a pleasant meal, talking about it, doing nothing. Spot has had his way with us for too long. He's gone too far. Do I need to spell it out? He came to our house. He killed my dog. Father would have had him *shot* for that!"

Edward was surprised, and secretly gratified, by this burst of vehemence. It was Joseph's quick trigger that he had hoped to tease into activity. That was why he had spared him from the police and why he had humiliated him before his fiancée. His sister had never shown any interest in the family business before, and, although he had witnessed the Italian side to her personality—the temper, the sudden eruptions of fervour—he had never seen it in this context. She had always been ambivalent—or perhaps even slightly embarrassed—about the family business, or so he had thought. He saw now that he had misread her. It was a mistake that he was pleased to have made.

Joseph nodded avidly. "She's right. Edward and I talked about it while we were walking here. He has an idea of what we need to do. You should listen to him."

Violet sipped her brandy, her eyes glittering over the rim of the tumbler. "Very well." She turned her cool gaze onto him. Her lips had a firm line, like lips that seldom smiled or spoke. "Tell us, then, Edward—what would you do?"

There was a portentous crack from the woods nearby and they automatically looked out of the window. The tops of the pines and the fir still flexed, but if any tree had fallen, it was too dark for them to see it.

"Well?"

Edward got up and walked to the window just as the wind threw a hard spray of rain against the panes. He winced at it, and then, his back to them all, took a breath and picked his words very deliberately. He had anticipated this, readied himself for it, and, after coming so far, he did not want to fluff his lines. "You can't just ignore him any more," he said, his tone calm and even. He spoke as if he were addressing a classroom of children who were not listening very well. "Spot isn't going to settle for Soho, he wants everything. There's no other choice—you *have* to fight back now. If you don't, he'll finish you off and then there'll be nothing left for the family. No business. No income. No position. Nothing. He'll take it all—this house, even, if he wants it. You don't have anything to lose and it still isn't too late. But you need to make a statement."

She regarded him coolly. "What kind of statement?"

"Something he can't ignore."

PART SIX

London
April 1946

64

ST MARK'S WAS THE PARISH CHURCH nearest to Halewell Close. It was a Norman building, laid out in cruciform shape and with seating for three hundred. Violet had hired a London florist to dress the building for the wedding and it had taken three days until she was satisfied: armfuls of flowers had been arranged in vases and tied to the ends of the pews and the altar was lit with twenty large candles that spat and sputtered, throwing dancing shadows across the walls. It was cool and crisp behind the thick stone walls. Plenty of the seats were taken but there were spaces. George Costello and Jack McVitie and the other men who had been arrested at Honeybourne were all absent. Billy Stavropoulos was absent.

Edward allowed himself the indulgence of a private smile. Joseph had looked for Billy for three days with no success. He seemed more and more convinced of his guilt to the point that just the mention of his name now would trigger his temper. Edward didn't have to do anything to foster his suspicion. Edward was proud of his work. He had engineered things so that Joseph would reach his own conclusions and everything else had followed naturally from there. He thought that it had been masterfully executed and, tonight, he would start to snip away the loose ends.

Joseph had asked Edward to replace Billy as Best Man and he had graciously accepted. That really was the icing on the cake, he thought. He allowed himself a moment of smugness. His fingers closed around the box in his right-hand pocket and he pulled it out.

Eve and Joseph were gazing at each other happily. Edward stared out into the crowd beyond. There were plenty of faces that he recognised. He drew his gaze forwards and, at the front, there was Chiara. She was one of Eve's bridesmaids. She was wearing a peach-coloured dress, the same as the others, and the colour suited her. She noticed Edward's eyes on her and she smiled at him softly.

The vicar arranged Joseph and Eve so that they were facing each other. At his direction, Joseph took the ring and slipped it onto Eve's finger.

"I now pronounce you man and wife."

Joseph bowed his head and kissed Eve. As he withdrew, and before he turned to the congregation, he looked to his side, at Edward, and smiled.

* * *

THE RECEPTION was to be held in the garden of Halewell Close. A large marquee had been erected on the main lawn, and, within it, thirty tables had been arranged, each of them set for ten guests. Bunting had been draped across the surrounding trees and lanterns hung from their boughs. A second, smaller marquee abutted the first and it was here that the meal was to be prepared and served. The food was to be provided by the kitchen at Claridges. The catering tent had been crazed with activity all day. There had been a generous budget for ingredients, and Ruby Ward had provided everything they could possibly have required. They peeled and diced vegetables, prepared consommés, butchered meat. Those not invited to the service parked their cars on the lower lawn, an array of sparkling metal and chrome worth many thousands of pounds. Immaculately dressed waiters and waitresses distributed glasses of champagne as the guests assembled inside the tent. Edward took a flute and drained it in a single, thirsty gulp.

"Hello," Chiara said as he sat down next to her on the top table. "You look very handsome."

He kissed her on the cheek. "And you look lovely. That's a beautiful dress."

She smiled at him, a little shyly. "Are you enjoying yourself?"

"Yes, of course—but it's all a little, I don't know—"

"Hectic?"

"Well, yes—exactly. And strange."

"The people who aren't here?"

"Exactly."

They both looked out across the space: the bar was jammed tight and children scampered between the tables.

"I do wonder about my aunt sometimes," she said with a long sigh. "This is typical—any excuse to show off. I think Joseph would have preferred something a little quieter, but he wouldn't have had much say in the matter."

Joseph and Eve were in the middle of the table, to Edward's left. They were beaming with happiness, his hand resting atop hers on the table. Violet was next to Joseph. Eve's parents had not been invited.

"No news about Billy?" she asked.

Edward hesitated, seeking earnestly for the truth. "Not that I've heard," he said. "It's very strange."

"Joseph is convinced he's the one who spoke to the police."

"So it must be possible."

"I heard him talking to Violet about it yesterday. It's been days since anyone saw him. It doesn't look good, does it?"

"No," Edward allowed. "It doesn't." He took a gulp of his champagne, pleased with himself again. It was astonishing the difference it made. He felt more confident, more in control, and he felt that that confidence must be obvious in his posture and bearing, and on the ease with which he could put all the right expressions onto his face. All the doubt that he had felt... how foolish he had been!

"Joseph will kill him if he finds him," Chiara confided.

Edward nodded, thinking that that wouldn't be necessary.

The meal was pleasant. The cook had prepared a seafood starter, followed by breast of chicken. The food was excellent and the drink flowed freely. The conversation was boisterous, fuelled by the alcohol, and Edward soon forgot his anxiety.

The dishes were cleared away and, eventually, one by one, the others left the table until Edward and Chiara were left alone. Edward suddenly felt an overwhelming closeness to Joseph's sister. The strength of feeling took him by surprise. Edward stayed at her side all evening, and after Joseph and Eve had taken their first dance he suggested they join them. She pressed herself against his body as they spun around the dancefloor, her head nestled into the space between his chin and shoulder. Her scent drifted into his nostrils, floral and sweet, and as he glanced down he saw that her eyes were closed and a smile was on her face.

He allowed his mind to wander. He would have to leave soon. He was going to kill Billy tonight. He had thought of it before as a means to end all the trouble he was causing, but there had always been another way. Now, though, there was not. All the possibilities had narrowed down into this one, unavoidable, point. He led Chiara around the floor as other couples joined them. Murder was distasteful to him but sometimes it was a necessity. Once you had accepted that it was simple enough. He felt peaceful at the prospect.

65

FIERCE APRIL RAIN WAS LASHING down outside the tent. It was a little before two and the party was still going on, the band striking up again and the sound of happy laughter followed Edward as he left the tent. Time to go. He put on his overcoat and regretted not bringing his umbrella. He had spent a couple of pounds on his hair this morning and the rain was going to make a terrible mess of it. He waited beneath the canvas awning and stared out into the empty gardens, the rain falling so hard that the driveway was running like a river.

He collected his car and set off back to London. The drive was easy, with no traffic to delay him. He allowed himself to think. Billy wasn't what you'd consider clever, but he was cunning. He knew, beyond a shadow of a doubt, that, if he could, Billy would use the advantage he had over him for as long as he stayed in Soho. He was full of hate and jealousy, and he had been given a dreadful weapon to use against him. He would hold it over him for as long as he needed, using the prospect of it to have him do whatever he wanted. The money? That was just the start. Edward knew he had no other choice but he reminded himself that it was all Billy's fault. It could all have ended up very differently.

Edward collected Jimmy and then set off for Southend. They reached the garage at the edge of the town just before three. There was a Humber parked next to the closed café. Detective inspector Charlie Murphy was smoking out of the open window. Edward slowed and parked alongside. Rain ran off the brim of his trilby as he left the shelter of the car and skipped around the deeper puddles. He opened the door and slid into the passenger seat. Jimmy got into the back.

"Evening, inspector."

"He's in the boot," Murphy said. "We've had him in a cell for a week. Fair to say he's not happy."

"Thank you."

"What are you going to do with him?"

"Probably best you don't know."

"Yes," he said, sucking down on the cigarette. "Probably." He flicked the dog-end out of the window.

"What's going to happen to the men you arrested?"

"They'll be weighed off. I'm guessing they'll get a two-stretch. With good behaviour, they'll be away for eighteen months." He looked across the car at him shrewdly for a moment. "That's what you wanted, wasn't it? George and his thugs out of the way for a bit."

"It's like you said—things have been running away with themselves. It was all unnecessary, all that aggravation. Something had to be done."

"And you're going to do it?"

"Someone has to." Edward smiled at him. "It's for the best."

"What about Spot? You said—"

"That's in hand."

Murphy indicated the back of the car with a jerk of his head. "What did he do?"

"Made a very serious misjudgement."

Murphy took another cigarette from the packet and lit it. His face looked jaundiced as the lights of a passing lorry raked through the car. "You and me are square, then," he said.

Edward gave him the keys to his car. "We are."

Murphy opened the door but paused. He turned back to face him. "Just so we understand each other," he said, "this was a one-time thing. We're not friends and we're not allies. You do what you do and I do what I've got to do. I'm still going to clear up Soho."

"I understand."

"You know what happens if you get in my way? There won't be any more favours, Fabian. You'll be nicked just as quickly as the next man."

Edward nodded. He felt a jolt of irritation: he was powerful now, and he wanted Murphy to acknowledge it. "There's another side to that coin, inspector. If you put me in a spot where it's you on the one hand and my liberty on the other, if you've got me boxed in and out of choices, let's be clear about one thing: you will *not* get in my way. We've done business together now and I can't say that I'd feel good about it, but you've got to know: I won't hesitate."

"Then we understand each other."

"Perfectly."

"Get rid of the car when you're finished with it."

* * *

BILLY STRUGGLED and bucked, his heels clattering and then catching against the lip of the boot, but his shackles were secure and Edward yanked him out. Billy tried to scream, the noise muffled by the rag they had jammed into his mouth. He made himself a dead-weight, the toes of his shoes scraping muddy troughs into the grass verge as they dragged him onto the wooden jetty. Their boat was waiting for them, bobbing on the swells. Edward stepped onto the deck first and then, pulling hard, he dragged Billy after him.

Jimmy went into the wheelhouse and made the preparations for casting off. It was a small fishing skiff, fifteen feet from bow to stern, and powered by a small motor. It belonged to a friend who owed Jimmy a favour. He turned the ignition to switch on the engine and unknotted the mooring ropes. The rag must have dropped out of Billy's mouth for he exclaimed, loudly, "What is this?" His voice was full of panic. "Who are you? Please, I ain't done nothing to no-one. Come on, mate. Let me off." Edward took him aft, hauling him down the shallow flight of steps into the room below where there was a tiny kitchen and store. He left him on the floor and went up on deck.

Jimmy started the engines. The noise seemed horribly loud but no-one came. They sailed out of the harbour, the engine chugging and then, when the navigation lights at the end of the harbour were at their backs, he opened the throttles and they picked up speed, cutting through the glassy water and leaving star-speckled froth behind them.

They sailed for an hour until the only evidence of the town were the pinpricks of light on the dark shoulder of land behind them.

"This is far enough," Jimmy shouted. He cut the engines and the boat drifted, rising and falling on the swells, quiet save for the ticking of the engine and the soft slap of the waves against the hull.

Edward propped himself against the rocking of the boat and went back down to the kitchen. Billy was on his knees, his shoulders braced against the cooker. He heard his feet on the steps, his head turning in that direction. "Please," he said, "Tell me what I've done. I'll put it right, I swear I will."

"Shut up, Billy."

Edward went behind him and looped an arm around his waist and dragged him towards the steps.

"Fabian?"

Billy lifted his legs up and kicked against the wall, knocking Edward over and landing atop him. "Hold on," Jimmy said, coming down to help. They took him at the shoulders and ankles and, together, they hauled him up the stairs. The sack bulged as he strained at his shackles but they were too tight. They dropped him in the middle of the deck.

"Fabian?" Billy pleaded from behind the burlap sack.

Jimmy handed him the carving knife he had brought from the kitchen. Edward pulled it back and stabbed Billy in the chest, two times. The knife cut a gash through his shirt and into the flesh beneath, filling with a line of blood as Edward watched. Billy fell back and bucked against the floor, writhing, twisting. He gave a roar that frightened Edward with its loudness and strength and he clambered atop his thrashing body, stabbing him with the knife two more times, into the neck, slashing with the edge of the blade, again and again. He stabbed downwards again, on his knees now, blood splashing from each fresh puncture, and, for an instant, he was aware of tiring as he raised and stabbed, and still Billy thrashed, his shoulders straining, his hog-tied legs jerking up and down. Edward freed himself, stabbing again and again, holding the knife in both hands, the tip pointing down, and plunged it, hard, right into Billy's heart. Billy's body suddenly went limp, relaxed and still. Edward shuffled backwards on his knees, straightened his back, tried to regain his breath. He looked down: Billy was motionless, and covered in blood. He stared at him, searching for a sign of life—a gasp, a bloody sputter—but there was none. He was afraid to touch him now, afraid to touch his chest or feel for a pulse, but he did, taking his wrist between his thumb and forefinger. There was a pulse, faint and indistinct, and it seemed to flutter away as he touched it, as if the pressure of his own fingers quenched it. In the next moment, it was gone.

He pushed up with his legs and stood, a little unsteady. He looked down at Billy's wiry form on the floor and felt a sudden disgust. It was his fault that he had had to do this. Jimmy unhooked the boat's anchor and attended to the body, feeding the rope through the space between Billy's shackled wrists and his back, looping it three times and knotting it expertly. The rope was long, maybe fifty feet, but the sea was deep here. The anchor would drag the body down and hold it beneath the surface. It might drift, but they were far enough from shore that that wouldn't matter. Jimmy heaved the rusting metal anchor onto the side and pushed it over. The rope unspooled rapidly until it grew taut on Billy's body, and by that time they had manoeuvred his torso over the gunwale. Edward could tell from the buoyancy of the rope that the anchor was not yet at the bottom.

The sacking had worked free around Billy's head and, as they hefted him up, it flapped loose. As his body balanced on the gunwale the clouds crept aside and moonlight was cast against the water. His face was lit, frozen, the lifeless eyes, the briny froth from a large wave crashing over his head. Edward thought of his leering grin, what he had seen and what he might have said. Fuck you, Bubble, he thought. Fuck you, and fuck you, and good riddance. He found a sudden surge of anger and shoved upwards, hard, flipping him at the waist so that his body inverted, his legs splashing as they slammed against the surface of the water. The body went straight down, sucked away into the blackness until there was no sign that it had ever been there at all.

It's finished, he thought, suddenly filled with a wonderful happiness. Done. He laughed, as he had often laughed alone, with similar relief after awful moments.

Jimmy went back to the galley and returned with a bottle of spirits. He cleaned out two dirty tumblers and poured double measures. Edward drank his. He thought how stupid and unnecessary Billy's death had been but how he only had himself to blame. He was a selfish, greedy, cruel bastard who had sneered at him and threatened his father, threatened his family, threatened his future and the rewards he had worked so hard to attain, threatened the life that he deserved. He looked out at the sea, the rain hammering a drumbeat against the roof of the boat, and he said, low and calm, the tightness in his throat gone: "Billy Bubble, it was all your fault."

Jimmy went into the cab and the engines started again with a splutter. The boat lurched forwards and picked up speed. He spun the wheel and they carved around so that the coast was before them again. Edward went forwards and rested against the wheelhouse. He was soaked to the skin: he ignored the rain and the sprays of spume. The boat cut through the rising swells, ascending and descending, a long, easy pattern. He collected a bucket and mop and went back to start to clean up the mess.

Eventually, the buildings of Southend came into view again.

66

THE SUN HAD RISEN from behind grey, dispiriting clouds during the drive back to London but the gloom still persisted. Edward had taken Jimmy back to his flat where they had embraced quickly, arranging to meet later. Edward would have liked to have stopped, perhaps had something to eat or even to sleep for an hour or two, but there had been no time for any of that. He would have to manage without. He had been full of adrenaline during the drive and, now that things were drawing faster and faster towards the conclusion that he had engineered, he was alert with the anticipation of what was to come.

Two more tasks, he kept reminding himself.
One task for Joseph.
One task for him.
Two more things to do and then they would be done. And then, finally, he would be able to relax.

He parked outside the warehouse in Soho. A sign above the doorway announced the building as belonging to SMC Cartage & Co but he knew that the business had been appropriated by Jack Spot as a front for his own black market operations. He sat with his feet propped against the dashboard, an unlit cigarette hanging limply from between his dry lips. His eyes were black and empty. He reached into the back for the 9mm Sten submachine gun that was resting on the bench seat. Ruby Ward had provided it for him yesterday.

"Come on," he grumbled to no-one in particular. "Come on."

His thoughts ran to the jungle and the war. He wondered how war did strange things to a man. Every minute you were living in fear. The expectation that the next bullet would be the one that finished you. That's got to damage you, he thought, hasn't it? Got to change something about how you are.

There was no point in dwelling on what had to be done. It was necessary: that was enough. He had learned that lesson in Burma and he had put it into practice with Billy. Some things in life just had to be sorted out. You got on with it as best you could. You did your best not to remember the things that you had seen and done, even though those memories came back to you anyway. He had done things that men who had not served would not have credited, and certainly would not have understood: killed in cold blood, destroyed property, stolen whatever he wanted. Billy could not possibly have comprehended it. None of them would have been able to, not unless they had been there. Joseph was the exception. He had been there, and he knew. He knew that the tasks they were performing this morning were necessary, too.

He thought of how he had developed a hard shell, like being dipped in lead. He had been scared more than he had ever been scared in his life. He had done things, maybe because he was following orders, but he had done them anyway. After a while he did not even think about them anymore; they became as mundane and routine as cleaning his rifle or changing his socks. He had done them like you might scratch an itch.

And this?

Compared to those things, this was a walk in the park.

He rolled the cigarette between his fingers. He gripped the stock and the barrel of the Sten.

A private car turned the corner and headed towards him out of the gloom, blooms of sodium yellow light from its headlamps suffusing the rain-smeared glass. He watched as it parked ahead of him, next to the entrance to the warehouse.

The car's doors opened.

He unslotted the magazine of the Sten, tapped it against his knee to clear any blockages, slotted it back home and recocked the weapon. His hands slid to the barrel and stock, closing around the gun, the metal cold against his skin. It was an excellent weapon and he knew precisely how to use it. He tightened his grip.

Four men got out of the car. They were only a little late. Edward had called Spot's man, Eric, yesterday night. He was Dick MacCulloch and he explained that he was driving the consignment of whisky down from Scotland this morning. He said that he could deliver it to wherever Spot preferred; the man had swallowed the story without question. There was no reason for him to be suspicious. He had played the conversation out properly, even negotiating the amount that he wanted in exchange for the booze. Eric had driven a hard bargain and Edward had only acceded to his price reluctantly. He had been impressed with his own performance. The price didn't matter a jot: this wasn't about money. There was to be no whisky. A payment would be made but it would be by him, and not be the sort that they were expecting.

The men laughed as they unlocked the warehouse's broad double doors, the noise of their mirth breaking the lumpen silence. Perhaps they had been out in Soho celebrating? Why not? It had been a good few days for them. The news was promising for Spot and his goons. The Costellos were out of business and the way was clear for them to dominate the West End. That was what they were all saying. London, and all the opportunities it offered, was theirs for the taking.

Edward tightened his grip around the stock of his Sten gun. He pulled his scarf up around his face, opened the car door and stepped outside. He held the submachine gun vertically, muzzle down, shielding it against his leg and torso. The morning air was cold and fresh. The sun was breaking between the chimney stacks of the hat factory at the end of the street, sparkling through the smoggy drizzle. The men had gone inside. Edward crossed the pavement and followed them. There were no windows, and the only light was the grey murk from the doorway. Boxes and crates were stacked up against the walls. The four of them had their backs to him. They were moaning that MacCulloch was late, that his tardiness risked a clip around the ear. They had things to do. Places to be.

Edward moved quickly, closing the distance, bringing the Sten gun up, aiming it at waist height.

They were ten feet away.

"Lads," Edward shouted out.

The four men turned.

Their good humour drained away, their mouths fell open, fear washed through their faces.

He fired. The gun rattled and cracked, spitting and bucking in his cradled grip. He sprayed bullets, swivelling at the hip to bring all four men within his arc of fire. Spot's heavies danced backwards, arms aloft, jerking like marionettes. One tripped and fell backwards against the wall. Another toppled across the bonnet of an old car that had been parked inside the warehouse, bullets thudding as they passed through his body into the sheet metal beneath, the burst windscreen crashing over him like fragments of ice. Another collapsed into a stack of boxes that fell over him, spilling bolts of cotton and silk. Edward fired for twenty seconds until the magazine ran dry and then he paused, breathless, the sudden echoing din replaced by a deep silence.

He walked back to his car and dropped the Sten gun into the open boot. He got in, started the engine, and pulled away from the kerb. He passed the open door at walking pace: the Spot men were scattered around inside like fallen ninepins, blood pooling on the concrete floor, running down into the drains. The blood ran down onto the copper shell casings, slicking across them.

Edward pressed the stick into second gear and accelerated away.

67

JOSEPH DROVE SOUTH at around about the same time, making good time until Whitehawk where the car was absorbed into a crawling queue, caught between busses that crunched through their gears as they struggled uphill and myriad other vehicles, all of them jammed tight. Impatient drivers pressed their horns and jerked their cars to within inches of their neighbours. Every spare seat was taken: battered pre-war Morrises, sporty Packards, a pair of youngsters hitching a lift on the running boards of a Humber. Queues of racegoers who had been unable to find a seat on a bus plodded alongside the road, heads down. The noise rolled over them: the distant ululation of the crowd, backfiring exhausts, snatches of distant music, babies crying in hot cars.

He had never been as nervous as this. It had taken Edward a day to persuade him that what they were intending to carry out was necessary. He had reminded him of Tommy Falco and it was that, eventually, that had made the difference. It was not their fault that it had come to this. Spot had been increasing the pressure for weeks.

Lennie Masters.

Tommy Falco and the other men at the Regal.

The violence all across the West End.

Even Chiara's bloody dog.

Edward had explained it colourfully. You don't pull a tiger by the tail, he said. Joseph could understand that. Spot had boxed them into a corner. He was taunting them, daring them to retaliate, daring them to do *something*.

Well, then. Fine. Now they would.

They would give him exactly what he was asking for.

The road finally climbed up Race Hill and as he crested it he was rewarded with a view out over the sprawl of Brighton and, beyond, the green and white of the sea. He rolled the car into the car park, locked it and set off for the track. Loud-speakers set onto the roofs of vans advised the racegoers where best to put their money. Children squabbled. A few punters were already drunk, staggering towards the gate to be parted from the rest of their funds. He paid the entrance fee and followed the tunnel under the course and came up again in the ten-shilling enclosure. He slipped through the crowd, treading discarded tickets into the mulch underfoot, crunching over the shards of a glass that someone had dropped. He concentrated on everything around him. He saw the names of the bookies set out on the blackboards propped up behind their stands: Rogerson and Taggart and Mitchell and Tavell. They stood on home-made platforms, crates and boxes, reaching out over the passing heads of their potential customers like the two-bob preachers at Speaker's Corner. They boomed out the odds, touting for business. They tic-tacked to each other and the odds on the blackboards were rubbed out and changed. Joseph looked beyond the enclosure to where the sun lit the white Tattersall stand across the course, a few horses cantering into position at the start. One of them whinnied, the sound carrying on the breeze.

He stopped and looked more carefully.

Where was he?

The brightening sky.

The clouds of dust over the course from the thundering of the horses' hooves.

The torn betting cards and the short grass towards the dark sea beneath the down.

Where, where, where?

And then he saw him. There, standing before Tavell's stall, was Jack Spot. He was eating a currant bun. Joking with Tavell. Not a care in the world. Joseph pulled his trilby tightly against his head, tugging down the brim so that as much of his face was obscured as possible. The horses from the first race of the day set off, the sound of their shod feet thundering as they came around on the rail. He got closer. A young man with oiled, blond hair stood on a wooden step paying out money.

Joseph reached into his pocket and felt for the revolver.

The horses turned onto the straight and accelerated towards them.

"Jack!" he shouted.

The big man looked up. Joseph noticed all the small details: the crumbs from the bun that had stuck around Spot's mouth, the fat knot of his tie, the faces around them that warped from jollity to fear as they saw the glint of the revolver and realised what that must mean. Spot opened his mouth as if to speak, opened and closed, the crumbs dropping from his mouth onto his coat and the floor, and Joseph fired, twice into the body, and Spot fell backwards into the stand. He slid down the blackboard, his coat rubbing off the odds. Joseph followed and stood over him.

The horses went by with a deafening drumbeat of hooves.

Spot put up his hands to ward him off.

"Please," he mouthed.

Joseph ignored him, aimed at his face and fired.

EPILOGUE

Halewell Close
June 1946

THE WEDDING OF Mr. Edward Henry Fabian and Miss Chiara Grace Costello was arranged for the last Saturday in June. It was only three months after Joseph's wedding and yet if the cost of financing yet more festivities was difficult for the Costellos to absorb, it was not obvious from the scale and grandeur of the occasion. Expensively engraved invitations had been dispatched to six hundred guests, twice as many as had attended the wedding of Joseph and Eve. Once again, the reception would be held in the grounds of Halewell Close, with the marquee—this one much larger—erected over the etiolated markings that were still visible on the grass. The party would go on all day and into the night, the entertainment provided by the best swing band in Soho. It would be lavish and no expense would be spared. That was Violet Costello's preference and Edward had been delighted to indulge it. After all, there was more money now. And he wanted people to remember the day. He wanted it to be more elaborate, more memorable than Joseph's.

After all, in so many ways, the party was his coming out.

There had been rumours of an upturn in the family's fortunes. Jack Spot's humiliation at the racecourse had seen him in full retreat, even before the unsolved death of his four lieutenants. That bloody morning's work had been dubbed "The Upton Park Massacre" by a wide-eyed press that had become entranced by the casual brutality of the killings. One thing was for sure: it had led to the rebalancing of power in the West End. Those businesses that Spot had taken from the Costellos had been returned to them. The flow of strong-arm money from the shebeens, spielers, pimps and prostitutes that he had diverted now flowed into the Costello's coffers again. The death of the four men served as a stark reminder of what happened to those who crossed the family's path, and suggestions to local businesses that it was in their best interests to 'work' with the family were now accepted without resistance. For the first time in months, the Costellos started to expand their sphere of influence. And for the first time in years, they were the dominant force on the racecourses once again. People were saying that they were swimming in new money.

The guests had travelled out of London in the morning and headed west into the Cotswolds. Their bridal gifts were envelopes stuffed with cash, handwritten cards inside each envelope announcing the donor so that Edward and Chiara might know who was responsible. The cards established the measure of the respect each donor felt for Edward and wished him and his beautiful bride the best for a long and happy life together. Others had provided gifts: crates of wine and magnums of champagne; gold and diamond bangles; a diamond encircled watch and wristlet; a gold fob watch; silver-plated Rhodium coated pens; a carved rosewood necklace; a pair of gold and amethyst cufflinks; three gold safety pins; an Italian cameo brooch. A distant aunt gave them a sterling silver letter opener from Aspinal of London and Edward absent-mindedly ran his finger along the edge and up to the sharpened point as they surveyed the heaving table where the gifts had been deposited.

The motivation for these kindnesses was not unsullied, and Edward knew it. Each guest hoped that he would remember them fondly and, in time, acknowledge their respect with a favour. The men and women were drawn from across Soho and the West End and they had all heard the talk. Edward Fabian had become the most influential person within the family. He taken the place of the incarcerated George Costello at Violet's side, and it was his counsel that she took. The ceremony binding him to Chiara had simply been the public confirmation of what everybody already knew: Edward was family now. It had been him, with Joseph, who had seen off Jack Spot. It had been him who had overseen the family's recovery and the expansion of their interests. He was not someone to cross or trifle with and, all agreed, he was destined for big things. There was no harm in trying to gain capital with him now.

Edward stood with his bride at the entrance to the marquee, shaking the hands of the men and kissing the cheeks of the women. He accepted their compliments with good grace, offered the hope that they would enjoy the evening and moved on to the next in line. He felt superb, perfectly ecstatic. He greeted everyone respectfully, with a kind and personal word to each that was calculated to encourage a sense of familiarity. He wanted his guests to think that he was someone who made an effort. He felt in control and it seemed impossible to him that anything could go wrong. Joseph was next in line and he hugged him, pounding him on the back and welcoming him into the family. Violet followed and he stooped to allow her to kiss him on the cheek. Jimmy Stern, at the wedding as his uncle but under an assumed name, took his nephew's hand and held it.

"Look what you've done," he said.

"Everything's going to be alright now. We don't have to worry about anything."

"Well done, my boy. I'm proud of you. Your father would be, too."

Jimmy squeezed his hand and, as he left him with Chiara, Edward felt moisture in the corner of his eyes.

"Are you alright?" Chiara asked him gently.

"Yes," he said. "Just happy."

For he was. Everything about the day had been perfect. He compared it to Joseph's wedding; everything was simply *better*. The ceremony at St Mark's had been more beautiful, the aisles bedecked with armfuls of roses and lilies and a storm of multi-coloured confetti as the couple emerged, blinking, into the sunshine. Chiara's engagement ring was more elegant: fourteen solitaire diamonds surrounding a twelve-carat oval blue Ceylon sapphire set in eighteen-karat white gold. Edward had commissioned Crown jewellers G Collins & Sons to make it and it had cost him seven hundred pounds. It was elegantly understated and yet very obviously expensive, easily surpassing the gaudy bauble that Joseph had presented to Eve. And his wife, who looked so luminously beautiful in her dress, was superior in every way to Eve.

He squeezed her hand and leant over to kiss her. He had proposed two days after he had disposed of Billy and then gotten rid of Spot and his men. The notion had been on his mind since before then, but his decisive action to secure his own future and the family's position in town made it the obvious next step to take. It was difficult to imagine how his stock could rise any higher, and the union would serve to preserve and deepen it. He would be family, once and for all, and all the silly talk of his leaving and returning to medicine could be finally put to rest. He had demonstrated the benefits he could bring to the business and now he would entwine it more tightly around himself. He would involve himself with every last aspect of it, enmeshing himself in it so completely that he would be impossible to disengage without causing expensive damage. It would be impossible, even when George and the others were released from jail. By that time—and he guessed he had another two years before he had to consider the problem of Georgie the Bull—he would be so deeply submerged that they would not be able to contemplate going back to the way things had been before.

He looked around. It was a boisterous and good-natured crowd, fuelled by a free bar that had been well-stocked by Ruby Ward. Topics of conversation included the police car that was ostentatiously parked at the gates of Halewell Close and the gimlet-eyed detective who regarded the guests as they turned off the road and set off along the long drive to the house. Some recognised him as detective inspector Charlie Murphy, fresh from his successful prosecution of George Costello and the other men who had been arrested at the army base.

Mention of the police inevitably led to disgusted observations that Billy Stavropoulos was still missing. This led to the presumption—which had become something more than a presumption—that he had been responsible for what had happened. He was a grass, a snake, and he would, people suggested, be dealt when he was found.

In turn, the conversation turned to the murder of four of Jack Spot's soldiers: Frank "Hock" Gusenberg, his brother Peter "Goosy" Gusenberg, Reinhardt Schwimmer and Richie Moran. The men had been gunned down in cold blood by anonymous hitmen. The bloody executions were seen as a reprisal to the shooting of Lennie Masters and Tommy Falco, and had driven Spot out of the West End. It had led to the reinvigoration of the family's fortunes. No-one knew whether Edward Fabian was involved, but no-one doubted the effect that he was having. Violet was relying on Edward's counsel and everyone agreed that the results had been remarkable. The family had been at a low ebb, its influence diminishing. It had seemed as if its twenty year rule at the head of the underworld was at an end. But no-one thought that now.

* * *

VIOLET COSTELLO sat down next to him with a wide, friendly smile.

"Aunt," Chiara said.

"Darling. Having a good day?"

"It's wonderful. Thank you."

She shooed away her gratitude with a wave of her hand. "Now, then, my dear—would you mind if I bent your husband's ear for a moment?"

"No—"

"Just me and Edward, if you don't mind? Your sisters are at the bar—I'm sure they'd like to speak to you."

She frowned but quickly mastered it. She leant over and kissed Edward on the lips.

Violet squeezed her hand. "Thank you, darling."

"Don't be long with him."

She left them alone.

Violet allowed a passing waiter to hand her a flute of champagne. She took one for Edward and, too, and handed it to him.

"Cheers," she said.

"Your very good health."

They touched glasses.

She placed the flute down on the table and stroked a finger around the rim. "You got what you wanted," she said.

"As did you."

"Yes," she said. "Don't think I'm not grateful for your help, Edward. I am grateful. Things would have been different without you—I'm not too proud to admit that. But let's not pretend about any of this, alright? I know what you are. You have plenty of similarities with Spot. You were not all that different, not when it comes down to it. You're ambitious. Greedy. You want to take the things this family has for yourself."

"I don't know what you mean, Violet."

"Edward, *please*. You're not talking to Joseph. A little respect."

He sipped his drink and, without looking at her, replied in a low voice: "So why did you give me and Chiara your blessing, then?"

"The lesser of two evils, I suppose."

"What?"

"Call it a marriage of convenience. You can help us— you have helped us—I'm not denying that."

"You don't think I'll look after her?"

"I don't really care what you do."

It felt like the ground beneath him was slipping a little. "Why are you talking like this?"

She stared at him. Her eyes were crystal clear, as blue with cold as they had been when he had met her for the first time. "Because I want there to be no misunderstandings between us, Edward. This family's legacy is the most important thing in the world to me. When I'm gone, I want to be sure that the family name will continue. My father worked too hard for too long to fritter it all away. I know that Joseph will never be able to take that responsibility for himself. He's too simple—not cunning enough. The same can be said for my brother. My nieces are either disinterested or incapable and, at the end of the day, they are women—and I know better than anyone how difficult it is for a woman to make a mark in this world. So it is difficult to see how any of my brother's children could manage all of this without help. I suspect you arrived at the same conclusions yourself."

Edward did not answer.

"You, on the other hand are cunning and ruthless. You don't have scruples. But remember this: you'll always be an outsider. You might have married Chiara but you will never be family. Not real family. Not blood."

He flushed. "Let's see what Joseph and Chiara think about that."

She waved that aside and took another sip from her glass. "That doesn't really matter." She smiled thinly at him and, again, he was put in mind of a predator addressing its prey. "There's one other thing you should know. I had a letter from Victor last week. He's coming home. Next month, or the month after that. He is everything my brother was, and more. He's better than Joseph—you won't be able to pull the wool over his eyes quite so easily. He'll see you for precisely what you are. A parasite. A leech. And we won't need you then. You will be of no further use. And Victor will brush you off."

* * *

THE GUESTS SPREAD out beneath the huge marquee, some dancing on the wooden platform that had been set out as the dance-floor, others sitting at long tables piled high with food and gallon jugs of wine. The bride sat in her beautiful dress at the raised top table with both of her sisters—her maids of honour—together with her other bridesmaids. The band finished the first half of their set and broke for refreshments. A young Italian tailor from the Hill picked up a discarded violin, wedged it awkwardly beneath his chin, and began to sing a Sicilian love song. Edward walked around the perimeter of the tent, trying to forget the conversation with Violet. He managed to smile warmly at those guests who caught his eye, a few of the men reaching back from their tables to shake his hand. Joseph was sitting with Eve, his hand resting on her knee beneath the table. Jimmy was in conversation with an older woman Edward did not recognise, a smile playing on his lips. Violet, Chiara and her sisters were talking animatedly.

Edward found his way to the entrance of the tent. It was a beautiful evening, shafts of golden sunlight falling on the freshly cut lawns that rolled down to the lake. He allowed himself to daydream. He imagined their honeymoon, landing in Sicily, the first time he had returned there since the accident that had seemingly doomed him to a life without the status he cherished. He thought about the burning sun, the startlingly blue sea, the sluggishness in the air. He thought about the woman in the harbour, the furious argument after she had confronted him and then, eventually, his hands pressing down on her shoulders until her thrashing and kicking became spasmodic and, finally, stopped.

A foul memory he would try and forget.

It meant nothing now.

He turned and looked back at Halewell Close, the imposing spires rising above the ridge of the marquee. It was a marvellous place and it was such a shame that it had been allowed to fall into decrepitude. The Costellos did not really appreciate it. It was just another bauble to own for them. Edward saw it for what it was, respected all the history that it must have seen, and valued it.

Damn Violet.

Damn Victor.

Damn them both.

He would have the house, in due course, and when he did, he would look after it properly.

He caught himself. For a moment, it felt as if it were something that he must have imagined. Was it all real? Had he really done it? Perhaps he was still in the jungle; a fever dream, sweating under canvas somewhere.

He walked away from the tent, down the sloping lawns to the boathouse.

He smelt the aromas emanating from the cook tent, felt the moisture on the breeze coming off the lake.

He wasn't imagining it. It was true. He *had* done it. He would have the house, and one in France, and one in Italy. He would keep his London apartment. He would have cars, all the newest models, and a new suit whenever he felt like one. He would have everything that he wanted. Everything that he deserved. He ran his fingers along the splintered balustrade that guarded the drop to the water below and thought back to the night he had stood with Joseph on the same spot, and agreed to rob a house with him. It was less than a year ago although it seemed longer than that. He looked into the gently rolling waves, stirred by the breeze, and thought of Billy Stavropoulos. There had been a week of bad dreams in the immediate aftermath of that night on the sea. Billy would appear at the foot of his bed, dripping wet, with seaweed festooned over his head and across his shoulders, limpets stuck to his face. He would stand over Edward's sleeping body, staring down at him, his eyes a filmy white as salt water puddled around his feet. Sometimes, when the dream was at its worse, Billy would be joined by a second figure. A woman, barnacles on her fingers like rings. Occasionally, every now and again, Jack Spot would loom behind her, a bloody hole cratering the middle of his face. Edward would stir with a sudden start, sweating, wondering for that first instant of wakefulness what was real and what was the dream. After the first week, the nightmare passed. He rarely had it now.

He turned back to face the marquee. The evening sun was low; he had to shield his eyes and yet it was still getting cold. He allowed himself a final moment of peacefulness before he made his way back up the lawn and into the tent.

He was intercepted before he was halfway there.

"Jack Stern?"

His stomach plunged.

"Excuse me—Mr. Stern?"

He turned.

A man was coming towards him.

He was solidly-built, in his mid-forties, and carried a leather briefcase. He had salt-and-pepper coloured hair, cut very short on the sides, and a solid jaw covered with just a little too much flesh, like the rest of him. His face was the very picture of inscrutability. One couldn't tell a thing from that face, Edward thought. Whoever he was, he was a professional.

"I'm sorry?" he said. "Do I know you?"

"My name is Arthur MacCauley," he said. "I'm a private detective."

"A private detective?"

"My client has engaged me to try and find the man in this photograph." He reached into his briefcase and took out a newspaper. He held it up: it was the article that Henry Drake had written with Edward's picture next to it. "This is you, isn't it?"

"Yes. That was almost a year ago."

"Yes, I know. It only just came to my attention. How about this?"

Edward looked at the photograph that the man held up. It was of a young man, in his early twenties, his hair cut fashionably short, his skin fresh and clear. He was well dressed in a dinner jacket, a white shirt and a black bow-tie. He was next to another man, similarly dressed, his arm around his shoulders. Both of them were smiling broadly, staring right into the camera. It was him. He could remember where the picture had been taken.

Cannes.

Eight years ago.

A world away.

Another lifetime.

"No, that's not me."

"Please, Mr. Stern. Really?"

"I'm sorry," he protested, "but it isn't."

He lowered his voice a little. "Let's not make a scene, Jack. Alright? What do you say? I know today's your wedding."

"That's right—it is my wedding. And you're trespassing, sir. If you don't leave I'm afraid I'm going to have to call the police."

He smiled at him. Completely unthreatened. "You want to do that?"

Edward almost turned away from the man, ready to leave him there on the lawn, but he stopped and, in that second, he anticipated his defeat and the consequences of it. Exposure. Disgrace. Scandal. He changed his mind. No, he thought. He wasn't finished. He could carry this off, just as he had carried everything off before. The show wasn't over yet. He fabricated a sigh. "Jesus Christ. But at least let me smoke a cigarette first?"

"And then we go back to London."

He reached into the pocket where his cigarettes were and felt the sharp point of the letter opener. He turned and pointed down the lawns to the lake and the boathouse. "It's quieter down there. We can talk about whatever you want."

"After you," MacCauley said.

IF YOU ENJOYED THIS BOOK…

…feel free to drop Mark a line at mark@markjdawson.com

Word-of-mouth is crucial for any author to succeed. If you enjoyed this book, please consider leaving a review, even if it is only a line or two. It would make all the difference and would be very much appreciated.

Amazon US
Amazon UK
Barnes & Noble
Kobo

If you want to get an automatic email when Mark's next book is released, sign up here. Your email address will never be shared and you can unsubscribe at any time. His website is at www.markjdawson.com and you can get in touch with him on Facebook and Twitter.

The Soho Noir series begins with THE BLACK MILE. For a free sample of the first chapter, read on.

CHAPTER 1
MONDAY, 10th JUNE 1940

DETECTIVE INSPECTOR FRANK MURPHY stepped away from the girl's body and went to the window; the yelling from the crowd outside was louder. He pulled the thick black-out curtains aside. It was dusk, eight o'clock, a silvery moon rising above the rooftops. An ARP Warden walked his rounds; tarts and their johns found their alleys; tail-gunners from the Piccadilly Circus Meat Rack flounced theatrically, touting for trade. The noise was coming from the junction with Frith Street, away to the right. A large crowd had gathered outside the Vesuvio Restaurant. A dozen bobbies had formed a buffer and two mounted officers kept skittish horses in line. Frank watched as a pair of men were led out of the front door, escorted on either side by lads from Tottenham Court Road C.I.D. The crowd bayed as a couple of the woodentops stepped up to clear a path to the Black Maria parked by the kerb.

The restaurant's large plate glass window shattered as a brick was flung through it.

"It's getting worse," Frank said. He watched as the two men were put into the meat wagon. Locals hammered their fists against the sides. "What a mess."

Detective Sergeant Harry Sparks was going through the girl's belongings. "Mussolini getting chummy with Hitler, that's that as far as I'm concerned—we can't take chances with 'em. Risk of a Fifth Column, that's what they're saying. Best keep them out of the way for the duration."

Frank let the curtain fall back across the window. "Maybe," he said. He turned back into the room. It was a tart's lumber, a cheap single room where punters would come up to get what they'd bought with their oncer: five minutes of slap and tickle and a dose of the clap so bad it'd peel the jewels right off. Cheap furniture, dirty clothes strewn about, unwashed pots and pans in the sink. Squalid. The business transacted inside was gruesome and desperate but it was hardly novel. Frank had seen plenty of rooms like this in Soho and Fitzrovia, especially in the last month.

A neighbour had noticed the door had been shut for three days and had stopped the local bobby. The woodentop had put his size twelve through the flimsy door and discovered the poor girl. Her body was spread out across the single divan. Her tongue protruded from between bluish lips and the bruises around her throat were dark and evocative, the shape of fingers from where they would have met beneath her chin. She had been stabbed a dozen times, probably more than a dozen, and her blood was on the walls, the floor, soaked into the bedding.

"What do you want me to do, guv?"

"Wake Spilsbury up—he better take a look."

"What do you reckon?"

Frank looked at the girl: seventeen or eighteen if she was a day, a grim and brutal life cut short. He'd been working on the case like every other detective on the manor and he recognised the handiwork. "It's him."

He was sure. He'd only taken five days' rest this time.

Whoever this poor doxy was, she was one of his.

Number five.

THE BLACK MILE is available at Amazon UK and Amazon US.

PRAISE FOR THE BLACK MILE

"This is far and above the best small/independently published novel I have ever had the pleasure of reading." The Kindle Book Review.

"A damned fine novel." Ivan Cotter.

"Fabulous atmosphere; believable characters; great story line. Historical crime thriller that (hate to say this) I couldn't put down!" Gill Hughes.

"Excellent hardnosed thriller." Neil Baldwin.

"Has you hooked from the beginning to the end." Michelle Pritchard.

"The further I got through The Black Mile, the harder and harder it got to put it down, and the longer my reading sessions became. An extremely satisfying thriller, heartily recommended and I look forward to Dawson's next book." Jim Cliff.

"A measure of a book to me is one I would read again and The Black Mile is just such a book." Bob Hammer.

"Mr. Dawson is a great storyteller." Annette Gisby.

"Excellently written, very well researched, this is an interesting story grippingly told." Sarah Hague.

"Wonderfully atmospheric period crime novel." Carlo Dusi.

"A fantastic read." Steve Tooker.

"The book is like a 40s, Soho, English style Homeland or Killing ... I loved it." Chris McCafferty.

"Clever, suspenseful, historically spot-on." Brian Levine.

ABOUT THE AUTHOR

Mark Dawson works in the film industry. He lives in Wiltshire.

Made in the USA
Middletown, DE
12 October 2018